ALL HALLOW'S EVE
BY
ALEX URQUHART

All Hallow's Eve
© Alex Urquhart 2018

DEDICATION

To Mrs. Drews, the best third grade teacher that Oregon has ever seen, and the first person to ever tell me that I had a talent for creative writing. Thank you, and sorry that I ended up writing about murder. Nobody is perfect.

TABLE OF CONTENTS

SEVEN DAYS BEFORE
HALLOWEEN

The Wolfmask smeared the blood from his gloved fingers against the wall. With a flamboyant flourish, he touched up the O in the word *look* so that it was a perfect circle. He dabbed his finger into the vial of red liquid once more, buttressing the substance on the tip of his appendage so that the next line of blood would be thicker. As with any organic matter that had been preserved for a long period, the aroma in the air would be repulsive to most. But the Wolfmask loved it.

The surface he painted on was like sandpaper: rough and unwelcoming. It made it difficult to produce an aesthetically pleasing font, but that wasn't the look he was going for anyway. He wanted it to be nefarious and evil. What was the point of drawing a taunting message in blood if it looked neat and welcoming?

A loud clunking sound outside made the Wolfmask snap his head to the right at the source of the disturbance. The massive industrial building he had chosen had been abandoned for years, and although it had windows, the grime made it impossible to see outside. A great number of innocuous things could've made the noise. It was probably nothing but a small animal out in the wilderness. However, the Wolfmask stilled for a few moments just to make sure that no one would attempt to intrude upon his endeavor and catch him quite literally red-handed. After he was satisfied with the lack of a subsequent sound, the Wolfmask went back to work.

He had become much more proficient at this particular task since he had enough practice. Once the police finally stumbled upon his initial message, they might find it more amusing than anything. Although an exceedingly simple work of art, his previous ineptitude led to a splotchy and childish final product. Since he only had one attempt at it, he had to leave it as it was, no matter how much the imperfection ate at him. Now he was doing the last bit of prep work and waiting for the first domino to fall.

With one last slash of his hand through the air, the Wolfmask finished the E. His message was complete. Reclining his head so he could focus a bit more, he read the sentence in full. The first thing he noticed was a rogue line of liquid seeping down from the H in the second word. He supposed it helped make the message more menacing, but truthfully, it gnawed at his inner perfectionist. *Ah well,* thought the Wolfmask, and he turned away. Extraneous detail was no longer something to dwell on. The chosen few were at Death's door, and the game was about to begin.

SIX DAYS BEFORE
HALLOWEEN

Albert Amos let out a deep, guttural sound of frustration. He moved the cursor on his computer screen backward, targeting a word he had misspelled. He deleted the entire word and retyped it instead of just the infringing letter. His father had always told him it was better to start anew than to try and polish a turd.

Amos winced when he took a drink of his coffee and felt how much it had cooled down. If a stranger were to sip it, they would think he had made it iced. It was just a by-product of his inability to multitask, even to the point of drinking a beverage while typing up a report. It didn't help that the report was about a tweaker who had tried to murder his offspring by sticking the thirteen-year-old kid's head in the oven. There was conflicting information emanating from both parties involved, and thus, the report demanded all his attention.

The office was inordinately loud today. Usually he and his colleagues could keep the noise down to a dull roar, but it appeared everyone was performing work at maximum capacity—and volume. He tried to not let the sound of keyboards and phone conversations distract him from transcribing an interview he had conducted with the cheap Zoom H-1 audio recorder. The interview was scatterbrained already.

From one row of cubicles over, the sound of arguing reached Amos's ears.

"Lady, please, you can't just waltz in here—"

"I can do whatever I damn well please. The last time I checked, it wasn't illegal to walk through the police station."

"No, but our detectives are very bu—"

"They can decide, not you, Goatee."

Just from this hilarious interplay and the sound of the voice in question, Amos guessed someone was interacting with Sergeant Tom Thompson, the only officer at the station who had a distinctive goatee.

"Please, ma'am, can you just come with me?"

"Yes. After I speak with a detective."

"Ma'am—"

"This isn't the fifties anymore, Goatee. You don't have to call me ma'am."

As Amos stood up from his chair, an old woman appeared in the opening to his cubicle. She was large and reminded Amos of a hamster. Her flabby cheeks were tinted red, and her gray hair stuck out in a plethora of different directions. A pair of huge glasses was perched on the bridge of her nose, increasing the size of her pupils through the lenses. She wore a tacky teal blouse with purple flowers and black slacks that looked tight around her large posterior.

"Are you a detective?"

"Yes. And a preoccupied detective at that," replied Amos, glancing down at the report that begged to be finished. Thompson shuffled into the opening of the cubicle with a ruffled and guilty expression on his face.

"What are you preoccupied with? Collecting overdue library books?"

Amos couldn't help but smile. There was nothing more amusing than a senior citizen who had lost the ability to filter sharp comments.

Thompson raised his voice. "Okay, ma'am, you

need to leave."

"No, Tom, it's fine. That was a little rude of me. I'm sorry," Amos said, looking at the woman.

The woman froze and looked nonplussed for a fleeting second, with her jaw slacking and her forehead uncoiling. It was as if she was expecting Amos to have her physically thrown out of the station while he stood in the doorway and proclaimed, "And stay out!"

Amos looked kindly at the old woman.

"I'm Detective Albert Amos." He held out his hand.

The woman firmly grasped his hand and pumped it down once before relinquishing her grip.

"Lorna-Mae Johnson."

"Nice to meet you, Mrs. Johnson." Amos offered a friendly smile in her direction.

Lorna-Mae looked around the station like an owl that was scanning for mice, apparently unable to bring herself to say that it was nice to meet Amos too. She honed her focus in on Thompson, who was hovering on the exterior of her personal space. Amos immediately caught on to what she was insinuating.

"I got this, Tom. Don't worry about it," Amos said while subtly winking at Thompson.

A relieved expression broke over Thompson's face. He mouthed, "Thank you," and walked back in the direction from which he had come.

Amos put a warm smile on, attempting to be kind. "So, what can I do for you, Mrs. Johnson?"

"You can explain *this*." Lorna-Mae withdrew a small piece of folded-up paper from her pocket. She handed it to Amos, and he unraveled it at the crease.

On the paper were five words.

WHO'S NEXT? ALL HALLOW'S EVE.

The words were followed by a horizontal X and a curved line underneath it, forming the shape of a smiley face of sorts. But it wasn't a jovial insignia. It looked like an emoji that was supposed to indicate a dead person.

Amos stared at the note for five long seconds.

"What is this?"

"It's a note. Left by the man who murdered my nephew."

"What?"

"Did I speak it in Spanish? I said it's a note left by the man who murdered my nephew."

"The man who—"

"Murdered my nephew. Correct." She took a step forward as if being closer to Amos would help him understand the situation.

Amos furrowed his brow and spread his lips, totally perplexed. "Who's your nephew?"

"Devin Johnson."

Amos tapped his fingers on the desk while he

tried to recall the name from any cases he had worked. The year before, Amos had played a minor role in cracking the largest serial murder case Oregon had ever seen. That had involved young women though. Not any males. Other than that case, there weren't many homicides on file from the past ten years.

"Name doesn't sound familiar. How old was he?"

"Twenty-one. But that won't help you. The reason you don't remember the name is because the police thought he had just left town," Lorna-Mae said.

"And he didn't?"

"No, he goddamned didn't! Did you not hear what I just said?" the old woman shouted. Amos noticed heads in nearby cubicles turned in his direction.

"Take it easy. I'm just trying to understand. So why did they think he left town?"

Lorna-Mae clicked her tongue in annoyance. "Well, they *said* it was because he had just gotten fired from his job. He was late on his rent payment for like the third time and had gotten an eviction notice. I made the colossal mistake of telling the police he had talked about moving to Sacramento before."

"Sac—"

Lorna-Mae waved her hand. "He has a friend

there or something. All his family lives in Oregon."

Amos let this sink in. He thought he remembered something about a young man a few years ago initially being investigated as a missing person.

"When was this exactly? When did he go missing?"

"Halloween night. 2012."

Amos raised his eyebrows.

"Exactly," the old woman said, as if she had been totally validated.

"Well . . . that is interesting. Then again, just because he disappeared on a particular date doesn't automatically translate to foul play."

"I know that, you knob," hissed Lorna-Mae, and a yearning to chuckle tickled the corner of Amos's lips. "It was also the last time I ever heard from him. Even if he did leave, don't you think he would at least get in touch with someone in his family?" The woman was so close to him now that Amos could see every wrinkle and mole on her decrepit visage.

"And anyway, how do you explain *that*?" Lorna-Mae jabbed her finger at the note that she had given Amos. He looked down and reread the red font. WHO'S NEXT? ALL HALLOW'S EVE.

"To be honest, this could be a great number of things," Amos said while gazing down at the note. "I know that sometimes local bands often do marketing campaigns like this to get people to come to shows."

Lorna-Mae rolled her eyes so hard it looked like she had fainted while still standing.

"Well—"

"This is a taunt! That is what this is!" Lorna-Mae snatched the note out of his hands and waved it around in the air before slamming it back down on his desk. "Whoever this is is taunting me. He killed Devin, and now he's going to kill someone else on the same day five years later!"

Amos closed his eyes to regain his composure following her outburst. He did feel a bit of sympathy for the woman, despite her rudeness, but all this interaction was distracting him from the task at hand. He didn't want to tell her to just leave, but he also didn't want to give into her ideas without having more information. He quickly came up with a hasty plan to placate her.

"Alright, Mrs. Johnson. Why don't you sit down?"

Lorna-Mae looked at him like he had asked her for her Social Security number. She stared daggers at him for several seconds without moving. Amos grabbed a chair from the empty cubicle across from his and brought it closer to him. He gestured toward the chair, hoping that she would either sit or simply leave. She looked around the room for a moment like a paranoid cat, and then slowly placed her huge derriere in the cushion. Amos opened one of the drawers beneath his desk and pulled out a yellow notepad and a pen.

"So first . . . where did Devin work?" He waited for her response.

"Excuse me?"

"You said he got fired and that's what sort of triggered his downward spiral. Where was it that he got fired from?"

"Oh my, I don't know. He was the dishwasher in a kitchen. It was a restaurant and bar. I think it had 'house' in the name."

"The Tap House at Nye Creek?"

"That's the one."

"Okay. And where did he live?"

"Some rundown apartment not far from there. The Tap House, I mean. I think the apartments were called Western Village? They're closed now though. Owners died. Their kids inherited it and have been trying to sell it for years but can't find a price that they like," Lorna-Mae replied. "Anyway, yeah, that's where he lived. His rent was only like five fifty a month, but since he worked a minimum wage job and spent half his time at the bars, it was no wonder he couldn't pay it."

Amos wrote casually, half-listening and half-scribbling. She was coming at him with information fast, but most of it was probably going to be useless anyway.

"And so he disappeared on Halloween in 2012? When was he last seen?"

"His neighbors saw him leave his house and get into his car at around eight p.m. Don't know where he was headed, but that was the last time anybody saw him."

Amos nodded, penning everything down onto the sheet of paper.

"Did the neighbors say whether he had lots of stuff in his car?"

"Huh?"

"Well, if he really was leaving town, you would think he would take all his belongings with him. Especially if he was being evicted anyway."

"I don't think they really paid much attention, to be honest." Lorna-Mae shrugged. "It's an apartment. People come and go."

"Right. Well, anyway. No one ever saw him again? Or heard from him?"

"Nope." Lorna-Mae pressed her lips together.

"Do you remember what number his apartment was?"

Lorna-Mae squinted her eyes, trying to recall the specifics.

"Uh, yeah. It was 333."

Amos wrote this down too.

"Thanks. So, the detectives who looked into this never considered it to be anything other than a kid leaving town?"

"No. As soon as I let it slip that he had been talking about moving down to Sacramento, it seemed like they kind of just let the whole thing go." Lorna-Mae scowled as she remembered the officers she had spoken with before.

"And, aside from the fact that it happened on Halloween, do you have anything else that makes you think he was murdered? What makes you certain he's even dead?"

"He came and saw me every couple of weeks!" Lorna-Mae snapped. "And I haven't heard anything from him in five years. And I'm not the only one. My brother, Devin's father, lost all contact with him too. Their whole family hasn't heard anything. They were sort of estranged from him, but me and Devin were close. If you knew my nephew, you would know he isn't like that. He may have been a bit lazy, but he sure as hell wouldn't just disappear."

"Okay, okay. That makes sense. I'm not trying to get you riled up, Mrs. Johnson. I know this must be hard on you."

Lorna-Mae again rolled her eyes with such intensity that her pupils completely vanished for many moments.

"So how did you come by this?" Amos gestured to the note.

"It was left in my mailbox this afternoon at approximately two thirty. My mail comes then and I always check it within ten minutes of it arriving. I know the perpetrator did it then because the note was left on top of the mail stack."

Amos nodded, a little amused at the preciseness of the woman's routine.

"Have you considered it could just be a prank?"

Lorna-Mae quivered with incredulity, her cheeks flushing maroon. "A prank? I'm seventy-four years old. Who would want to prank me?"

Amos wanted to remark he could think of a great many people who would find it funny to fuck with a crotchety old hag like her, but on the risk of being called yet another old-timey insult, he withheld this comment.

"Alright, well, I will look into this and get back to you with what I find. What's your number?"

Lorna-Mae wrote down her phone number on a sticky note that Amos supplied and handed it over. Amos promised that he would get back to her as soon as possible.

"Yeah, well, if you don't, I'll come barging in here again and find someone else who will!"

"Can I keep this?" Amos held the note.

Lorna-Mae just glared at him for a few seconds and didn't even respond to his question. She picked herself up out of the chair and stormed off in a huff, leaving the note behind.

What a lovely woman, thought Amos.

"Shit!"

Amos tried to put pressure on the wound, but it was too late. Crimson began bubbling on his chin, and he immediately felt nauseated. He reached for a piece of toilet paper to stymie the flow, but once he pressed it against the gash and saw the blood seep through, he was on the verge of puking. Amos held his hand to the edge of the counter, determined to steady himself, and he turned his head away from the bathroom mirror, trying to avert his eyes from his own DNA.

"You alright, hun?" Anita called from the bedroom.

"Yeah, I'm alright. Just cut myself shaving."

"Aw, I'm sorry, babe. Do you feel sick? Is there anything I can do?"

Amos smiled, touched by his wife's endless compassion for him.

"No, I'm alright. Thank you though," he said.

He stood there for at least a minute, looking down at the bathroom floor. Finally, when he was almost 100 percent sure the bleeding had ceased, he looked back up into the mirror. A now-sealed cut was visible on his right cheek. Sweat glistened from the top of his large bald spot as his body worked to fight the distress signals emitting from his brain.

Amos supposed that the world would find it ridiculous a detective who often investigated violent crimes would have such a strong case of hemophobia, so he kept it as private as he could. Only his wife, his partner Stevie, and a couple of his colleagues knew of his deep-seated fear of blood.

After taking a few deep breaths to settle his nervous system, Amos found a Band-Aid from the cabinet above the sink and placed it haphazardly against his cheek. He didn't even care that it was crooked. If he looked at the wound for much longer he would lose it.

Amos rounded the corner and came back into the bedroom. Anita lay sprawled on the bed on her stomach, wearing only a large tee shirt and white panties. She was reading some magazine that offered various home-decor solutions. Once she caught sight of Amos, she flashed her beautiful smile. Every time she looked at him it was like the first time she ever saw him.

"Aw, babe, the Band-Aid is crooked."

"Yeah, well . . . lots of things in life are crooked," Amos said sheepishly.

Anita giggled. "That doesn't even make any sense, hun."

Amos took off his shirt, readying himself to crawl into bed next to her. He looked down at his body and noticed the hair on his chest seemed to be longer than it had ever been in his life. He supposed he ought to trim it down a bit to avoid looking like he had a tangle of weeds on his chest, but the hair did provide coverage of the several layers of fat that clung to his torso. As Amos looked down at his wife, slender and beautiful, he couldn't help but feel like an unsightly beast. They were the exact same age, but forty-five years of life had taken much more of a toll on Amos's exterior than it had Anita's.

Amos reclined backward until he was looking up at the ceiling from under the covers. He wasn't ready to go to sleep yet, so he hadn't bothered turning off the light before he had lain down. He stared at the grooves and notches next to the lamp above and became lost in thought. A couple minutes later, Anita aroused him from his stupor.

"What is it, hun?"

"Oh, nothing."

Anita immediately frowned and maneuvered her mouth in an expression of impatience.

"Al, don't play that game."

Amos smiled, tickled by his wife's insistence on curing the ailments of all those around her.

"Nothing is *wrong,* per se. I just have a weird feeling."

"About what?"

Amos turned his attention toward Anita. Her brown eyes burned into his. Though kind and gentle, Anita had always had a fierce spirit that made people want to tell her everything there was to tell.

"Oh, just something that happened today," Amos said finally. "This old kook came into the station and started talking about her missing nephew. She was completely adamant that he had been killed, but she said that the investigating officers were convinced that he had just left town. At first, her rambling and general demeanor just made her seem like a nut. And after she left I pulled up his file and we had indeed left the case open with a note on file that he *did* just leave town. But something just feels . . . off."

"What do you mean?" Anita furrowed her forehead in concentration.

"I don't know. It just seems like we didn't do all that we could. I know this is probably just a coincidence, but the kid disappeared five years ago on Halloween night."

Anita rocked forward a little in surprise.

"Wow," she said emphatically.

"Yeah. But, I mean, the detective who worked on the case before is Ted."

Anita nodded. Ted Leery was one of Amos's good friends and probably the most thorough detective they had on the force. If he didn't reach any strange conclusions about the nature of Devin Johnson's disappearance, then who was Amos to say it was possible foul play?

"I know you really respect Ted. But he isn't an omniscient guru, you know? There is a chance that, once in a blue moon, Ted might make a mistake. And besides, you're a pretty good detective yourself," Anita said, with a soft expression on her face.

"Well . . ."

"If something is bothering you about this, then look into it!"

Amos nodded absentmindedly, but he wasn't convinced. He had always been well-versed in the art of self-doubt.

"I know you're doing that thing where you try to convince yourself you're wrong, but you have always underestimated your ability to sense when something is amiss. Trust your instincts. They are virtually always right," Anita said with a heartwarming smile.

Amos couldn't help but return the grin. Even after nearly twenty years of marriage he was still as smitten with her as he had always been. He leaned forward, and although it caught Anita off guard, he swooped in for a kiss.

"I love you, you know that, right?"

Anita's cheeks turned pink.

"Albert, will you stop being so cute and just listen to my advice?"

Amos looked back toward the ceiling, and eventually the smile started to fade.

"Okay. I'll look into it."

FIVE DAYS BEFORE HALLOWEEN

Amos and Ted Leery sat uncomfortably close to each other. Amos could smell Ted's overpowering cologne since he was in such near proximity to him. Amos never understood why good-looking men like Ted needed to wear cologne. Surely his chiseled jaw and perfect hairline were enough to attract women. Not to mention every time Ted flashed his exorbitantly white smile, Amos swore he could hear females everywhere fluttering their eyelashes.

Across from Amos and Ted was someone who

was the opposite of attractive. With a forehead so large that it made him look like a Neanderthal, and a veritable cloud of body order lingering around him, Police Chief Scott Dozer rambled on at an uncomfortably fast pace, sounding like an auctioneer. He was in the middle of lecturing the pair in front of him on how poor of an idea it was to start reinvestigating a case without a body, and as he went on and on, he seemed to be getting redder and redder in the face.

"Listen, Albert, I appreciate what you're trying to do. But the kid was telling people that he was considering moving to California, and he had just gotten an eviction notice. I'm not going to waste time and resources looking into something that has no bearing on keeping the people in this town safe."

Ted looked at Amos, and in unison, they both rolled their eyes (a gesture that their boss thankfully missed). Dozer tended to get preachy, especially when he had to explain why he was telling people no.

"Chief, all I want to do is look around the kid's apartment and interview a couple people who live in the houses nearby," Amos said.

Before Dozer could shoot this idea down, Amos immediately turned to Ted.

"Tell him what you told me, Teddy."

Ted looked at Dozer in apprehension before replying. "I will admit that I had a lot on my plate at the time of Johnson's disappearance."

Dozer leaned forward bullishly. "But you don't think there is anything here, do you?"

Ted looked over at Amos apologetically before he responded. "I don't think so. But I don't see why it could hurt to look into it a bit deeper."

Dozer shook his head in frustration and then pointed at Amos. "When did the always-practical Albert Amos start wearing a tinfoil hat, eh?"

Amos frowned, a little offended. Ted looked over at him while wearing an expression that said, "Don't listen to him."

"Chief, I didn't even *have* to run this by you. In all likelihood, there would be one or two ten-minute interviews and this would be wrapped up. I could've done that without your permission, but I came to you out of courtesy," Amos said, and as soon as he said it, he knew it was the wrong thing to say.

"Don't you threaten me with insubordination," Dozer hissed while turning a brilliant shade of maroon.

"Okay, okay, okay. Chief, I see your position. Albert, I understand why you want to look into this with the note and what not," Ted said, referring to the taunting smiley-face sticky that was now stored in evidence. "How about this? Why don't you go down to Tuck Parker's house and interview him for the oven case? It's down by Devin Johnson's old apartment, isn't it? And if you manage to wrap up the interview quickly and find yourself probing around Johnson's apartment complex, then that should be okay, shouldn't it, Chief?"

Dozer opened his mouth to respond, but then closed it. Ted had this effect on people where he could rationally explain both sides of an argument and help the parties arrive at a compromise without much effort at all. Dozer began to lean back into his chair and placed his thick arms behind his head, flashing the tattoo of the large dog on his inner bicep.

"Fine, Amos," Dozer said irritably. He would only refer to Amos by his last name when he was pissed. "Go and interview Tuck Parker, and if you have time, stop by the kid's apartment. But I swear to God, unless you find about a dozen bodies and the fucking cure for cancer in there, don't come to me and try to reopen this thing. Got it?"

"Got it," Amos replied shortly. Dozer waved his hand in the air, indicating their dismissal. Amos and Ted simultaneously rose from their seats and nodded at Dozer before leaving the room.

As soon as they were back in the main office with all the cubicles, Amos turned to Ted.

"Hey, Teddy, thanks for that. I really appreciate it."

Ted grinned, showing off his excessively white teeth.

"No problem, buddy. No problem at all."

"Oh, you know I already went and talked to Tuck Parker, right?"

Ted's grin seemed to grow even wider.

"I do, but Dozer doesn't, does he?"

Amos laughed heartily and clapped Ted on the back.

"I suppose I should just interview him again just to cover my tracks. But anyway, I owe you one."

Ted chuckled and walked in the direction of his cubicle. Amos was a little surprised Ted had covered for him. Ted had always been somewhat of a puritan; he was never one to break the rules. But he was also a good friend. Apparently, that took priority in this circumstance.

As for Tuck Parker, Amos was already dreading seeing him again. Parker was the drug addict Amos had spoken with earlier in the week who had attempted to stick his teenage son's head in his oven. The charges had been dropped because the kid had changed his story, but the state was still trying to see if it could build a case, and thus, Dozer had told Amos to interview Parker and see what came of it. He had given Amos this task earlier in the week and said it wasn't "high priority," so Amos could see why Dozer had assumed he hadn't done it yet. It looked like Parker was going to have to be interviewed again, which was a shame, as he was one of the most deplorable human beings Amos had ever met, and the first interview had yielded squat. Parker had basically refused to divulge anything, so Amos didn't see why that would change. But if it meant getting a chance to inquest into Devin Johnson's disappearance a bit more, then he was going to do it. After all, he had to keep his promise to Anita.

"So . . . are you saying that you *did* do it? And that it was *self-defense*?"

The tattooed man in front of Amos cracked his neck in such a peculiar fashion that he briefly reminded Amos of a snake.

"Yeah, man. The kid charged at me in the kitchen. Grabbed a knife and started comin' at me with it."

After finishing his sentence, Tuck Parker summoned up a large clump of saliva from deep in his throat and spat it right onto the carpet without a second thought. Amos felt the strong urge to get up and leave, but he remained motionless on the torn-apart brown chair that was pressed against the wall. He shouldn't have been surprised. Cleanliness wasn't Parker's forte. In the kitchen to Amos's right, stacks of what looked like mail teetered on the edge of the table. Right next to the spot where Parker's saliva had hit, there was a darkened brown stain, and not far away from said stain, there was a heap of dog shit Amos had almost stepped in when he was weaving through the disgusting living room. Amos guessed the excrement had been produced by the Doberman pinscher that was chained up in the backyard and looking forlorn.

"You realize that the charges were dropped because Cade gave a different story two weeks ago, right? Not because of a lack of evidence?"

Parker's eyes swelled. Apparently, he had been oblivious to the fact his son had changed his tune, and now that he was realizing he had just reopened the can of worms, the man looked positively flummoxed.

"How would I know that? He's with his moms."

Amos almost felt an urge to laugh at the sheer stupidity of the situation.

"So . . . you got him in a headlock, pressed his head into the oven, turned it on, and held him there . . . as an act of self-defense?"

"Yeah, man, that's what I just say, isn't it?"

Amos cringed. Improper grammar was one of his biggest pet peeves.

"I'm sorry, Mr. Parker, but I just find it hard to believe that a thirteen-year-old would make you feel like your life is in danger."

"Man, he grabbed a fuckin' knife!"

"A sentiment I also find hard to believe. I interviewed Cade two days ago, and he was completely calm, rational, and respectful. Not some punk kid trying to off his dad."

"You think you know my kid better than me?" Parker's veins bulged in his neck.

Amos looked at Parker and felt repulsed. Every visible inch of skin was covered in ink. Among these tattoos was the name KELLY, a full-blown graphic of the grim reaper, a malevolent-looking snake, and a skull-and-bones pirate flag. In his earlobes were two of the biggest black gauges that Amos had ever seen. His teeth were an awful yellow with spots of black intermingled throughout. Although Parker was somewhat thin, his biceps bulged threateningly; they were on full display since the man was wearing a white tank top. Every few moments, Parker would scratch his neck like he was swatting at a bug and look around the room in a frenzy. Amos would bet his house that Parker was either on meth or heroin. His wild, drug-fueled mood swings combined with his muscular stature made it near impossible to believe that shoving Cade Parker's head in an oven was an act of self-preservation.

"I don't think I know Cade better than you, Mr. Parker. I just think you're full of shit."

Parker's eyes widened, and he stood up and

marched forward until his face was within inches of Amos's.

"Wanna run that by me again?"

Amos stared right back at Parker, repulsed but undeterred.

"Unless you want to spend the next few years of your life as someone's bitch at the state penitentiary, I suggest you back up, buddy," Amos replied irritably, as though Parker was a particularly irksome gnat. "I know that drugs can sometimes shorten a person's fuse, but you're about six inches away from aggravated assault of a police officer, which can get you up to fifteen years in Oregon. And you may be dumb, but not even a two-bit tweaker is that dumb. But prove me wrong, Mr. Parker. I'd welcome it. And Christ, take a damn Altoid. Your breath smells like that pile of dog crap on your carpet."

Parker snarled and gnawed on his bottom lip. Eventually, reason seemed to overtake his fury, and he retreated onto the couch.

"Look, Mr. Parker," Amos said. "I have more than enough to give to the DA now, and you could do some significant time. So we can do this the hard way, and it will likely end with you spending the next ten years in a cell, or you can drop this self-defense bullshit and make a formal confession and set your sights on a plea deal that will chop years off your sentence."

Parker smiled, and Amos noticed he was missing at least two of his teeth.

"Fuck that."

"Excuse me?"

"Fuck that. And fuck you. Get out of my house."

Amos smiled and shrugged.

"Hard way it is," he said simply.

Without another word or glance in Parker's direction, Amos got up from his seat and strode toward the front door, which was still ajar. With his stomach turning and his blood boiling, Amos crossed the threshold, stomped down the steps, and purposefully walked through Parker's front lawn, taking care to track mud from the nearby planter through the grass. He had a feeling Parker was watching him from his living room window.

Once Amos was back in the driver's seat of his company-issued Dodge Charger, he cursed in frustration. He wasn't upset Parker hadn't given him a formal confession; hell, this whole venture was just a ploy so that he could go and snoop around Devin Johnson's old apartment anyway. But it did aggravate him when informants or suspects spoke to him with such disrespect. It also surprised him in a way. A person of interest just draws more attention when they act like a jackass.

Amos turned the key in his ignition and merged onto the street without even looking for oncoming traffic. He sped away, using the gas pedal as an outlet for his frustration. He was suddenly going so fast he almost missed the right turn that would take him to Western Village, but jerked his steering wheel just in time. Amos peeked into his rearview mirror, making sure no one behind him saw his uneven driving, but alas, a red Mini Cooper rushed past, and Amos was positive the person driving it hadn't missed his fitful maneuver. *Oh well,* he thought.

Amos drove two more blocks until he saw a ramshackle cluster of buildings to his right. The parking lot was totally vacated, so Amos swung his vehicle into a spot that was within proximity to the nearest rundown structure. After his engine was off, he hopped out, and took a gander at his surroundings. The nearest houses were more than fifty yards away, as a giant field separated the former apartments from the closest neighborhood. *Well, shit,* thought Amos. Canvassing an area for possible witnesses who could provide some sort of information was always an iffy proposition if it took place well after the fact, but doing so when the logistics wouldn't yield a plausible informant anyway was a fruitless endeavor. The more logical route would be to try and contact friends and family, but that would also be more difficult, as most of Devin Johnson's family no longer lived in the area and Amos had no clue who the boy called friends.

Amos looked toward the ground in disappointment. He knew this was a long shot anyway. Heck, Devin Johnson was probably still alive. There was just something about the whole thing: the note, the way Lorna-Mae was so strong in her convictions, and the fact that it had happened on Halloween. Most years the holiday didn't mean much, but a mysterious disappearance on the Day of the Dead? It all led to an unsettling feeling lingering in Amos's gut. But there was nothing he could do. And he had already kept his promise to his wife by coming here.

Before he got back into his car, Amos looked up at the apartments in front of him. They had suffered major decay, and there were at least seven ivy strands crawling up the outer walls. The buildings were tall and, for some reason, menacing. Perhaps it was the degeneration of the exterior. The place looked more like a haunted house than an abandoned apartment complex. Amos's eyes fluttered over everything. For a moment, he tried to convince himself to just get back in the car. But for some reason, he moved inside the complex and toward the staircase that would take him up to the third floor.

Amos trudged up the stairs, and by the time he made it to the landing he was looking for, his thighs were burning. He was surprised at how many rooms the architects had packed onto one floor. It was one of those urban developments specifically made for low-income housing, so the high volume of apartments was a little jarring. Generally, with this kind of place, there were limited spaces available.

He continued down the row of apartments, passing 316 and 317. Eventually, he made it to the one he was looking for: 333. Devin Johnson's old apartment. For some reason, Amos's pulse was beginning to ascend. He froze, looking back over his shoulder, as there was a bizarre sensation in his gut. There couldn't be anyone around; this place was deserted. So why did he feel like he was being watched? He looked back across the apartment building and saw a room adjacent to the one he was about to enter on the opposing landing. The blinds were open, the darkness inside hollow. Amos tried to ignore the voice in his head that was telling him a set of unfriendly eyes could be lingering in the darkness. He turned forward, gripped the handle to the door, and turned it gently. Surprisingly, it was unlocked.

The door swung open, and Amos was greeted by exactly what he thought he would be: absolutely nothing. There was no leftover furniture, nor a fridge. The light blue walls were dusty and blank, offering no hint someone use to live here. He shook his head, frustrated that he had tricked himself into thinking this foray would produce any sort of desirable results. Amos walked over the threshold and looked in the small room that doubled as a living area and a kitchen. There was another door across from him that he guessed led to a bedroom. He quickly moved across the living area and opened the door.

The bedroom was miniscule. There was enough space to fit a queen-sized bed and not much else. The only thing in the room was a closet on the opposite wall. Amos rolled it open. It was so tiny it couldn't even fit the most conservative of wardrobes, so it took him about two seconds to figure out there wasn't anything of note inside. He turned and stared at the vacant walls. Even though he wasn't even sure what he was looking for, he knew that it wasn't there.

Oh, Albert, he thought. *This is why it never pays to follow every aimless lead.* Amos shook his head and smiled at nothing in particular. He had always prided himself on being rational. Even-keeled. Calm. Only going where the facts lead. Sometimes, Anita had even accused him of being *too* pragmatic. "Where is your sense of adventure?" she had once asked. This is where spontaneity got you. Looking at an abandoned apartment where nothing interesting had ever happened. Amos felt a bit foolish. *Waste of time,* he thought as he exited what was once Devin Johnson's bedroom.

As Amos was about to make his way back onto

the landing, something made him do a double-take. Behind the door, a weird crimson color clashed with the blue paint beyond. Amos gripped the door and swung it shut so that he could get a clear view of what he was looking at. On the wall, there was a large horizontal X drawn with a splotchy curved line underneath it. It was the same dead-like smiley face that had been on the note Lorna-Mae had given him, but blown up. Amos leaned in, and a curious iron-like smell reached his nose. Suddenly, a wave of nausea hit him like a freight train. The face had been drawn in blood.

Amos plugged his nose and ripped the front door open. When he was back onto the landing, he couldn't control himself. With a massive retch, he threw his body toward the railing and vomited onto the grass below. He spent many moments doubled over, trying to catch his breath, and spitting the taste of bile out of his mouth. His hand began fumbling in his pocket for his phone.

Seconds later, he was on the line with dispatch.

"Yeah, hi, this is Detective Albert Amos. I'm at 1455 Southwest Second Street. Apartment 333. I have found a probable violent crime scene. Send forensics. And quickly. The blood on the wall is still fresh."

FOUR DAYS BEFORE
HALLOWEEN

From outside, everything looked tranquil. It was a balmy fall day, sixty-five degrees, but with a casual breeze that acted as a coolant for anyone not stuck inside. Leaves listed lazily down the sidewalk, and the American flag in front of the large gray building fluttered half-heartedly. To an outsider, it would appear that a sense of malaise had overtaken the Newport Police Department. But inside, people bustled about so fast it appeared as if the various sergeants, detectives, and lieutenants were preparing for the impending apocalypse. A typical Friday. Bad things always seemed to happen just before the weekend. It was like people let their guard down knowing that bliss of their days off was just around the corner.

Amos sat at his desk, staring at the picture of Devin Johnson he had printed out. The kid was tall and wiry, with glasses and a pale complexion. He reminded Amos of a meerkat or a weasel. The photograph was stacked on top of a manila folder that was stuffed full of the pages of documents that Amos had collected, all of which pertained to Johnson.

Earlier that day, there had been a head-on collision on Highway 20, nine miles east of Newport. A young woman had been sending a text to her friend and had only realized that she had crossed the yellow line when she saw a Ford F-150 barreling toward her. Early reports on scene indicated the woman had suffered two broken wrists, a lacerated spleen, a collapsed lung, and several fractured ribs. The driver in the other car hadn't been so lucky. Fifty-seven-year-old Stephan Forsyth's body was in the process of being transported to the morgue. That was the tragedy of the whole thing: the innocent had been slaughtered and the guilty would survive, albeit likely facing charges of manslaughter and reckless endangerment.

Every cubicle seemed to be possessed by talk of the collision. Only Amos and Ted Leery were currently focused on looking for links and possible witnesses to the young man.

Amos stared at the picture of Johnson, lost in thought. He was suddenly jolted out of his stupor by an enthusiastic voice.

"So, you finally learned to minimize the porn tabs on your computer? What a momentous occasion!"

Amos spun around in his chair, and was greeted by a devious and energetic smile and a punch to the arm.

"Ow! Jesus, Stevie."

"Oh, don't be such a pansy, Al."

The young brunette bounded into his cubicle like a puppy, pulling a chair behind her to sit in. Her dark hair was in a ponytail that wagged back and forth on the back of her head, and her straight teeth remained on display as she continued to grin. Stevie Hutchins placed her rear into the chair and drew closer to Amos.

"I don't think you know how hard you hit," Amos said wearily.

Stevie stuck her bottom lip out in a mocking expression.

"Aw, poor baby. You need a Band-Aid? Maybe a tampon?"

"That doesn't even make sense."

Stevie giggled, and the energetic, breathtakingly attractive smile remained plastered to her face. Amos always had to work with all his might to try and suppress any sign he was attracted to her. If he ever flirted with Stevie or made any sort of offhand comment, no matter how benign, rumors would abound that he had a thing for his much younger, much more attractive partner. Such was the nature of a small town. And the last thing he needed was gossip that made him sound like a crusty old creep.

"How was Kauai?" Amos looked back down at the picture of Johnson.

"Just fuckin' dandy!" Stevie said.

"What did you guys do? All the touristy activities?"

"Well, we went snorkeling and hiked Mount Kawaikini. But Aaron got sick halfway through the trip and had to stay at the hotel so that kind of put an end to that sort of stuff.

"Oh, that's rough. I'm sorry," Amos replied in a monotone voice. He was unable to conceal his indifference to a young, attractive couple that wasn't able to have a perfect vacation.

"No worries. Our hotel was right on the water anyway so I just got to suntan for most of the week."

"You do look quite a bit tanner," Amos said,

trying to push the thought of Stevie in a bikini out of his mind.

"Thanks, Al!"

"Did you just get back in yesterday?"

"Nah, two days ago. Wanted to have a day to decompress before I came back to the station."

"Understandable." Amos nodded.

"What are you working on?"

"The Johnson case."

"The what case?"

Amos looked over at Stevie in surprise. Obviously since she had just returned from vacation, there was no possible way she would be cognizant of anything pertaining to Devin Johnson. But since he had spent the last day totally absorbed in all the details of Johnson's disappearance, it was still odd to hear a newcomer completely oblivious to everything that had happened.

"Oh Jesus . . . where do I even start?"

"At the beginning, numb nuts."

Amos sighed. He took one heavy breath, and then launched into an explanation of what had taken place in the last forty-eight hours. When he reached the part about the same dead smiley face being drawn in blood on the wall of Johnson's old apartment, Stevie's mouth fell open so far that her lips looked like they were about to crack.

"Oh. My. God. Are you kidding me?"

"Not kidding, I'm afraid."

"It was the same face that the aunt gave you on the note?"

"The very same," Amos replied with a perfunctory nod.

Stevie's eyes bulged like they were about to pop.

"So you think it was a homicide? And the killer is taunting her?"

"Taunting her. And playing with us."

"What did the note say again?" Stevie rubbed her forehead as she tried to recall what Amos had told her.

"It said, 'Who's next? All Hallow's Eve.'"

"So he's saying he's going to kill someone else this Halloween?"

"That's what *I* am gathering from the message, yes."

Stevie rubbed her forehead in disbelief. "Jesus Christ. This is *huge*."

"I know."

There was a long lull as Stevie looked around the cubicle, thinking about everything that Amos had told her.

"So wait, whose blood was it on the wall?"

"Yesterday, forensics ran it through several databases with no matches. However, Johnson didn't have a criminal record, so he wouldn't be in any databases. So we brought in Johnson's father yesterday evening for a genealogical DNA comparison since he lives in Newport, and the results came in this morning. There is a ninety-nine percent chance that it was Devin Johnson's blood on that wall," Amos said darkly.

"Jesus. Is the blood fresh?"

"It was fresh to the wall. But old. It had just been preserved."

"Holy cannoli oil," Stevie responded in awe, while fiddling with her ponytail. Amos had long ago picked up on this as one of Stevie's nervous ticks. Whenever she was experiencing stress or was deep in thought, she would play with her hair.

"Are you the only one working on this?"

"No, Ted is in on it too," Amos replied. "We have kind of been double-teaming this since you were gone. He has been looking for any possible witnesses who saw Johnson on Halloween night in 2012. I'm trying to get in contact with the neighbors who watched him leave his place. I have been attempting to figure out where the boy was headed when he left his apartment. I talked to Verizon, and they should be faxing over the texts that came from Johnson's phone that night any minute now."

Stevie nodded.

"And what does Dozer think about this whole thing?"

Amos smiled in exasperation. "Let's just say he wasn't exactly thrilled with what I found."

"He can't stop this now, can he? If Johnson's

blood was on the wall in that insignia it must be the killer's signature," Stevie said. "No matter how much of an obstructionist Dozer is, he can't impede this, can he?"

"You bet your ass he can," quipped Amos. "If it were up to Dozer, we would be all writing speeding tickets. Anything that's complicated or takes time to investigate gives Dozer a pulmonary embolism."

Stevie shook her head in annoyance.

"Well, we can only hope he lets us do our jobs. Have you had any luck yet? Any leads?"

Amos shrugged. He didn't have anything, but for some reason, he never liked disappointing Stevie. He was her mentor, and although he was only twelve years older than her, he often thought that she considered him a father figure.

"Well, not a *lead* per se . . ."

"Jesus, Al, just say no."

"Alright then, no."

"What about Ted?"

"Not that I kno—"

"Speak of the devil!"

Ted had suddenly come into view, and the expression on his face was a little unsettling. Stevie looked up at him and her eyes seemed to zero in on his lean torso, which caused Amos to feel a slight twinge of annoyance. Stevie was engaged and living with a young man named Aaron Wright. They had been together for five years. Yet, every once in a while, she would look at Ted like she was ready to be mounted by him right then and there. Amos liked Ted, but he would also often feel jealous of his boyish good looks and charisma.

"What's up, Teddy? Find anybody?"

Ted shook his head vigorously.

"Not anyone connected to Devin Johnson. But curiosity got the best of me, and I expanded my search."

"Expanded your . . . what?"

"Have you ever heard of Luke Ledoux?"

"Luke who?"

"Ledoux."

Amos furrowed his brow in befuddlement. "Who the hell is that?"

"Someone we're both going to be very familiar with in the coming days. Here, come with me. Both of you."

Luke Ledoux wasn't exactly a looker. With a nose so pointed Amos felt like it could be used as a weapon, and bucked teeth that would put a beaver to shame, the morbidly obese seventeen-year-old was quite homely.

Ted had maximized the tab on Safari so that the

online story from the *News Times* blanketed the entire screen of his MacBook. The headline, which was in bold, was striking:

Teen Disappears In Suspected Suicide

"Jesus. This is how it all starts," Amos said while leaning over Ted's shoulder.

"I know," Ted replied quietly.

Stevie was on Ted's other side, transfixed by the headline on the computer.

"A 'suspected' suicide? Meaning the physical evidence wasn't conclusive?"

"No, meaning a body was never even recovered," Ted said simply.

"Then how do they know it was suicide?"

Ted gave Stevie a condescending look. Amos would never tell her this, but he knew for a fact that Ted didn't care for Stevie.

"*They* know because we told them. I brought up the kid's file." Ted grabbed a manila envelope and tossed it in Stevie's direction. "He had been on Zoloft for years and had tried to kill himself twice before. Also, we used the GPS on his phone to determine his last known location on the night he died. Guess where he was."

"I have no id—"

"The bridge," Amos added.

Ted clicked his tongue and pointed at Amos,

confirming his assertion.

"He jumped off the bridge?"

Amos nodded, but Ted shook his head, giving hilariously unintentional opposing responses. "No, I don't think he did. But we were made to think he did."

Stevie frowned in concentration as she stared at the picture of Ledoux. "But why do you think that? What makes you think this was foul play? If the last known location of a previously suicidal teen was a bridge, logic would dictate that he jumped off it of his own volition, no?"

Instead of using a verbal response, Ted simply opened the manila folder. On the first page, which gave the basic details of everything the department had gathered about the disappearance, he used his index finger to scroll until he found the lines of text he was looking for. Stevie and Amos both leaned in and read simultaneously.

Time of Disappearance: Approximately 10:17 PM.

Date: 10-31-2007.

"So what you're saying is . . . you think there is a

killer living in Lincoln County. But he only kills every five years. . . on Halloween night?"

Dozer looked at Amos as though he were suggesting that Biggie and Tupac were secretly still alive and living in Cuba. His eyes were wide, his lips were caved in and a vein was bulging in his neck.

"I know it sounds crazy—"

"You're goddamn right it sounds crazy. It sounds asinine."

"Boss, look. We found—"

"Wait! Stop right there. Instead of *you* telling *me* what you found, *I* will tell *you* what you didn't find. A body. In fact, you haven't found any bodies at all," Dozer said angrily. "And yet, you're dropping that on me? A 'serial killer'?"

"Technically he has to kill three people to be considered a serial killer." Amos tried to sound as smarmy as he could. He was irritated Dozer was focusing all his attention on him, even though Ted was in the office too.

Dozer was turning purple and moving his lips, trying to find the best insult to hurl at Amos. Before he could, Ted stepped in.

"Chief, you have already said Devin Johnson's death has to be viewed as a homicide."

Dozer looked over at Ted with his brows raised. Being that the detective was usually so submissive, Ted was the chief's favorite subordinate, and the look on Dozer's face was one that reflected a feeling of mini-betrayal.

"Teddy, we ain't talking about Johnson here. We're talking about Luke Ledoux, aren't we?"

Ted pursed his lips and shrugged his shoulders. "You have to admit that a young man in the same age bracket as Johnson who also vanished on Halloween night is, at the very least, suspicious."

"But like I said, you don't have a *body*! No body, no investigation. Unless you find that same goddamned insignia drawn in blood on Ledoux's fucking wall," Dozer mumbled.

"Stevie is bringing up Ledoux's old address now. Once we have it, the three of us are going to go scope it out," Amos said.

"Then scope it out, and if you find anything, then come talk to me. But now, there is absolutely no reason to throw around the phrase 'serial killer'!"

Amos had to use all his willpower to hold in the comment he wanted to make, that Dozer was the only one who had even said serial killer.

"Why are you even bringing this to me now?" demanded Dozer.

Amos looked over at Ted, and the two exchanged apprehensive glances. They both knew the fury Dozer was exhibiting was nothing in comparison to the rage they were about to induce. Nobly, Ted took the lead.

"We think we need to bring patrol in and prep them for this. If this guy is planning something for Halloween, we need everyone on alert."

Instead of turning a deeper shade of red and cussing them out like Amos was expecting, Dozer's face broke into a smile. It was a forced thing and seemed more like a grimace than a grin.

"No," he whispered.

Amos looked over at Ted, and the two swapped exasperated expressions.

"What?"

"No," Dozer said, and his voice was quite a bit louder this time.

"But—" Ted began.

"No!" Dozer yelled, his voice amplified to a decibel Amos had never heard it reach before.

Abruptly, Ted stood up with a look of fury blazing in his eyes and left the office without another word. On his way out, he took great care to slam the door. Dozer didn't even flinch at the sound before focusing his attention on Amos. His eyes narrowed, and it was as if he was daring Amos to challenge him on his stance. Amos knew that, for now, the battle had been lost. Therefore, he stood up, holding eye contact with Dozer before he turned to the door and left the office.

Once he was back in his cubicle, Amos was shaking in anger. Whenever he was filled with unmitigated rage, he found it impossible to focus.

Instead of trying to distract himself and find an outlet for his anger, he simply stewed in it, letting it marinate until he felt like screaming. The same thoughts kept scampering through his consciousness like persistent rats, gnawing away at his Zen. *Fucking Dozer. Always the obstructionist.* This wasn't even close to the first time that his boss had impeded progress on a case, but this situation was the direst. If another young man died, Amos would not hesitate to put the onus of blame on his boss. They had all of the proof they needed to bring in reinforcements. Did Dozer just not care about the children in the community enough to want to increase the scope of this thing? *Fucking spineless bastard.* Every time he thought of how irrational it was, Amos would feel a pang in his chest that gave him a strong desire to pick up his Mac and chuck it across the room.

He couldn't believe his boss could be so thick. After all, Dozer had okayed a forensics team sweeping Devin Johnson's apartment, and begrudgingly agreed to bring in Johnson's father for a DNA comparison. He had even *told* Ted that Johnson's disappearance had to be reopened as a probable homicide. So why was it so hard to believe that Luke Ledoux's death was nefarious in nature too? Why had he gotten so angry at them for suggesting it?

Dozer had only been in his position for a year.

His predecessor, Mickey Mulvaney, had stepped down after the department had been put under fire by local and national media regarding the way it had handled a serial murder case that had gone unsolved for thirty years. The press had called Mulvaney incompetent and the department negligent. Several of Mulvaney's subordinates had been fired, and one had even been arrested for impeding and affecting the investigation. The whole thing was an utter fiasco, and Dozer had been under a microscope since he had been hired to succeed Mulvaney. So perhaps *that* was why he was so resistant to the theory that Amos and Ted had presented. Maybe he couldn't bring himself to consider the idea that a case that could potentially bring the NPD a veritable avalanche of media attention might have just fallen into his lap, after one like it had cost the last chief his job. Dozer was just trying to save his own skin. Either way, he was being moronic and stubborn.

Amos was so absorbed in pissing himself off about the whole situation he didn't hear Stevie enter his cubicle, and he jumped when she spoke.

"I've got it."

"Christ, Stevie! When are you going to stop doing that? You almost gave me a heart attack."

Stevie chuckled. "You can't be that stressed out. And if you are, having a heart attack might behoove you. Death is definitely a viable solution to excessive stress."

"Hardy, har, har," Amos replied acrimoniously.

"Anyway, it's 353 Southeast Seventh Street."

"What are you—wait! Ledoux's old address?"

Stevie gave a sarcastic thumbs-up. "Can't get anything past you."

Amos didn't say anything, but started frantically looking around for his phone and his keys.

"What are you—"

"Go get Ted. We're going there now."

Amos looked to his right, noticing how high-end the neighborhood they were passing through was. Each house seemed to grow in girth and height as they moved along; apparently, the nicest homes were tucked into the far corner of the street. Southeast Seventh came to a halt at a dead end, and the gravel road morphed into a cliff. Below, Amos could see buildings he knew to be a part of the Bayfront. The confluence of brush and trees made it difficult to get a good view of Yaquina Bay, but Amos had a feeling the aesthetics would improve once you were on the second or third floor of any one of the beautiful homes surrounding him.

From inside the company-issued Dodge

Charger, piloted by Ted, Amos sat in the front passenger seat while Stevie looked cooped up behind them. Ted, as always, remained calm and collected as he drove the car about ten miles slower than was necessary. Amos was secretly thankful Ted wasn't his partner. Although a brilliant detective and a shrewd mind, Ted was far too cautious and adhered a little too tightly to the rules for Amos's taste. He was almost unbearably squeaky clean. Stevie, on the other hand was bold, sometimes brash, and unafraid. It made things less daunting when you had someone by your side who would never back down.

Ted pulled up next to a baby-blue house that was just on the precipice of being a mansion. It had three stories, and Amos guessed each story had at least five rooms, minimum. Stevie had discovered the Ledouxs had moved away from this house shortly after their son had died. However, they didn't sell the house. And though no one had lived in it for some time, the place looked perfectly well-kept.

Ted parked the car right in front of the black mailbox that had the numbers 353 plastered on it. He, Amos, and Stevie all simultaneously got out of the car and began walking up toward the front door.

"I don't even know why we're doing this if you don't want to enter the house, Ted," said Stevie irritably.

"Look around, Stevie." Ted's voice dripped with disdain. "Somebody has obviously been taking care of this place for the Ledouxs. This lawn couldn't have been mowed more than a week ago."

"So your banking on the off chance that this caretaker, whoever he or she is, is going to be cleaning precisely when we come knocking?"

"Or maybe this person stays here in return for taking care of the house."

Amos looked over and smiled as he noticed how many strides Stevie's short legs had to take to keep an even pace with the two taller men. Once they climbed up the steps to the front porch, Ted raised his fist and clunked it three times on the door. There was only silence in response to the knocking; no distinguishable bustling or extraneous noise came from within. After ten seconds, it was abundantly clear that no one was home.

"Well, this was a waste of time," Stevie said cheerfully.

Ted ignored Stevie's brashness and took out his phone and began texting someone. Stevie sighed; Amos knew that Ted was purposefully trying to irritate her now.

Instead of trying to break the tension between them, Amos tried the door handle for shits and giggles. While twisting, he was expecting to meet resistance. But there was none.

"It's unlocked."

Ted looked up from his phone in surprise and a mini-smile broke out on Stevie's face.

"Well come on then! Let's go!"

"No!" Ted stopped them with his hand out. "This house still belongs to the Ledouxs. If we went in there now without their permission or a warrant we would be trespassing."

"Suit yourself, but I'm going inside." Stevie shoved his hand out of the way and walked around him.

"Wait!" Ted began, but Stevie had already pushed the door open and crossed the threshold. With a shrug and an apologetic look in Ted's direction, Amos followed her.

The interior of the house matched the exterior in glamour and opulence; a massive wooden staircase sprouted up in front of them and an appealing shiny tile floor spread out below. The place was pristine. In fact, it almost looked like no one had ever lived there at all. There weren't even any furnishings, nor were there leftover belongings.

Ted hissed as he passed through the doorway behind them.

"If we get caught doing this I'm throwing you under the bus, Stevie. No way am I sticking up for you to Dozer."

Stevie pretended not to hear him and moseyed forward toward the staircase.

"What do you think, Al? I'll go upstairs and

you two look around here? We're specifically looking for that insignia, aren't we?

"I mean, of course. But if anything else strikes you as odd or out of place don't hesitate to bring it to my attention," Amos replied, looking into the nearby living room, which was adjacent to a hallway.

"Roger that."

Ted made sure that Stevie was all the way up the stairs before turning to Amos. "Man, I can't imagine what it must be like to deal with *that* every day. You deserve a raise."

Amos smiled and shrugged. "I will admit that she does get a little overbearing at times. But she's fearless. And not afraid to take risks. Which, considering my personality type, is something that is needed in our partner dynamic. And she's driven. She works harder than most of the people in our department."

Ted look unconvinced. "Whatever you say."

The two men meandered into the living room, which was absent of any furniture. The walls were completely blank. The only noticeable object in the room was a coiled line of cable burgeoning up from a tiny hole in the ground Amos guessed used to connect to a TV. No dead smiley faces leered at them, nor did any old blood glimmer from the walls.

After making certain that nothing of note was

in the living room, Amos turned and ducked into the kitchen. He was expecting Ted to follow, but instead, the man went back in the direction that they came.

"I'm going to look at the other rooms down the hallway," he said.

Amos nodded and continued into the large kitchen. The floor was vast and looked incredibly barren without any sort of table in the middle of it. He checked the cupboards, and found those empty too. He swiveled about but saw nothing of great significance. Somewhat surprisingly, the large and magnificent Sub-Zero fridge that must've served the Ledouxs had been left behind. For no reason in particular, Amos gripped the handle of the fridge and swung it open. Inside, there was a single item: an opened can of Pepsi.

There was a dull hum in the background, indicating that the fridge was still on. *Odd,* thought Amos. The electricity was still on, so someone must have been in the house somewhat recently. Perhaps the soda belonged to the caretaker, whomever it was. Amos shut the fridge and gave one last sweeping look around the kitchen. His concentration was broken by Ted's voice from across the house.

"Al! Come look at this!"

Judging from the excitement in Ted's voice, he had found something of consequence. Amos hurried out of the kitchen to the living room. When he entered the hallway that Ted had gone down, he became a little confused. There were two doorways on either side and none of the four doors was open.

"Where are you, Teddy?" Amos called.

"In here!" Ted shouted. His voice sounded like it came from behind the last door on the right. Amos opened it and found Ted crouching on the floor. He had his phone out and was utilizing the flashlight application to shed light on the ground. The room beyond contained a water heater, and although it was otherwise bare, Amos guessed it used to be home to a washer and a dryer. Amos looked over Ted's shoulder and mentally zoomed in on what he was looking at. There was a clearly displaced floorboard and what looked like a ladder that led to a dark chasm underneath it. The basement.

"I found it like this," Ted said eagerly. "This floorboard was already like this. And look at it. You can see fingerprints in the dust."

Amos felt a leap of excitement in his gut.

"Let's go."

Ted nodded and started climbing down the ladder. Once he had scaled down several steps, Amos began making his way down too. It was a short climb, perhaps only six feet or so. However, the darkness was so enveloping that it was impossible to see anything that surrounded them.

Amos hopped down off the ladder onto the concrete below and stood next to Ted, who was shining his flashlight around in a circle.

"Do you smell that?"

"What?" Amos smelled the air. "Oh, yeah, now I do." The smell was so strong, it almost made him gag.

Through the darkness, Amos could see Ted's eyes bulging. "What do you think that is?"

"Well, we're in a basement. Chances are, it's probably a dead rodent or something. Maybe a raccoon."

By the light of his phone, Amos saw Ted shake his head.

"Not going to lie, this is pretty damn creepy."

Amos laughed. "Well, if the killer is down here waiting to ambush us, at least we will know that we were right about this whole thing."

"Yeah. That is a comforting thought," Ted said sardonically. They both chuckled, while Ted pointed his makeshift flashlight against the wall.

"Where the hell is the light switch in here?"

Taking his cue, Amos brought out his phone and accessed the flashlight application. He gyrated everywhere, almost spasmodically. Once the light passed over the bulky object suspended in the center of the room, they seemed to let out a collective gasp.

"What the *hell* is that?"

After a few seconds of stunned silence, the two crept forward, while Ted focused the light on what they had both seen. The object was light brown and red and appeared to be levitating in the center of the room. Ted pointed his phone upward, and with horror, Amos realized what they were looking at. The carcass of a deer, bloodied and ripped apart, had been hung from the roof of the basement. It had been disemboweled.

Amos began to retch, feeling stomach acid rising in his throat.

"Oh my God." Ted pinched his nose.

What was most jarring was the way the dead deer had been placed. Instead of a noose around its neck, two ropes had been tied to its front legs. The legs were being pulled in opposite directions, making the deer look vaguely like Jesus on the cross. Amos would've almost preferred the deer being hung by its nape. The way it was placed gave it an oddly humanoid feel. It was as if they were looking at an actual dead body.

Fighting past the urge to vomit, Amos swiveled the beam onto the wall opposite him. It took him seconds to find what he was looking for: the color red. In his chest, his lungs seemed to compress; it was as if the blood had reached out in the form of a hand and taken an ironclad grip on his diaphragm.

Amos moved past the deer, making sure to breathe through his mouth. When he was within several feet, he was able to get a clear view of the red stain. Sure enough, he was greeted by the same dead smiley-face insignia, blown up even bigger than it had been on Devin Johnson's wall. This time, it was also accompanied with writing underneath the face. Amos leaned in, reading what was written.

THE WOLF'S PREY, BE NOT DECEIVED. HE FEASTS AGAIN ON ALL HALLOW'S EVE.

"The wolf?"

"Yep."

"Is that what he's calling himself?"

"I guess . . ."

Anita brought the glass to her face and sipped her wine absentmindedly. She had already finished two glasses of the bottle of merlot in front of her, and Amos noticed her sentences were beginning to become short and choppy. Unlike most people, Anita seemed to have a firm grasp of when she was getting drunk, and she always consciously tried to suppress every sign of it, thus the diminutive speech. Amos had a glass of wine in front of him as well, but it was mostly untouched. They sat at the dinner table, and every sound made around them seemed extraordinarily loud. Perhaps it was the creepy conversation.

"So the deer was some sort of prop?"

"Huh?"

"Well, it said, 'He feasts again'?"

"Right."

"A lot of gray wolves mainly eat deer in the wild."

Amos couldn't help but smile and raise his eyebrows. His wife had always possessed the most random shreds of superfluous knowledge, including, apparently, a wolf's culinary habits. "My wife, part-time consumer of wine, part-time zoology apprentice."

Anita let out a deep belly laugh. "You know that I know things."

Amos shook his head. He always thought his wife would make a fantastic *Jeopardy* contestant. At Amos's company Christmas party, there was an annual game of trivia, and he and Anita won every single year.

"Trust me, I know. Sometimes it feels like you know everything."

Anita smiled and brushed Amos's nose flirtatiously with the tip of her finger.

"If only that were the case. Might be able to actually keep you in line there, mister."

Amos chuckled and leaned in for a small kiss. Once he withdrew his face, Anita started speaking again.

"To me, it seems like it's all just a show, you know? That basement. It feels like he's saying the real 'feast' is going to happen for him when he kills on Halloween. Not that he's insinuating cannibalism or anything. Seems metaphorical. But if he is, that would explain why Johnson and Ledoux's bodies were never found?" proffered Anita.

Amos stuck out his tongue in disgust. "Wow, babe, thanks for that lovely thought."

Anita grinned widely. "I'm just saying! It would make sense," she said, and it appeared as though she was being facetious. "So you don't know if it's Ledoux's blood yet?"

"Well, not necessarily. But I would bet my right nipple that it is."

Anita raised her nostrils and puckered her lips. "Uh, can we find something else to wager?"

Amos laughed. "Well, it's going to take a day for forensics to come back with the results, so in that time, you can think of a better bet."

Anita placed the wineglass down on the kitchen table, and gave Amos a piercing stare. Amos looked in her eyes and felt goose bumps race down the back of his spine. Sometimes she could literally extract information from his brain at will.

"Are you okay?"

"What?"

"Are you *okay*? The scene sounds pretty . . . gruesome. Sometimes you do this thing where you act all jovial and lighthearted to try and mask your true feelings." She wasn't speaking in an accusatory tone; she was simply trying to get at the heart of the matter.

"Honey, I'm fine. Honestly, this doesn't even crack the top five in worst things I have had to look at in my career."

Anita continued to stare at him dubiously.

"Okay, *okay,* it was a little gross."

"A little? It sounds disgusting!"

"I just can't get the image of that mutilated deer out of my head. It was the way it was staged. It looked like a crucifixion or something." Amos shuddered.

"I'm sorry, babe. That sounds awful."

"The whole thing was just theatrics by this guy. Just some sort of twisted scene that he envisioned."

Anita nodded, her expression soft. "Yeah, but still. I can see why you're shaken by the whole thing."

"Yeah."

Amos broke eye contact with his wife, looking around the kitchen. Every few seconds, his mind went right back to the deer; bloodied, shredded, and suspended in midair like some sort of possessed avatar of the killer.

"So what does Dozer think about the whole

thing?"

Amos looked at his wife and gave her a meaningful grin.

"Oh, he's just *thrilled.*"

Anita chuckled and took another big gulp of wine.

"See, Dozer is in a tricky position. Before we found this, he wanted to downplay it. Like because of everything that happened with Mickey and the Nowhere Girls, he just couldn't bring himself to admit that a case like this had fallen into his lap," Amos explained. "But *now,* he's dead set on avoiding all the mistakes Mickey made. The clunky police work and shoddy investigation by Mickey's detectives over all those years. After he saw the scene, he's all about dedicating everybody's time and resources to catching this guy."

"What do you mean?"

"He already has me, Ted, Stevie, and Bonner working on it," responded Amos. "Bonner was working on a separate case like usual, but since he's technically Ted's partner, Dozer made Ted bring him in on it. Then he was talking about bringing two other detectives in too. And we're already discussing an all-staff meeting the day before Halloween to try and prep for whatever this guy has up his sleeve."

Anita nodded and her eyes began to lose focus as she concentrated on everything Amos had told her.

"So you think he's going to kill again?"

In the ephemeral moment before he answered, Amos' thoughts gravitated towards the face that had kept flickering back into his consciousness over the past few days. The bright blue eyes, the lazy smile. Back when Amos was a deputy, he had developed an amicable relationship with a sixteen-year-old kid named John Kimball. His friends had called him Johnny K, or sometimes, Special K. Amos had caught the kid skipping class one day back in '04. Ol' Johnny K had been smoking weed with his goons at a spot that the teenagers called the Top of the World. Amos had given the kid a break, with the agreement that he would never be caught with another roach again. He had encouraged Johnny to stay in school, and they had kept in contact for many months, speaking on the phone and even meeting each other for the occasional banana split. He wasn't sure what it was, but Amos had seen potential in the kid. Some sort of raw smarts that he thought would translate in the world. That was why it was so devastating when the Coast Guard had dragged him out of Yaquina Bay two years later. A suicide. And Amos had never found out why. There didn't seem like there *could* be a logical why. But the onus was on him. He had failed John Kimball.

Finally, he answered his wife. "If we don't stop

him, yes."

Anita nodded, trying to downplay the trepidation Amos knew she felt.

"And who is the guy you're going to talk to tomorrow?"

"Oscar Gutierrez, the caretaker of the Ledouxs' house."

"Like just to see if he ever saw anybody suspicious?"

"Well that, among other things," Amos admitted.

Anita froze and she immediately picked up on the fact that there was something else Amos was insinuating.

"Other things?"

Amos looked at her, unsure if he should continue. His wife was his wife, but it was definitely a breach of protocol to share these kinds of details with anyone who wasn't involved in the investigation, even though every detective did it.

"Correct."

"Such as?"

"Well, we spoke to the Ledouxs. All I can say is that the entrance to the basement was well-hidden. The only people who knew about it were the Ledouxs themselves and Oscar Gutierrez."

THREE DAYS BEFORE HALLOWEEN

"You look like shit."

Amos looked up from his computer. Stevie leaned against the wall of his cubicle. She was drinking from a cup of Starbucks coffee and looked at him curiously as though he were a docile animal at the zoo that was refusing to move.

"Thanks, Stevie. Glad you're here to lift my spirits."

"It's Detective Stevie Hutchins, isn't it? Not Spirit Lifter Stevie Hutchins?"

"Anyway, I barely got any sleep last night," Amos explained.

"Why? Did Anita not let you have sex with her?"

Amos frowned at his partner. "Don't make jokes like that."

"I'm not joking! I wouldn't have slept with you last night either," Stevie teased.

"I don't even know how to respond to that. But no, sexual frustration wasn't the problem. It was that deer. That *scene.*"

The smile on Stevie's face melted away.

"Jesus. When did you become such a pussy, Al?" She was still being facetious, but there was an underlying sense of exasperation hiding behind her jokes.

"Did you *see* it? I mean, come on. How could I forget something like that?"

"You know I *did* see it. You're not supposed to forget it. Just the opposite. This is what we signed up for. You knew what you were getting into. What you guys found down there wasn't even that bad. Do you remember the Vickers guy a couple years ago? That was ten times harder to look at than this was."

Amos shrugged and remained silent. He wasn't going to waste effort trying to reason with her. Sure, Burt Vickers blew half of his head off with a shotgun. But from the moment they walked into the room they knew what that was. This was a complete mystery. One that had a strange, occult-like vibe to it. It was almost as if what they had found was supernatural. That was what had stuck with Amos and caused him to lose sleep.

"When is that caretaker guy coming in?"

"He should be in here any moment."

"Are you going to interview him alone?"

Amos shrugged his shoulders. "You can come in if you want."

"Not a good idea, Al," a snide voice interjected from nearby.

Sliding into Amos's view was Lawrence Bonner, or as Stevie disdainfully referred to him, the Law Boner. His skin was as pale as Amos had ever seen and dozens of freckles were glazed on his pastel cheeks. His hair was jarringly red and a pair of thick-rimmed glasses sat preciously on his small nose. Bonner was short and stocky with muscular arms and bulging pectoral muscles struggling to stay inside his tight white polo.

Stevie saw Bonner and rolled her eyes. "Shit. Turns out the devil appears even when you aren't speaking about him."

"Always so charming," Bonner replied with a sarcastic smile.

"Why shouldn't I sit in on the interview?"

"Because the point of an interview is to *listen,* something you're inherently incapable of."

"Fuck you, bonehead."

Amos raised his hands in a gesture that was

intended to stop the conflict.

"Okay guys, enough. Lawrence, she can take part in the interview if she wants to. Stevie, try to refrain from the name calling, okay? This could be a long case, and I don't need you two trading barbs the minute we start working on it," he said, sounding like a disappointed parent.

Bonner shrugged. "Suit yourself, Al."

Stevie gave Bonner a soul-crushing glare, before turning back to Amos. "What about Ted?"

"What about him?"

Stevie furrowed her brow, looking confused. "Don't you want to give him the option to talk to the guy too?"

"He isn't here."

Stevie frowned. "Why is he not here?"

"He's interviewing a witness in the Bay Haven rape case," Amos replied.

"That is more important than this?"

"I think he said it was the only time that worked for the guy he's interviewing."

"Well by all means! Who cares about serial murder? We have to make sure we adhere to everyone's work week!" declared Stevie mockingly. Amos laughed but Bonner remained stoic.

"So should I sit in on it too?"

Amos looked over at Bonner, considering the question he had posed.

"I don't want three people in the room. Might

be too distracting for him. One of you can come in with me."

"Which one?" Bonner asked in his nasally voice.

"I don't care. Why don't you rock-paper-scissors for it?" Amos said, subtly patronizing Bonner.

"Since I'm your actual *partner,* and he's just a ginger, I say it should be me," Stevie interjected.

Amos burst out laughing at this, and when he saw how displeased Bonner looked, he tried to instantly quell his amusement. But it was too late; Bonner was already offended. Before Amos could apologize for laughing, he muttered something indistinguishable that sounded like it had the word *fuck* in it and stormed off in a huff.

"God, I hate that guy," Stevie hissed.

"I know, but could you try and at least play nice? He's going to be in on this thing with us for however long it takes us to catch this guy."

"'No promises," said Stevie cheerfully.

Amos shook his head and was about to turn back toward his computer when Dozer suddenly appeared over his shoulder.

"He's here. Gutierrez. He's waiting for you in the questioning center."

Oscar Gutierrez fidgeted in a stiff metal chair. He was extremely skinny and appeared to be somewhat malnourished. A copious amount of gel had been distributed throughout his short, black hair, which was spiked up in the front. His eyes were a light blue that was on the verge of gray, which contrasted heavily with his brown skin. He was wearing a white tank top and filthy-looking jeans that were torn at the knees.

Amos and Stevie sat down across from him. When they introduced themselves, he shook their hands, but remained silent. Whether it was nerves or some sort of language barrier that kept Gutierrez silent, it came across as a little abrasive.

"How is it going, Mr. Gutierrez?"

Gutierrez shrugged.

"Thank you for coming down to meet with us."

The man didn't say anything. His eyes just shifted back and forth between them.

"Let's get down to brass tax. So, you know the Ledouxs? How did you meet them?"

"My soccer league," Gutierrez replied with a mild accent. "Jamie, Luke's father, was one of the organizers."

"And this was just a recreational league, correct? There wasn't any money involved?"

Gutierrez crumpled his eyebrows.

"You had to pay money to join so you could

have a jersey and cleats and stuff. But no, there wasn't any prize money for winning or anything. Why does that matter?"

"Just let us ask the questions, please," Stevie replied.

"No, no, it's okay, Stevie. I get that it seems like an impertinent question. The reason I asked that, Mr. Gutierrez, is for the purpose of gathering background information on everyone we talk to. It just helps us to understand relationships, in case they become important later," Amos explained.

"Oh." Gutierrez still looked confused.

"Anyway, you're friends with Jamie Ledoux?"

"Right."

"How did you come to be the caretaker of his house?"

"I work in landscaping, so I always just used to do yard work for Jamie, because he hated doing that sort of work. I did odd jobs on and off for like three years. Then Luke died," said Gutierrez, bowing his head.

"Did you know Luke?"

Gutierrez nodded. "I didn't know him well. But I knew him. He was a good kid."

Amos nodded and glanced over at Stevie. She stared at Gutierrez through beady eyes as though she was skeptical of what he was saying.

"I imagine it was difficult for you to endure something like that." Amos pretended to be sympathetic.

"Not for me. But seeing what it did to that family. That was the real tragedy of it. It destroyed Jamie," replied Gutierrez.

Amos looked down at the notepad in front of him, trying to hone in on what question to ask next. He didn't want to be blunt, but he knew sometimes being straightforward led to more genuine responses. He threw caution to the wind.

"So did you ever think that Luke *didn't* commit suicide?"

For a few seconds, Gutierrez's face showed utter bewilderment and confusion. "What?"

"Did you ever think he didn't commit suicide?"

"What you mean?"

Stevie leaned forward and her voice was dripping with disdain when she replied to Guiterrez's question. "I think you know what he means."

Gutierrez looked over at Stevie, and his eyes narrowed. "Actually, I really don't."

Amos reclined in his chair and regretted his decision to bring Stevie in with him. They were unintentionally doing the good-cop-bad-cop routine, but that wasn't what Amos was going for.

"We have reason to believe that Luke Ledoux was murdered."

Gutierrez's eyes bulged and his mouth fell open.

"No. No. Impossible."

"Why do you say that?"

"Because he jumped off the bridge. Jamie told me. Jamie wouldn't lie to me."

"I don't think he intentionally lied to you, Oscar. I think he was probably ignorant of his son's fate," Amos replied.

"But why? Why do you think this?"

Amos and Stevie exchanged glances, before both looking back at Gutierrez.

"We found a message from his killer, along with Luke's DNA."

Gutierrez's mouth stretched open even farther.

"What the . . . Where did you find this? Are you sure it was Luke's blood?"

"Positive," Stevie said. "The results came back from the forensics lab this morning."

"And as to where we found it, that's actually why we wanted to speak with you in the first place."

Gutierrez looked totally nonplussed. Amos hadn't mentioned to him on the phone what they had found at the house. He had just told him that he needed to speak with him about suspicious activity that revolved around the Ledouxs.

"We found it in Jamie Ledoux's house," said Stevie. She was staring at the man across from her with such intensity that Amos almost told her to stop.

Gutierrez went pale and his forehead crumpled in total bamboozlement.

"What the hell? The Ledouxs' house? That isn't right. Why are you—"

Gutierrez suddenly stopped speaking, and an ominous, knowing expression passed over his face. For several seconds, he stayed silent. Then, his bottom lip quivered.

"Am I like . . . a suspect in this or something?"

Amos shook his head. Even though he wasn't ready to say that Gutierrez *wasn't* a suspect, he knew it would be detrimental to tell him that they were considering him one.

"No, no, nothing like that. We spoke with Jamie on the phone and he said that you were the only other person who knew about the entrance to that room." Amos tried to keep his voice measured and relaxed. "And because it was so well-hidden, we figured that it would be difficult, although not impossible, for a stranger to break into the house and find it on his own. The main thing we wanted to ask you was: have you ever shared the knowledge of that basement with anybody else?"

Even though Amos had attempted to reassure Gutierrez, the man looked positively terrified. Maybe it was a natural reaction for a person to become frightened when he was in any way implicated in a violent crime, so Amos didn't want to assume he was scared because of guilt, but it was a little unnerving to watch nonetheless.

"N-no, I never told nobody about it. Why would I? It's not exactly dinner table conversation, you know?"

"Right, that makes sense," Amos said delicately. "Like I said, it isn't totally out of the realm of possibility that the intruder just found it on his own."

Gutierrez nodded rapidly several times.

"So what do you do when you go to the Ledouxs' house anyway?"

"What do you mean? I mow the lawn. I wash the windows. I mop the floors. Normal stuff, you know? Just whatever Jamie asks me to do." Gutierrez's eyes flitted around the room like he was expecting it to collapse at any moment.

"Does he pay you pretty well for it?"

A flash of irritation scampered across Gutierrez's face. "That is a little personal."

"Answer the question," Stevie demanded.

"He pays me like two hundred dollars every time I go over there."

Amos leaned in like he hadn't heard him correctly.

"Two hundred? Is he planning on moving back here or something?"

"Huh?"

"That's a lot to pay to take care of a house that you aren't even living in," Amos said in disbelief.

"What? Do you think I'm going to tell him to pay me less?"

"Well, no. It's just odd."

Gutierrez shook his head, and it looked like there were at least a thousand other places that he would rather be than sitting in a stuffy room with a balding middle-aged detective and his spunky female partner.

"He still visits Newport sometimes. And he stays at the house when he does. I think it just reminds him of his old life. Before the tragedy."

"Wait, Jamie still visits the house? How often?"

Gutierrez shrugged. "Not often. Only a couple of times since they moved away."

After a few seconds of penetrating silence, Amos said, "Have you ever noticed anybody suspicious around the house?"

Gutierrez shook his head.

"Like I said, I never knew anything about this. This whole Luke thing. I was never looking for anybody suspicious. Why would I? I was just the caretaker of their house."

"So you have been taking care of this house every week for the last five years?"

"What? Of course not. It doesn't need care that often. I only go over there when Jamie asks me to."

"And how often is that?"

"Shit, I don't know! Like once a month."

Amos pursed his lips and narrowed his eyes.

"What?" Gutierrez sounded panicked when he saw Amos's reaction.

"Oh, nothing. It's just, Jamie made it sound like you were over there a lot more often than that."

"You need to take that up with him then, because I really don't go over there that much at all."

Amos glanced over at Stevie, and she still watched the man across from them like she didn't believe a word he was saying.

"You're saying that you only go over to the Ledouxs' house once a month, and when you do, you haven't noticed anyone suspicious?"

"Yes. Right. I mean—no, I haven't noticed anyone suspicious."

"And this is the first time you ever considered the possibility that Luke was murdered?" Amos asked.

"Yeah, obviously. I'm . . . blindsided by this whole thing!"

Amos believed him. The man seemed genuinely surprised by the news. Could this have been a stellar bit of acting? Sure. But Amos always tried to stay on the nonparanoid side of suspicion, and it didn't seem like Gutierrez was the type of person who could put on such a show. He looked over at Stevie one more time, and then back at Gutierrez.

"Okay. Thank you for your time, Mr. Gutierrez."

Once Gutierrez had left the station, Amos went right back into the questioning center with Stevie not far behind him. Once they were inside, Stevie got within six inches of Amos's face.

"What do *you* think? *I* think he's hiding something."

Amos looked at her in incredulity. "Excuse me?"

"There is something that he's not telling us."

Amos rolled his eyes. "Listen, Stevie, I don't want to downplay your intuition, and your gut is usually right, but not this time," he said. "There is no way that man was lying. Did you hear what he said?"

"I'm not deaf, Al, of course I heard what he said."

"Then explain to me why he would freely admit to not telling anybody about the basement. Don't you think if he were hiding something he would've said he had told multiple people?"

"Well, I think—"

"Let me finish," Amos said. "Don't you think if *he* was responsible for what was in that basement he would've told us that he did see somebody suspicious as a way to deflect attention from himself?"

Stevie opened her mouth like she was going to reply, and then shut it once she realized she didn't have an adequate comeback.

Amos gave a curt nod of his head. "That's what I thought."

"I didn't say he was the killer, dick! I said he knew something that he wasn't telling us!"

Amos felt his gut sink. Stevie's natural response when someone defied her was anger. And whenever she got angry, Amos would start to be condescending. It wasn't something he tried to do. It was just a defense mechanism that he subconsciously went to.

"You may be right. But I don't think so. Our job is to find evidence. Not speculate. Not guess."

Stevie bit her bottom lip and shook her head. She silently mouthed the word "guess," and it was as if she had become so indignant she couldn't even speak properly. She made an about-face and walked off. Amos's stomach continued to descend, but he knew that she wouldn't stay irritated for very long. Stevie wasn't one to hold a grudge, and she knew that he wasn't usually one to just pass on her instinct and assumptions. Their working dynamic was generally very strong, and hopefully she would quickly understand that the occasional disagreement wasn't something to hold onto.

Once he got back to his desk, Amos couldn't help but start to ruminate on what Stevie had said. He didn't think Gutierrez was hiding anything. But for some reason, as he continued to dwell on it, he began to have a feeling in his gut that something *was* acutely awry. It didn't feel significant. And Amos was absolutely positive that the Mexican caretaker wasn't the man they were looking for. But for some reason, he had an inkling that he would be speaking to Gutierrez again.

ONE DAY BEFORE
HALLOWEEN

Amos had never felt it this hot so late into fall. In Newport, sixty-five degrees was considered a balmy summer day. And yet, somehow, it was seventy-two degrees outside, not exactly ideal conditions for twenty-two people to be packed into the same room in full police regalia. Everyone was sweating, and the room was possessed by the faint smell of body odor. Amos had a feeling that Bosworth, a 300-pound black man who everyone called the Bos, was responsible for the majority of the smell. For whatever reason, the Bos had a particular proclivity for putting onions and garlic on everything he ate, and the scent exuded from his body whenever he started to sweat.

Amos, Ted, Stevie, and, somewhat comically, Bonner, stood in front of their colleagues while Ted was in the middle of his speech. Dozer sat behind them with his arms folded next to the whiteboard that had every name and significant detail of the case written on it. The pictures of Luke Ledoux, Devin Johnson, and Oscar Gutierrez were all plastered to the whiteboard, along with blown-up photos of the two crime scenes the police had found. The dead smiley-face insignia was shown in a photograph, but had also been drawn on the board by Amos to buttress the significance of it. Finally, a large map of Newport had been placed on the center of the board, and Ted was currently pointing at certain sections of the map.

"Two units will be patrolling every five-block radius, starting from *here*." Ted continued, "To *here*. Your designations for which blocks you will be patrolling will be emailed to you later today by Albert. There are certain neighborhoods that will be intentionally neglected. We can't cover every single block in town, so the ones we figure will not warrant a large amount of people will have to go uncovered."

An arm shot up into the air. Officer Dave

Dieter sat there with his hand petrified above the rest of his body like a Nazi salute.

"Yes, Dieter?" Ted tipped his chin to the man.

"Yeah, I'm a little confused."

"Doesn't take much to confuse you," Stevie said loudly. Everyone in the room started laughing, but Dozer waved his arms, trying to get his officers to stay silent.

"Please keep comments like that to yourself, Hutchins," Dozer snarled.

"I don't get what we will be looking for," Dieter continued, unfazed.

Ted glowered in Dieter's direction.

"Dieter, we have literally been explaining—"

"You have been explaining the details of the case," Dieter interrupted. "And while it's interesting to see these crime scenes, and learn more about the ins and outs of this thing, I don't understand what you want us to be looking for, other than that smiley-face thing and a body next to it."

"We don't really know who we're looking for," Ted countered. "In all likelihood, we won't be notified of any illicit activity until after it's already begun, and hopefully we can respond fast enough to prevent a homicide. Keep an eye out for anyone that looks to be menacing or particularly suspicious. Or anyone wearing wolf-related regalia. The killer called himself 'the wolf' in his little drawing here."

"Teddy, do you realize how vague that is?"

Bosworth interjected from the back row of the seats that were filled with officers. "And it's Halloween. Everyone is going to be wearing masks and shit. How are we supposed to differentiate actual menace from a costume? And 'wolf regalia'? What does that even mean?"

"Well, Bos—"

"Do you really think that this guy is going to abduct his target right out on the street?" Sergeant Tom Thompson made a skeptical noise after he spoke and his goatee bobbed up and down as his mouth contorted to make the noise.

"It's not like this guy is going to be wandering around with a bloody axe talking to the devil," Officer Kevin Beadle said, a blond and wiry man standing against the wall at the back of the room.

"Sure you don't want us looking for the actual devil?" Bosworth joked. "Seems like it would be an easier task."

Without warning, Dozer stood up from his chair and shouted one word.

"Enough!"

Everyone else in the room froze and stared at Dozer as though he had fired his gun at the roof. A piercing silence filled the void, and everybody remained virtually motionless, as if moving would make them the target for Dozer's displeasure.

"Enough jokes and goofing off like a bunch of kids in junior high!" Dozer yelled, looking at

Bosworth in particular. "While you're all busy laughing your asses off, this guy is stalking his next victim. I know you're all a bunch of fucking comedians, but I can't stress how *serious* this case is. We need to find this guy. He has literally *told* us that he's planning to kill somebody tomorrow. And if we don't stop him, you're all going to be thrown under the bus like this department was with the Nowhere Girls. I don't like it, but that is the reality."

Everyone in the room seemed to fidget uncomfortably. It was as if the pressure that Dozer had just placed on all them had caused them all to physically move.

"So when will this all start?" Bosworth looked positively perturbed in response to Dozer's outburst. "When do you want us to begin patrols?"

"Five p.m.," Amos replied. Every set of eyes shifted from Dozer over to Amos, and his voice caught in his throat for a second when he realized he was about to speak in front of twenty-two people. "Devin Johnson and Luke Ledoux both disappeared hours later than that, but we feel confident if this guy is going to try and abduct someone, he will do so at night, so we want to make sure everyone is out and about by sunset, which will be a little after six."

Dieter leaned forward with an obtuse expression on his face. "Do you think we should be on the lookout for teenage boys?"

"Yes, Dieter, we do think he will be targeting a young man." Ted nodded. "Luke Ledoux was seventeen. Devin Johnson was twenty-one. So I think we're looking at an age range of anywhere from sixteen to twenty-five."

"And are we going to move forward any special preparations to alert the young men in the community?"

Amos and Ted looked at each other.

"I will get back to you on that," Amos replied. "We're in a tricky spot, see. We don't want word to get out about how big of an operation we're running in case it scares this guy off. But we do want to have some sort of warning out there so that the target demographic can be more vigilant when they are out and about."

"What if we just tell them that there has been suspicious activity in the area lately and to be on their guard?" proffered Beadle.

"Because that is a vague and virtually useless proclamation. Suspicious activity could mean anything, and if we heed a warning like that, all it will do is create mass confusion," Amos replied. "Trust me, we're working on an answer to that question, officer. Obviously, it's imperative that we find a solution, since the lives of our kids hang in the balance." The face of John Kimball flitted through his mind after he said this.

For five seconds, the room kept quiet, as various deputies, sergeants, and lieutenants contemplated the ominous nature of what they were being tasked with. It was like everyone had realized how huge the case was due to the sentence that Amos had just vocalized. The jovial, wisecracking mood had been extinguished. Smiles had morphed into stone faces, and a proverbial rain cloud hovered over them as worry began to dominate the collective consciousness of the cops in the room. It was one thing to talk about murders in the context of words on a whiteboard. Once Amos had vocalized the endgame of the killer they were chasing, everyone had become filled with a slight sense of dread. Bosworth finally broke the silence with a single word.

"Jesus," he said while shaking his head.

"I know," Amos said. "I know. This is . . . big."

"That's one word for it," Bosworth mumbled.

For a while, no one said anything. People looked for the next person that had a question. But no one raised their hand or spoke.

"So if no one has any further questions, I think that's it. We will be meeting in here again tomorrow before we all depart to give one last rundown of the game plan, as it were. I know you guys all have work to do, so I will let you get to it. And with that, I will see you all in here tomorrow."

The scraping of chairs against linoleum rang

out as all the officers rose in sync. When everyone had turned their backs and were walking toward the door, Stevie leaned in close to Amos's ear.

"This is going to be a shit show," she whispered.

"Why do you say that?"

"Look at them. They don't want anything to do with this. Most of these guys think they shouldn't have even been brought in on this. They think it's our job."

Out of the corner of his eye, Amos could see Bonner smirking, and he knew that the red-haired detective was holding in a snarky comment.

"So you think they won't meet our expected, uh, performance standards?"

"I think they probably won't even do anything unless they see something that's like . . . *really* suspicious," Stevie replied. "I don't want to say they are going to try and make us look bad, but that is what it feels like."

"They better not if they know what is good for them."

Dozer brushed up against Amos's left shoulder as he walked by. After looking at the door to make sure everyone else was out of earshot, he turned to face the four of them. Stevie gazed at him in apprehension; Bonner just looked smug as if he was about to receive some sort of praise. Ted and Amos remained somewhat ambivalent to Dozer's presence. They both knew he would likely try and threaten them somehow, but neither of them cared.

Dozer snarled as he began to speak. "Listen. I have been working my goddamned ass off to improve the department's reputation over these last few months. And I'm not going to have some asshole who thinks he's smarter than all us tarnish that. You best believe that if there is a homicide tomorrow night, and the guy gets away with it, it's your asses that are on the line."

"You're saying that we're responsible if they don't do their jobs?" Stevie gestured at the last of the patrolmen who were departing the room.

"I'm saying that it's up to you four to instill in them how important this is. If an employee doesn't do his job, that falls on the person who told him how to do his job, don't you think?" Dozer's foul coffee-breath wafted into Amos's nose.

Amos wanted to make a comment about how Dozer had just implicated himself as well, but he simply nodded. He needed to get to work, and arguing with Dozer would delay the inevitable. Dozer stayed standing there as if he was daring one of the four of them to back talk him. When none of them did, he gave one last angry grunt and stormed off.

"He seems cheerful," Stevie said.

Amos glanced over at Bonner and noticed his smug expression had been wiped away and replaced by an offended scowl. With a dramatic turn of his head, he angrily walked off toward the offices. Once he was gone, Amos turned to Ted.

"I'm going to call Principal Dodd and try to arrange a meeting with him in the morning. I will let you know what he says. Other than that, I guess I will see you tomorrow."

Ted looked at Amos meaningfully. It took Amos a minute to read his expression, but when he did, he was surprised.

"What is it, Teddy?"

Ted shrugged. "I don't know. I guess I'm just nervous. It's one thing chasing the bad guy knowing he could strike at any time. But when he actually gives you a deadline . . . there is a hell of a lot of pressure."

Amos offered a consoling hand on Ted's shoulder. It wasn't like Ted to show weakness, so Amos knew he had to make his advice good, otherwise Ted wouldn't confide in him again.

"Look, Teddy, we're going to catch this guy. It's not like we're chasing a ghost or something. I know he thinks he's cleverer than we are, but I promise you, he's not. Anyway, what is Dozer going to do? Fire you? You're the reason we're doing this stuff in the first place. Luke Ledoux. That basement. That is all on you. So relax. Dozer's bark is worse than his bite."

Stevie stood in the background with her arms

folded, and Amos could tell that she was eavesdropping on the conversation.

"Yeah. I know. Thanks, bud," Ted said with a small smile.

"Anytime," Amos replied with a matching grin, and Ted walked off.

After Ted was gone, Amos and Stevie were the only two people left in the meeting room. Stevie was looking at Amos like she was about to laugh.

"What?"

Stevie had a mischievous expression on her face. "Oh nothing. I know I'm your *actual* partner, but I was thinking Ted would make a good life partner for you."

"Shut up, Stevie," Amos replied. Stevie laughed, and the pair began walking side by side toward the office. She continued to chuckle a little as they went toward their respective cubicles.

"You realize you're going to be out there with me tomorrow night, right? You better not piss me off, or it's going to be a long night."

Stevie was still chuckling for a while, but eventually it faded. Slowly, her face morphed into something more serious.

"I have a feeling tomorrow is going to be a long night regardless."

HALLOWEEN

8:32 a.m.

Coby Conner woke with a start, causing his hand to slam onto the desk with a loud *slap.* Heads turned in his direction, and he hastily wiped the drool off the corner of his mouth and leaned back casually as though nothing had happened. Unfortunately, Mrs. Parrish hadn't missed the gesture.

"Coby, I know first period can be rough on an eighteen-year-old, but *please* try and stay awake," she said from the front of the class.

All the students around him erupted into laughter, and Coby felt his face heat. He tried to not look to his right because he knew Cassandra Klay would be looking at him, and having his crush laugh at his expense wasn't exactly how he wanted to start his day.

"As I was *saying,*" Mrs. Parrish continued. "The juxtaposition of the characters in this scene are a direct allegorical comparison to the New Testament; that is to say that Lewis is consciously, and overtly I might add, trying to assert the two main characters as Jesus and Matthew . . ."

Almost immediately, Coby began to totally tune out. It was virtually impossible for his brain to analyze literature at any time of the day, let alone the morning. Like most of his cohorts, Coby was never one to get the recommended eight hours of sleep. He always paid the price in Mrs. Parrish's AP English class, but he never seemed to learn his lesson. At least, the trade-off of more sleep in exchange for better retention of shitty literature wasn't worth it in his eyes.

With a slight turn of his head, Coby began to furtively stare in Cassandra's direction. He was so deeply infatuated with her that even looking at the side of her head or the glimmer of her earring was strangely satisfying to him. Months ago, Coby's dad had offered up a collection of somewhat profound advice on his attraction to Cassandra. Basically, the thesis of what he had told Coby was that putting someone on a pedestal never ended well for either party, and that as much as it seemed like high school romance was the center of the universe, in time he would neither remember nor care whom he obsessed over when he was eighteen. It had been good advice, and had helped Coby feel better at the time. Eventually, he had gravitated right back toward her. Cassandra had told him several times that she had no interest in him other than as a friend. In a way, this had made his attraction grow stronger.

Coby noticed Cassandra was frowning in concentration as she appeared to be paying rapt attention to what Mrs. Parrish was saying. He wondered if she could perhaps feel him staring at her or something, and was trying with all her might to not look in his direction. Quickly, Coby turned back toward the front of the class, and resumed not paying the slightest attention to Mrs. Parrish's lecture.

Halloween wasn't what it was when Coby was a kid. Back in elementary school, everyone would come to school wearing costumes; if you *weren't* in some sort of fancy ensemble you would stick out. As a senior, nobody dressed up. Besides the building anticipation for parties that were going to take place later that night, Halloween was just a normal day. As Coby looked around the room, he mentally counted only three people who seemed to be celebrating the holiday. One was Mrs. Parrish herself. Like most uninspired and underpaid teachers, she had simply donned a witch's cap and a distinctly un-witchlike purple shawl draped around her shoulders. Perhaps it was the only thing that she could find in her closet that didn't clash with the five-dollar cap. Other than Mrs. Parrish, only a girl named Rebecca Flynn and a boy named Ben Rogers were dressed up. Flynn was one of the quiet, nerdy girls who seemed to have an engrossment with anime, and thus, she was supposed to be one of the characters she envied, with a tight black skirt, a white blouse, and jarring makeup. Rogers was dressed as the Joker, purple suit and slicked-back green hair on full display. Coby secretly admired their gusto. Most of his other peers were too afraid of the scorn they would receive to put on a costume.

Mrs. Parrish's dull speech was interrupted by the phone ringing on her desk. She looked irritated, as if the phone itself had decided to put a stop to her soliloquy. Stomping over to her desk, Mrs. Parrish picked up the receiver. "Hello," she answered as if speaking to a telemarketer. After a few seconds of silent listening, Mrs. Parrish mumbled something indistinguishable and hung up the phone.

"Coby, you're wanted in the office."

The entire class broke out into a rousing chorus of "Oh," uniformly ribbing Coby as though he was in deep trouble. For a few long seconds, Coby sat in the back of the class looking unnerved.

"I think they meant now, Coby," Mrs. Parrish said.

Coby gave one last look around the room before standing up. He walked through the narrow path in between the two rows of desks, feeling the heat of twenty sets of eyes on him. One of his friends, Sean, intentionally stuck out his foot as Coby walked by, causing him to stumble. A small snicker broke out through the classroom, and Coby playfully punched Sean in the arm.

"Boys, please," Mrs. Parrish said sternly. She was one of those high-school teachers that felt better suited to teach fifth graders; she talked to everyone as though they were young children.

Coby brushed by Mrs. Parrish without making eye contact. He took one last glance back into the room and saw Cassandra staring at him with beady eyes and a minor frown. Coby felt a pang in his gut, stewing about her facial expression as he departed the classroom. He knew that as the day went on he would make up a million different reasons in his head for why he had made her angry. Such was the unhealthy nature of his infatuation with Cassandra.

The hallways of Newport High School had been deteriorating for some time. There were a couple of brown stains on the ceiling from leaks on the roof, and occasionally, a displaced tile stuck out like a sore thumb. The place was totally empty, as everyone was still in various classes throughout the building.

As Coby ambled down the middle of the hallway, he felt a little worried. He had no idea why he had been called to the office. Although not a great student, Coby was far from a trouble maker. He had never been suspended nor received detention. Perhaps it revolved around some sort of extracurricular activity. He was on the Leadership Committee and he also helped organize pep rallies, so maybe it had something to do with that. Coby tried to suppress the thoughts that warned him of impending trouble as he sauntered through campus.

Eventually, Coby got to his intended destination. There was a window to the main office where visitors could speak to one of the office workers and next to it, a large door. Through the window the middle-aged, overweight blond secretary named Dawn was writing notes on a formal-looking sheet. Dawn seemed to feel his presence without Coby saying a word, and she looked up with a vague, unfocused expression on her face.

"Hello there, dear."

"Um, hi, Dawn," Coby replied. He could tell by the way she had greeted him that she had forgotten his name.

"What can I do for you?"

"Mrs. Parrish said that I was supposed to come to the office. I'm not sure why."

For a fleeting moment, Dawn looked at him curiously as though she didn't quite understand. Then, as if a lightbulb had turned on behind her eyes, an expression of understanding spread across her face.

"Ah, yes! Coby Conner. Your father called the office and is on hold. He wants to speak to you. Says it's urgent."

Coby looked at her with a mixture of consternation and skepticism. It had to be a mistake. If his dad had wanted to talk to him he would've just called his cell.

"Uh, are you sure it's my dad?"

"Yes, dear, I'm sure," Dawn replied.

Coby frowned. His mother and father were both currently in Southern California visiting his grandparents in Rancho Cucamonga. His mom had texted him that morning and told him that today they were all simply staying inside; it was going to be too hot to do any sort of blissful Californian activity, so he couldn't imagine why his dad would be calling. With a dubious countenance, Coby walked through the door to the office, and Dawn pointed at the phone sitting in the back corner. The light on the phone was blinking red, apparently signaling that someone was still on hold. Coby hurried over to the phone and picked it up.

"Hello?"

For several seconds, the other end of the line stayed silent. Then, a bizarre growling emitted from the receiver. It was a weird noise. It reminded Coby of some sort of African predator that he had seen on National Geographic. The growl continued for two seconds and then ceased.

"Hello?" Coby repeated.

Finally, a deep, warped voice answered him. It sounded demonic.

"He comes for you tonight. Death."

With a distinct *clink,* the line went silent.

Coby felt a chill run down his spine as he looked at the phone as if it were some diseased thing. Initially, his heart thumped rapidly and wild thoughts ran through his mind. But then, a more calming voice floated to the front of his consciousness. *Probably just one of my friends fucking with me,* he thought. There were many likely culprits who would think it would be funny to impersonate his dad and leave a sinister-sounding message. Sean, Danny, and Carson all came to mind. Coby smiled as he realized that it was all just a gag. He turned to look at Dawn as though she would be in on it, but all her attention was still focused on the piece of paper in front of her that looked like an itinerary. Coby hung up the phone and approached her.

"That wasn't my dad."

Dawn looked up at stared at him. "Excuse me?"

"You said that was my dad, but it wasn't. I think it was a prank caller. Probably one of my friends," Coby said with a small smile.

Dawn cocked her head to the side, her thin lips agape. "What? No, it was your father. I just spoke to him a few minutes ago."

"Well, whoever you talked to was probably pretending to be him, but I can guarantee you that whoever I just talked to wasn't my dad."

"Why do you say that?"

Coby looked back at the phone and shook his head as he thought of what the person had said.

"It was like a demonic voice. They were using some sort of voice changer. And they said that death comes for me tonight or something."

In response to this, Dawn looked concerned and fairly embarrassed.

"Oh my . . . I'm so sorry, Mr. Connor," she said. "A prankster? That's—I . . . I'm very sorry."

"It's alright, Dawn. No worries. Gave me an excuse to get out of class," Coby joked, trying to assuage her embarrassment.

"Hold on," Dawn said, suddenly sounding confused. "I'm almost positive that whoever I spoke to was an adult."

Coby froze for a second.

"What? Why do you say that?"

"It sounded like a grown man, not a teenager."

"Hmm. That's odd." Coby doubted Dawn's ability to analyze the age behind the voice she had heard.

"That was a grown man I was speaking to."

"Yeah. Well anyway, it wasn't my dad. At least, I don't think so. Maybe I will give him a call or something."

"You better," Dawn said, pretending to sound self-assured.

Coby exited the office and gave Dawn a wave through the open window.

"Well anyway, sorry to interrupt . . ." He nodded to her work. "Whatever you're doing."

"Oh no, my dear, no problem at all. Have a good day," Dawn said. She still looked mildly embarrassed.

"You too."

As Coby walked away, he pulled out his cell phone and started scrolling through his contacts. *Fucking dicks,* he thought. Whoever it was that had prank called him had just made him walk all the way across campus for no reason. He wasn't sure why he was even calling his dad. He would have no idea what Coby was talking about.

Moments later, Andrew Connor answered the

phone.

"Hello?"

"Dad?"

"Coby? Shouldn't you be in class right now?"

"Well, I was," Coby replied. "But I just got called to the office, and the secretary said you had called for me."

There were several long beats of silence as Andrew cogitated on what his son had just said.

"What?"

"I went into the office and she said you were on hold. So I picked up the phone and this warped voice was on the other end. It sounded like the devil or something. And it said, 'He comes for you tonight. Death.'"

Andrew made a grunting noise that was supposed to indicate his confusion.

"What the hell? Who was it?"

"I think it was one of my friends or someone just screwing with me," Coby replied. "Like a Halloween prank or something."

"That's what you kids call a prank? Jesus. I'm glad I'm not a part of your generation." Andrew chuckled.

"So you definitely didn't call me then?"

"No, no I didn't. Although if you don't get right back to class I might start calling and making death threats too."

Coby guffawed loudly, and it reverberated

around the empty halls.

"Yes, sir. Going back there now. Hope you and Mom are having a good time."

"You betcha. Talk to you later, bud," Andrew replied. "Tell your friends to get a life."

Coby smiled to himself and put his iPhone back into his pocket and headed back in the direction of Mrs. Parrish's class.

9:02 a.m.

Gordon Dodd leaned forward in his chair, squinting through his glasses. At first, he simply looked over at Ted like he wasn't seeing him properly. Then, he gave an exasperated chuckle.

"No way. I'm not doing that."

"Mr. Dodd—"

"I said no."

Amos looked at Dodd curiously. He wasn't quite sure what the man was objecting to.

"Listen, sir, we don't want to cause any trouble for you," Amos said.

"That is exactly what you're doing!"

"We're just trying to make sure all your students are safe."

Dodd opened his mouth, stammering at this suggestion.

"Do you realize how much of a, pardon my French, *clusterfuck* that would create? Parents would demand their kids get sent home. The phones would be ringing off the hook. It would be absolute chaos here. And all because you think some weirdo who drew a creepy face on a wall might be coming to get us? Why is it *my* responsibility to help you two do your jobs?"

Amos shook his head irritably. "Like I said, we're interested in the safety of your students, not in your assistance finding the culprit."

"What do you want me to do?" Dodd demanded. "Call an emergency assembly? But only for the boys? And then tell them, 'Hey, make sure you don't get *murdered* tonight, kids. Happy Halloween.'"

"Not at all. Hopefully, 'Don't get murdered' is already in your curriculum," Ted replied without missing a beat.

Dodd shot Ted an irate glance. Apparently, he was the only one who was allowed to be sarcastic.

"Look, *pal,* isn't this sort of against your, uh, what's the word . . . mandate? Like sharing this with me. I'm an unaffiliated third party," Dodd said contemptuously. He glanced down at the photograph on his desk Amos had provided. A six-by-eight version of the dead smiley-face signature glinted evilly underneath Dodd's desk lamp. "I thought homicide investigations were supposed to be clandestine. But here you are asking for help from someone whose main job is to decide whether teenagers get detentions or suspensions for skipping class."

Amos reclined back in his chair and looked over at Ted, who was seated next to him and glaring at Dodd with a fiery disposition. The two of them were packed into the office like chickens in a coop, while Dodd sat with a copious amount of arm space behind the desk separating them. Amos hadn't expected to meet this much resistance; or for that matter, any resistance at all. He had called the day before to schedule the appointment with Dodd, and although he had not fully explained the case, the principal had struck him as benign and pleasant over the phone. Now that Amos and Ted were sitting in front of him and had explained the true nature of what they were dealing with, Dodd had become very rude, and for the life of him Amos couldn't figure out why. They had shared only the most important details of the case with him, and he had become more and more disgruntled as they went along.

"I'm not sure what you're so frustrated about," Amos said.

Dodd shifted around uncomfortably. "When I agreed to this meeting, I was unaware you were going to make such a request. And I had no idea this would be so, uh, unsettling."

Amos thought for a moment about what to say next before resorting to a tried-and-true police interrogation technique, albeit one that was usually reserved for suspects and not malcontent principals.

"Mr. Dodd, I'm a severe hemophobic. Do you know what that means?"

Dodd looked flabbergasted for a few seconds, with his jowls quivering and his face flushing with color. He started stuttering in confusion.

"I-I, no, what are you even ta—"

"It means I'm afraid of blood," Amos continued before Dodd could finish. "Even my *own* blood. Whenever I see blood, I feel sick to my stomach. I can't breathe. My chest feels tight. Ironic for a cop, right?"

"What are you even—"

"I was the one who *found* that bloody signature on the wall of Devin Johnson's old apartment. You remember Devin Johnson, don't you? He went to school here."

Dodd turned a little pale, and he looked disturbed.

"The point is, sometimes we should leave behind our own well-being for the greater good," Amos said. "Trust me, this whole thing disgusts me too. But this isn't about me. This is about these kids."

"You think I don't consider my students' safety of paramount importance? Of course I do! But if you think I'm going to create mass panic to circumvent a threat that may not even be *real* . . ."

"Trust me, Mr. Dodd. It's more than real."

Dodd opened his mouth again, but then closed it without responding. His magnificent handlebar mustache twitched as he debated what to say. Amos noticed in that moment that Gordon Dodd looked a bit like a walrus, with his ridiculous facial hair and wrinkled neck. However, instead of extraneous blubber, Dodd had layers of muscle packed onto his stocky body. He was a weird mix of masculine and something much geekier; what with his wiry glasses and bizarre mustache. Seemingly out of nowhere, Dodd's vexation started to ebb away as he began speaking again.

"Look, I appreciate what you're trying to do here. But we have over three hundred male students that attend Newport High. Do you think it would be *prudent* to get them all together and tell them about this? It would spread like *wildfire.* And what if it turned out to be nothing at all? They would go home and tell their parents, and then the district office would start fielding calls, questioning how we handled it . . ."

Ted used his left hand to gesture emphatically. "But think about the opposite, Mr. Dodd. Think about if someone was killed, and the parents found out that you knew about this guy beforehand. You would get all the blame."

Dodd glowered over at Ted for a second, and his face flushed red once more as he looked back at

Amos.

"How about I just speak with you? And not your hot-headed partner?" he asked without any sense of irony.

"He's not my partner. But he does voice a valid concern, Mr. Dodd."

Dodd bit his lip as he ruminated on what Amos had said. He glanced toward the window and seemed to digest the sunlight flooding through, and when he looked back at Amos, his facial expression had changed yet again.

"What do you suggest I do?" His voice was suddenly calm again. Amos was almost taken aback by the random, erratic changes in Dodd's demeanor. It was startling, and Amos wondered if Dodd was bipolar or something. It would be an unusual quality for someone in a position of authority.

"I suggest that you make a school-wide announcement. Be it a call for assembly or simply over the intercom, wish the students a happy Halloween," Amos replied. "Tell them that the police have been monitoring suspicious activity in the neighborhood, and tell them to be vigilant. Have a prepared statement. Don't try and scare them, and don't share any details of the case, but give a substantive warning."

Dodd gave a slight shake of his head, and clicked his tongue. "I don't think so, guys. I really don't."

At that moment, Ted shook his head irritably, rolled his eyes, and got out of his chair.

"If anything happens, this is on *you.*" Ted made sure to point forcefully at Dodd before turning and leaving the office.

"Please just do *something*, Mr. Dodd. Thank you for your time," Amos said as he got up as well.

Dodd said nothing in response to this. He simply stared in Amos's direction. Therefore, with a gauche bow of his head, Amos left in Ted's wake.

"What a *prick.* What was the school board even thinking, hiring a guy like that?"

"I know . . . I had heard some rumors about Dodd before, but I didn't expect him to be so . . . abrasive."

Amos and Ted were walking side by side in the school parking lot, heading in the direction of the visitor parking spots where each of their respective vehicles was anchored.

Amos looked over at Ted. "What do you mean? What kind of rumors?"

Ted shrugged. "Oh, I don't know. I shouldn't spread them around if they aren't true."

"No, tell me, Teddy. What kind of rumors?"

Ted looked around the parking lot, making sure

that no one was lingering on the periphery or within earshot of them.

"Nothing that would explain why he was such an asshole," Ted explained quietly. "Just . . . There have been whispers of his infidelity for years."

Amos stuck out his bottom lip and raised his eyebrows in consternation. "I'm surprised he's even married."

"Yeah, to a woman named Deidra. Really sweet lady."

"How do you know her?"

"Just from around town."

Amos nodded with his mouth slightly ajar in an expression of understanding. The two men reached the spot in the gravel where they had to depart from each other's company before they could get in their cars, so Ted gazed around the parking lot one last time before looking Amos directly in the eye.

"All I know is, if Dodd does nothing, and one of his students gets murdered, he's almost as guilty as the killer in my eyes."

3:25 p.m.

"I don't believe you fuckers."

Carson, Danny, Sean, and Landon all erupted with laughter.

"I'm telling you, Coby, it wasn't us." Carson chuckled while he spoke. The giggling made his statement far less believable.

"This is like that *Scream* movie from the nineties," Coby muttered, feeling annoyed but also amused.

"Never seen it," Sean said, his frumpy, untamed hair flopping in the light breeze.

Coby looked at Sean in disbelief. He often forgot his friends weren't movie buffs like he was.

"You haven't seen *Scream*?"

"I just said that, ding-dong."

"Have you guys seen it?" Coby looked incredulously at the other three. Landon and Carson both shook their heads, but Danny nodded.

"Yeah, I seen it when I was a kid, I think."

Coby pointed his stubby finger at Danny. "You *saw* it when you were a kid."

"That's what I just said, didn't I?"

"Anyway, it's about these teenagers that are being stalked by these two killers. And the killers call their victims with a voice changer and ask them questions about horror movies and shit," Coby said.

Sean laughed sarcastically. "How is that in any way like this?"

"Well, you guys called me with a voice changer—"

"It wasn't us, idiot!"

Coby stopped talking and looked down at the ground. Out of the five people in their group of friends, Sean was the one that he liked the least. He was a tall, good-looking guy who seemed to believe popularity in high school was the pinnacle of all human existence. His arrogance was only matched by his inherent naivety, although Sean pretended he was much smarter than he was. Coby often wondered if he hung out with the four of them so that it would make him look better.

While Sean was a definite hunk, the rest of the group was quite the motley crew. Carson was just over five foot four, and he seemed to be missing a distinguishable neck. He often reminded Coby of a penguin, although not as plump. Danny was wiry and blond and looked like a weasel. Landon appeared tall and stocky from the front, but once you got on either side of him, you realized that he was trending toward fat. It looked like he was trying to grow a beard, but all that he had achieved was the traces of what resembled pubic hair along his jawline. As for Coby, he was average height and scrawny, with brown hair and a small nose. Although not ugly, nobody had ever accused Coby of being handsome. He had a girl in middle school tell him one time that he was a "plain Jane."

As the five friends ambled down the sidewalk, the breeze picked up. It wasn't as warm as the day before, but it was still sweltering for Halloween in Newport. They were each wearing tee shirts and shorts, and Carson had flip-flops that slapped against the pavement as they meandered along.

Whenever it was sunny out, the late afternoon became Coby's favorite time of day. The euphoria of escaping from the doldrums of a stuffy classroom and out into the golden outdoors was palpable, and everyone seemed to be in a good mood.

"So what did the message say again?" Landon frowned in concentration.

"Oh don't pretend that you don't know."

"Seriously, Coby, it wasn't me!"

"Out of all you, you're the most likely candidate, Landon," Coby replied.

"Why do you say that?"

"Because you think you're the funniest."

"I *am* the funniest."

"So you admit it was you?"

"No, dude, I swear, it wasn't me!" Landon replied, half laughing.

Carson clicked his tongue impatiently.

"*Anyway*, Coby said the message said that death comes for him tonight."

Coby nodded, but also stuck his index finger in the air to indicate that there was more to it.

"It said *he* comes for you tonight. Like death was the he."

"Oh, who cares!" Sean said loudly. "It was obviously just a prank. Can we move on now?"

The smiles were wiped off all their faces, and their jovial nature was replaced by something more reserved. Sean was, in a way, the leader of the pack.

When he spoke, everyone listened. Therefore, instead of continuing to joke about the message, everyone remained quiet for a while, as if speaking might provoke Sean's wrath. Finally, it was Carson who decided to brave the silence.

"So what time do you want us over at your house tonight, Sean?"

Sean shrugged, as if he was ambivalent to the idea of the rest of them showing up at all.

"Just sometime after eight. That's when people are going to start showing up."

"How are you going to get alcohol for everybody anyway?" Landon asked, sounding perplexed.

"My dad's liquor cabinet for one, and then Frank is going to buy us beer," Sean explained. Frank was one of Sean's dad's employees. He was in his late twenties and seemed to be trying to live vicariously through the teenagers, as he was their most frequent supplier of booze.

Coby frowned. "Won't your dad notice if liquor is missing from his storage?"

"Dude, he doesn't give a shit. He left me home alone on Halloween night. What does he expect?"

Coby didn't say anything in response to this, but was secretly thankful Sean and the others remained ignorant to the fact that his parents had also left him home alone. He didn't want any ideas thrown around about moving the party to his place.

His ten-year-old brother, Mack, didn't need to be exposed to that.

"How many people are coming anyway?" Landon said in his throaty voice.

Sean raised his hands toward the sky in a "beats me" type gesture.

"Maybe, like, fifty?"

"Jesus," Carson muttered.

"What? Is that too many for the imp to handle?" Sean ruffled Carson's hair. Carson irritably pressed Sean's arm away and looked disgruntled.

Landon froze suddenly. "Hey, who's that?"

It took several moments for Coby to realize who Landon was referring to. He scanned the area in front of him and finally his eyes locked onto someone who was far away. Some forty yards in front of them, a tall figure stood leaning against the hood of his red pickup truck. The man was way too distant for any of them to see who it was, but Coby could make out that he was wearing a black shirt and blue jeans. The figure remained motionless, and Coby was positive the man was staring at them.

Landon put his hand over his forehead to block out the sun. "Is he looking at us?"

"I think so." Coby squinted, trying to see better.

"Should we flip him off?" Sean suggested. "Didn't his mother tell him that it's rude to stare?"

"Don't do that," Carson whispered.

"Why are you whispering, bro? He's, like, an entire football field away," Landon said.

The rest of them burst into laughter, and even Carson had to crack a smile. Through his guffaws, Coby kept his eyes on the man. He couldn't see any distinguishable facial features from the distance they were at, but Coby had a gut feeling he didn't know who the person was. A few seconds later, the man walked around to the driver's side, got in the truck, and the headlights switched on. The vehicle was only in place for a moment before it drove off in the opposite direction.

"That's a little . . . odd," Coby said.

Sean glanced over with a pompous look on his face. "It's probably your *Scream* killer. Death comes for you tonight, remember?"

The others laughed heartily in response to this, but Coby became surly. He wanted to tell Sean to blow it out his ass, but he held the comment in, letting it stew in his stomach. Every once in a while, he felt a strong urge to clock Sean right in his smug teeth. In fact, he wasn't sure why he was even friends with the guy; all Sean brought him was occasional rage and frequent self-doubt. However, he had never acted on his vexation. As angry as he felt sometimes, Coby wasn't conflict-oriented. He had often gone great lengths to avoid an argument. Instead of coming to blows, Coby would become quiet and brood, letting the others continue to engage in their usual banter.

"Oh, Cobes, I forgot, I think Cassandra is coming tonight," Sean said suddenly.

At first, Coby didn't process what Sean had said. He hated when Sean called him "Cobes" as though they were best pals. However, once it resonated, Coby perked up.

"She is?"

"Yeah, dude, she is. And let's just say she knows how to have a good time when there is alcohol involved," Sean said mischievously. "Last time I was at a party and she was there she could barely walk she was so trashed."

Coby stuck his bottom lip out and gave a sardonic thumbs-up that he pumped into the air a few times. "Oh, lovely."

"Hey, he'll take it any way he can get it, right, Coby?" Landon added.

"Fuck you, guys." Coby smiled. He thought it was disgusting to contemplate what they were insinuating, that it would be easier to make a move on her when she was drunk. Also, Cassandra had told him point-blank if he were to hit on her anymore, she would stop talking to him altogether. So even though he didn't vocalize this thought, he knew trying to get all alpha male on her during the party would be off the table.

Sean chuckled again, swooping his hair out of his eyes as the breeze gained strength.

"All I know is, it's going to be a party to remember," he said.

4:02 p.m.

Mack didn't give any indication he heard the door open when Coby walked through. He just continued to mindlessly shoot digital soldiers on the TV screen, pretending that he was still alone. Mack had a headset perched precariously around his ears, and seemed to be silently digesting everything that his fellow game players were saying through the wireless earphones. When Coby dropped his backpack on the wood floor, he heard an obscenity screamed by someone who was talking to Mack on the headset.

"You know Mom said you aren't supposed to use those, right? They are only for me."

Mack looked at Coby through narrowed eyes. His shoulder-length dirty blond hair curtained his face so heavily that it looked like a lion's mane.

"Are you going to tell her?"

Coby gave Mack a stern look. "I will if you don't put them away now. You shouldn't be listening to stuff like that. You're ten."

"I hear stuff like that from you all the time!"

"Shut up." Coby frowned and plopped down on the couch. He took out his phone and scrolled through his Facebook feed, while Mack continued to play the same shoot-'em-up game on the TV, surrounded by various innocuous items on the floor. The house was a tad unkempt at the moment. Coby's parents still had five days left on their vacation, and although he had told him he would keep the place clean, he wasn't going to start cleaning until the day before they got back.

Coby suddenly had a question float to the forefront of his consciousness that perplexed him.

"Wait, Mack, how did you get home? Wasn't I supposed to come pick you up? You were supposed to text me."

Mack continued to look at the TV, determined not to make eye contact with his brother.

"Mack?"

"I walked," Mack said quietly.

Coby's eyes bulged. "Damn it, Mack! You know you're not supposed to walk by yourself!"

"It's like four blocks," Mack whined.

"I don't care. It isn't up to me. Mom and Dad said you aren't supposed to walk."

"You walk all the time! You just walked home now!"

"But I'm not a little kid, Mack! And I was with friends. Tell me you didn't walk by yourself." Coby already knew the answer. When he was greeted by only silence, his suspicions were confirmed.

"Jesus, Mack." Coby shook his head and buried his face in his right palm.

Mack's bright blue eyes welled up with tears as he was stricken by an apparent mix of guilt and fear.

"Are you going to tell Mom and Dad?"

Coby rolled his eyes. "No, because then I will get in trouble too. For letting you walk home by yourself. Somehow, Mom will make it my fault."

Coby looked away, frustrated with his kid brother. His parents had relegated the duty of looking after Mack completely to him, and he hadn't realized how much of a task it was going to be to babysit for such a prolonged period while they were down in Southern California. Whenever Mack stepped out of bounds, it wasn't only worrisome because of the child's personal safety, but it also meant Coby wasn't doing an adequate job taking care of him, which didn't sit well with their parents.

"Are you mad at me?"

Coby glanced back at Mack and noticed that he looked like a puppy dog terrified of upsetting his owner. In an instant, Coby shifted from scornful to empathetic. There was a part of him that only Mack could speak to; perhaps it was just an innate desire to protect his younger sibling that lowered his outer defenses, but no one else could make Coby into a pushover like Mack could when he stared at him with those big eyes.

"Nah, buddy, I ain't mad at you. Just don't do it again."

"I won't," Mack replied earnestly, and he looked back at the TV screen. Coby sighed, a knowing smile spreading across his face. He was terrible with discipline, and he knew that Mack had not learned his lesson.

No more than ten seconds later, Mack snapped his head back in Coby's direction.

"Hey! You're taking me trick-or-treating tonight, right?"

Coby closed his eyes, only remembering his obligation now that Mack had mentioned it.

"Oh my God, I totally forgot about that."

Mack flashed an expression of sudden worry and set the Xbox controller down as he turned to face Coby, ready to plead with him.

"You're going to, right?"

"Aren't you a little old to be doing that?"

"I'm in fourth grade!"

"Do you even have a costume?"

"Well, yeah."

"I actually was going to go somewhere tonight."

Mack frowned. "You were? Where were you going to go?"

"Just to see some friends."

Mack rocked forward incredulously, his blond hair falling in front of his face. "You're going to leave me sleeping alone on Halloween night?"

"I'll be back by, like, midnight at the latest.

You will only be alone for a while."

Mack shook his head and seemed to shudder at the thought of sleeping in a house by himself for a few hours.

"So wait . . . You're not going to take me trick-or-treating then?"

Mack stared at Coby in desperation, and his pupils somehow became twice as large, enhancing his cuteness. Once more, Coby melted on the inside.

"I don't have to be there until, like, nine. So I can take you at, like, six or so. It might not be totally dark for a bit, but I'm sure you will still get lots of candy."

Mack's eyes instantly lit up. "Woo! Cool! Thanks, Coby!"

Coby nodded. He wasn't exactly ecstatic to walk around the neighborhood with a ten-year-old candy fiend who would likely be dressed like Batman, but he would probably only have to do it an hour or so anyway.

"Can we watch a movie too?" Mack looked hopeful.

Coby considered this for a moment. "Maybe. If we have enough time. But it has to be a scary movie."

"Deal!" Mack said excitedly. "Can it be gory too?"

"Maybe a little." Coby gave his little brother a devious smile. Mack beamed with his entire face, radiating hyperactive energy.

"Can we order pizza?"

"Don't push it," Coby said.

4:04 p.m.

The car bottomed out with a loud *thunk* as Coby careened into the McDonald's parking lot. Mack, who was sitting in the passenger seat, bugged his eyes out and looked at Coby in anguish.

"Whoops," Coby said sheepishly.

Coby whipped his maroon 1991 Honda Accord station wagon into a vacant parking spot at the back of the lot. He had to pump the brakes with vigor as the car slid into the narrow area, so that it wouldn't barrel into the side of the West Coast Bank that was now across from him. The brakes of the Honda were a little shady. If you didn't urge it to stop with all the strength in your foot, it would continue to drift forward lazily like its heart wasn't really into it. Such was the plight of old cars.

Mack twitched irritably. "Why do you have to park so far away?"

"So nobody bangs into Mervin, slick," Coby replied with a click of his tongue. Even though the Honda, which was named Mervin, was kind of a piece of junk, Coby had worked all the past summer to save up the money to buy the vehicle, and it possessed more than a little sentimental value to him.

Mack shook his head and folded his arms grumpily.

"Just stay in the car then," Coby said in exasperation. "I won't need your help."

"But then I won't get to pick the movie!"

"Tough shit. I'm paying for it. I get to pick."

"Don't say that word, Coby! Mom told you not to cuss!"

Coby ignored his brother and got out of the car, taking care to slam the door shut so that it would startle Mack, and he was rewarded with a slight flinch. Giggling to himself, Coby walked across the parking lot and toward the movie rental kiosk that was placed next to the side door of McDonald's. It was better that Mack not come anyway, because if he did, the process of choosing a movie would take twice as long. Coby grabbed the red mesh-like cover that was used to protect the glass, and touched the "Rent a Movie" option that was displayed on the screen. Since it was Halloween, the kiosk had taken it upon itself to amass its stockpile of movies with horror flicks. Coby scrolled through several B-movie options, including the remake of *Piranha* that had been released in 2010. *Probably a little too gory,* thought Coby. He kept swiping through movies until he came to a section that seemed to be classic scary movies. When it came to this classification, Coby had a strong preference for the older stuff; horror seemed to be the only genre that produced exceedingly awful films as time went on.

After a brief search, Coby's eyes zeroed in on the original *Halloween*. In an instant, his mind was made up. He had a feeling Mack had probably never seen it, and though it was quite creepy, its scares came with a slower psychological delivery as opposed to the typical jump-scares you'd find in horror movies. Plus, there was gore, but it wouldn't be too gratuitous for Mack's eyes. With a feeling of self-satisfaction in his gut, Coby withdrew his debit card from his pocket and swiped it in the designated slot. Seconds later, the DVD came out in a square red case. Coby snatched it and turned around, heading back to his car.

While he was strutting back in the direction he had come, something caught Coby's eye from afar. He had been walking with his vision focused on the pavement, but a brief flash had interrupted his fixation with the ground. It took him a few moments to identify what had taken place, but then, it happened again. The driver of a red pickup in the far corner of the lot was flashing its lights at him. Coby froze. *What on earth*, he thought. Coby tried to get a better look at who might be behind the wheel, but the truck was too far away, and Coby was nearsighted. Figuring it must be someone he knew, Coby continued to walk forward, determined to get a better look at the driver. The truck flashed its lights two more times in Coby's direction.

"Jesus, dude, stop, I get it," Coby muttered under his breath.

Without warning, there was a loud revving as the engine of the pickup turned over. Coby stopped, unnerved by the noise. The red truck moved forward, and Coby was almost able to make out a face behind the windshield. However, at the last second, the truck turned to the right and increased its speed. It stopped briefly on the precipice of Highway 101, before swerving to the left and speeding off.

What the fuck is with this day, thought Coby. With a start, he recalled the vehicle that the unidentified figure had been leaning against on his walk home. It had been a truck. A red pickup truck. He thought about it for a moment longer and a strange sensation began to creep up his spine. Was it the same person behind all these bizarre occurrences? Who would be that determined to screw with him? He told himself that it had either been someone he knew, or just a coincidence. But deep in the recesses of his brain, something told him that neither of these conclusions was correct. He pushed the thought aside forcefully.

Coby swung the door to his car open and found Mack sitting in the front seat with his face pressed against his fist.

"What took you so long?"

Coby didn't answer. He could've offered a stock platitude about trying to decide what movie they were going to watch being the cause of his delay, but he didn't want to waste the effort. With a flick of his wrist, he turned Mervin's engine on and gripped the gearshift, putting it in reverse.

Mack's eyes lit up eagerly. "So what movie are we going to watch?"

"*Halloween*," Coby replied.

Mack frowned in confusion. "That's what it's called?"

"Yeah."

"What's it about?"

Coby looked over his shoulder and began to move the car backward.

"It's about this crazy guy who breaks out of a mental hospital and stalks these babysitters."

"Stalks?" Mack looked befuddled.

"Yeah, like, uh, follows. Like he's going to try and kill them."

"Does he succeed?"

Coby looked over at Mack and gave him a mischievous smile.

"You're just going to have to see what happens, aren't you?"

6:02 p.m.

The hoodie got tangled on his head, causing Coby

to briefly lose his vision as he fought through tangles of thick polyester and cotton.

"Son of a bitch!" he shouted. It took him a few seconds to rearrange his dark blue sweatshirt and pull it down all the way to his waist. Once he did, he glanced in the mirror and brushed his hair out of his eyes. He wasn't exactly dressed for success, but he didn't look terrible either. Coby heard Mack's voice waft into his room.

"I heard that."

Coby jumped, realizing that Mack was in the adjacent hallway. He toggled on the door handle, fighting with the lock he had fastened earlier. Once he had successfully outwitted the door, he pulled it open and saw Mack standing there. He was wearing a black costume and a metallic silver mask, with the hood of his cape pulled over his head. Mack had chosen to dress as the *Star Wars* supervillain Kylo Ren.

"Aren't you a little short for that outfit?"

"What? Doesn't it fit?"

"It was a reference to—oh never mind. You look good."

Coby looked away from Mack and took one last glance at himself in the mirror. His hair was currently in open rebellion and sticking up in seemingly three different directions. But he didn't have hair product, and no amount of water could tame the beast on top of his head. So, resigned to his follicle fate, Coby sighed and left his room.

"Alright, let's go. Do you have your bucket?"

"Well, duh. How else am I going to carry candy?"

Coby shook his head irritably. "Well, where is it then?"

"By the front door."

Coby fiddled in his pocket, making sure he had his keys. "Alright then. We're off!"

Coby led Mack through the hallway and out of the front door, locking it behind them after Mack had grabbed the orange plastic pumpkin he was using to collect candy. The street outside had giant coniferous trees stretching overhead from each side. The trees themselves looked spooky, casting bizarre shadows on the road as the sun was just beginning to set. Underneath the trees, thick blackberry bushes and other fauna bunched up together, creating a veritable wall of vegetation. Every time Coby walked past the brush at night, he frequently imagined someone leaping out of the bushes and attacking him. It had always caused him to take a wide berth and walk in the middle of street. He knew no one was ever going to jump out, but it was just habit by now. Mack had to take several strides to keep up every time Coby took a step, and he began breathing heavily as he walked alongside his brother in the middle of the road.

"Slow down! You're walking so fast!"

"Maybe you're just walking slow."

"I'm going as fast as I can!"

The Connors lived in a small house tucked into a cul-de-sac in a neighborhood with a generally elderly demographic, so no one else was currently on their street but them. Most of their neighbors were most likely not even aware it was Halloween, and if they were, they were not going to be partaking in any candy-bequeathing festivities. All of the front porch lights of the neighboring houses were off. Therefore, Coby had decided to take Mack out onto Eads Street and trick-or-treat in a busier area. It was a little early to be going out, but it wouldn't be much longer before the sun had set and small children were out in force.

At the first house they stopped at, the brothers were welcomed by a couple that looked to be in their forties. They greeted Coby and Mack with a warm smile. Coby had already told Mack he refused to say "Trick or treat," and that Mack was going to have to shoulder all the responsibility of it. After Mack had barked out the three words, the couple had exchanged pleasantries with Coby for a few seconds before dropping a Three Musketeers bar into Mack's pumpkin bucket and waved them along their merry way.

The next house they hit on Eads was armed with a decorative repertoire of Halloween-themed knickknacks. Five sizeable jack-o'-lanterns were displayed on the deck and a vibrating plastic ghost was haunting them with electronic-powered *Oh*s. Once they knocked on the door, a large gentleman answered. He was quite overweight, and had long brown hair and glasses. He instantly reminded Coby of someone who might do software work at a computer company. Once the man's eyes caught sight of Mack, he grinned.

"Trick or treat!" Mack shouted.

"Ah, man, I think I'm going to drop in two pieces of candy for someone dressed as Kylo Ren!"

"That's the spirit," Coby replied. He knew this man was the exact kind of person that a *Star Wars* character would speak to. The man grabbed two miniature Snickers and dropped them into Mack's bucket.

"Thank you!" Mack turned around and bounded off the deck.

Coby gave the man a small wave and followed Mack.

For thirty minutes, Coby took his younger brother to various houses around the neighborhood, collecting all manner of sweets. There were some houses that did not answer their call, but the ones that did were full of welcoming, festive individuals who seemed to be enjoying themselves almost as much as Mack. After they had hit their tenth house, the sun had finally set and the streets were teeming with children collecting candy. Coby was a little eager to depart from the crowd, so he took Mack down Eighth Street to a collection of houses that weren't being bombarded by kids.

Eventually, Coby and Mack reached a house that was on the corner of Eighth and Benton. The lights were on and the pathway was beset by lit carved pumpkins, so Coby figured that this would be a good house to attack. They climbed up three small stairs until they were in front of a large wooden door with an old-fashioned brass knocker. Coby knocked and waited. Moments after he had done so, the door opened, and they were greeted by a kind-looking old man with soft white hair and squinty eyes.

"Trick or treat!" Mack said enthusiastically, and the old man smiled.

"Well, hello there! Happy Halloween!"

Coby smiled at the man, and patted Mack on the shoulder.

"Our little *Star Wars* fan here would like some candy if you can manage it."

The old man chuckled heartily. "Oh, I think I can manage a piece or two. What's your preference, kiddo? Butterfinger or Reese's?"

"Reese's!"

"Say please, Mack."

"Please!" Mack said, inflecting a more soothing tone into his voice.

"You betcha!" The old man rifled through a

bucket of goods on a chair behind his door. At first, he fingered two candy bars, but then he looked up for a second, shifted his focus back on the bucket, and grabbed a handful more.

"Oh, no thanks," Coby said. "I don't need any."

"It isn't for you, champ," the old man replied. "I only give out candy to those wearing costumes."

"Fair enough. But my friend here doesn't need that much," Coby said, trying to be polite but firm as he put his hand on Mack's shoulder. "He already has quite a bit."

"It isn't all for him! It's for both of them."

"Both . . . ? Who are you talking about?"

"Your friend!" The old man pointed toward the street.

Coby and Mack turned around simultaneously. Coby's gut clenched and his heart skipped a beat. Across the street, underneath a stop sign, a figure stood like a sentinel, looking right at them. The figure was tall and wearing black, with a mask covering his face. The mask was dark gray, with two eyeholes cut underneath the spiked ears. A wolf.

Coby gazed over at him with a series of chills shooting down his spine. The figure just continued to stare back, unmoving. Coby waited for the man to do something, but he just stood there.

"Who is that?" Mack grabbed onto Coby's arm.

"I'm not sure."

"You don't know him? I thought he was with you." The old man sounded perplexed. "He was walking right behind you when you were coming up the street."

Coby looked back at the old man.

"No," he said slowly. "He isn't with us."

Coby turned back toward the street, and now the figure was cocking his head to the left while maintaining his gaze.

"It's probably just some prankster," Coby said, but his voice shook. He put his arm around Mack's shoulder and drew him in tight. Mack quivered in Coby's grasp.

"Maybe you boys should come inside," the old man said, staring across the road.

Coby and Mack turned around and appraised the friendliness of the old man. He had a bit of a hunch and was decrepit; there was no possible way he could be a threat. Coby seriously considered following the man inside. But then, his senses came to him. He wasn't just going to take his ten-year-old brother in a stranger's house, no matter how benign he appeared.

"No. Thanks though," Coby said.

The old man looked at him in surprise. "Are you sure?"

"No, really, it's fine," Coby replied shortly.

The geezer's face turned a little surly. "Suit yourself. Happy Halloween."

The old man backed up over the threshold and shut the door in Coby's face. For a couple seconds, Coby stood there, a little flabbergasted at the fact that the seemingly genial old man had just cut them off so abruptly. Then a horrifying realization poured over him. He and Mack were now alone with the man across the road. Coby whipped his head about and pulled Mack behind him in a protective gesture. However, once he saw the street, he slacked his body from its tense position. The man in the wolf mask was gone.

"Don't be scared, buddy. It was just some moron's version of a practical joke. He's probably just following random people around and trying to freak them out. It's Halloween, remember?"

"It's just weird, you know?" Mack said in a small voice, keeping as close as he possibly could to his brother.

"I agree, it's pretty weird. But it's nothing to be afraid about. Nobody is going to attack you."

The two of them had decided to end their trick-or-treating venture for the night and were heading home, walking as fast as they could without running. Coby had made sure to take the route to their house that would be the most crowded, and although he spoke to his brother in a consoling tone, his heart beat at breakneck speed. After all the oddities that had taken place that day, it seemed hard to believe that the man in the wolf mask was just a random, creepy coincidence. But Coby didn't want Mack to throw a fit; it wouldn't behoove either of them to panic.

Coby led Mack through a bevy of children and their parents, passing them like they were on a freeway.

"I'm sorry we couldn't stay out for longer, buddy."

"It's alright. I want to go home too. And I wish Mom and Dad were there."

Coby gave a long, hard look at his brother. He couldn't see his facial expression due to the Kylo Ren mask, but he knew that Mack was still beset by trepidation. If only he knew about the phone call that Coby had received at school earlier in the day.

"Do you believe me about the wolf guy?"

"Yeah, I think so," Mack said unconvincingly.

"Trust me, buddy, it's nothing to worry about. Just some punk trying to fuc—I mean mess with us."

Mack nodded through the mask, and Coby patted him on the head. They weaved through several more kids and a few of their parents looked over at Coby in irritation, as though him walking past them was a great injustice. It took the brothers ten minutes to make it back to the street that their house was on, and when they rounded the corner of Kruger Lane, they saw the same familiar, haunting trees casting weird shadows next to a wall of brush. Coby led Mack on the complete opposite side of the street this time, determined to not even get close to the shrub. He knew logically there was no one there, but he couldn't help but imagine what it would be like to see the man in the wolf mask peeking out from behind the bushes.

6:15 p.m.

"It's only been an hour and my legs are already stiff."

"You can get out and stretch them, Stevie. If we need to leave it's not like I'm just going to bail on you."

"I wouldn't put it past you. I know you're always in the market for a new partner."

"But that would mean you would get a new partner too. So . . . I'm sure Bonner would be happy to have you," Amos deadpanned.

"Ew! I would rather have literally anybody as a partner than the Law Boner."

"How about Ted? That would be interesting to pair a suit like Ted with someone who has a certain proclivity for bending the rules."

"At least Ted is good looking."

"Yes, I suppose that is the most important thing to look for in a detective, isn't it? The best ones are always good looking."

The car that they sat in was parked at the edge of a cliff on the west side of the Yaquina Bay Bridge. They were sitting about fifteen feet under the bridge, looking down at the bay below. Amos had tried to convince Dozer to let him take his normal vehicle, but Dozer had insisted everyone drive more low-key rides to avoid the suspicion of any potential suspect, and thus, he and Stevie had ended up in an unmarked 2013 Ford Crown Victoria. They had spent the past hour driving along aimlessly, unsure of what they were supposed to be looking for.

"Look at all the lights down there," Amos said, referring to the Bayfront. "It's just a normal night for everybody but us."

Stevie's face was then beset by half a smile. Sort of a frisky, sarcastic thing. "Uh-oh, are you getting all philosophical on me?"

"It's just . . . I can't help but think of some young kid out there, having a good time with his friends while he's unknowingly being stalked." Once more, those bright blue eyes of John Kimball seemed to gleam at him in the dark. His skin, sallow and tinged with green as the mortician unzipped the body bag for Amos to see. It had been thirteen years now since then. And yet, it felt like every young teenage boy ambling about with his friends on this evening was Special K, like Amos could finally make things right if he saved them all from the demon that was lingering in the shadows.

"Oh, even better, you're getting all morbid on me."

"It's just weird to think about, you know? That right now, there is a killer within a few miles of us." Amos looked out at the sky in apprehension.

The darkness had taken full control now, giving the town an eerie feel. A wisp of fog had descended on the Bayfront, shrouding the tallest buildings with a layer of opaqueness.

"Good job, Al. You have sufficiently creeped me out now."

"I'm just saying, it feels like the deck is stacked against us. We don't even know what we're looking for. If something happens, we won't know about it until it's over with."

Stevie chewed on the inside of her cheek as she thought. "You mean someone will die?"

"I was trying to say it a bit more eloquently than that, but yes."

"Eloquent isn't my style."

"This I know," Amos said sardonically.

"Anyway, that won't happen."

"What?"

"No one is going to die tonight."

Amos looked away, gazing over the water. The

murky, musty bay was illuminated by all storefront lights nearby. He could see the dock beneath the Abbey Street Pier, which had approximately eight sea lions piled onto it, all looking exceedingly indolent and lethargic. From above, people stared at the sea lions, occasionally shouting something at them. The Bayfront was usually tame during the nights, but since it was a festive holiday, many people were milling about.

"How can you be so sure, Stevie?"

Stevie gave Amos a fierce look, and for once, she spoke in a totally serious tone. "Because we aren't going to let that happen."

Amos shrugged. "I like your confidence, but I'm not so sure. Like I said, we don't even know what we're looking for."

"But we also don't know if he's even going to go through with it."

Amos gave Stevie a skeptical look, raising his eyebrows and collapsing his lips inward. "We know he has gone through with it twice before. Maybe even more than that."

"Except there have been no other Halloween night disappearances in Lincoln County or any of the surrounding counties."

"None that we know of," Amos replied ominously.

"Oh, Jesus. If you want to start chasing ghosts, be my guest. But I'm going to focus on what's tangible."

Amos looked back down at the dock. He noticed that there was now a large harbor seal attempting to assert its dominance on the sea lions by invading their territory, but the lions were having none of it. They each took turns barking aggressively at the newcomer, and a couple of them even slapped at the seal. Eventually, the invader gave one last look at the bouncers guarding the dock, and dove back into the bay.

"I just feel helpless."

Stevie gave Amos a genuine look of empathy. "I know, Al. But this isn't all your responsibility. You aren't a superhero. You can't stop every bad thing from happening."

"I never said I could."

"But you still try to do so. I really do admire you trying to spare everyone from some unspeakable fate. But that isn't how the world works. Not everyone is going to be saved. All I know is, you have a strong heart, a shrewd mind, you're the best detective I know, and you're going to do everything in your power to stop this man . . . or woman."

Amos looked Stevie in the eyes and was touched, feeling a rush of affection for her. She was rarely sappy or consoling, so he wanted to savor the moment.

"So sack up. Stop being a pussy and let's go

out and find this asshole."

"And she's back," Amos said.

Stevie laughed and Amos turned on the engine of the Ford. He let it warm up a little bit before he put the car in reverse and started backing out, ready to begin patrolling again. The traffic was sparse; there were only a few cars out on the roads to impede their progress.

"It isn't a woman, by the way."

"Huh?"

"Our killer. It's a man."

"You don't know that! It very well could be a woman!" Stevie replied earnestly.

"Ninety-one percent of all serial killers are male. For that matter, nearly half of all killers are white males."

"You keep saying that he can't yet be called a serial killer. Two vics, remember? It has to be three before we can use that particular phrase."

"One more equals three," Amos said.

Stevie sighed. "You can bust out all the stats you want, but there is a chance it could be a woman."

Amos didn't feel like arguing with her. He simply drove on the roundabout under the bridge and came back to Highway 101. The neighborhood that they had been tasked with patrolling was in between the highway and Elizabeth Street. There were only a couple houses on each block, but the street stretched out a couple thousand feet, so they basically had to do giant, narrow loops repeatedly.

"All I know is, get ready to hoof it if we see anyone dressed as a wolf," Amos said.

"Ha, okay." Stevie gave him a sarcastic thumbs-up. "I will keep an eye out. But you really think someone who is smart enough to evade police for ten years would just walk around wearing a wolf mask after what he wrote on the Ledouxs' wall?"

7:05 p.m.

The couch they were sitting on was wide, but Mack was sitting inexorably close to Coby as they watched Michael Myers stare at his next target. The incident with the man in the wolf mask seemed to have sufficiently disturbed Mack's Zen. Every few minutes he would glance toward the sliding glass door that led out of the living room and into the backyard, anxiously anticipating someone to be there. Coby had told Mack several times not to be afraid, but it seemed that the situation had slipped out of his grasp. Mack was consumed with nervous energy.

As it was while watching all movies with Mack nowadays, the kid seemed to feel the need to vocalize every time he had a question about the plot. "Why is he following her? Why not someone else? Is she going to die?" Eventually, following eight queries, Coby had told Mack to shut up and watch the movie. After a couple more attempts, Mack had settled in and had stopped trying to guess what would happen before it did.

Although *Halloween* was at times quite terrifying, Coby had forgotten that it was a bit of a slow burn. For the first hour or so of the movie, there were simply various shots of Michael Myers lingering in the background while numerous characters failed to notice his presence. There wasn't a ton of action, and thus, after his nervousness faded, Mack's eyes were beginning to droop as sleep threatened to invade his consciousness. He was still wearing much of his Kylo Ren ensemble, just without the mask. Coby hadn't had the heart to tell him to take it off and put on his pajamas, so they had sat down on the couch while Mack was still costumed, put the movie in, and the kid had broken into some of his candy. Now, Mack was beginning to drift off into dreamland.

Once Mack was all the way out, Coby stealthily slid off the couch and walked into the kitchen, hungry for a snack. He had eaten a sandwich before he had taken Mack trick-or-treating, but that was hours ago, and he felt ravenous. Coby seemed to be at the stage of his life where no matter how much he ate, he always felt a sense of dull hunger. His mother frequently referred to him as a bottomless pit. What most people considered to be a meal, Coby perceived as a snack. He poured himself a bowl of cereal and stacked two bananas and a package of Twinkies in his arms and ambled awkwardly back into the living room, carrying more than what was comfortable.

Ten minutes later, the food was gone and Mack was still asleep. Coby started to watch the movie again, ambivalent to the fact that he had missed a chunk of it. He had seen *Halloween* multiple times, so he didn't fret over missing a scene or two. He focused on the screen, and he realized that he had tuned in just before another murder was about to take place. *Perfect timing,* thought Coby. He waited in silent anticipation for Michael to strike. Just when the killer leapt out from his hiding place, Coby heard a noise he knew hadn't come from the movie.

Thunk.

Coby jumped and his chest tightened. He looked for what had produced the noise. His heart pounded frenetically and the hairs on his arms stood on end. Coby glanced back toward his sleeping brother. He quickly flipped his head back around, frantically searching for what had made the noise. Moments later, he heard another noise, but this one was much softer: the sound of something light hitting the ground. Coby scanned every inch of the room until he noticed something that hadn't been there before: a postcard. It sat directly underneath the mail slot of the front door. It hadn't been there when they had come in from trick-or-treating. Somebody had just dropped it through.

Trying to stay as quiet as he could, Coby got off the couch and tiptoed over to the front door. Once he had made it to his intended destination, he looked down at the postcard as though it was some sinister omen. He crouched down and picked it up, bringing it closer to his face. The only light in their living room was coming from the TV, so it was hard to see. However, it didn't take Coby long to realize what the real problem was: there was nothing on the postcard. It was made of thin cardboard material, but it was a totally blank white canvas.

Coby looked back at Mack, as though his sleeping brother might have some answers for him, but the ten-year-old remained in a deep slumber. Coby focused his attention on the card and flipped it over. There was something on the other side drawn in red ink. A horizontal X with a small curved line on the nether side. A smiley face. One that appeared to be dead.

Trying to remain calm, Coby kept staring at the insignia with a mix of foreboding and confusion. What was it? What was it supposed to indicate? The culmination of all the events of the day had finally begun to make Coby consider the possibility someone was threatening him. He wondered whether it would be prudent to call his parents and relay everything that had happened.

Suddenly, Coby's stupor was broken by a loud cry.

"Ahhh!"

Coby jumped and turned around to face his brother. Mack's eyes were bulging out of his skull and he was covering his mouth.

"What? What is it?"

"He was there! Outside! He was looking in through the glass door! The wolf man!

Instead of going toward the glass, Coby immediately marched down the hall toward his parents' bedroom, putting the postcard in his pocket.

"Where are you going? Don't leave me alone!"

"Get behind the couch. Now!"

Mack scurried off the cushions and scrambled around to the back of the sofa, eclipsing his body from the view of the glass door.

"Keep quiet. And still. I will be back in ten seconds."

Coby ran down the hallway and burst into the last door on the left. He slid his parents' wooden closet door open and focused on what he had come for: the three-and-a-half-foot-long case with the padlock on it. With his fingers trembling, Coby put in the combination as fast as he could, and removed the lock. Once the case was open, Coby picked up the gun, knowing that there were shells in the chamber but that the safety was on. He pointed the Mossberg down at the ground like his father had always taught him when they had gone shooting together, and he jogged quickly back through the hallway and into the living room.

When Mack saw what Coby was carrying, his eyes bulged wildly. "Where did you get that? Is that a real gun?"

Coby didn't answer, but slowly approached the sliding glass door, raising the shotgun. Keeping his eyes on the door, he whispered to Mack, "If anything happens to me I want you to go lock yourself in Mom and Dad's room and call the police with the phone in there."

"Coby, don't!" Mack hissed. "I'm so scared."

"Be quiet. Keep still."

Coby approached the glass, keeping his eyes tuned for movement. The patio outside wasn't lit up; there was a switch by the door that would turn on the backdoor light. Coby got right next to the switch, taking one hand off the shotgun and keeping it taut, ready to turn on the light. He took a deep breath and flicked his index finger up, instantly shedding light on their entire tiny backyard. There was no one there.

Feeling a bead of sweat running down his forehead, Coby absentmindedly wiped at his face. He seemed to be having difficulty swallowing, and his heartbeat was so pronounced he could audibly hear it inside his ears. His breath was shallow and he had to consciously make an effort to push the excess air out of his lungs. He shot a glance down at the shotgun and realized with a jolt that the safety was still on. Coby hurriedly pressed the miniscule button on the side of the gun, readying it to fire. He scanned the area outside back and forth like a prison tower searchlight, trying to eliminate the possibility of impending danger.

"Do you see him?"

"No. He isn't there."

"He probably left when I screamed."

Coby looked at his brother over his shoulder. Suddenly, he came to an epiphany. He cocked his head to the right, furrowed his brow, and opened his mouth slightly.

"Wait, how would you have seen him if this light was off?"

For a second, Mack's mouth expanded and contracted rapidly as he searched for a quality answer. It reminded Coby of that moment when a child is caught in the act of doing something wrong and starts scrambling to not get in trouble.

"I just saw th-the shape of him, I guess. Like I saw the pointed ears," Mack replied, no longer whispering.

"And hold on . . . You were out cold a second ago."

"So?"

Coby sighed and felt an immense sense of relief spreading out through his chest, mixed with extreme irritation at his brother. His heart rate began to even out.

"So could you have maybe been having a nightmare or something?"

"No! It was real! I was fully awake!"

"But I still don't get how you could've seen anything with the patio light off."

Mack made a wild gesture with his right hand. "I told you, I just saw the shape!"

Coby shook his head in exasperation. He couldn't believe he had allowed himself to get all worked up. "Mack, you didn't see anything," Coby said flatly.

"No, I did! I swear!"

Without another word, Coby stormed through the living room and back down the hallway to their parents' bedroom. Making sure to click the safety on, he put the gun back in its case in the closet. He hesitated for a moment, looking at the padlock discarded on the ground. Some sixth sense was telling him to keep it unlatched in case he needed quick access later. He obeyed the intuition, leaving the lock set off to the side, and with a little extra oomph, Coby shut the closet door.

"Don't put it away! What if he's still out there?" Mack called from the living room.

"No one is out there, Mack."

Coby thought of the postcard with the strange insignia in his pocket. Someone had been on their front porch within the last couple of minutes. But for all Coby knew, the same person could be going door to door and dropping in postcards with dead-like smiley faces on them through everyone's mail slots. He couldn't think of any reason why someone would do that, and he was almost fully aware of the active cognitive dissonance his brain was concocting. Did he not believe it was related to the man in the wolf mask because he just didn't want to believe it? Regardless, Coby wasn't ready to full-on panic quite yet. It wasn't like the man had dropped the postcard through his mail slot, sprinted into their backyard, and pressed his face against the sliding glass door. Logistically, that would be next to impossible. The gate to the backyard was locked and it was also almost eight feet high. It seemed unlikely someone would be able to scale it, especially in such a short amount of time, while not making any noise. Also, it was completely unfeasible Mack would've seen him in the darkness.

Coby walked back into the living room,

glowering at Mack.

"If you do that again I'm going to kick your butt."

"Do what?" Mack sounded offended. His forehead was screwed up and his lips puckered out a little.

"Cause a ruckus like that. You almost gave me a heart attack."

"He was there! I mean, at least I think he was!"

Mack suddenly looked ashamed.

"Now you aren't so sure, are you?"

Mack's eyes began to well up with tears.

"I'm . . . I'm sorry, Coby. I thought I saw him."

Coby looked at Mack, wanting to rage and scream and use his little brother as an outlet for the fear he had felt. However, he couldn't bring himself to inflict emotional harm on the child, no matter how much strife Mack had caused him.

"Buddy, it's fine. Just don't do something like that unless you're *positive* you see something. *The Boy Who Cried Wolf*, remember?"

"Okay," Mack replied quietly.

After a moment of silence, Mack suddenly looked up, frowning at Coby.

"Why were you by the front door anyway?"

Coby turned his head away, internally debating whether to tell the truth.

"Nothing, no reason. Just thought I heard trick-or-treaters outside."

"Oh."

As Coby headed back toward the couch, Mack seemed to try and tune in to what was happening in the movie, focusing his eyes on the screen. In a split decision, Coby walked over to the Blu-ray player and hit the STOP button.

"Hey! What are you doing?"

"I think you've watched enough of this movie for tonight."

8:30 p.m.

Mack didn't look the least bit ready to fall asleep. His self-created disturbance had made him nervous and jittery. After he had turned off *Halloween*, Coby had switched on a friendlier movie that was playing on ABC Family, but it hadn't held Mack's attention in the slightest. Every few minutes, Mack would hear some sort of noise outside and jerk his head around. Now, Mack lay underneath the topmost covers of his bed in his pajamas, and his eyes shifted around wildly every few seconds.

Coby had come in to say good night after Mack had brushed his teeth. He was watching his brother with empathy. Mack wasn't just milking it. He was experiencing genuine fear.

"Are you okay, buddy?"

"Yeah."

Coby gave Mack a piercing look, trying to

convey he was unconvinced.

"I'm just a little scared. That's all."

Coby walked closer and stood next to Mack's bed.

"Buddy, there is nothing to be afraid of. The guy we saw while trick-or-treating was just messing with us."

"Okay. But I think I really did see something outside of the door in the living room too."

Coby shook his head. Even though he was experiencing some of the same worries, he was the older brother. He had to make his younger sibling feel safe. "No you didn't, buddy. It was just your imagination. Remember how Mom always tells you about how great of an imagination you have?"

"Yeah, but—"

"There wasn't anybody outside."

Mack pulled the sheets closer to his face while looking at the ceiling.

"I'm going to be right here in the house with you anyway, okay?"

"Promise?" Mack looked dubious while he stared directly at his older brother.

"Yeah," lied Coby.

Mack bobbed his head a little and turned over onto his side, preparing himself for an attempt at sleep.

"If you need anything, I will be downstairs. Okay?"

"Okay."

"Goodnight, buddy."

"Goodnight."

Coby flipped the light switch, casting Mack's room into darkness. He gave one last look at the lump that was his brother, walked into the adjacent hallway, and shut the door. For a couple seconds, Coby placed his ear up against the door to Mack's room, making sure that no nefarious noise was emitting from it. Hopefully Mack would go right to sleep and not wake until the morning.

Coby withdrew his head from the door and immediately pulled his phone out of his pocket. Ignoring the feeling in his gut that something was awry, Coby typed out a quick text and sent it to Carson:

Pick me up in 20 minutes.

8:53 p.m.

Coby heard the rumbling sound of an engine outside of his house. He quickly patted his pockets, making sure he had his wallet, keys, and phone. Sure enough, a small vibration against his thigh let him know that his cell was indeed there. Coby pulled it out and looked at the screen:

Outside.

He stared up at the ceiling one last time. He hadn't heard any noise from the room in the past fifteen minutes and was sure that Mack was asleep. Suppressing the guilt he felt, Coby crept toward the front door. If his parents knew he was leaving Mack alone, they would kill him. Yet Coby knew deep down that if someone was in danger, it wasn't Mack. *He* had received the creepy phone call that morning. *He* had seen the strange man leaning against his truck. And he had been the one to find the postcard. The cognitive dissonance was there; he knew he was rationalizing a potentially poor choice. But Cassandra was beckoning. Sean had said she would be there. And he had to go. She was so intoxicating to him that it was like a magnetic force was pulling him towards the party. Any chance to see her, any time he got to spend in her presence, was worth the potential pitfalls. How often did he get to be with her of class? The opportunity to see the girl he was hopelessly infatuated with in a nonschool setting outweighed the guilt he felt for leaving Mack behind.

Coby silently torqued the handle to the right, pulling the door open. With one last glance back at the house, Coby slid his body through the space he had created and silently pulled the door closed.

Seconds later, he was hopping into the front seat of Carson's white Ford F-150. It was a massive truck that Carson used to overcompensate for his peaky stature. The truck had been supplied by Carson's father, a wealthy real estate mogul who had inherited the family business.

The system stereo deck inside the truck was emblazoned in blue, lighting up Carson's face from behind the steering wheel.

"What's up, man?"

"Nada mucho, amigo. You ready to party?"

"As ready as I will ever be."

Carson revved the engine and drove off down the street. He and Coby engaged in some small talk, bantering about who may or may not be at the party while they pulled onto 101 and sped off in the direction of Sean's house. Coby was hesitant to tell him about what had transpired over the past couple of hours. Carson was much easier to confide in than the other friends in the group, but Coby still was worried about sounding like a paranoid kook. After all, did anything happen when it boiled down to it? He had seen someone in a creepy costume on Halloween. Later, he had found a postcard. Even if it did mean something, none of his friends would think that it did. Even Carson. Therefore, Coby stewed in his anxiety and tried to let the banter distract him, but it didn't.

The Ford F-150 traveled north on 101 past the Walmart at the far end of town before Carson took a right on Sixty-fifth Street. The street morphed into a hill that sloped downward toward Big Creek Park. Just before the park, a street forked off to the left, leading to Sean's house. The house was, for all intents and purposes, only a couple of rooms away from being a castle; it had three stories and seemed to occupy the entire block.

The Ford traveled slowly down Loomis Street and, from outside, it appeared the party was well underway. The entire building seemed to be vibrating and various vibrant colors shot out from the windows from what looked like a strobe light. Carson pulled the truck up against the sidewalk and put it in park.

Carson looked over with mischievous eyes. "Well, let's do this."

He and Coby hopped out of the truck, shut their doors, and started walking up the pathway to the booming white house. It was tucked far enough away into the corner of the street that there weren't any neighbors around to make noise complaints or knock on the door and tell them to quiet down. Also, the neighborhood was sort of off the beaten path; there wouldn't be any cops patrolling Big Creek Park unless there was a reason for them to do so.

If a swath of law enforcement were somehow beckoned to them, Sean had developed a contingency plan to combat the minor in possession charges that everyone would face. There was a police scanner that Sean kept on him that would light up and make a beeping noise if there was a cop car in the vicinity. If it began to go off, Sean would hit the breaker that would turn off all the lights and music and everyone would retreat down to the basement and lock the door. By the time the police made it, the partygoers would all be filing out of the basement door and into the woods to hide. It was an elaborate escape plan and had been successful twice before, although a couple of stragglers had been slapped with citations both times.

Carson walked in front of Coby as they crossed the lawn, scaled the three steps to the porch, and assembled themselves side-by-side in front of the door. With one last look at Coby, Carson pulled out his phone and typed a text to let their hosts know they were outside. Knocking or ringing the doorbell would be a superfluous gesture with how loud the music was. Ten long seconds passed while thumping tunes played in the background before the door finally swung open. Sean, with his hair frazzled and a giant pair of sunglasses covering his eyes, looked at the newcomers.

"Finally! I was wondering when you assholes were going to show up!"

Coby appraised Sean, looking at his ridiculous outfit. He wore green swimming trunks and a maroon bathrobe with no shirt underneath. Five strands of multicolored beads draped around his neck like it was Mardi Gras.

Coby's eyes swelled incredulously. "Dude, did you start drinking before you got dressed?"

"Shit, man, it's a Halloween party! Why didn't you two jerkoffs dress up? Anyway, I can get more trim dressed like this than you can in a suit."

"More STDs too," Coby replied cheerfully.

Sean ignored this comment and stepped aside to let them in. Behind him were at least twenty people packed onto a makeshift dance floor, all humping each other to the beat of the Drake song blaring through three giant black speakers. Most of the people were wearing costumes; only three or four were not. Coby saw the Lambert twins, two short and stocky juniors at Newport High, dressed as Mario and Luigi. Behind the Lamberts were several preppy sophomore girls Coby didn't know dressed in fishnets and wearing cat ears. Next to them, someone was in a gorilla costume, dancing spasmodically like he or she had just done a line of cocaine. Finally, Coby's heart jumped into his throat as he zeroed in on Cassandra dancing in the throng of people. She wore tight blue Spandex shorts and a small top with the Superman logo emblazoned on it, as well as a red cape. He had glanced at her midlaugh where her attractiveness seemed to be at its peak, and several butterflies fluttered around in his stomach.

"Do you think she will fuck you if you just

keep staring at her?"

Landon suddenly appeared over Coby's left shoulder. Unlike Coby and Carson, he had taken the time to put on a costume. He wore a strange vest and had a bald cap covering his head, making him look a little like Mr. Clean. His pudgy arms weren't covered by sleeves and he was wearing camo pants. In his right hand was a red Solo cup that discharged a potent whiskey smell.

"What are you supposed to be?"

"Bane!" Landon shouted over the music. "From *Batman*."

"Where's your mask?"

"How am I supposed to make out with any hot chicks if I'm wearing a mask?"

"There isn't hardly any hot girls here anyway," said Sean, who was still standing behind them.

Coby looked out at the dance floor and noticed at least six attractive females, including Cassandra.

"Your standards are too high, man."

Sean saw Coby looking over at Cassandra and smiled sarcastically. "You're right, I should just be obsessed with Cassandra too."

"I'm not obs—"

"Yes, you are," a new voice said. Coby looked to his right and burst into laughter. Danny, tall and wiry as ever, was in a massive yellow banana suit.

"Nice costume, man! Better not get too close to that gorilla," Coby said.

"You shouldn't get too close to that gorilla anyway," Landon muttered, and the four friends collectively stared at the person in the gorilla outfit who was now doing a very aggressive version of the sprinkler dance.

Carson walked past them, swiveling his head back and forth. "Anyway, where is the booze?"

"Kitchen." Sean pointed into a room to their left that led away from the dance floor.

Coby and Carson both went in the direction that Sean indicated, which was a short hallway that only had a few people lingering in it. The end of the hallway transformed into an archway that segued to a magnificent kitchen with marble counters and perfectly kept tile floors. In the middle of the kitchen was a large counter that had all the alcohol displayed in a perfectly organized fashion: Cases of beer on the left, hard alcohol in the center, and red Solo cups on the right.

"Damn. Nice spread," Carson said in awe.

Several girls stood behind the counter and chatted away, oblivious to the two boys' presence. When Coby and Carson approached the alcohol, they got a couple quick glances from the girls, but nothing substantial. One of them even gave Coby a dirty look, as if he had done her a great dishonor by getting closer. He quickly grabbed a Keystone off the counter and turned to leave the kitchen with Carson right behind him.

As soon as he made his way down the hallway and back into the living room that was serving as a dance floor, Coby heard someone scream at him.

"Oh my God! Coby!"

Coby looked over and saw Cassandra walking toward him with her arms out. Just from one quick look at her, Coby guessed she was absolutely trashed. Her pupils were large and unfocused and her cheeks were flushed red. Also, she had never regarded him with that much enthusiasm before.

"Hey, Cass," Coby said, and she threw her arms around him and embraced him in a tight hug. Coby felt a swooping sensation in his stomach. Hugging her was fairly abnormal; she only allowed him to embrace her once in a great while. Coby noticed once he was in her grasp that she was carrying a small half pint of Fireball Cinnamon Whisky.

"How are y-you?" Cassandra slurred.

"I'm good," Coby replied, his heart leaping through his chest like it had learned how to fly. For some reason, at the beginning of any conversation Coby had with Cassandra, he would lose all of his ability to coagulate a coherent sentence that was more than a couple of words. Eventually, after speaking for a while, he would relax and become more suave, but not by much.

Cassandra backed out of his arms and appraised him up and down. "Why aren't you d-dressed up,

Cobes?"

Cobes, huh, thought Coby. Now he was sure she was completely hammered. If she ever realized she had called him a pet name after she sobered up she would be wrought with embarrassment. At least that was what he assumed from the way she regarded him most of the time.

"Just didn't feel like it. So you're Superman, huh?"

"Super*woman.*" Cassandra giggled and brushed Coby's nose with her index finger.

"Gotcha. Feeling pretty buzzed?"

"Y-you could say that." Cassandra stammered her words, and she chuckled so hard that the laugh seemed to throw her off-balance. "What about you?"

Coby looked down at his still unopened can of Keystone.

"Just got here."

"Well l-looks like you've got some catching up to do. Here, let's go outside!"

"What?" Coby asked, bewildered.

"Let's go on the back deck! You need to get drunker!" Cassandra shouted. Quite comically, the song playing ended right when Cassandra was shouting, and "You need to get drunker" reverberated around the entire room. A tiny smattering of laughter broke out, but Cassandra remained incognizant of it.

"Come on!" she shouted, grabbing him by the wrist.

"Uh, okay." Coby let her lead him through the crowd. He looked back and saw Carson, Landon, and Danny all looking at him with gleeful expressions and Carson gave him a thumbs-up. He turned his head back around and had to bob and weave through various costumed bystanders as Cassandra shoved her way unceremoniously through the crowd. Various faces gave anguished and consternated looks as they walked past. No one could believe that Cassandra was showing Coby attention. It was widely known that he was infatuated with her, but that she had no interest in him. And he had made a fool of himself more than once with his behavior towards her, a fact that none of his peers missed. Most of them thought his obsession with her was creepy at worst, and pathetic at best.

Cassandra led Coby through another room and then tried to push open the sliding glass door that led to the back deck. However, the door stayed latched.

"What is with this thing?"

"Um, Cass, it's locked." Coby reached around her and flipped the lock so that the door could open.

"Oh, right," Cassandra replied with a puerile giggle, and then she opened the door and stepped through. Coby followed, wondering why she was so insistent on being alone with him.

Once they were outside, Coby felt the cold bite at his hands. The temperature seemed to have dropped ten degrees just in the minute that he and Carson had arrived at the party. As he set his Keystone down on the railing of the deck a gust of wind tore through Coby's hoodie like a cleaver and he couldn't help but to chatter his teeth. Cassandra acted like it didn't bother her at all. It was probably the heat from all the liquor in her system.

"Now this is more like it!" she exclaimed, rather loudly.

Cassandra did a strange pirouette and faced Coby, holding the Fireball out toward him.

"Drink, mister!"

Coby gulped in mild trepidation. He wasn't generally a fan of Fireball. It was far too sweet and usually led to a wicked hangover. But Cassandra could've been offering him a glass of urine and he probably would've taken a small sip just to satisfy her. He unscrewed the top and drank a little from the plastic flask. After a second, he made a move to stop drinking, but Cassandra grabbed the bottom of the half pint and held it in place, forcing him to take a longer swig.

"That's it, Cobes. That's it."

After Cassandra finally let him stop and inhale, she gave another girlish giggle. She had made him chug at least a quarter of the bottle.

"You'll feel it here in a minute," she said, as though he had no idea how alcohol worked.

Once she was turned around, Cassandra went back to sipping on the whiskey herself and looking into the woods at the edge of Sean's backyard. There was a bout of prolonged silence as she seemed to be lost in thought, while Coby waited anxiously for what she would do next. A faint sound of nearby crickets wafted through the air, and the few stars that weren't covered in clouds were twinkling overhead.

"It's so pretty out here," Cassandra said. "I've always liked Halloween. It's my favorite holiday."

Coby didn't answer. Those two thoughts seemed to be totally disjointed and unrelated, so he wasn't sure what to say.

"Why didn't you dress up, Coby?"

Coby looked at her, feeling a little impatience. "I already told you. I just didn't feel like it."

"But why?"

"I don't know . . . I just didn't want to look silly."

"You wouldn't have. You never look *silly*."

Cassandra looked directly into Coby's eyes and moved a fraction of an inch closer. Coby felt a little out of breath and his heart thudded against his chest.

"Well, thanks, Cass."

"I love it when people call me that," Cassandra said with another tiny giggle.

Coby looked away from her, positively uncomfortable. He fidgeted with the front pocket of his hoodie and, for some reason, he desperately wanted to change the subject.

"Hey, Cassandra, I have a question."

Cassandra looked a little disappointed that he had not called her "Cass" again.

"Yes?"

Coby looked out toward the trees. He wasn't sure why he was bringing it up and he knew doing so would be a bad idea, but he couldn't help himself. From deep within, a festering and unpleasant feeling yearned to break out.

"Why did you glare at me today?"

Cassandra looked dumbfounded. "Huh? When?"

"When I got up in Mrs. Parrish's class."

"I don't know what you're ta—"

"Yes, you do," Coby said forcefully.

At first, Cassandra continued to look flabbergasted. Then, suddenly, the drunken and euphoric energy was zapped out of her and her expression turned to reflect anger.

"Oh stop being dramatic. I hate it when you do this! You're so sensitive. I didn't mean to glare at you. And even if I did, what is the big deal? Stop being such a baby."

"Okay, okay! I'm sorry I brought it up. Sheesh," Coby said, stepping away from her.

Cassandra put a pouty expression on her face and begrudgingly took another swig of the whiskey. Once she finished her prodigious gulp, she started rambling again.

"You know, if you weren't so sensitive and didn't overthink things so much, maybe I would actually give you a chance."

Coby almost started laughing at this sentence, even though it instantly began gnawing at him. "That's not true."

"Yes, it is! You're actually a great guy—"

"Actually?" Coby shook his head.

"But then you do that! You overanalyze everything and expect like . . . perfection out of me. I didn't mean to glare at you this morning, and yet, here you are acting like I was intentionally trying to hurt your feelings. You always expect me to act a certain way. Say certain things. And it's exhausting. But if you weren't such an overthinker, I would be interested in you, believe it or not."

Coby felt goose bumps rising on his arms. "You would?"

Cassandra looked at him with an intense look in her eyes. "Yes."

"But . . . why?"

As soon as the word escaped Coby's lips, he realized how childish and pathetic it sounded. But for some reason, Cassandra's face softened and she looked at him like she never had before.

"Because you're good. And like . . . actually good. A lot of guys pretend to be good guys, but you are, you know? You never have bad intentions."

"Well, thanks."

"And you're smart," Cassandra continued. "And funny. And cute."

Coby felt that same swooping sensation in his chest, like his torso was lighter than a feather. "And you're not just saying that because you're dru—"

Before Coby could finish his sentence, Cassandra fell into his arms and kissed him. Her lips pressed firmly against his and her hands draped tightly around the back of his neck. Coby's eyes bulged, realizing what was happening. A dream he had had for two years was finally coming true. It ought to have been magical and pacifying. Coby should've been able to feel the sparks as their lips touched. His nose ought to have been filled with the marvelous aroma of her perfume. And yet, all he smelled was the fetid scent of alcohol on her breath. All he felt was her wet, squishy lips. And instead of being satisfying, it was just repugnant. Somewhere, in the deep recesses of Coby's brain, a fuse ignited, burning slowly but surely as she continued to suck on his face. This is the only way she would take him? Drunken and sloppy? It was patronizing. It was condescending. *So, I'm only good enough for you when you're hammered?* thought Coby. With a giant *squelch,* Coby pulled his face away from hers.

"This is fucking disgusting," he spat.

Cassandra looked at him like he had struck her. Before she could respond, Coby stormed back into the house, slamming the sliding door shut and leaving Cassandra out in the cold.

9:17 p.m.

Water rushed steadily into his hands, creating a quickly draining pool. Before it was totally empty, he splashed the liquid into his face. Coby grabbed the towel from the rack nearby, first drying his hands and then his face. He gently dabbed the fabric against his forehead, but slowly his pushes became fiercer until he was rubbing the towel with such barbarity and vexation he was surprised his skin didn't peel off. He hurled the towel to the ground and unleashed a guttural scream from deep within his chest. If there was anyone in the hallway outside the bathroom, they would think he was having an ignominious bowel movement.

"Fuck!" Coby shouted. "God damn it!"

He pictured her sloppy lips, still tinged with the cinnamon of the Fireball Whisky, pressing against his mouth. He saw her eyes, unfocused and hungry for attention. Anyone's attention. Another wave of fury pulsed through him, and he kicked the small trash can with unbridled fervor. Coby paced back and forth in the small room, rubbing his hand through his hair.

A vibration in his pocket made his tantrum cease. He pulled his phone out, desperate for a distraction from his acrimonious fit. But his rage was only increased when he looked at the short text message on the screen of his iPhone. It was from Cassandra.

Come out back. Let's talk.

"Jesus Christ!" Coby kicked the trash can again, but not with as much force this time. *What does she want now?* he thought. He figured she was just going to scream at him and try and put him in his place. Hell, she might have even summoned one of her goons to try and intimidate Coby. It wouldn't be the first time. Coby had had at least three different guys over the years text him and try to harass him into leaving Cassandra alone when he would get overzealous with his attention, either by texting her too often or saying something too affectionate. Whenever she got upset with him, she would turn to whomever her actual boyfriend was at the time and force him to threaten Coby. One time, one of her more irascible partners, Jake Hanes, had pinned him up against a locker at school and told him that if Coby ever talked to her again, Jake would kick his ass. The result had been three long months of seeing Cassandra walk past him in the halls and looking awkwardly at the ground, avoiding eye contact or conversation. But then, she had broken up with Jake and Coby had gravitated right back to her. It made Coby disgusted with himself. After all she had put him through, he continued to crawl back to her like an abused pet. It was the forbidden fruit. He wanted what he couldn't have. It was human nature, but with who Coby was and how intensely he seemed to experience every feeling, it was like the worst thing in the world.

Coby exited the bathroom, and the noise of the booming music downstairs became louder once more. He trudged his way down the stairs, feeling like he was walking the Green Mile. Best case scenario, Cassandra would be outside, ready to unleash a verbal berating. Worst case, someone would be waiting to instigate a physical fight. He knew he shouldn't even go outside, but he had to see this through. As angry as Coby was with Cassandra, he needed to know what she had to say. He made his way through the throng of people on the dance floor and received several uncomfortable glances from people who had seen him storm past in a huff several minutes before. He kept his head down, not wanting to make eye contact as he went through the familiar adjacent room and approached the sliding glass door. A quick look out back didn't yield a sighting of Cassandra or one of her goons, but he guessed they were waiting for him farther down the deck. With a deep breath, he pushed the door open and slid outside.

This time, the chill cut into him with such power that he gasped. Coby looked for Cassandra, but she was nowhere in sight. The deck was completely empty.

"Hello? Is anyone here?"

All he heard was silence. He kept his ears tuned for any noise that would signal someone else's presence, but none came. Coby looked over the deck, seeing the shape of trees at the edge of the lawn. They bristled as the wind moved through them. It was completely dark in the woods, and for a brief second, he imagined something lingering just out of sight.

Coby turned around, looking back inside the house. He could still see people dancing through the passageway to the living room beyond, but no Cassandra. A glimpse of yellow that was likely Danny's banana suit flashed across the hallway, followed by what looked like a bald head. Coby wanted to go back inside and talk to his friends. He was yearning to relay what happened with Cassandra. He felt they wouldn't believe him. Before he went back inside, he took one last gander at the yard and the woods beyond.

For some reason, Coby had an eerie feeling in his stomach. Something deep inside of him was urging him to go inside. He wasn't quite sure what was causing him stress, but it felt strange and sinister. He surveyed the yard, looking for anything out of place. Finally, on the third pass, he saw it. A bright LED flicker near the edge of the woods.

What the hell? thought Coby. The light seemed to be coming from a miniscule crevice that was dividing two trees. It was tiny and vivid, causing specks to appear in the corners of his eyes as he stared at it. Coby took a few steps toward the stairs that led down to the yard, full of curiosity and apprehension. Suddenly, when he was on the last step, he heard a loud *crack* emit from the woods behind the light.

Coby froze. *No,* he thought. *No, this isn't right.* Something was off. Instead of taking a single step closer to the light, he made an about-face and went back into the house.

9:20 p.m.

Stevie belched loudly as Amos turned his vehicle onto Second Street, and Amos inhaled the malodourous scent of her burp.

"Jesus, Stevie. Have you been eating beef jerky?"

Stevie pretended to frown in concentration.

"I don't think so. Maybe I did. Not sure."

Amos rolled his eyes and focused his attention

back on the road. They had now been patrolling for four hours. The most interesting thing that had occurred was a kid sprinting across Highway 101 in an area that wasn't a designated crosswalk. There hadn't been any reports of attempted abductions, or men in wolf masks. In fact, now that Amos thought about it, they had only seen a few trick-or-treaters all evening. Two other officers *had* busted a party of high-school kids out on the Bay Road, much to the likely chagrin of Dozer. Dozer had specifically said not to waste time crashing any parties, which was the police's usual detail on Halloween night. Apparently the two officers in question had not received the memo.

Stevie looked at Amos with a confused expression on her face. "Where are you going?"

"We've been patrolling the same block for hours. I think it's time we expand our search for a while."

"Oh, boy, look at you, you rebel. If Dozer gets wind of this—"

"How would he? How could he possibly know that we abandoned our block for a few minutes?"

"Wouldn't be surprised if he was tracking this car." Stevie pretended to look over her shoulder.

"Even Dozer ain't that paranoid." Amos pressed harder on the gas. Once they got to the highway, Amos turned left, cruising north past Moby Dick's.

"You never answered my question."

"Huh?"

"Where are you going?"

"Nowhere, really. I'm doing a loser lap. That's what the kids call it. Driving aimlessly around town."

"Goddamn, Al. You sound like you should be in a rest home," Stevie said in faux disgust.

"I'm not *that* old."

"You sure? Only an old fart says the phrase, 'That's what the kids call it.'"

Amos smirked. He reached for the dashboard and turned up the radio. They were listening to 97.5, the classic rock station, and an AC/DC song was blaring.

"Every AC/DC song sounds the same," said Stevie, shaking her head.

"That isn't true at a—"

Amos's sentence was interrupted by the tune of a new song. It was a generic tune, one that he had heard many times before. It took him a second to realize that it was his own ringtone. Trying to keep his eyes on the road, he pulled out his phone and quickly glanced at the screen.

"It's Ted."

"Why is he calling?"

Amos ignored her question and answered his phone. "Hello?"

"I've got something." Ted sounded out of

breath.

Amos's pulse instantly started racing. "What? What do you have?"

"The police station just received an anonymous tip. Like not 911. The actual police station. You will hear dispatch issue an alert here to everyone in a matter of moments. I wanted to reach you first so you could get a head start and get out to the scene before anybody else does," Ted said, and his voice sound incredibly strained.

"What happened, Teddy?"

"I'm not exactly sure. The anon caller said there was an assault and shortly thereafter, shots fired. He wasn't very descriptive. It sounded like he feared for his own life. He hung up before he could tell us who was calling."

"Jesus Christ. Where is it?"

"1600 Elm Street. It's up an old logging road in Toledo."

Amos frowned. "Toledo?"

"Yeah."

"Alright, we're on our way."

Amos hung up the phone and pressed the gas pedal nearly all the way to the floor. The car lurched forward and Stevie grabbed her seat on each side.

"Jesus, Albert, slow down! What's going on?"

"I need you to type an address in on the GPS."

"What?"

"Now!"

Stevie started fumbling with the GPS. "Okay, what is it?"

"1600 Elm Street. Toledo."

Stevie typed in the address and hit ENTER. Instantly, the little GPS screen showed a sprawling map of Newport in teal and blue and an illuminated red line that was their route. Amos sped as fast as he could down 101 until it curved to the right onto Highway 20. He went so fast around the corner that the car seemed to lean onto two wheels.

"You're going to kill us before we even get there, Albert! Slow down!"

"I can't!"

"Why not?"

"Because we have to get there first!"

"We have to get *where* first?"

Just then, the police scanner went off. The woman manning the dispatch broadcasted to all the cops in the area.

"We got a 242 out in Toledo. Possible shots fired. Address is 1600 Elm Street. Repeat, 1600 Elm Street. All officers please respond immediately."

"Shots fired?" Stevie repeated in awe, as dispatch continued to ramble on about the possible crime.

Amos didn't answer, but continued to go as fast as the Ford Crown Victoria could go. Highway 20, the longest road in the continental United States, had dozens of curves. Amos swerved around each of the twists, not taking any care to pump the brakes.

"How did Ted—"

"Anonymous tip. Whoever it was reported the assault. But they didn't call dispatch, they called the police station."

"They called the police station?"

"Right."

"What the fuck? Who was it?"

"No idea," Amos replied. "Ted said the guy sounded like he was in fear for his life and hung up the phone before they could even ask who it was."

Stevie didn't respond to this. Out of his peripheral vision, Amos saw her subconsciously move her hand down toward her belt. He knew that she was reaching for her gun like it was a pacifier.

Toledo wasn't especially far. It was technically only six miles from Newport, but because the road was so curvy, it usually took locals at least ten minutes to make the commute. Amos wasn't sure exactly where Elm Street was, but he had a vague idea. On the east side of the miniature town that was Toledo, the landscape morphed into several different logging roads that ran for miles and miles. It was likely the address they were heading to was in an exceedingly secluded spot. If it was in any way related to the crime they were all patrolling for, perhaps this was intentional by the perpetrator.

As Amos continued along at eighty-five miles per hour, he worried about two different things. One, he was going twenty miles over the speed limit. Since the car they were in was unmarked, someone could technically pull them over for speeding if they wanted to. The citation would be negated as soon as Amos flashed his badge, but they would lose valuable time and not be the first ones to arrive on scene. Secondly, Amos was concerned about the Toledo Police Department. They were obviously way nearer in proximity than he had been, so there was a chance one of their officers could get there before he did. Amos had to hope the small interlude between when Ted had called him and when dispatch had broadcast the 242 would be enough to allow him to be first.

"Starting to feel a little queasy," Stevie remarked as they rounded yet another curve. She continued to hold her seat with one hand, her gun with the other.

"Sorry, partner. Can't do anything for you."

"Wasn't asking you to," Stevie replied. Amos glanced at her, and she indeed looked a little pale.

"If you have to puke, do it out of the window."

"I'm sure this Audi behind us would be absolutely thrilled to get a bunch of vomit on her windshield." Stevie looked in the rearview mirror on the passenger side.

Once they hit Toledo, the automated voice from the GPS spoke to them.

"In thirty feet, turn right."

Amos obeyed the command, turning sharply to the right in front of the Dairy Queen that served as the guard tower of Toledo. The road twisted even more dramatically along Thirtieth Street. Within seconds, the automated voice spoke once more.

"In twenty feet, turn left onto Prescott Avenue."

Amos looked at the GPS, a little surprised. He thought the address would be farther into the city. Once he came to Prescott Avenue, he turned sharply. The road turned into a steep hill, robbing the car of speed. It chugged up the summit until they reached a portion where the street flattened out. This didn't last long, however, as the pavement dove back down, morphing into a huge slope. At the bottom of the hill, the trees started to cling together until they were in what could be rationally considered a forest. The disembodied voice emitted from the GPS again.

"In six miles, keep right onto Elm Street."

Amos and Stevie looked at each other in disbelief.

"Six miles? Jesus, this place is out in the sticks," Stevie said.

Amos shook his head, a little annoyed at how much farther they had to go. For all he knew, the teen who had been assaulted was also the one on the receiving end of the gunshots and was bleeding out in the woods.

Five minutes later, the street forked off into two different directions thirty feet ahead. The path to the left was paved and looked like it led back to the highway. The path to the right was a gravel road that hooked sharply into the woods.

"In twenty feet, keep right onto Elm Street."

Amos banked the car to the right onto the gravel path. It was barely even a logging road; the area intended for travel was so narrow that one slight unintentional flick of the wrist and the Ford would be stuck in the mud. Elm Street slowly curved even farther to the right and ascended upward until it was another steep hill. The trees were so close to the vehicle on either side that Amos or Stevie could've rolled down their respective windows and reached out and touched the leaves. There was no sign of any other police cars in the area. At least they appeared to be the first on scene.

"In one mile, the destination is on your right."

Amos glanced over at Stevie in anxious anticipation. She had a look of steely resolve on her face, as if she somehow knew they were about to confront the man they were looking for. She still had her hand on her gun and fingered it incorrigibly. Amos looked back at the road. The narrow pathway only allowed for him to go approximately ten miles an hour. It was as if the car itself was feeling the suspense as they drew closer and closer.

Eventually, they came to a large clearing. The forest made a semi-circle around the clearing, and in front of the line of trees, there was a mammoth industrial building. On the side of the building, Amos could clearly make out the numbers 1600. Underneath the address, large swaths of an orangeish-brown color ran down into the ground. It took him a second to realize that it was just rust. The rest of the building was a dark gray and looked filthy. The place appeared to have been abandoned for quite some time.

Stevie leaned forward in disbelief. "This is it?"

"Guess so," Amos whispered back.

"Why are you whispering?"

"I don't—sorry, didn't even mean to."

Amos drew the Ford closer and closer until they were within ten feet of the building. He put the car in park and switched the engine off before looking over at Stevie.

"You ready?"

Stevie didn't even answer him, but grabbed the handle to her door and thrust it open, swinging her right leg out of the vehicle. Before Amos got out he radioed dispatch and announced their arrival.

"Roger that, F-22. Two other units only half a mile out," replied dispatch.

Amos set the radio down and got out of the car, creeping up next to Stevie. Simultaneously, they pulled their guns out of their belts and began slithering toward the building. Stevie also unhooked the flashlight from her midsection and turned it on, shining it on the entrance. The door to the building was a thick metal that seemed to be hanging off its hinges. Each of the detectives got on either side of the door and Stevie gave Amos a small nod. Amos gulped and then banged on the door several times.

"NPD! Is anybody in there?"

No response.

"This is the police!" Amos shouted. "Is anyone inside?"

Still no answer.

"We're coming inside and we're both armed. If we see any sudden movement we *will* shoot."

Silence.

"Okay, let's go," Amos whispered.

With adrenaline coursing through his veins, Amos got in front of the frame, raised his weapon, and pulled the door open. It was pitch-black inside. Stevie shined the flashlight through the entryway, illuminating a small portion of the building in front of them. The entire structure was one giant room. Stevie turned the flashlight in a circular motion, but nothing of significance made its way into their line of sight. The roof of the building was at least twenty feet high, and as Stevie pointed the light upward,

Amos could see three or four cracks in the ceiling.

"This place looks ready to collapse," Stevie whispered.

Amos ignored her and called out into the opaque space in front of them. "Hello? Is anybody there?"

Amos listened intently for a response, but all that he heard were the reverberations and echo of his own voice.

"No one's here, Albert."

Amos lowered his weapon and looked around the room. It was hard to see anything, but Stevie appeared to be right; there wasn't anyone or anything inside the giant room with them. However, this wasn't consoling to Amos. In fact, it made his unease increase greatly. If someone had seen an assault and heard gunshots, why did everything in front of him look like it hadn't been touched in decades? Something was amiss.

From far away, Amos heard sirens.

"Looks like the cavalry is on its way," Stevie said and continued to brandish the flashlight in all different directions, illuminating new portions of the structure. As she passed over the opposing wall, something caught Amos's eye.

"Wait! What's that? Go back to that!"

Stevie froze and pointed the flashlight back toward the center of the wall. Their eyes both locked in on it at the same time: the color red.

"Oh Jesus."

Amos rushed forward with Stevie in his wake. He knew what he was going to find there, but he hoped he was wrong. Alas, the same dead smiley face leered down at them from the wall, this time at least ten feet in circumference. Much like the Ledouxs' house, there was writing underneath the insignia:

THE WOLF'S DECEIT, THEY DROP LIKE FLIES. NOTHING HERE EXCEPT YOUR EYES.

Amos stared at the message, dumbfounded.

Stevie's mouth expanded in horror. "What does that mean?"

Amos didn't reply. He continued to stare at the last five words. *Nothing here except your eyes.* It only took him a moment before everything clicked.

"Oh, *shit!*"

"What? What?"

Amos made an about-face and jogged back to the door, fumbling in his pocket for his phone. But there was no need to call anyone; the sound of tires disturbing gravel and loud sirens outside signaled the arrival of more cops.

"Albert, what is it?" demanded Stevie. "Where are you going?"

"Come with me. Hurry."

Amos burst through the door to the building

and saw that seven police cars had pulled into the clearing. He approached the nearest vehicle and a blond patrolman named Colin Vega opened the door.

"Detective Amos, what is—"

"Officer, I need you to get on your radio. Tell dispatch we're going to need a forensics team out here. Everyone else needs to get back to Newport immediately."

"What are you talking about? What is going—"

"Albert!"

Amos turned to his left and from a nearby vehicle he saw Lawrence Bonner striding toward him.

"What is going on? Did you find the vic?" The man looked out of breath.

"There is no vic. There were no gunshots either. At least not here."

"What do you mean? You just said we needed to radio for a forensics team!" Vega interjected.

"We do. But we don't have a body."

"Then what the hell do we have?"

"A diversion," Amos said.

9:30 p.m.

Something slammed against Coby, nailing him in the ear. For a fleeting moment, pain dominated his senses. Then the anger came.

"Whoa, man, watch where you're fucking going! That hurt!"

The person in the gorilla suit continued to dance rambunctiously. He had either not heard Coby's complaint, or simply didn't care. Making sure to glower at the gorilla, Coby pushed his way through the clump of people on the dance floor. He could see the bright yellow of Danny's banana suit near the other side of the floor and guessed Landon and Carson were somewhere nearby, so he plowed toward the spot of yellow. Eventually, Coby found all three of them leaning up against the railing of the stairs by the front door. Danny wobbled and bobbed his head as he sipped on the Corona in his hand; he looked to be either drunk or under the influence of a hallucinogenic drug.

"Where the fuck have you been?" Landon demanded.

"I was outside," Coby replied, massaging the ear that had been struck by the gorilla's elbow.

"Why were you—wait! Were you out there this whole time with Cassandra?"

"No, not the whole time."

Landon raised his eyebrows. "Were you *inside* with Cassandra?"

Coby shook his head quickly. "No, no, nothing like that. I came in a couple minutes ago and went upstairs to the bathroom because I was pissed."

"Why were you pissed?"

Coby sighed. He looked to his left and then to his right, making sure Cassandra wasn't within earshot. "She made out with me a little bit."

At first, Landon looked utterly nonplussed. Then his jaw dropped open. Next to him, Carson mouthed the words, "No way."

"She *kissed you*?"

"Yeah, man."

"Then why the fuck are you pissed?"

"Because it was gross, man. She was only doing it because she was drunk. I don't know how to explain it." Coby shook his head.

"That makes *no* sense," Landon replied. "You've been obsessed with this girl for years. And now you're mad at her for kissing you?"

Coby didn't say anything. He didn't want to try and rationalize it.

Carson leaned in, looking bemused. "So you just stopped kissing her and left?"

"Well, yeah. I was that mad. I went upstairs for a bit, but then she texted me to come back outside. So, I went out there again, expecting to get yelled at, but she wasn't even there."

"Huh?"

"She told me to meet her outside, but she wasn't even outside."

Landon and Carson looked at each other as if they didn't understand. Danny continued to bob his head to the music, remaining completely ambivalent to the entire situation.

Carson looked left and then right, bamboozled. "So where is she now?"

"No idea. Thought you might know."

There was an interlude in the conversation. Suddenly, Coby remembered what had driven him to come back inside.

"Oh! And something super weird happened when I was on the deck just now. It looked like someone with a flashlight was in the woods behind the house."

"What?"

"Yeah, I was just standing out there and it looked like someone was shining a flashlight."

Landon's face was instantly inundated with concern.

"Shit, man, what if it's the cops?"

Carson rolled his eyes. "Yeah, I'm sure a cop is just out there stumbling around in the woods."

"Maybe he's trying to go all covert ops to bust us or something."

"Covert ops with a bright flashlight?"

"It's probably just a hobo or something."

Landon's eyebrows ascended incredulously. "What bum has a flashlight?"

"Where's Sean? I kind of want to tell him," Coby interposed, thinking of the brownie points making out with Cassandra would earn him with Sean.

Carson shrugged. "I mean, you could. But I think he's a little preoccupied at the moment."

"With what?"

"A girl."

Coby shook his head, half-exasperated but also half-amused.

"Oh, hey," Danny said. It was as if he had woken up from a deep slumber and was greeting them all. They all looked at him for a moment, perplexed.

"Hey," Landon drawled.

"I brought something for you guys." Danny smiled naughtily. His eyes were unfocused and large, and Coby could tell that he was as high as a kite.

"What did you bring?"

"Follow me. Let's go upstairs. I'll show you."

Danny stumbled his way up the stairs. The others all looked at each other apprehensively. Landon clicked his tongue and then trekked up the steps behind Danny. Carson followed suit, and although Coby was a little worried about what Danny was about to show him, he ascended the staircase as well. When they got to the landing on the second floor, Danny gestured at a door at the end of the hallway.

"In here," he said.

"Wait, this is the bathroom." Coby placed his hand on Danny's shoulder to stop him.

Danny nodded with a bizarre smile. "I know. But it's probably the only room that locks."

Ignoring the disapproving look on Coby's face, Danny knocked on the bathroom door. When there was no response, he turned the handle and walked into the room. The other three did as well, and although it was spacious for a bathroom, having four people inside made it cramped.

Carson shook his head with a skeptical grunt. "This had better be good, Dan."

Danny didn't reply, as he fumbled in his jeans pockets underneath his banana suit. Eventually, he withdrew a Ziploc bag with several chunks of something Coby couldn't identify at first. When Danny fingered the chunks, Coby leaned in and saw what they were: mushrooms.

Coby backed up. "No way. I'm not doing that."

Danny looked up at Coby with a mystified expression. Landon burst into laughter.

"Oh my God, Danny, really? Shrooms? You're going to do shrooms here?"

"Yeah man, so are you."

"Not me. I'm not doing that," Coby repeated.

"Oh come *on*, Coby."

"No, dude. No way."

"What do you think is going to ha—"

Carson suddenly stepped forward with his chest inflated. "I think we should."

Coby looked over at Carson, aghast. Usually,

Carson was the voice of reason. In response, Landon smiled wryly in anticipation.

"Well, if Carson is going to then I pretty much have to, don't I?"

Almost in unison, the other three boys looked at Coby, determined to make him give in.

"Guys, I'm paranoid enough as it is. There is a reason I have never done anything that will make me hallucinate. Hell, smoking *weed* makes me anxious."

"Just have a piece of one. You'll barely even feel it," Danny said.

"Come on, man. If Carson is going to do it then you can do it!"

"Fuck you, Landon," Carson muttered.

Coby looked at the Ziploc bag, feeling conflicted. Part of him wanted to let loose, but he knew deep down that eating the mushroom would be a mistake. The first time he smoked marijuana he felt like he was on the verge of a heart attack because he had become so anxious, so he knew that his personality wasn't one that was conducive for hallucinogens. And yet, he would never live it down if he refused.

"Man, if this ain't peer pressure . . ."

"Dude, you don't have to do it," Carson said.

"No, you don't have to," Landon said. "Just know that I will forever think you're a pussy if you don't."

Coby sighed. "Fuck it. Fine."

Landon clapped loudly, pursing his lips in triumph. "Alright! I knew you had it in you!"

Coby rolled his eyes wearily. "Yeah, yeah. When I'm hyperventilating in the fetal position here in fifteen minutes I'm blaming you."

Danny passed out the mushrooms, divvying them up so that the larger chunks stayed with him and Landon, while the smaller parts went to Coby and Carson. Coby held the small, rubbery psilocybin aloft in his hand with a sense of unease building in his chest.

Landon had an amused expression on his face. "Well, should we cheers or something?"

"Sure," Danny replied. "Happy Halloween, guys! Have fun in wonderland!"

The friends all raised their mushrooms in unison. With one last calming breath, Coby popped the fungus into his mouth and chewed. It didn't have much of a taste, but the texture was disconcerting. It felt like he had bitten into an eraser. After several chews, he swallowed. *No going back now,* thought Coby.

As soon as Landon had consumed his mushroom, he made a move for the door handle, but Danny stopped him.

"Not yet, man. Wait for it to kick in."

Landon frowned and cocked his head to the side. "What, just wait in here?"

"Yeah, man. Just for a little bit."

"You want us to just chill in here?"

"Yeah. No big deal."

Landon stepped back into the bathroom. For ten minutes, the friends stood around the toilet, making half-hearted attempts at conversation. In the background, the music from downstairs could be heard thumping along, albeit much more muffled. Truthfully, everyone but Danny was waiting to feel the effects of the drug they had just taken. Eventually, after the time had elapsed, Landon reached for the door again.

"Screw it. I'm going."

Carson held his hand in the air, trying to get Landon to stop. "I don't even feel anything, man!"

"I don't care. Let's go back downstairs."

Landon pulled the door open and stomped out of the bathroom. With a heavy roll of his eyes, Carson followed him, looking distressed. Danny simply shrugged and went out too. Coby followed suit.

As soon as they were out on the landing again, the music became amplified beyond belief. It seemed it had been turned up in the time they had spent in the bathroom. They all trudged down the stairs, gazing onto the dance floor below. Someone had turned off the regular lighting, and all that was left to illuminate the crowd of people was a strobe light and a colorful disco ball. Somehow, it seemed like even more people had found their way out onto the dance floor. At least fifty bodies packed into what was once Sean's living room.

The rap song blaring made Coby's ears ring. It felt like his entire skull was gyrating along with the music, and he felt a slight tingling in his head. They all slithered their way to the dancing throng of teens in front of them and Coby saw several new costumes he hadn't noticed before, including someone wearing a Guy Fawkes mask and another person donning a Batman cowl.

Next to him, Landon pumped his arms to the rhythm of the music. The move looked extremely silly, and Coby laughed. With a flick of his wrist, he shifted his arms in a noodlelike motion, trying to one-up Landon in ridiculous dance. Carson turned around in front of them and did a spastic version of the robot. Danny jumped up and down with his arm in the air holding a triumphant fist. For three long songs, the friends all danced wildly, possessed by the spirit of fun. By the end of their ritual salsa, Coby noticed a warm sensation in his head, and his eyes tripped out every time the strobe light flashed.

Coby felt a small tap on his shoulder. He turned to his right and was greeted with a hard palm to the cheek.

"Fuck you, asshole!"

Cassandra's face was inches from his. Coby's heart jumped into his throat. His cheek felt hot, and he knew the portion where she had struck him was flushing red.

"Ow! What the hell?"

"You're such a dick!"

"Did you seriously just slap me?"

Cassandra seemed to take this as a challenge. Cocking her hand back, she went to slap him again, but Coby was ready for it and caught her arm. Landon continued to dance, oblivious to the drama taking place. However, Carson watched both of them with fearful eyes, looking unsure of whether or not to jump in.

Coby held Cassandra's arm in the air and made fierce eye contact with her. "Stop! Just stop!"

Cassandra yanked her arm back and glowered at Coby as though he were the scum of the earth. "Why? Am I too *disgusting* for you?" Every time she spoke, Coby could smell the alcohol on her breath.

"Oh, so is this why you texted me to come back outside? You just wanted to smack the hell out of me?"

Cassandra froze with a flummoxed expression on her face.

"What are you talking about?"

"Your text."

"What text?"

"Uh, you texted me to come back outside like fifteen minutes ago."

"No, I didn't!"

"Jesus, Cass, how drunk are you?"

"I don't even know where my phone is! I have been looking for it for, like, an hour!"

"What?"

"I think I set it down somewhere weird or something because I can't find it. I didn't *text* you."

In that moment, time froze. The music blared on, but somehow, Coby could only hear the beating of his heart. Cassandra's face was warped in his vision, and the voice of the rapper in the song became much deeper as if it were playing in slow motion. It was like he had been simultaneously bludgeoned over the head by the drugs and the reality of what had just been said.

Coby felt a strong wave of nausea hit him like a wrecking ball. He thought he was going to vomit, but no bile rose in his throat. With a jerk, Coby turned around, looking to get out of the gaggle of people. He heard Cassandra call to him from somewhere far away, but he pressed through the crowd away from her, trying to escape the claustrophobic dance floor. Terror dominated his senses, and the various masks people wore seemed ten times bigger and more menacing. He looked to his left and the gorilla stared at him as if it were ready to pounce. He glanced to his right, but the Guy Fawkes mask leered at him. Coby let out a small shriek and continued to swim his way through the sea of people. Every costume induced a fresh pulse of dread. A vampire. A monstrous clown. A wolf.

Coby's heart missed a beat. Standing motionless in the crowd of people, the man in the wolf mask stared at him from afar. Coby blinked several times, trying to rid his consciousness of the boogeyman. It was just a hallucination. It had to be. A product of the bad trip he was on. The man couldn't be here, infiltrating the party. And yet, there he stood, frozen like a statue, watching from across the room. Coby waited, paralyzed by fear. Everyone around the wolf danced without a care in the world, unaware of the menace that blended in with them. Before he could think of what to do next, the wolf stepped forward. Coby swiveled around and began to flee, letting out a guttural bellow.

He pounded his way through several bystanders, catching elbows, shoulders, and knees alike. As he charged, Coby looked for Danny, Carson, and Landon, but they had disappeared in the horde of people.

"Carson! Carson!" Coby screamed, but his cries were drowned out by the music. He chanced a quick glance backward and saw the wolf still coming toward him, sliding through the crowd. Coby continued to shove his way in the direction of the staircase, hoping his friends would come into his view, but they didn't. The music pounded against his eardrums, and the only thought he had was to get away from the chaos and his pursuer. He rounded onto the staircase, finally free of the herd of his peers.

Coby stampeded up the stairs, taking three steps at a time. After what felt like an eternity of climbing, he was back on the landing, which was fully lit by three overhead lamps. He sprinted as fast as he could, but his legs felt heavy, like he was wading through quicksand. He didn't dare look back. He passed three rooms on each side of the hallway, including the bathroom he had come from ten minutes before. Making a split-second decision, Coby opened the last door on the left and ducked into the room, shutting the door behind him.

Near-silence enveloped him. Almost at once, he realized the mistake that he had made. Here he was alone, no one to help him. The devil approaching. His younger brother far away and helpless. It was the drugs. They had clouded his mind. Made him panic. The only thought he had had was to put as much distance as he could between himself and his pursuer. And now he had played right into the wolf's hands.

Coby could still hear the pounding music, but it was muffled. Inhaling wildly, Coby doubled over and tried to regain his breath, looking around the room. Most of it was occupied by a king-sized bed. Realizing the sound that his ragged breathing was making, he clasped his hands over his mouth. He looked down at the doorknob, seeing there wasn't a lock. Coby pressed his weight against the door, determined to keep it shut. After several long seconds of waiting, nothing happened.

Coby leaned forward on his forearms, pressing even harder. The door creaked in protest, and he internally cursed the noise it made. He was on the verge of hyperventilating. *Exhale,* thought Coby. *Exhale.* It was what his dad had always said to him when he was stressed.

Where was the wolf? Had he not seen Coby charge up the stairs? Surely the man was coming for him. But there was no sound of someone in pursuit. No footsteps, no movement. Besides the music playing from downstairs, Coby heard nothing. There was light flooding into the dark room from the crack underneath the door. Coby wanted to lay flat on the ground and peek into the hallway beyond, but that would compromise the barrier he created to protect himself.

Coby looked behind him and saw a window out of the bedroom. The roof of what he assumed was the garage was just underneath the window. If he could walk out onto the roof, perhaps he could find a way down to the lawn and make his escape. Just before he was about to dart to the window, he heard a soft *clunk* come from the landing.

Staying totally still, Coby waited for the sounds

of further movement. He pressed his ear against the door, listening and planning a subsequent move. If he tried to flee through the window now, the noise would alert the wolf-man to his precise location. He continued to debate what to do next, attempting to not give into the terror pulsing through his system brought on by the shrooms. Something caught Coby's eye. Below him, the light underneath the door had become eclipsed by darkness.

Before he could process the change, the door flew open, catching him in side of the head. It blasted about with such force that Coby was hurled backward, falling onto the bed. The wolf lurched through the entryway, pouncing onto Coby like a lion. With one hand, he gripped Coby's throat, while the other slashed through the air like a scythe. Coby only had a millisecond to defend himself, and somehow he caught the man's wrist with his right hand. He was expecting to see a knife protruding toward his face, but instead, something much smaller lingered in front of his right eye: a needle. Coby kept both eyes on the needle as it moved closer to his nape. The man was strong, but Coby pushed against the needle-wielding arm with all his might, able to keep him at bay. He thought his throat might collapse under the pressure of the man's grip. Even if he managed to hold the needle, he would surely be strangled in a matter of seconds. He looked at the gray mask perched inches from his face and saw a set of eyes burning at him. It would surely be the last thing Coby ever saw.

Just then, two more people burst into the room, laughing and half-clothed. Sean and a tiny redhead draped around his shoulders stumbled forward toward the bed. At the same moment, their eyes found Coby and the demon on top of him crushing his neck. For the tiniest space of time, their faces held the traces of amusement from the joke Sean had apparently just told. Then their expressions morphed into that of unbridled horror.

Sean stepped forward. "What the hell are you doing, man?"

Instantly, the wolf relinquished his grip, causing a suction noise like a vacuum to emit from Coby's mouth. He leapt off the bed and charged toward the new pair in the room. The redhead let out a piercing scream and sprinted back the way she had come. Sean, however, held his ground. He swung wildly at the wolf, but the man ducked and Sean's fist hit air. The wolf caught him around the midsection, tackling him to the ground. He quickly punched Sean twice in the jaw, leaving him looking woozy.

Coby watched for a second, debating assisting Sean with the fight before giving in to cowardice and scrambling off the bed and toward the window. He unlatched the window with a *click* and pushed it open. Instantly, the wolf's head snapped around toward Coby. Sean used this to his advantage, and unleashed a hard blow to the man's chin, causing him to careen backward. With the man briefly reeling, Coby crawled through the window and hopped down onto the roof, looking back at the ongoing combat.

Coby saw the wolf dodge a subsequent punch and watched him retaliate with a forearm shiver to Sean's throat, causing Sean to gag. The wolf leapt off of Sean and charged toward the window, making a move to climb out onto the roof, but slipped for a second. This quick stumble gave Sean enough time to launch himself from the ground, hitting the man on the back of the knees. The wolf fell forward, slamming his forehead on the wall.

With the two people still grappling in the room behind him, Coby turned around and rushed toward the edge of the roof, looking at the lawn below. It was more than a comfortable jumping distance, and Coby felt sure he would injure himself if he tried. However, just to the right of the lawn there was a truck parked in the driveway with its back end facing the garage. The bed was covered with a blue tarp. He wasn't sure what was underneath it, but the tarp itself was probably enough to stymie the force of Coby's landing. With a deep breath, Coby looked back toward the window and saw Sean and the demon continue to struggle. Sean had his arm around the man's neck, lifting him upward in a headlock. The man fumbled for something in his pocket. For a second, something glinted in the air. Before Coby could warn him, the wolf plunged the knife backward, stabbing Sean in the shoulder. Sean let out an ear-splitting screech and tumbled backward, falling onto the ground.

Coby's blood curdled and his stomach dropped, but he didn't wait a second longer. He jumped off the roof, pointing his body toward the truck. In midair, his torso shifted forward. With a loud *crunch,* he hit the bed of the truck, landing on his hip. Fumbling with the tarp, Coby rolled over and hopped out of the bed onto the driveway. He only noticed the stark pain in his hip as he broke out into a full sprint. His injured side begged him to slow down, but he couldn't. *Don't stop. Don't stop,* thought Coby. He ran with all the force in his legs, knowing that the wolf was likely not far behind.

9:57 p.m.

"Why are you driving so fast? You don't even know where we're going!"

Amos looked over at Stevie with a grumpy expression on his face. "Hopefully we will find out soon enough."

He rounded around a curve on Highway 20, knowing Newport was now only a mile away. But even as he drew closer, there was a sinking feeling in his gut. Due to the well-placed diversion, the killer had created a twenty-five-minute window to do the deed without the presence of police, as virtually every cop in Newport had sped out to the scene in Toledo.

Stevie gripped onto the handle above her door, balancing herself as Amos rounded about another curve. "Whose DNA do you think it was on the wall this time?"

"Truthfully, I'm not sure. Could be either one of the victims. Luke Ledoux or Devin Johnson. Or it could be an unidentified third vic."

Stevie rolled her eyes. "Thanks for that insight, Sherlock. I'm glad we have narrowed it down to literally anyone."

Amos didn't even crack a smile. He kept his eyes focused on the road, brooding on what was likely the third impending homicide. To think an innocent person might be being murdered made his stomach turn inside out.

"I feel like we should do the opposite of whatever's obvious."

Amos let silence hang in the air for a second before responding to Stevie. "What are you talking about?"

"It's all a game, isn't it? I think he views us like chess pieces. Trying to manipulate us into making moves that would behoove him. He set up multiple crime scenes, knowing it would augment the presence of officers involved in this case, right? The theatrics with the deer and the insignia . . . it's like he knew exactly how to set up something we would all be a part of, so when it came time to *make* that call, the entire department would go out to Toledo."

Amos scrunched up his forehead, trying to follow the point she was making. "So do the opposite of whatever's obvious, because he's always one step ahead?"

"Right."

"But what would that entail exactly? How would we even go about doing that?"

"Well—"

"Like right now, for instance. What would doing the opposite of what's obvious look like?"

Stevie gave Amos a look of indignation.

"There is no need to patronize me, smart-ass."

"I'm not! I genuinely want to kn—"

Amos's response was interrupted by the sound of static on the radio, signaling something about to broadcast. Amos exchanged one quick apprehensive glance with Stevie before the woman's voice began speaking.

"Officers, we got a 245 near Big Creek Park. Please respond immediately. Possible stabbing. Address is 424 Borneo Drive."

Stevie's mouth fell open. She attempted to speak, but Amos waved her down and turned up the volume on the radio.

"Be advised, suspect is still at large. White male, approximately six foot three, wearing a gray mask resembling a wolf, black pants, and a long-sleeved black shirt."

"Jesus Christ," Amos said under his breath.

Stevie looked over at him with her mouth still agape. "He's even wearing a fucking wolf mask."

Amos didn't reply. The adrenaline surging through his nervous system made him shake. His mind whirled at a mile a minute. The code, 245, was for an assault with a deadly weapon, not homicide. So perhaps the intended victim had escaped, or, at the very least, wasn't yet dead. Stevie apparently arrived at the same conclusion moments after he had.

"So the vic must have survived?"

Amos pursed his lips. "So far, I guess."

Stevie nodded in triumph. "We're going to get this fucking guy, Al. And this time he isn't going to kill anybody."

Amos looked in the rearview mirror for a second and noticed he was as white as a ghost. However, the fear he felt intermingled with excitement. Stevie was right. They might have just lucked out. Truthfully, he had never foreseen a conclusion to this case where someone else didn't end up dead. But the killer's diversion plan had been successfully enacted and the victim had *still* managed to survive. Perhaps this thing wasn't going to end with more death after all.

"What's the quickest way to Big Creek Park?"

Amos gave a quick shrug, rounding the car around another curve. "Probably the gravel road that runs behind the elementary school. Takes us right there."

"Isn't that a one-way street?"

"Yeah, well . . . we're the police."

Finally, the car began to descend the slope of Highway 20 into Newport. Amos made a sharp turn on Eads Street and sped toward the road that would take them to Big Creek Park. They traveled down the gravel until they were zooming past the park on the right. Eventually, they came to a cluster of upscale houses. The automated GPS told them to keep traveling north until they were in a neighborhood tucked away in the farthest corner of town.

"Take a right here," Stevie said quietly. Amos obliged, and as soon as they did, he saw lights flashing in the distance.

Amos squinted until he saw what was producing the light.

"The paramedics got here first."

"Good," Stevie replied firmly.

When they had traveled thirty more feet, they pulled up next to a gargantuan white house that had at least fifty people milling about outside of it.

Numerous vehicles were parked all along the sidewalk, and in the driveway, an ambulance was stuffed next to a red pickup. Amos put the car in park just beyond the driveway, but he made sure he wasn't blocking the ambulance in.

"Dozer's going to be pissed."

"Why?"

"He told us not to bust any parties . . . but it looks like we just did."

In response, Amos scoped out all the people milling around outside the house and saw that Stevie was likely correct; most of the bystanders were teenagers in costumes. Several of the teens were talking on their phones and looking frantic. The lawn many of them were standing on was covered in debris, including a glittery substance, balloons, and what looked like toilet paper.

Amos shook his head. "He attacked someone at a party? Doesn't seem very discreet."

"Look, though, Albert. Everyone is wearing masks. He would blend right in," Stevie replied, pointing at some of the people.

"Come on then. I'm guessing we don't have much time."

Amos got out of the car and Stevie followed suit. He warmed up his vocal cords, clearing the phlegm before he began to bellow at the teenagers.

"Everyone, sit down! Police! Sit down on the ground and stay where you are! Stay clear of the

house! Down! Now! This is the police!"

The stragglers all glanced at him, and one by one began sitting down. Amos approached one of the paramedics, who had a clipboard and was writing something fervently. He was a short, redheaded man with an insane number of freckles.

Amos raised his palms toward the sky. "What happened?"

The paramedic glanced up from his clipboard, looking confused. "Who are you?"

"Detective Albert Amos. This is Detective Stevie Hutchins." Amos nodded toward Stevie.

"Jesus, it took you guys look enough. You're the first cops on scene. An eighteen-year-old kid named Sean McVey was stabbed in the shoulder by a masked perpetrator."

"Where is he?"

"Inside. Upstairs. We're tending to him now. We were just about to put him on the gurney. He isn't in great shape. Probably will survive, but lost a lot of blood."

"And the attacker escaped?"

"Far as I know," the paramedic said. "We didn't really ask that many questions."

Without another word, Amos strode across the lawn and crossed the threshold of the front door. The interior was decorated with chic paintings and iconoclastic photographs, giving off the air of wealth. And it was probably a safe assumption that the owners of the house *were* well-off, as the building was just on the fringe of being a mansion. The furniture had all been pushed to the outer rim of the massive space, making way for what Amos assumed was the now-abandoned dance floor. On the opposite side of the room a staircase led up to a second landing. There were three small projectors attached to the stairs shining colorful patterns along the dance floor, and hanging from the roof there was a disco ball. Amos quickly clambered up the staircase and saw a paramedic lingering in the doorway of the last room on the left.

The man with dark brown hair and heavy eyebrows eyed him up and down. "Who are you?"

Amos quickly pulled his badge out of his pocket and flashed it at the paramedic while striding down the hallway. "Detective Albert Amos. Is the victim inside?"

The man nodded. "Yeah, but just a heads-up, it ain't pretty."

Amos ignored this warning and rounded about into the room. Instantly, his lungs compressed so much that exhaling felt impossible. Sprawled on the floor next to a bed was a young man that was shockingly pale. His complexion contrasted strikingly to the prodigious amount of red that was pooled underneath him. He had a thick bandage wrapped around his shoulder, but it didn't seem to be totally containing his wound, as crimson still blossomed through the white wrap. He looked up at Amos with a hazy expression on his face. Amos stayed several feet away from the young man, as if what had happened to him might've been contagious. Two paramedics were crouched down next to the boy, tending to his arm.

"Sean McVey?"

The handsome young man nodded.

"I'm Detective Albert Amos."

A heavy panting from behind Amos made him turn his head. Stevie had entered the room and was looking at Amos with a frown.

"Trying to ditch me or what? You know, you move pretty fast for a mid—" Stevie's voice caught in her throat for a moment as she saw Sean. "Jesus Christ."

"Uh, this is Detective Hutchins."

Sean looked at Stevie, and she waved at him awkwardly with a pitying expression on her face.

"This is probably a stupid question, but how are you doing?" Amos asked.

Sean looked over at Amos through squinted eyes as if he couldn't quite see him clearly. "A-alright, I guess. I mean, I just got stabbed, so . . ." His voice was quiet and raspy.

Amos tried to keep his vision focused on Sean's face and not the blood pooled underneath him. Every time his eyes crossed over the congealed substance, a wave of nausea blasted against him.

"So what happened?"

"I mean . . . where do you want me to begin?"

"Wherever you think you need to."

The scene was totally frantic. Red and blue lights flashed into the room from the adjacent window and the sound of approaching sirens blared through the walls. The EMTs on either side of the injured teen conversed about what they had to do next, making it difficult for Amos to keep his undivided attention on Sean. The kid shifted his eyes from side to side as he tried to summon a good starting point to his tale.

"Well . . . everybody came over to hang out. Like more people than I had planned on."

Amos noticed that Sean sounded inebriated.

"Wait. This is your house?"

Sean bowed his head sheepishly. "Yeah. Well, my parents' house."

"Right. Are they out of town?"

"Yeah. They're on vacation."

"So you threw a party?"

Sean appraised Amos with worried eyes.

Amos shook his head. "Don't worry, kid. There are more important issues to attend to, obviously."

Sean smiled for a second and then grimaced as one of the paramedics shifted his arm to the side. "Yeah. I threw a party."

"And you said more people showed up than you planned on?"

"Yeah."

Amos nodded. "I'm guessing you didn't keep track of who all was here?"

Sean didn't answer verbally, but gave a small shake of his head.

Suddenly, one of the paramedics snapped his head in the direction of Amos and glowered at him. The man had short black hair and a stubby nose.

"Can you not wait to do this until he's at the hospital? He's losing blood and we're trying to hurry."

"I'm not stopping you, am I? I realize his health is paramount, but you aren't ready to move him yet, and until you do, I think it's vital that we try and catch the person who did this to him before he gets too far away."

The man snarled at Amos, but didn't retort. Amos looked away from the angry EMT and back at Sean.

"So you got attacked? How did it happen?"

"Well, me and Kira were—"

"Kira who?"

"Kira Black. She's probably the one who called you guys. We had just come upstairs and were looking for a room. We came in here and I saw the guy on top of my friend Coby on the bed, choking him."

"What guy?"

Two more paramedics entered the room,

holding a large gurney. Amos and Stevie had to shift out of the way so that they could set the gurney next to Sean.

"The guy who stabbed me. He was wearing a wolf mask."

"So you said he was attacking your friend Coby? What is Coby's last name? And where is he?"

"Conner. And I don't know. He ran."

Amos crouched down next to Sean so that they were both on the same eye level.

"You said the guy wearing the wolf mask was choking him?"

Sean nodded.

"What did you do?"

"Well, as soon as I came in, the guy hopped off Coby and charged toward me. Kira instantly bailed. I stayed and fought him."

Stevie raised her eyebrows. "You fought him?"

"Yeah. He had me pinned at first, but then when he saw Coby trying to go through the window, he went back after him."

Stevie shook her head. "The window?"

"Yeah. *That* window." Sean pointed at the window that was just above the king-sized bed.

Amos and Stevie both looked toward the window, which was ajar.

"When I saw that he was going for Coby again, I knocked him down and got him in a headlock.

That's when he took out the knife and stabbed me."

"What happened to Coby? You said he ran?"

Sean had sweat beaded up on his forehead, and his breathing became labored. "Yeah. He escaped through the window. Not really all that surprising that he bailed. Coby has never been a hero." He said it with a sort of sardonic contempt but also like it was darkly amusing.

Amos looked back in the direction of the window. He quickly walked over to it and looked out. The roof was just a couple of feet underneath the opening.

"And what happened to the attacker after he stabbed you?"

Before Sean could answer, one of the paramedics got behind him and began to wrap his arms around Sean's midsection.

"We're going to lift you onto the gurney okay?"

Sean looked apprehensively at the other paramedic that had approached his feet. "Uh, okay."

Before Sean could say another word, the two men heaved him into the air and placed him gently on the gurney. Sean grunted in pain as he hit the makeshift bed.

"What happened to the attacker, Sean?"

Sean looked up at Amos and squinted. "He went through the window after Coby."

As Amos came bursting out of the house back onto the lawn, he saw several new police vehicles parked outside, all with their lights blazing. Some of the officers were talking to the remaining party-goers, while others were walking past Amos and into the house. Amos scanned the area until his eyes locked on Ted Leery, who was walking toward him, looking disturbed and panting. Ted's teeth seemed to be chattering; the blue overcoat he was wearing for warmth didn't seem to be working.

"Jesus, Albert. What the hell is going on? Someone was stabbed?"

Amos nodded, but didn't stop. He continued to walk briskly back toward the Ford Crown Victoria. Ted quickly made an about-face and took long strides to try and catch up with Amos.

"Slow down, Albert! Who got stabbed?"

"Kid named Sean McVey. They are bringing him down on the gurney now. But he wasn't the target."

"What? What the hell does that mean?"

Amos stopped for a moment, appraising Ted. "Come with me."

"Huh?"

"Get in the car. You, me, and Stevie are going to go look for Coby Conner."

Ted looked absolutely bewildered. "We're going to look for who?"

Stevie appeared next to Ted, her cheeks tinted pink.

"Coby Conner. Just get in the car. We will explain."

Ted still looked confounded, but instead of continuing to try and extract an explanation, he shrugged and followed Amos and Stevie to the car. As Amos circled around to the driver's side, Ted made a move to sit in the front passenger seat, but Stevie cut him off.

"Oh, I don't think so. I ride shotgun, pretty boy."

Ted flushed red. He bent his head awkwardly and shuffled into the back seat. Amos rolled his eyes at his colleagues before getting into the car himself. As soon as he was inside, he picked up the receiver for the police radio.

"Dispatch, this is Detective Albert Amos. Please put out an APB on Coby Conner. Eighteen years old. Approximately five foot nine. Brown hair. Brown eyes. Wearing a dark blue hoodie and jeans. Last seen in the vicinity of 424 Borneo Drive near Big Creek Park. If found, please bring into protective custody."

"Roger that, detective," the female voice of dispatch replied.

"Who the hell is Coby Conner?" Ted

demanded.

Amos glanced in the rearview mirror and noticed Ted looked inexorably uncomfortable in the back seat, with his long legs scrunched together and his head scraping the roof of the car.

"Coby Conner was our guy's original target, I think. Sean McVey, the stabbing vic, walked in on Conner being choked out by a man in a wolf mask. He went to Conner's aid, and after a brief physical altercation, the perp stabbed him. This all happened in an upstairs bedroom at McVey's party." When Amos said the word *party* he pointed over his shoulder at the house they were driving away from.

"But McVey survived? He was the one who told you this?"

"Yes. He got stabbed in the right shoulder. Lost a lot of blood, but it looks like he's going to pull through."

Ted ran his fingers through his hair and frowned in concentration. "So Conner got away?"

"Yes. While McVey and the perp were struggling, Conner escaped through an upstairs window. After the perp stabbed McVey, he went through the window after Conner."

Stevie glanced over at Amos with a questioning look on her face. "So you think Conner is still in the neighborhood?"

"Well, this all happened in the last twenty-five minutes, so, I don't think he could've gotten too far."

Stevie twiddled with her hair nervously. "But . . . what if the perp caught him?"

Amos looked at her with a weighty expression on his face. "Then we lose."

9:59 p.m.

Coby's hip hurt like hell, but he didn't dare stop running. He had taken an ill-conceived turn and was traveling down a gravel road with no houses or people in sight. But he couldn't turn around now. For all he knew, the wolf was still in hot pursuit. *Don't stop,* thought Coby. *Don't stop.* The lingering effect of the mushroom he had eaten still made every tree that lined the gravel road appear menacing and evil. However, the adrenaline rumbling through his nervous system seemed to be overtaking everything else.

Coby chanced a quick glance over his shoulder and saw nothing behind him. He continued to run, but slowed down a bit so he could fumble around in his pocket for his phone. When he pulled it out, his gut clenched in dismay. The screen had a spider web–like pattern on it, and was devoid of color.

"Oh, fuck!" Coby hissed, coming to a complete stop.

The phone must have shattered when he hit the bed of the truck. And it wasn't just the screen. The hardware on the inside must have been damaged as well, because the phone was lifeless. He spun around, preparing to be ambushed by the wolf. But there was still no one there. The gravel road he was on led down past the reservoir and into the wilderness. Continuing to travel down it would do nothing for his safety. There would be no one to help him nor any phones to use. He had to go back the way he had come. Yet, there was still the likelihood that the wolf wasn't far behind. Coby looked over at the edge of the road. The forest clumped together so thick it was difficult to see into it. *Screw it,* thought Coby. Tucking his broken phone back into his pocket, he ran over to the edge of the trees and scrambled into the brush.

The blackberry brambles were thick enough that he could tuck himself down into a serviceable hiding spot. Once Coby was a few feet into the thick vegetation, he swiveled about and crouched down, looking toward the road. He tuned his ears to the sound of anyone approaching, but all that greeted him was silence.

Without warning, Coby's breathing became inordinately difficult. His heart beat so rapidly it caused his chest physical pain, and a feeling of nausea spread out in his stomach. He was in a stationary position for the first time since he had been attacked, and it was like the panic had finally arrived.

Coby began internally condemning himself for not heeding his instincts earlier. The disturbing phone call. The red pickup in the McDonald's parking lot. The man in the wolf mask leaning against the stop sign. The flashlight in the woods. How was it that he had ignored the part of his brain that had sent out all those disturbance signals? Was it because he saw what he wanted to see? Had he convinced himself that he wasn't in danger simply because he didn't want to be? As he stood there in the darkness, he felt impotent and foolish. This all could've been avoided if he had listened to the voice in the back of his head trying to tell him that something was amiss.

His hiding place totally eclipsed his body from the road, and thus, it was difficult to get a vantage point that allowed a clear view of the street. *What are you going to do now, Coby?* he thought. *Hide here until morning?* The cold bit at his outer extremities like a thousand tiny rats gnawing on his flesh. A gust of wind shook through the brush, blowing the thorny blackberry backward until it scraped against Coby's face. He recoiled in pain, but tried to subdue the noise from his chest.

Just then, he heard it.

Crunch.

Coby froze, momentarily ceasing the shaking of his battered body.

Crunch. Crunch.

Footsteps.

Crunch. Crunch. Crunch.

Coby wanted to flee into the forest and never return.

Crunch. Crunch. Crunch.

Slowly, the outline of a massive figure slid into view on the street. The wolf slowly crept his way forward, reminding Coby of an actual predator stalking its prey. His head swiveled back and forth, and his feet took the smallest of steps. If he was at all shaken by the fact that the police were likely on the way, it wasn't reflected in his demeanor.

Coby tried as best as he could to remain motionless. He became aware of how loud his breathing was in that moment, and he tried to hold it in. As soon as he closed his lips, his lungs felt like they were tearing apart. He tried to continue to hold, but he couldn't. He had to unhinge his jaw and try to quietly inhale. The move produced a sound like air escaping from the world's tiniest balloon. It wasn't much of a noise, but it was enough. The wolf stopped. His head turned slowly in the direction of the trees where Coby was hidden.

Coby knew it would be best to run now. Although he wasn't positive that the wolf could see him, he was certain the man knew exactly where he was thanks to his laborious breathing. He looked behind him, making sure that there was a path wide enough to charge through into the forest beyond.

Crunch. Crunch. Crunch.

Coby's head whipped about. The wolf had again started to walk down the street. Apparently, he remained ignorant to Coby's presence after all. Relief washed over Coby like a bucket of warm water. He bowed his head and let his breathing become regular. Was he going to get out of this after all?

While distinctly hearing the crunching of the wolf walking away from him, Coby waited in his hiding spot for what felt like an eternity, although it was likely only two or three minutes. Once he was certain the man had traveled far enough, Coby peeked his head out and craned his neck to the left. Indeed, the figure was still walking down the gravel road, approximately forty feet from where Coby was crouching. The road curved up ahead to the right, and Coby watched as the silhouette of the demon disappeared around the bend.

Coby exhaled, dropping his head to his chest. His diaphragm rose and fell rapidly, moving his chin back and forth. *My God,* thought Coby. *Oh my God.* His legs felt like noodles that wouldn't continue to support him for much longer. With a start, he internally started cursing himself. *What are you doing, idiot? Fucking move!*

Feeling like some sort of inept Spider-Man, Coby slid his body precariously through the brush until he was back out on the road. Still facing the bend the wolf had rounded, he crept back in the direction of Sean's house. The sound of the gravel being disturbed underneath his feet made him want to scream, but there was no path forward that would be quieter. *Fuck it,* thought Coby. With a burst of his legs, he sprinted, tearing down the road at breakneck speed, no longer caring about the noise it made. The crunching of the gravel eventually changed to slapping as the road morphed back into the paved section of Borneo Drive. In the distance, Coby could make out the outline of Sean's house. It was some fifty feet away.

Coby felt a sharp pain in his knee. He wasn't sure what had caused it; perhaps the wild burst had done something to one of his tendons or ligaments. All Coby knew was, he had to circumvent his momentum. Once he slowed down, his knee felt like it was being pierced by needles. *Don't stop now,* he thought. *You're almost there.* But he couldn't start running again. At least for a minute, he had to stay stationary and catch his breath. His knee and hip were throbbing in pain.

Exhale, thought Coby. *Exhale.* He imagined his dad's soothing voice and hands on his shoulders as he coaxed him into softer breathing. *Exhale.* Eventually, he seemed to regain control of his body. *Exhale. Just breathe.*

The sound of a dull, rapid slapping reached Coby's ears. It almost reminded Coby of a bird flapping its wings as it prepared for flight. It was the same noise that had been made when he was running on the pavement just a second ago, except now it was getting louder by the second. Coby whirled about and felt his stomach contract in terror. The wolf was running at full speed, charging right toward him.

Coby screamed.

The man bowled over him like a linebacker, knocking him off his feet and onto his back. The earth-shattering landing knocked the wind out of Coby, and although he intended to let out a cry of agony, all that he could muster was a strange rasp from his throat. Immediately, the wolf struck him forcefully across the jaw with his fist, bouncing the back of Coby's skull against the pavement. Disorientation flooded his senses. He wasn't sure which way was up, nor what up even meant. All he could process was a malevolent hand that reached for him. Coby tried to bat it away, but he didn't know where his own arm was.

The face of the wolf leered down at Coby. Once more, the hand enclosed around his throat and something miniscule and sharp glinted in front of his face. It would only be a matter of milliseconds before the needle penetrated him, and this time, he couldn't catch the arm that was wielding it. As he lay there, he felt a rush of heat in the back of his head, and he wondered if his skull was cracked. His eyes caught a flash of the color red. Surely he was bleeding out and was about to die. But then, why was he also suddenly enveloped by a gleam of blue?

The pressure on top of him released, and Coby was left reeling for a moment on the ground, still discombobulated due to the blow to the back of his head. From far away, he heard the screech of what sounded like spinning tires and a curious smell of exhaust wafted into his nostrils. Coby tried to lift his head, but it was too much effort. The world spun. Through his confusion, Coby arrived at the conclusion that the wolf was no longer on top of him. Instead, the sound of that familiar dull slapping reached Coby's ears. No more than a minute later, there was a large man wearing dark blue kneeling by his side.

"Are you okay?"

Coby couldn't even respond to the officer before he passed out.

10:06 p.m.

"Which way do you think he went?"

"Probably up Sixty-fifth Street. Back toward the highway. That's what I would do if it were me. Simultaneously put as much distance between myself and my pursuer while also going toward the place where there is going to be the most people."

Ted scoffed from the back seat. "He wouldn't

just find the nearest house and knock on the door?"

Amos shook his head as the headlights of the Ford rounded a curve and the pavement began to slope upward. "The nearest house? Look around, Teddy. The nearest house is three blocks east. It would be just faster to go to the highway."

Stevie twisted about and looked at Ted. "And besides, he was running like hell while being chased by a psychopathic killer in a wolf mask. Probably wasn't spending a lot of time thinking anything besides, 'Must go faster.'"

As they drove along, Amos subconsciously put himself in Coby's shoes, realizing how afraid the boy must've been. And confused. Why was this man trying to hurt him? From an outsider's perspective, it was probably so random and traumatizing. There he was, at a party cutting loose with his friends, and then a stranger in a macabre mask follows him into a room and tries to strangle the life out of him. How could you make any sense of that? Hell, this was probably what all victims of serial killers felt: wild fear, but confusion as well.

The car crept up Sixty-fifth Street, traveling slower than fifteen miles an hour. Amos didn't see any point in going fast; the boy was likely still close by and they might miss him hiding somewhere if they went too fast. Amos had received a brief description of Coby from Sean before the EMTs had loaded him into the ambulance, but he didn't have a clear-cut image of the teen in his brain. Brown hair, brown eyes, average height, not fat but not exceedingly thin. They had searched for a driver's license in the car's computer system so that they could bring up a picture, but they had not been able to pull him up. Either Coby was short for something or it was the kid's middle name.

Left and right they looked. There were trees all around, no buildings or any other indication of development. After the house they had come from, the neighborhood had turned barren, like every sign of life was hiding in the brush.

"Should we call out his name?"

"He isn't a dog, Stevie."

"Well, thanks, Teddy Bear! It really helps now that I know we aren't actually looking for a dog."

"Guys, not right now."

"He's right, Teddy Bear. Maybe patronize me another time," quipped Stevie.

Amos looked up in the rearview mirror and saw a look of absolute resentment on Ted's face.

After traveling a mile and noticing nothing but more foliage, Stevie rolled down her window.

"Coby!" She shouted it so quickly that it sounded like one syllable, and the noise seemed to echo off the trees.

"Shush!" Ted hissed. Stevie ignored this and shouted the boy's name again. No response.

"What if the killer is nearby? He's going to

know we're coming!" Ted whispered.

Stevie looked back at him. Amos could tell that she wanted to offer a sarcastic retort but was holding it in for his sake. She shook her head and went quiet.

Eventually, they pulled up to the end of Sixty-fifth Street at the edge of Highway 101.

"So, should we turn onto the highway?" Stevie suggested.

Ted shook his head. "No way. If he went out onto the highway this whole thing would be over by now. We would've already gotten the call that he had been picked up. Flip a U-turn."

Amos swung the car back around and drove back down toward Sean's house. When they were back on Borneo Drive, Amos saw the police lights from Sean's house still flashing against the night sky. There were even more people milling about now, and several new vehicles were pulling up to the sidewalk. Frantic crying teens in costumes sprinted up to the newly arrived cars, meeting what Amos assumed was their parents.

Before the car could reach the house, Ted blurted out, "Turn right here." Amos looked at him in surprise, but obliged. They cruised down Wayward Way, another mostly uninhabited block. There were a couple of houses at the far end of the street, and then a dead end.

"Wait, who is that?"

Twenty feet ahead of them, Amos saw the silhouette of a large figure sulking down the street with his head bent down. The man wore black pants and a thick black jacket, but Amos couldn't see any other distinguishable features from his current vantage point. He hit the gas pedal with more force, and sped up until they pulled up alongside the figure. The man's hood was pulled up and he was looking toward the ground, so Amos couldn't see his face.

Stevie rolled down her window. "Hey there. How's it going tonight?"

The man turned his head toward them, but Amos, Stevie, and Ted were not greeted by a face. They were greeted by a pointed gray mask.

For a moment, time froze. The man with the wolf mask stared into their car, and Amos was too shocked to find any words. Before he had another moment to react, the man took off running down the street.

"Hey! Stop!" Stevie shouted, and she fumbled with the passenger-side door handle. Ted threw open his door and pounced out of the car like a jaguar, chasing after the man. Within seconds, Stevie was out of the car and in full pursuit too, just behind Ted's streaking body. Amos put the car in park, and by the time he got out, he was already far behind the chase, but took off running anyway.

As he sprinted, Amos saw the man in the wolf

mask duck past the dead-end sign. Ted was only a few feet away from him. Amos pumped his arms with vigor, trying to quicken his pace, but it was no use. He was too far behind to make any difference. Up ahead, the man disappeared into the forest behind the yellow sign. Ted and Stevie bolted after him.

Ten seconds later, Amos was moving past the same sign. He had found a bout of strength in his legs and was finally moving at a healthy pace. However, he had lost sight of the people he was in pursuance of and his breathing was ragged and sparse. He wasn't used to physical exertion, and he knew he couldn't run for much longer.

Amos slid his way into the forest. After a few feet, he noticed that his legs started to turn over rapidly. At first, he thought it was because his body was adapting to running. Then he realized it was because the forest floor was beginning to slope down. As soon as he came to this epiphany, the ground became exceedingly steep. He attempted to stymie his momentum, but his chest swung forward like a pendulum, and his feet were off the ground. With a vociferous crash, Amos hit the dirt and his legs rolled over him. He stuck his arms out to grab onto something but there was nothing to stop his thunderous tumble down the hill. He rolled and rolled, hitting roots, branches, and blackberry bushes alike. Every time his body bounced off the ground, he grunted in pain. Finally, after at least ten rolls, he came to an unceremonious stop at the bottom of the hill, his face planted in the dirt.

Amos stayed still for a moment, waiting for the onslaught of pain. However, it never came. Perhaps the adrenaline in his system warded off the effects of his injuries. With a precipitous shove off the ground, Amos clambered to his feet. He swiveled his head back and forth, looking for where the others had gone. They had vanished.

"Jesus Christ," Amos hissed. He dug through his right pocket for his cell phone and the flashlight application that would illumine the area around him. Before he could locate it, a sound of brush rustling behind him made him gyrate about. Amos reached for his gun as he gazed at the spot that had moved in the bush ahead, preparing to be attacked.

Without warning, a hand clasped on Amos's right shoulder, making him flail and thrash wildly. His elbow caught the person behind him and he heard a yelp of pain.

"Ow! Fuck, Al. What are you doing?"

Amos pressed his hand against his chest and made a face of exasperation. "My God, Stevie, you scared the piss out of me."

"I thought you heard me coming!"

Amos shook his head and bent over. "Jesus. I'm getting too old for this shit."

"Agreed. You are pretty old."

Amos scowled at his partner. The moment felt ill-suited for levity.

"Where's Ted? And the perp?"

"I don't know. I fell down the hill and lost them," Stevie replied. She held up her palms, displaying mud and scratches that were ubiquitous on her body.

"You too, eh?"

Stevie's eyes bulged and the corners of her mouth twitched. "No way. You fell down?"

"Yeah. Great couple of stealthy detectives, aren't we? Come on, let's go this way." Amos pointed behind Stevie. "Ted can't be too far."

Right on cue, Ted called from somewhere nearby. "Albert? Stevie? Where are you guys?"

"Here!" Amos called back.

"Come over here! I've got him in cuffs!"

With a leap of triumph in his gut, Amos clapped Stevie on the back enthusiastically.

"Let's go!"

Amos waded through a bevy of vegetation that seemed to sprout up from every direction. Stevie followed in his wake, and she stuck so close to him that he could feel her hot breath on the back of his neck. After several steps, he seemed to lose track of where Ted's voice had emitted from several seconds before.

"Where are you, Teddy?"

"Here!"

The call came from a spot to the left of them. Amos bulldozed his way through several plants until he came to a small clearing. On the ground, Ted sat sprawled over a large figure that was in a heap. The man had a set of handcuffs restricting his arms, and his face was buried in the dirt. Ted seemed to be using all the strength of his legs to keep the man pinned; his arms were shaking with the tension.

"Alright, alright, help me get him up," Ted said, out of breath.

As Amos strode over to the pair, he noticed the wolf mask had been discarded onto the ground several feet away. Once he got closer, the pinned man raised his face from the dirt. Amos's stomach seized.

"No. Way."

Ted looked at Amos, appearing flabbergasted.

"You know him?"

Amos nodded slowly.

"I sure do. That's Tuck Parker."

10:44 p.m.

Amos took one last gander at the open manila envelope, trying to mentally prepare himself as much as he could. He began rereading the first paragraph to try and help ensure memorization.

Stevie stepped toward him. "You ready for

this?"

Amos sighed. He consolidated the forms in front of him and shut the folder. "Yeah, I guess."

"What's wrong?"

Amos bobbed his head from side to side, trying to indicate that he wasn't quite sure how to put it into words. "I don't know, it just feels like there is a lot riding on this. Since he left behind no viable evidence at any of the scenes, I know that a confession is paramount."

"I'm sure something will come up. I bet they will find the knife that he used to stab McVey."

Stevie was referring to the team of officers still down by Big Creek Park, sweeping the area for the bloody weapon Parker had discarded when he was fleeing.

"Yeah, but if they don't, we're screwed. It's only a matter of time before he asks for a lawyer."

"Well, then we better not waste any more time, huh?"

Amos gathered the folder and stood up. He also picked up the bottle of water that he had set on his desk. Stevie looked at him with narrowed eyes.

"For our guest," he said roguishly. She gave a half chuckle, and then they began to walk side-by-side, heading for the questioning center. Before they could reach their intended destination, their path was blocked by a sweaty Dozer.

"Helluva night, huh?"

Amos stopped walking. Dozer leaned against the wall to his right, using his arm to support the weight of his body. Instead of the usual spruce attire that a police chief would wear to the station, he was wearing a dark blue tee shirt, and when he leaned, he flashed the weird dog tattoo that was on his bicep. Dozer was perspiring even more than usual and he looked truly exhausted.

"Helluva night is right. Have you been here all evening, Chief?"

Dozer nodded wearily. "Been trying to manage the clusterfuck from the tranquility of the office."

Stevie laughed loudly. "Yeah, this place is the zenith of Zen. We should start doing yoga classes here."

Dozer didn't reply. He fanned himself off with the hand that wasn't buttressing his weight against the wall while looking at Amos. "So Tuck Parker, eh?"

Amos nodded hesitantly. He thought he could pick up a trace of skepticism in Dozer's voice. "Yeah. Tuck Parker."

Dozer maintained piercing eye contact with Amos. It was like he was scanning him, trying to somehow pick up on Amos's true thoughts.

"You really think he's our perp? You think he was clever enough to set up all these ostentatious scenes all over the city and lead us on this wild goose chase?"

"I don't know, boss. All I know is, Sean McVey was stabbed by a man in a wolf mask. And we found Tuck Parker near the scene of the crime, wearing a wolf mask."

"But that is the thing, isn't it? You think someone who was cunning enough to set up that deer and that scene out in Toledo would be caught walking two blocks away from where he stabbed some kid less than a half hour before? And wearing the mask when there were two other witnesses that could corroborate McVey's story?"

"What do you want me to do, boss? Skip the questioning? Let him go?"

"Not at all. Just approach this with a grain of salt."

Amos nodded curtly, wishing Dozer would get out of his way. However, the tall, burly man just stood there, fanning himself off as if he were in the Sahara Desert.

"Why don't you interview the Conner kid first?"

Amos raised his eyebrows in incredulity. "He's here already? Weren't they going to take him to the hospital?"

"He refused," Dozer replied quickly. "Said he was fine."

"Didn't Bosworth find him unconscious?"

"Yep. Bos said it looked like he had a concussion. Our guy was literally attacking him seconds before Bos showed up, for Christ's sake. And my guess is the guy heard the sirens and fled. But anyway, the kid refused to go to the hospital. Kept saying he had to go back home and take care of his ten-year-old brother."

"But you brought him here?"

Dozer nodded. "Yep. Bos said that once he told Conner that it looked like we had caught the guy, Conner was a little less stressed about getting home, and a little more inclined to come to the station. Probably wants to scope Parker out for himself . . . if he's the guy, that is."

"And how is the McVey kid doing?"

"He's going to make it. He's in the ICU right now, but we just got word that he's in stable condition."

"So where is Conner?"

"Waiting in the lobby. I didn't want to bring him in before we were ready. Bos is out there keeping him company. Unless you want to interview him now and Parker later?"

Amos felt a kink in his neck because he shook his head with such force. "No. Parker first."

Dozer pursed his lips. "Suit yourself."

With that, he turned about and walked back in the direction of his own office. As soon as he was out of earshot, Stevie whispered, "Why is he so apprehensive about this guy?"

"When you meet Parker, you'll see. Doesn't

exactly seem like a criminal mastermind."

"What does he seem like?"

"Just kind of a whack job. A two-bit junky."

Stevie put on a fake eager expression. "Sounds lovely. Can't wait to meet him!"

Amos guffawed and started walking again in the direction of the questioning center.

"Is Ted coming in with us?"

"No. He's over in his cubicle doing some research on the Conner kid before we interview him."

Stevie frowned. "Research?"

"Yeah. I think he's trying to establish a link between Conner and the other vics."

"But we didn't find a link between Ledoux and Johnson? So why would there be a link between Conner and one of the other two?"

Amos shrugged. "Just covering our bases."

Finally, the pair approached the questioning center. They both stopped, looking at each other in trepidation. Stevie raised her shoulders like she was inflating herself to prepare for battle.

"Alright. Let's do this."

Amos gave her a small nod and opened the door. Sitting at the table with his wrists cuffed together was the ignominious, vile creature that was Tuck Parker. A lot of times, with perps, it was almost difficult to envision them committing the crime they were accused of. They spoke soft.

Looked normal. But not Parker. He looked like he had put at least a few heads in the oven. The tattoos all over his body were more menacing now than they had been during the two interviews Amos had conducted with Parker previously. His filthy, mangled hair congealed to his forehead, and his whole body was covered in dirt. When the detectives entered the room, he looked at them maniacally and bit his lip. It wasn't an expression of fear; it seemed more like he was suppressing pain. The gauges in his ears swelled his lobes to a disgusting size. They almost looked like miniature wings.

"Hello, Mr. Parker." Amos pulled out one of the two chairs that were opposite the man, while Stevie sat in the other. "Didn't think we would be speaking again so soon."

Parker didn't say anything. He shot a frenzied glance over at Stevie, and she glowered back at him. He scratched at his arm.

"Do you want a bottle of water, Mr. Parker?"

Parker's face curled into a weird smile. He didn't answer the question.

"Alright then. Not thirsty." Amos left the bottle of water on his side of the table and began tapping his fingers absentmindedly. For a good twenty seconds, he let the silence hang in the air. The only noise in the room was the dull tapping that came whenever Amos would drum his fingers on the surface in front of him. He maintained eye contact with Parker, trying to make him as on edge as possible. If there was one thing that made virtually every person in the world uncomfortable, it was silence. The man stared back at Amos. It was as if they were both determined to not be the one to break the void.

"You know, I had you all wrong, Mr. Parker." Amos opened the manila folder that he had brought with him. "I guess this is why you shouldn't judge a book by its cover. But you know what? I had you pegged for an idiot, Tuck."

Parker's face transformed into a leering, mocking expression.

"Putting your own kid's head in the oven? It's so stupid it almost sounds like it was done sarcastically. No one could really be that dumb, could they?"

Suddenly, Parker let out a bizarre laugh so high in volume that it made Stevie jump. Amos was caught off guard as well.

"Something funny?"

Parker continued to giggle wildly. From the corner of his mouth, a trail of saliva ran down his chin as the insane laugh morphed into a wheeze.

"But maybe you aren't dumb at all, Tuck." Amos pressed on through the man's bizarre mirth. "Maybe it's just a front. You knew the kid would refuse to take the stand against his own father, and when he rebuffs the subpoena, his mother will be held in contempt of court, not you. Were you trying to paint yourself as some drug-addled, hot-headed punk so that we wouldn't catch on to your true nature?"

Parker was laughing so hard his eyes welled up with tears.

Without warning, Stevie slammed her hand on the table. This time it was Parker's turn to jump. Stevie's voice was amplified and harsh when she spoke. "What the *fuck* is wrong with you?"

Parker looked at Stevie, his eyes bulging. For a second, he looked afraid. Then, a malign grin spread out on his face, and he jabbed his index finger at Stevie. However, no words came out of his mouth.

"Keep shoving that little prick of a finger in my face, and it's going to get snapped in half."

Again, Parker chuckled. He withdrew his finger and coiled his fist while beginning to rock back and forth in his chair. It was truly a bizarre sight; Parker still hadn't said a single word, and he was acting like a particularly volatile patient at an asylum.

Trying to press on from any further brusqueness from Stevie, Amos continued with his line of questioning. He viewed Parker as emotionally fragile, and his goal was to metaphorically shake him into talking.

"So, what's with the insignia, Tuck? What kind

of warped acid trip produced this?" Amos slid the manila folder across the table. He had displayed the picture of the bloody dead smiley face that had been painted on the wall of Devin Johnson's former apartment. Parker looked down at it, and his smile seemed to fade. With his right hand, he picked up the manila folder and brought it closer to his face.

"What, you don't recognize your own handy work, Mr. Parker?"

Parker instantly set down the envelope and slid it back across the table, looking distraught. Once more, he began itching his arm, but this time, his strokes were much more feverish and penetrating to his skin.

"Wait a minute, I know what is going on," Stevie said softly to Amos.

Amos looked over at her, feeling confused.

"He's going through withdrawals," Stevie continued with a knowing expression on her face. Parker's eyes shifted back to her, and his upper lip curled into a snarl.

Amos eyed Parker and began to smile.

"Ahhh. I imagine it's hard to keep up a silent treatment while your body craves heroin, isn't it, Mr. Parker? First the wild agitation? That is the initial stage. Then later comes the illness. You'll be puking up probably a quarter of your body weight. Can't imagine how awful that will be for you."

Parker closed his eyes in response to this. It

reminded Amos of a little kid, one that was attempting to shut his or her eyes and make the external irritant questions go away.

"Look, Tuck . . . we aren't going to let you go until you talk. At the very least we can charge you with resisting arrest. There is no way you will just be free to go. You're going to be trapped in this stuffy little room with me and my colleague until you talk."

In response to this, Parker made a strange whistling noise through his teeth. Eventually, his hissing changed into words.

"I . . . ain't . . . talkin'."

Stevie threw up her arms in faux rejoice. "He speaks! Hallelujah! Praise Jesus, Mary, and Joseph!"

"Fuck . . . *you.*"

"You're not really my type though, Tuck. I prefer men whose teeth aren't yellow and whose ears don't look like slices of Canadian bacon."

Parker muttered something under his breath that wasn't totally audible, but it distinctly sounded like it rhymed with the word *bunt.*

Stevie stood up and leaned across the table, getting inches from Parker's face. "Want to run that by me again, slick?"

Parker bared his teeth at her. For several seconds, he simply breathed in her face, taking great care to exhale right in her nostrils. Stevie didn't back down, showing no sign she was disturbed by the foulness of his breath. Finally, Parker's face broke into another nefarious grin.

"You got a pretty little mouth there, girl," he whispered. "You use it too much, but it sure is pretty. I like 'em like you. Tiny and tight. But with a little *spunk*. Yeah. . . I'm sure you could take a *mean* dick."

Stevie raised her open palm into the air, cocking back. Just before she was going to strike him, Amos caught her wrist.

"Hey, hey, hey! Stop, Stevie, stop!" Amos had had to stand and put his arms around Stevie's waist, holding her back from leaping across the table while she struggled against him.

"Fuck you, asshole! I will *end* you! I will kick your balls back up into your pelvis, you fucking slime!"

Amos continued to try and restrain Stevie, who was thrashing around like an angry bull. Parker was laughing dementedly again and clapping his hands. Amos managed to subdue Stevie's arms, but she was still wiggling, trying to break free. "Stevie, *stop*! Enough! Stop!"

Finally, Stevie's body slacked and she stayed motionless in Amos's arms, breathing heavily.

"Just relax, partner."

Amos maneuvered Stevie's body around in a circle, turning his back to Parker. Once she was facing the door, he released her.

She made a move like she was going to go back to the desk, but Amos held his arm in front of her.

"Nope. Out."

Stevie looked up at him, and her face was beet red from the surge of fury. "Huh?"

"We're going out. Come on."

From behind them, Parker's cacophony of laughter had gotten so loud that it was like nails on a chalkboard. Stevie glared at him, looking like she still wanted to break his nose.

"C'mon, partner. Please?"

Stevie looked back at Amos, and her facial expression softened. With one last menacing glance at Parker, she left the room.

"I'm sorry, Albert."

"It's okay. We have all lost our cool before."

"No, like . . . I should've known that he was going to try and bait me like that. I'm sorry. If I had made physical contact with him it would've been over."

"Good thing I stopped you, huh?" Amos offered her a small smile. Stevie's hair was ruffled so much that a few large strands were drooping in front of her face. Amos tugged one of the strands and tucked it behind her ear.

"You aren't mad?"

Amos smiled. In that moment, he felt a rush of tenderness for Stevie. The fact that she had almost gotten into a brawl with a murder suspect and her number one concern wasn't disappointing him was cute. He reached out and patted her on the shoulder.

"Nah, partner, I ain't mad. We just can't let him get the upper hand like that, you know?"

Stevie nodded. "Yeah. Obviously. So, what are we going to do now?"

Amos bit his lip and started walking down the hallway, indicating to her that she should come with him.

"We're going to sit on Parker for a bit. Not literally," Amos said with a glance back at Stevie, who chuckled. "We're going to let time play to our advantage and interview him again later. Get his anxiety built up a little more. For now, we will go talk to Coby Conner and see if he can confirm anything that would identify Parker. And also, this."

Amos stopped in the middle of the hallway and fiddled with a knob on the wall.

"What on earth are you doing?"

"Turning up the thermostat to the questioning center. Can't imagine it's fun to go through heroin withdrawals in a hot room, can you?"

Stevie's mouth dropped open, and she covered it with her hands while smiling. "I think that is a brilliant idea."

Amos smiled and made sure the knob was up to eighty degrees. A very small part of him felt a little guilty for the tactic, but if Parker *was* the killer they were searching for like it appeared, then it didn't matter if he was in discomfort.

"So should we go grab Conner?" Stevie offered.

"First we have to talk to Ted to see if he has gathered any pertinent information on the kid."

"Ah, right. That little snag."

Amos shook his head in exasperation. He rounded the corner of the hallway back into the cluster of cubicles that made up the main office and sauntered down the second row until he found Ted. The man's face was covered in scratches from running after Parker in the forest and a large bruise shined purple under Ted's right eye. Parker had caught him with a hard elbow in the ensuing tussle that had occurred in the brush.

"Ah, buddy, you look like shit."

Ted smiled. "Yeah, well . . . that's the price you pay for this job, I guess." His smile faded as he saw Stevie lingering just behind Amos.

"So did you find anything on Conner? We're about to go talk to him."

Ted shook his head and reclined in his chair. "I didn't find a link to Johnson or Ledoux if that is what you mean. I found something, but it isn't connected to this case."

"What is it?"

"In 1997, Coby's mother, Dana, was raped. They never caught the guy who did it."

Amos ran his fingers through his hair as he thought. "Any suspects?"

"Yeah, actually. Guy named Leighton Jones. Registered sex offender. Had a laundry list of crimes that were sexual in nature, but he never had an extended prison sentence. Anyway, the file says that he was the prime suspect, but they were never able to confirm it. Dana Conner didn't report it until months after it happened so there was no DNA evidence to tie to Jones."

"Wait, Leighton Jones? Wasn't he the key witness in the Nowhere Girls case? The one who was murdered?"

Ted nodded and clicked his tongue. "You got it."

"That's bizarre."

Ted looked down at the sheet of paper in front of him and ran his finger down it. "I think that is it though. Coby seems to be just a normal kid. Never gotten into any kind of trouble far as I can tell."

"Okay, thanks," Amos replied, turning to leave.

"Do you want me to come and sit in on the interview?"

"Nah, Teddy, that's fine. You're good."

"Okay. Then I'm going to go back down to the

McVey house and try and talk to more possible witnesses. Some of the kids are here at the station downstairs waiting to be interviewed but most are still drunk, and none of them said they even saw the perp anyway. Hopefully there will be a stray neighbor or something back on Borneo."

"Sounds good," Amos said, giving Ted a thumbs-up before walking away. Stevie followed him.

Amos walked in the direction of the lobby, weaving through more rows of cubicles. Eventually, he and Stevie got to the door that led outside. Just before they were about to go through, the door swung open. Bosworth lumbered through the frame, but stopped when he saw the pair of them.

"There you two are! I was wondering when you would show up. Better get this over quick. Kid is itchin' to get home."

Bosworth stepped out of the way and let Amos and Stevie come through. Sitting on a bench on the opposite side of the lobby was a young man who looked completely exhausted. His brown hair was sticking up in a multitude of directions, and he was reclined so far back on the bench that he had no semblance of posture whatsoever. On his jaw, Amos saw three deep scratches and a dark shadow. His pants had a large hole in them around the left kneecap, and the rest of his clothes were covered in dirt. He was holding a blue gel ice pack to the back of his head, and it looked like he was struggling to keep his eyes open.

"You must be Coby." Amos gave the kid a small smile.

Coby nodded, and when he did, he seemed to grimace in pain.

"How are you doing?" Stevie said in a tone Amos didn't hear frequently; she sounded warm and empathetic like a concerned mother.

Coby pushed himself up on the bench. "Fine. I mean . . . I'll be fine."

"I've been told you're trying to get home to see your kid brother," Amos said gently.

"Yeah. I am. He's probably sleeping, but he's home alone."

"Okay. We will make this quick and just try and get a brief rundown of everything that happened. Obviously, we'll need a more extensive interview later, but for tonight, we'll make it fast. Follow me."

Amos beckoned Coby off the bench, and the kid slowly got up. He followed Amos into the office and through the swath of cubicles. Stevie brought up the rear, and as Amos glanced back, he noticed she was staying inordinately close to Coby. Eventually, Amos came to a conference room that was unoccupied and showed the kid inside.

Coby walked over to the most comfortable-looking chair that was generally reserved for Dozer and plopped down in it. Amos and Stevie sat on the other side of him. Stevie gave Coby a smile once he was slouched in the chair. He was still holding the blue gel ice pack to the back of his head.

"So, our boss said that you might have a concussion. That you refused to go to the hospital."

Coby shook his head with fervor, which caused him to briefly squint his eyes in pain. "No, I don't have a concussion."

"But you lost consciousness."

Coby shrugged uncomfortably. "For like a few seconds."

Amos gave a mini-shrug. "If you think you're fine then, okay. Since you are eighteen, it is well within your right as a legal adult to refuse medical care. But concussions are nothing to mess around with. It's your brain we're talking about here."

Coby didn't respond. He looked up at the ceiling and played with the string to his hoodie with the hand that wasn't being used to brace the gel pack.

"So how did you lose consciousness?"

Coby rubbed the back of his head. "When the guy punched me, my head hit the pavement. I didn't pass out right away or anything, but I think it was the combination of being choked and my head hitting the ground."

"He was choking you?"

"Yeah. Both times."

"Both?"

"Huh? Oh, yeah, like when he attacked me at Sean's house and then when he caught up with me out on the street after that. Both times he was choking me."

"He was trying to strangle you in the middle of a public street?"

Coby shook his head again. "No. I think he was just trying to hold my head in place. He had a needle and was trying to inject me with it."

"A needle?"

"Yeah."

Amos exchanged a meaningful look with Stevie.

"But he never contacted you with the needle?"

"No."

Amos percussed his fingers on the table as his mind processed. What kind of substance did the needle contain? Perhaps something lethal?

"Okay, Coby," Amos said slowly. "I'm going to need you to take me through everything that happened tonight, starting at the beginning. Don't leave anything out. Put as much detail in as you can. Anything you tell us might help."

"Uh, okay. Only tonight though? Not the rest of the day?"

Amos leaned forward, sparked by a new curiosity. "Why? Did something happen earlier in the day?"

Coby nodded. "A lot of things happened earlier in the day."

"Hmm. Okay. Take me through everything then."

Coby shifted in the chair, preparing himself for his story. Stevie had withdrawn a notepad from underneath her jacket and was already furiously taking notes. Amos could make out the word "needle" written down in tidy handwriting at the top of the page.

"It all started this morning in class," Coby began. "Mrs. Parrish told me that my dad was on the phone for me in the office. I thought it was weird because I figured if my dad wanted to talk that he would just call my cell. Anyway, I went to the office and picked up the phone, and it was a really warped voice that answered. Like really deep. It reminded me of the devil or something. The voice said, 'He comes for you tonight. Death.' And then the phone call ended."

Amos felt the hairs on the back of his neck rise. "What time was this at? Approximately?"

"Oh, around eight thirty, I would say."

"And it obviously wasn't your dad then?"

"No. I called him right after that, and he said he hadn't been trying to call me."

"Did you tell anyone about this?"

"My friends, yeah. They thought it was just some guy fuc"—Coby closed his eyes as he corrected his speech—"messing with me."

Amos nodded. "And you never found out who it was? Did you receive any other strange phone calls the rest of the day?"

Coby rubbed his temple. "No, I never found out who it was. And no, I didn't."

"So what else happened today that was noteworthy?"

"Well, I walked home with my friends from school, and on the way home, there was this guy by a red pickup truck that was just standing there and staring at us. He gave me a weird vibe."

"A man? What did he look like?"

Coby shrugged. "Not sure, really. He was too far away. It looked like he was tall. Muscular. Dark hair."

Stevie jumped in. "Do you remember what he was wearing?"

"Um, jeans, I think. And a black shirt. It might have been a sweatshirt. I don't know, I was pretty far away."

"And he was just staring at you? Was this on Eads Street?"

"Yeah, it was. And yeah, that is what it looked like. Then he got in the truck and drove away."

"Do you remember what kind of truck it was?"

Coby frowned in concentration. "What, like what model? No. It looked kind of old. I saw it again up close in the McDonald's parking lot like an hour later."

Amos sat up a little straighter. "What?"

"Yeah. I had taken Mack, my little brother, to go rent a movie at Redbox. I was walking back to the car, and I saw the same red truck parked nearby, and he flashed his lights at me."

"Jesus," Stevie muttered as she continued to scribble down notes.

"He flashed his lights at you? Like he was trying to get your attention?"

Coby gave a small nod. "Yeah. He did it like four or five times. But before I could see who it was, he drove off again."

"And you're sure it was the same truck?"

"Pretty sure, yeah."

"What time was this at?"

"A little after four, I think?"

There was a tiny respite as Amos ruminated on everything Coby had just told him. It appeared the kid had been stalked by someone throughout the day, likely the same person who had attacked him at Sean McVey's party. Tuck Parker didn't have a vehicle registered in his name, though he did have a license. Perhaps the vehicle was stolen. Maybe they could even get in contact with McDonald's and see the footage from the parking lot around the time Coby had said the incident took place.

It was Coby who broke the silence next. "The creepiest thing though was what happened when I took Mack trick-or-treating."

"Oh yeah? What happened?"

Coby cleared his throat. "We were at the corner of Eighth and Benton, I think. We were getting candy from this old guy's house. He was actually the one who pointed him out."

"Pointed who out?"

"The guy who attacked me. The man in the wolf mask."

"You saw the man who attacked you at Sean's party earlier in the night too?"

"Yeah."

"What was he doing?"

Coby shuddered. "He was just watching us. He was standing against the stop sign, just staring. We turned around for a second to talk to the old guy who was trying to invite us inside, and when we turned back around the guy was gone."

"You said this was at the corner of Eighth and Benton?"

"Yes."

"What time was this at?"

"Like, six thirty, maybe?"

Stevie squinted her eyes like she was trying to concentrate. "Do you remember what he was wearing? Like, besides the mask?"

"It was all black. Like a long-sleeved shirt and black jeans."

"Did the black shirt have a hood?"

"I don't think so."

Amos looked over at Stevie. Up until that point, Parker had fit the description. But he had been wearing a black jacket with a hood. Not simply a long-sleeved shirt. Perhaps Coby had just not seen it properly. Or Parker had just changed clothes.

"Did you see him again at all before he attacked you at Sean's party?"

"No."

"Did anything else happen that struck you as odd up until the attack?"

Coby seemed to grind his teeth together as he thought. "Uh, I don't . . . Wait! Yes! Cassandra's phone!"

"Cassandra? Cassandra who?"

"Klay. She's in my grade. She was at the party."

"What happened with her phone?"

"So we were out on the back deck talking, right? At Sean's house. And we had sort of . . . an argument, I guess. So, I went back inside," Coby said. "Then like ten minutes later I got a text from her telling me to come back outside, so I did. I went back out on the deck. But she wasn't there. There wasn't anyone there. And then I saw a light at the edge of the woods in Sean's backyard."

Stevie had begun writing at an insane pace again. "A light?"

"Yeah. Like a flashlight."

"Did you go and check it out?"

"No. At that point my guard was up, and I thought it was weird, so I went back inside."

Stevie pointed at Coby. "Good thinking!"

"Thanks." The sides of Coby's mouth twitched like he wanted to laugh.

"So did you ever find Cassandra?"

"Yeah, not long after. She told me she never even sent the text and that she had lost her phone an hour before."

Amos raised his eyebrows. "Wait, what? She said she didn't even have her phone?"

"Right."

"So you think it was somebody trying to lure you out back on your own?"

"Exactly," Coby said with a tap of his hand on the table. "Right after Cassandra told me that is when I first saw him again. The wolf mask guy. He was inside the party, just standing on the dance floor in the middle of everyone. He was just staring at me."

"He was actually *inside* the party? Standing by everyone else?"

"Yeah. Just standing there. When I saw him I panicked and I ran upstairs to try and hide in the bedroom."

"Did you try and get someone else's help? Like one of your friends?"

Coby looked a little sheepishly. "No, I didn't. I, uh, wasn't exactly in a great state of mind."

"Like you were scared?"

"No, like he was drunk," Stevie replied bluntly.

Coby looked down at the ground, and he seemed like he was trying not to laugh again. "Something like that."

"Ah," said Amos delicately, trying not to smile. "So you ran upstairs to hide in a bedroom? And that is where he attacked you, correct?"

"Yeah. He pinned me on the bed, and the same thing—he was grabbing my neck and he had a needle. He was trying to stab me with it."

"Stab you?"

Coby twitched in irritation. "Well, inject me."

"And I'm guessing that is when your buddy Sean burst in?"

"Right. With a girl. I don't know what her name is."

"Kira Black," Amos replied. "We already had someone talk to her."

Coby didn't reply to this. He simply rubbed his eyes and let out a yawn.

"So Sean already gave us a rundown of what happened there. He and the assailant had a physical altercation, and you escaped through the window onto the roof?"

"Yep. Jumped in the bed of the pickup in the driveway. Oh, and while that happened, I did this."

Coby fumbled around in his pocket. After a couple of seconds, he pulled out a phone that had a large spider web–like pattern on the screen.

"Uh oh," Amos said.

"Yeah. Hence why I didn't call the cops right after it happened."

"Right. I was wondering about that, actually."

"Yeah. Phone was broken. When I realized it, I just took off running down the gravel road."

Stevie continued to scribble on her notepad as Coby spoke. "What gravel road?"

"I don't know the name of it." Coby sounded impatient. "The one right by Sean's house. It goes down past the reservoir."

"Was your assailant right behind you?"

"Well, he was behind me, but not like . . . *right* behind me. I had time enough to hide. When I was running, I realized that going down the reservoir road was stupid because there aren't any houses or anything down that way. No one to help me. So, I stopped and hid in the brush on the side of the road. I hid there for like a minute before he walked by."

"He walked past you? He didn't see you while you were hiding?"

"I thought he did at first, but he must not have because he just kept walking. Anyway, he kept going farther down the road, and once he was out of sight, I came out of my hiding place. I started booking it back to Sean's house. Like full-on sprinting. Eventually, I stopped because I thought I had lost him and my knee was hurting. Honestly, I was just trying to catch my breath. Before I knew it, I turned around and there he was, running right at me again."

"So that is when the second attack took place?"

"Yes. He tackled me in the middle of the street and clocked me right here." Coby pointed at his jaw. "Like I said, my head kind of bounced off the pavement. Everything that happened after that was a blur. I remember he was choking me. And the needle. But then next thing I know he was gone, and that big cop showed up and asked if I was alright. That's when I passed out."

"Do you know how long it was in between when the man got off you and when Bosworth showed up?"

"No, I really have no idea. Like I said, I was out of it." Coby rubbed the spot on his jaw that had the dark shadow.

"Understandable," Amos replied. He let silence hang in the air for a few seconds while Stevie continued to jot down everything Coby had said. When she was caught up, Amos veered a little and began a new line of questioning.

"The man we apprehended is Tuck Parker. Have you ever heard that name before?"

Coby looked much more alert. His eyes widened and he moved forward in his chair, sitting up a little straighter and turning his head slightly to the left as if trying to bring his right ear closer to Amos's mouth so that he didn't miss anything.

"Tuck? That's his name?"

"Yeah. Tuck Parker. It's short for Tucker."

"I have never heard that name," Coby said while shaking his head.

"Okay. Well, let's see if you recognize him." Amos nodded at Stevie, and she pushed forward a manila envelope she had brought with her, which she then opened. It took her a few seconds of shuffling through various files before she arrived at a mug shot of Parker. Stevie pulled it out and set it in front of Coby. With shifty eyes, Coby scanned the photograph up and down.

"I don't think I recognize him."

"You don't think?"

"No. I definitely don't recognize him."

Amos nodded, feeling a sinking sensation in his gut. He knew that interviews with witnesses or those directly involved with a crime rarely went like that; if there was a path of least resistance it would usually be nixed right away. And yet, he couldn't help but feel a pang of disappointment. He wouldn't tell Coby this, but in all likelihood, the man who had assaulted him had spent more than just the past seven hours stalking his target. It seemed probable that Coby had seen his attacker before, whether he knew it or not.

When Stevie began to speak again, her voice suddenly had a tad more urgency. "You said he was grabbing you around the neck, right? Trying to hold you in place?"

"That's right," Coby said shortly.

"So you would've gotten a good look at his inner wrist?"

Coby pursed his lips and shook his head. "I wasn't really looking at his wrist, to be honest."

"But would you have remembered if he had a unique tattoo if it was showing right in front of your face?"

Amos closed his eyes for a moment. *Of course.*

"I might, yeah," Coby said slowly.

"Tuck Parker has Chinese writing tattooed on the inside of his right wrist. I'm not sure what it translates to, but the letters almost form the shape of a snake. It's in bold black."

Coby looked up at a spot on the wall as he tried to focus on what Stevie had just said. His eyes misted over and his jaw drooped open slightly. After a few seconds of thinking, he let out a deep breath.

"No."

"No, what?"

"He didn't have a tattoo like that."

Amos felt his heart rate ascending. His mind was so muddled from such a long day that he couldn't process the new information.

"Are you sure you just don't remember him having a tattoo like that? You did just say that you didn't get a good look at his wrist."

"No. I said I wasn't focusing on his wrist. But I would've remembered something like that. And he didn't have a tattoo."

Amos didn't reply. He was bamboozled. Maybe Stevie had just misremembered which wrist the tattoo was on. He looked over at her, and she was making eye contact with him.

"Coby, do you mind if me and Detective Hutchins step outside for a second?"

Coby looked at him with an exasperated expression on his face.

"Or not?" Amos said.

"It's just, I really need to get home to my brother, and I thought you said this was going to be quick."

"I understand. Really, I do. But if what you told us is true, then there is a possibility that the man who attacked you isn't in custody right now. Do you really feel safe going home alone?"

"That Bosworth guy said that I would have a protective detail," Coby replied quickly. "That two cops would stay outside of my house overnight."

"And that is enough for you?"

Coby shrugged. "I think it kind of has to be. I need to get home."

"Okay. We can be done for now then."

Amos watched as Bosworth walked next to Coby with two other patrolmen not far behind them. They rounded about the corner of the hallway connected to the lobby and exited through the double glass doors that led outside. As Amos gazed at them, he felt unsettled. Something deep in the recesses of his brain was telling him to stop Coby from leaving. But he had no reason to do so that he could rationally explain.

From behind him, Stevie tapped his shoulder.

"So what do you think?"

"I don't know, partner. I really don't know."

"Do you think we should've just let him go like that?"

"He has a protective detail," Amos replied, but once he said it, he realized how unconvinced he sounded.

"Hopefully we didn't just put those deputies in danger too."

"Oh, don't be ridiculous. This guy isn't Michael Myers. He isn't just going to go on an unfettered killing spree."

Stevie flushed red. "Albert, you need to stop underestimating this man. He just stabbed a teenager at a crowded party and beat the snot out of another in the middle of a public street. How can you be so sure what he's capable of?"

"I don't know what all he's capable of, Stevie, but I know that there is a good chance he's in cuffs inside the questioning center at this very moment, and unable to do Coby Conner any further harm."

Stevie suddenly lowered her voice to a whisper. "Albert, you just said it. Our guy is cunning. He's an expert at deceit. The diversion, remember? Do you honestly believe that Tuck Parker is just putting on a facade of ineptness and is secretly a criminal mastermind?"

Before Amos could retort, Dozer's voice reached his ears from a few feet away.

"You two! Come here. I have to show you something."

Amos turned around and saw that Dozer looked extremely tense; he was almost snarling, and his forehead was wrinkled as he scowled.

"Everything okay, boss?"

"Just come with me. Now. "

Dozer turned around and strode down the hallway at a quick pace. Amos followed after him. He watched as Dozer rounded the corner of the hallway and expected him to take a right to the offices, but he didn't. He just kept walking straight. He stopped right in front of the questioning center.

"Look, Albert." Dozer pointed toward the window that was on the door. Amos peered in, and saw Parker leaning forward in his chair. In his hand, he was holding the water bottle that Amos had offered him, and he held it to his mouth, chugging powerfully.

"Drinking water. Mesmerizing."

He made a move to go inside. Before Amos could open the door, Dozer reached out his arm and grabbed him by the shoulder, holding him in place.

"No. Not that. That isn't what I was talking about."

Amos looked up at Dozer, and he was totally befuddled.

"Uh, what? Then what am I supposed to be looking at?"

"Look at the hand that is holding the bottle."

Amos gazed in again and saw nothing out of the ordinary in regards to Parker's hand.

"I'm not sure what I'm—"

"He's right-handed!"

Amos looked at Dozer in utter bewilderment. "So?"

"*So,* think about what happened to Sean McVey."

"What do you mean?"

"McVey had his assailant in a headlock when he was stabbed, right? And he was stabbed in the right shoulder. So if the suspect was right-handed, think about how he would've had to grip the knife to do that."

Amos felt a lump rise in his throat.

"He would have to grab the hilt so that the blade was facing toward him and then reverse thrust to make penetration," Dozer said, demonstrating the move. "Does that seem plausible to you?"

"I mean . . . I don't have a particular refined stabbing technique, boss."

"That's not—Jesus! Come here, Hutchins!"

Stevie raised her eyebrows and seemed to involuntarily back up.

"Now!" Dozer demanded.

"Alright, alright." Stevie extended her arms out in a "calm down" type of gesture. She walked over to Dozer until she was about a foot away.

"Now turn around."

Stevie turned so that she was facing Amos, and she looked positively vexed. Dozer slipped his right arm around Stevie's neck, but kept his grip slackened so that he wouldn't choke her. Over Stevie's right shoulder, Dozer looked at Amos.

"Okay, Hutchins, pretend like you're going to stab me. How would you do it?"

Stevie motioned her arm in the air, but didn't follow through. "It's kind of hard to mimic this without actually having something in my hand."

"Sorry, sweetheart, but I don't have a cleaver on me."

Amos reached into his pocket and pulled out a pen that he handed to Stevie. "Here, use this."

Once Stevie grasped onto the pen, Dozer continued his demonstration, with his arm around his subordinate in a faux headlock. "Okay, now how would you wield it if you were trying to stab me?"

Stevie clenched the knife in her fist so that the sharp end of the pen was protruding out of the space between her index finger and thumb.

"Okay, now if you were going to stab me like that, which side would you choose?"

With her right hand, Stevie brought the knife over her opposite shoulder so that the pen was pointing toward the left side of Dozer's torso.

"Shit." Amos scratched the top of his balding head.

Dozer pulled his arm so that it was no longer around Stevie's neck. "Exactly."

"So our killer is left-handed?"

"And Tuck Parker is right-handed."

Stevie nodded eagerly. "I told you, Al!"

Dozer turned to her. "What?"

"Well, Parker has a tattoo of Chinese writing on his right wrist. But Coby Conner said that his assailant didn't have any such tattoo. Also, when he described what the man was wearing, he said a long-sleeved black shirt. He said it didn't have a hood. But Parker is wearing a black hoodie."

Amos turned and looked through the window to the questioning center. There Parker was, scratching his neck rabidly and sweating from seemingly every orifice. He looked like he was ready to jump out of his own skin. If he wasn't the killer, why was he walking around the neighborhood that Coby had just been assaulted in while wearing the same wolf mask the attacker had? What would motivate him to do such a thing? A vision of Parker's house flashed across Amos's consciousness. Filthy, unkempt, and destitute. Stacks of unpaid bills sitting on the kitchen table. As Amos looked at Parker through the window, it clicked.

"Excuse me," Amos said suddenly and quickly opened the door to the questioning center and slid inside, leaving Dozer and Stevie looking stunned in his wake. Once he was in the room, he shut the door, whipped about, and strode right over to the table where Parker sat. Parker looked up at him, appearing nervous. When Amos slammed both of his hands on the table, Parker jumped.

"Jesus Christ, man!"

"Who paid you to do it, Tuck?"

"Huh?"

"The mask! Who gave it to you?"

"What are you talking ab—"

"Don't play stupid with me!" Amos screamed and Parker jumped again. "The game is up, Parker! You can stop wasting both of our time! Who gave you the mask? Who told you to be in that neighborhood?"

Parker didn't answer, but his face lost all its

color.

"Man, I don't even have to answer these questions."

"Of course you don't, but you aren't leaving this place until you do. Jesus, Parker! Do you even know what you have gotten yourself into?"

Parker rocked back and forth. "Man, why is it so damn hot in here? It feels like we're in a sauna."

"He has killed people, Parker. Two that we know of. Maybe even more."

Parker's eyes bulged.

"That's right, idiot! Look what you did to yourself! You're the number one suspect in a goddamned murder investigation!"

"I didn't kill nobody, man!" Parker screeched, leaning in with his hands clasped together so that it looked like he was praying.

"I know you didn't, moron. But I can promise you, however much money this guy gave you, it wouldn't be enough to cover your attorney fees if you refuse to talk and had to defend yourself in court," replied Amos relentlessly. "How much was it, Tuck? How much did he give you?"

Parker resumed his insane rocking, and although he wasn't saying anything, his mouth was moving. It was like he was lip-syncing to a nonexistent song.

"How much?"

Parker looked up and Amos saw that his

demeanor from the earlier interview had totally changed. Whereas before he came off as defiant, angry, and downright vicious, he now looked simply terrified. Being that Amos was still standing, he towered over his respondent, and as he leaned in further, Parker seemed to recoil.

"How much, goddamn it?" Amos shouted.

"Five thousand."

"Five thousand? He gave you five thousand dollars?"

"Yeah, that's what he gave me up front. He said if I went through with it he would give me five thousand more."

"And what were his instructions exactly? He just gave you the mask and told you when and where to wear it?"

Parker nodded. "Yeah, man, he just showed up on my front porch yesterday. He told me to just walk around that neighborhood for two hours, starting at nine thirty. He gave me the money and the mask and he told me to wear all black. He said that the police would try and arrest me, and that if I didn't talk, he would give me the other half of the money."

"I'm assuming he didn't tell you his name then? What did he look like?"

"I don't know, man. He was wearing a mask. The whole interaction lasted like ten minutes."

Amos was only inches away from Parker's

face. "What kind of mask?"

"The same kind he gave me!"

"Can you tell me anything else about this man?"

Parker began aggressively rubbing his left temple, and he momentarily stopped rocking back and forth as he thought.

"Well, he didn't talk normal. He was trying to hide it, but I think he had an accent."

Amos whispered so close to Parker's face that he could feel his own breath reverberating off the man's forehead. "What kind of accent?"

"I don't know, man. It was hard to tell. It almost sounded like a Mexican accent."

11:15 p.m.

It took Mack a long time to realize he was awake. Caught in limbo between the dream world and reality, he lay there for several long minutes, playing out the rest of the dream. He had been sitting in the back seat of the car; his mother had been driving and singing along to the soft country song wafting through the speakers. He had asked where they were going. She told him their destination wasn't much farther and continued to croon lyrics Mack couldn't quite hear. He had looked out the window and seen a blur of trees rushing by, but the image had been ephemeral. The car had stopped. He leaned around the edge of the seat to try and glimpse what caused his mother to pump the brakes of the car. But for some reason, he couldn't quite make out what it was. His mom had told him not to watch. "You don't need to see him," she hissed. And although he didn't view him with his own eyes, Mack had known in his gut that the man in the wolf mask was standing in the middle of the road. He had made Mack's mother stop the car.

That was when Mack had woken up, but it had taken him a prolonged period of time to realize he was no longer in slumber. His heart beat fiercely from the nightmare, and the sheet he was underneath adhered to him like a bandage. Once he became coherent, relief washed over him. He wasn't in a car. He was right here in his bed. And his brother was downstairs, ready to protect him. Mack looked up at the ceiling of his room and saw the glow of several luminescent plastic stars his father had plastered there for him. It was a pale imitation of the night sky, but it comforted Mack.

Mack closed his eyes, wishing he could fall back asleep without any effort at all. But he had never been that way. It always took him eons to fall asleep. On top of that, he was a light sleeper. The slightest noise or change in temperature would rip Mack from whatever dream he was having. It made it difficult to get a good night of sleep.

As he lay there, Mack thought of what had

happened earlier in the evening. He wished his thoughts would gravitate toward something else, but the more he tried to move his attention, the more the thing he wanted not to think about fluttered into his mind. The wolf-man leaning against the stop sign, staring at them. Mack pulled the covers over his face, as if being completely eclipsed by the sheets would protect him from all external torment. He thought of when he had been asleep on the couch earlier. He could've sworn he saw the wolf-man peering into their living room through the sliding glass door. Coby had been so adamant Mack hadn't seen anything. He said it had to have been Mack's wild imagination. But as Mack curled himself underneath the covers with fear dominating his senses, he was now sure that he *had* seen the same boogeyman leering at him from their backyard. His heart beat even faster as he pictured the gray mask pointing right at him.

Just relax, thought Mack. *You're safe now.* It was like his bed was some sort of protective enclosure, and he was determined to stay under the covers until he drifted back off to sleep again. As he clenched his eyelids tighter and tighter, determined to make himself sleep, an odd smell reached his nostrils. It was foreign; Mack instinctively knew it didn't belong there. It reminded him of the outdoors, raw and earthy. He couldn't place what it was. Reluctantly, he slid the covers off his face and rolled over in his bed, looking out at his room for the source of the smell.

It was so dark Mack couldn't see anything. His room was full of possessions he had been accumulating his whole life, and Mack could just see the edges of the various shapes. A pile of clothes. A box full of old Legos. His acoustic guitar he had already given up learning how to play. In the far left corner of the room, Mack saw the outline of something large and dark he knew to be the case to his guitar. So, what was producing the odd smell?

Mack shifted more in his bed, trying to identify the aroma. He scanned back and forth, looking for what he couldn't see. At the foot of his bed, he noticed his basket of dirty laundry. Perhaps the odor was emanating from there. Mack began to sit up, trying to get closer to the laundry. As soon as he lifted himself, he noticed the massive black shape in the corner of the room move.

His eyes instantly locked onto the shape. Mack suddenly felt robbed of air, like his lungs no longer functioned. Slowly but surely, the pointed gray nose moved forward in the darkness, caught by a beam of moonlight peaking in through the window. The wolf-man walked toward the bed, towering over the quivering young boy who suddenly hoped he was still dreaming. *Wake up,* thought Mack. *Wake up.* But even in his tired state, he knew the nightmare had seeped into reality. This was no dream.

Once the wolf-man was only a foot away from him, Mack screamed. However, his cry was quickly drowned out by the gloved hand clasping onto his face. The outdoorsy smell blasted into Mack's nostrils as he felt his breath rebounding off the glove. With his other hand, the wolf-man brought his index finger to his lips.

"I would keep silent if I were you," he whispered.

11:32 p.m.

Amos rapped on the door aggressively four times. Once he caught sight of the white doorbell, he pressed it emphatically for good measure.

"Jesus, Al. You're going to wake the whole neighborhood."

Seconds later, a cacophony of voices speaking in Spanish rang out from behind the door. Being he wasn't the least bit bilingual, Amos couldn't understand a word of what was being said. However, the tone of most of the voices sounded angry and panicked. After a veritable eruption of frantic screaming, the door swung open. An overweight woman with dark, wrinkled skin and heavy eyebrows gazed up at them. She was extremely short and round and reminded Amos of a gopher.

"Yes?" the woman said, her word bogged down

by an exceedingly thick accent.

"Yes, hi. I'm Detective Albert Amos. This is my partner, Detective Hutchins. We're here to speak to Oscar. We just spoke with him on the phone and he said he would be waiting for us."

"Yes, okay," the woman replied. She beckoned them inside and stepped out of the way. As soon as they walked in, Amos felt claustrophobic. Five other people were stuffed into the small room: an old man sitting in a rocking chair, two young children who looked like brother and sister, a pretty woman sitting next to them on the couch, and a toddler standing precariously between the woman's knees.

"Hello," Amos said awkwardly, bowing his head like he was a monk. None of the people responded, although the pretty woman forced a smile in his direction. Amos briefly wondered if any of them could understand him. Without warning, the old woman who had let them in shouted at the top of her lungs.

"Oscar! *Ven Aca! Ahora!*"

Amos jumped. The house they were in was tiny; there was no need to be yelling that loudly. Perhaps the woman was hard of hearing and didn't realize how amplified her voice was.

From the open door that segued into the kitchen, Oscar Gutierrez came walking through, looking irritated. Once he saw Amos and Stevie standing in his living room, he raised his eyebrows and pursed his lips.

"Hello again, Mr. Gutierrez," Amos said. "Is there anywhere we can speak in private?"

Gutierrez grinded his teeth nervously. "I have seven people living in my house, so . . ."

"Maybe we can step outside?" Stevie offered.

Gutierrez pointed his chin at the door. "I don't care. Sure. Let's step outside."

Amos nodded and opened the door that led back out onto the front porch. "After you, Oscar."

Gutierrez stomped angrily between Amos and Stevie. Amos exchanged a nervous glance with his partner and followed Gutierrez out with her right behind him. Once he shut the door, Gutierrez rounded on them with fury.

"What is the meaning of all this? Coming to my house at almost midnight! What is wrong with you people?"

"We did call you and let you know we were coming, Oscar," Amos said pleasantly, looking into the man's eyes with thinly veiled malice.

Gutierrez threw his arms up in the air. "That doesn't matter! This is ridiculous. What could possibly be of such great importance that you two *pendejos* had to come here at eleven thirty at night?"

"We have a prime suspect in Luke Ledoux's murder," Amos replied amicably as though he were talking about his weekend plans.

Gutierrez looked nonplussed. His eyes went from Amos to Stevie and back to Amos with a look of sheer bamboozlement.

"Uh, okay? Great. I'm happy for you. You came here to tell me this?"

Amos smiled. "Correct."

Gutierrez frowned. "Well, who is it?"

"You."

For several long seconds, Gutierrez stared at Amos with the same bewildered expression on his face. Then, he suddenly looked quite pale.

"Me?"

"That's right. You."

"But what . . . I don't understand."

Amos watched the man in front of him intently, looking for a rehearsed reaction. But Gutierrez seemed genuinely frightened and confused.

"Earlier this evening a young man named Sean McVey was stabbed at a party a couple miles away from here. We believe his assailant was the same man who murdered Luke Ledoux and Devin Johnson, and the one who broke into Jamie Ledoux's basement." Amos made piercing eye contact with Gutierrez. "Not far from the scene, we apprehended a man named Tuck Parker, who wore regalia that we believe to be the signature ensemble donned by the killer, and brought him to the police station. After a bit of questioning, Parker said someone showed up at his house two nights ago and offered him five thousand dollars to wear a wolf mask and parade around the neighborhood in question for two hours. Parker said that man had a Mexican accent."

For a fleeting moment, Gutierrez still looked horrified. Then, his face twisted in absolute vehemence. His brows were high, his cheeks contorted and flushed, and his eyes were inundated with pure rage.

"Are you fucking *kidding* me? A Mexican accent? Do you know how many people in Newport are Mexican?"

"No idea," Amos murmured, totally ambivalent about the answer.

"Close to a thousand!"

"I see. And how many of those thousand people have access to Jamie Ledoux's house?"

Gutierrez opened his mouth for a moment, trying to find the words to respond, but he couldn't.

Amos moved in a little closer and lowered his voice by a decibel. "Listen, in situations like this, we look at two things: who has the motive for the crime, and who has the means. You're the only known person who knew about Jamie Ledoux's basement. Meaning you're the only one who had the *means* to set up the scene with the deer. And you're the only one we have interviewed with a direct connection to one of the victims, and you match the one description we have of our killer. We haven't worked out what your motive would be yet, but you sure as hell have the means. You keep cropping up, Oscar. Why? Tell me why that is."

"I would never hurt Luke. Or anybody," Gutierrez said and rubbed his forehead. His anger seemed to have morphed into anxiety.

Stevie looked at Gutierrez curiously. Amos couldn't quite make out the emotion in her expression. She squinted at him like she couldn't quite see him properly. "Can your family verify that you were home tonight?"

Gutierrez looked around, and in that moment, he reminded Amos of a skittish cat. His eyes focused on Stevie's feet and he scratched his temple as he responded.

"No. They can't. I just got home a half hour ago."

"Where were you?"

Gutierrez didn't reply. He simply looked at the ground, and if Amos wasn't mistaken, it looked like his eyes were welling up with tears.

"Where were you, Oscar?"

"I can't say," Gutierrez whispered.

Amos shook his head in exasperation. "Oscar, you do realize how that sounds, don't you?"

"It's not like that."

"What's it like?"

Gutierrez closed his eyes, as if doing so could

magically transport him away from Amos and Stevie's presence. Amos waited for an answer, but he didn't get one, so he continued to press. "Weigh your options here, Oscar. You're the number one suspect in a *murder* investigation. If you have an alibi you need to tell us what it is. Because right now you sound pretty damn guilty."

"I can't tell you without . . ." Gutierrez stopped midsentence and looked around, clearly conflicted.

"Without what?"

"Without getting myself and . . . others . . . into a lot of trouble."

"It can't be worse than murder, can it?"

"*Jesus!* I didn't kill anybody!"

"Then what were you doing?" Amos demanded, feeling a strong desire to poke Gutierrez in the chest. Suddenly, the man flapped his arms like a spasmodic bird.

"Fine! Fine."

Amos waited expectantly, but Gutierrez was drawing it out as long as possible.

"Yes?"

With a long sigh, Gutierrez finally let go. "Drugs," he said quietly.

This time, it was Amos's turn to be baffled into silence. He turned to look at Stevie as though she would be able to explain what Gutierrez had just said, but she looked dumbfounded as well. It seemed to be too dramatic of an admission to be a lie. But contraband was the last thing that would have come to his mind when thinking of Oscar Guiterrez. Though the man didn't particularly look like he could be a murderer, he looked even less like a drug user.

"You were doing drugs?"

"No, no, buying."

"You were *buying* drugs? What kind of drugs?"

"Blow," Gutierrez muttered.

Stevie's jaw dropped and her nostrils flared. "You were buying cocaine? What is a family man such as yourself doing buying cocaine?"

"Shhh!" Gutierrez hissed, looking over his shoulder at the door. "Look, I wasn't buying it for me. I know what you're going to say, that that's what everyone says, but it's the truth."

Amos shook his head in exasperation.

"It's true! Look, the coke we got here in town comes in through the port. Fishing boats, you know? But they won't sell to most Mexicans. They don't trust us. They only sell to their friends."

Amos didn't fully understand. "And?"

"And, I know a guy who works on a boat. I've done work on his house. So, that is who I get it from."

Amos shook his head. "I still am not quite following."

"He resells it," Stevie said suddenly. "To his buddies that the real dealers won't sell to. Is that what you're saying?"

Gutierrez gave a small nod. Amos again was surprised by what the man had just copped to.

"You do realize that selling drugs is more of a crime than using drugs, right?"

"Look, this is only the third time I have done this. It's money that I need. Look at my house! We have seven people living in here, I work six days a week, and we're still poor. I'm not like . . . a drug dealer. Like I say, I have only done it three times now. And I only sell to two people."

Amos observed Gutierrez, trying to see if the man was telling the truth. Selling drugs seemed like a strange thing to confess to if it wasn't true. And if Gutierrez was guilty, wouldn't he just try and play it off like he was innocent altogether? Would he be smart enough to concoct an alibi that made him look culpable of a lesser crime?

Amos's cogitation was interrupted by a startling sentence from Stevie.

"He's telling the truth."

Amos looked at her in disbelief. "Excuse me?"

"I believe him."

Gutierrez looked almost as shocked as Amos. He looked at Stevie as though she had just shown him a superpower.

"Really, I do believe you. This isn't a trick. I honestly do. I think what you have told us thus far is true. But I also believe there is something you're still not telling us." Stevie stepped closer to him. "I knew it the moment we got done interviewing you at the police station the other day. You're no killer. But you know something. Something about this case."

"What are you ta—"

"After a certain amount of time doing this job and interviewing so many people, you can begin to differentiate between truths. I've gotten good at it, Oscar," pressed Stevie, narrowing the distance between her and her respondent. "I can tell when someone is telling the whole story. But I can also tell when someone is only telling a partial truth. And I have been able to smell that on you since the minute you started talking."

"You just said you believed me!"

"I do. But I also believe you're holding out for some reason. And I want to figure out why."

Gutierrez retreated a little and his back hit the door.

"On a normal night, I would arrest you right here on the spot. No ifs, ands, or buts. You would've been in cuffs about ten seconds ago. But we happen to be chasing a killer tonight. What are the chances of that? You're one lucky-ass man, Oscar. And here's how this is going to work. You're going to tell me what you're withholding. Then, I'm going to tell the narc guys that I got a tip from somebody that there are drugs in this house.

They are going to come and search the place. However, it's going to slip my mind until tomorrow morning. What you choose to do with that time and any . . . *materials* you may possess . . . is up to you."

"And what if I'm not withholding anything?"

"Then you go to jail for possession and distribution this very moment and won't see your family until Christmas."

Gutierrez scratched his head, looking truly torn. But he was hesitating. He wasn't pleading with Stevie. That told Amos he did know more than he was letting on. Amos again waited for Gutierrez to say something, but he just continued to look off into space and scratch his head, appearing to have a full-scale internal debate.

Stevie seemed to stand a little straighter, and spoke with strength. "The thing is, Oscar, we're not going to wait around here much longer. We don't have the time. So, if you don't decide in the next thirty seconds, the cuffs are coming out."

Gutierrez stared at her, looking like he wanted to call her a nasty name.

"The clock's ticking, friend."

"You don't understand."

Amos responded so quickly to Guiterrez that it almost looked like it startled the man. "What don't we understand?"

"It's not that I don't want to. It's my safety I'm

worried about. My family's safety."

Amos's mind processed information at light speed. "Safety? What do you mean? Did someone threaten you?"

Gutierrez closed his eyes again, and in doing so, he revealed that Amos had gotten at the heart of the matter.

"Who threatened you, Oscar?"

Guiterrez craned his neck around the detectives, looking left and then right as if he expected someone to be lingering there. "I don't know who he was."

Amos looked over at Stevie, and she had a triumphant look on her face.

"Tell us what happened, Oscar," she said.

Gutierrez began to grind his teeth again, filing away the tension in his mouth.

"About a week ago, I was supposed to go over and check up on Jamie's house, right? I don't always clean, but every two weeks I go over and check on the house for him, to make sure everything is alright. Well, when I went over there, I saw somebody in a truck pulling out of the driveway right when I pulled up. I thought maybe Jamie had had someone come over for some reason. I thought it was strange, but I didn't do anything about it. Later that night I got a call from a blocked number. It was a warped voice. Sounded like the devil or something. He told me that if I told anyone about seeing him at Jamie's house that he would kill me and my whole family."

"Did you get a look at the man's face?"

"No. I just saw the truck."

"What color was it?"

"God, I don't know. Maroon, I guess? Maybe light brown?"

"Did you do anything after the man called and threatened you?"

"Well, I didn't really know what to do. I was scared you know?"

"Right." Stevie nodded.

Amos wiped away a bead of sweat over his eyebrow before he asked his next question. "Did you ever try going back to Jamie's house after that?"

"No."

"Do you know if there was anyone else around that day that might be able to identify this man?"

Gutierrez raised his palms slightly into the air. "Not off the top of my head. There are people that live around there, obviously. Neighbors. Right across the street there is a house full of kids. Like in their early twenties or so. I don't know if it's a fraternity or something, but every time I go over to Jamie's I see a bunch of them always going in and out."

"A fraternity? How could it be a fraternity? The closest university is an hour away."

"Oh, yeah . . . right. Well they're college-aged kids, at least."

"Okay. And what day was this again? Remind me."

"Last Tuesday. Two days before I came into the station."

"Got it."

Stevie had pulled out her phone and was typing on the screen. At first Amos thought she was sending a very ill-timed text, but then he realized she was manually recording the conversation. Apparently, her mobile device had to substitute for a notepad at the moment.

"Listen, guys, I'm really scared here, you know?" Gutierrez said. "I don't know why I had to get wrapped up in all this, but somehow I did. And he said he would come after my family if I talked to anyone. You kind of forced my hand here. What am I supposed to do now? What if he comes here?"

"He won't. We're going to catch him first."

"So do *you* believe he's telling the truth?" Stevie said it apprehensively, like she was scared that Amos would say no.

"Yeah, I do."

"So you think the real killer talked to Parker in

a fake accent to try and make us think that Oscar was the guy?"

"Guess so." Amos put the Ford Crown Victoria in drive.

"So the real guy paid Parker to strut around the neighborhood in the killer's regalia so that once we caught him, we would find out that the man who paid Parker had a Mexican accent? A Mexican accent not unlike Oscar Guiterrez's?"

"Sounds like it."

"I wonder if he was planning on putting Conner's body somewhere public tonight after he murdered him, hence the need for an immediate fall guy."

"Maybe."

"And he was hoping that we would buy that Gutierrez was our perp."

"Yep."

"But wouldn't he realize Oscar would tell us about what happened the other day at Jamie's house?"

Amos let Stevie's question hang in the air for a few seconds. He wasn't sure what to say.

"I don't know, partner. None of this makes any sense."

Stevie didn't reply. She drummed her fingers on her lap, rocking in the passenger seat. After a while, she seemed to think out loud.

"So what's next?"

"We're going to have to verify Oscar's alibi with his drug-purveying friend that he met earlier this evening. But that can wait until tomorrow."

Stevie nodded as she pulled her seat belt across her body. "Okay, so, now that you have stated what we *aren't* going to do, can you tell me what we're going to do?"

"You're going to have to call the officers stationed outside of Coby Conner's house and give them a heads-up about the situation, while I drive to Jamie Ledoux's house."

Stevie frowned with her mouth slightly agape. "You're going to try and find more witnesses who saw the man in the reddish-brown truck? At this time of night?"

"Gutierrez said that across the street there were college-aged kids. And it's Halloween night. I would be willing to bet a pretty penny that they aren't asleep quite yet."

11:37 p.m.

Coby pressed the front door open as quietly as he could, but it still creaked in protest. He sighed in irritation. He desperately didn't want to wake Mack. If his brother saw Coby's battered visage, he would ask him what happened, and once Coby had relayed the story about the wolf's multiple attacks, Mack may never sleep again. Especially after Coby had promised him that he would be downstairs the whole time.

Once Coby was inside, he shut the door and turned around to gaze through the peephole. Across the street, two police cars were parked against the sidewalk. Coby could make out the hulking figure of the muscular officer who had driven him home still sitting in the driver's seat. He was eating something and engaged in some sort of banter with his scrawnier partner who was reclining on the passenger side. Coby supposed he ought to feel safer with the armed men manning the proverbial battlements and the fact that the wolf had already been apprehended by the police. But as he whirled about and walked forward in the darkness, part of him still expected to see a sentient dark figure standing in his living room, waiting for him. Why would they assign the protective detail if the man had been caught? He shuddered as every shadow cast by the various bits of furniture looked like the outline of a wolf. Was this how it was going to be from now on? Even though the wolf was going to be behind bars, would he start to see him in the shadows everywhere he went?

Coby trudged up the stairs. His head felt like it could split in two at any moment from when the wolf had bounced his cranium off the pavement like it was a basketball. His memory of the attack in the street was hazy; perhaps it was a combination of emotional trauma and the fact he had received such a forceful blow to his head. Coby absentmindedly ran his fingers through his hair, and even the slight brushing of the follicles caused a prickle of pain to run through his body. Perhaps he should've gone to the hospital. But the cop that examined him said his pupils weren't dilated and his cognitive function wasn't impaired, the two telltale signs of a concussion. Even though he was concerned about his head, Coby kept trying to reassure himself that everything was fine.

After he checked in on Mack, he would try to contact his parents himself. The detectives had attempted to reach Dana and Andrew Conner from the station, but they had not answered. Officer Bosworth had said their phones had gone straight to voice mail, so they must have been in a place without service. His mother had warned Coby that the pair of them would spend part of the trip staying at a hotel off of Highway 60 in Orange County, and that reception there was spotty at best. Coby had no idea what hotel they were staying at, so he couldn't tell Bosworth to call the place directly. Of course, the night that Coby had experienced the most traumatic event in his life had to coincide with an evening that the two people he needed to reach the most were out of range.

As he approached Mack's room when he was upstairs, Coby noticed how cold it was on the second floor. The chill bit at his hands and tried its best to penetrate his hoodie. Coby couldn't figure out what had caused the dip in temperature. He knew he had left the heat on when he had departed for the party earlier, and the first floor had been pleasantly warm. As he crept closer to Mack's room, something in the most cavernous cavities of his brain told him something wasn't right. Something was awry; he felt it deep in his chest. Once he was within a foot of the door, Coby's stomach did a somersault. Approximately two inches of space sat between the edge of the door and the latch. But Coby remembered firmly shutting it when he had wished Mack good night.

With a forceful shove, Coby moved the door open, curled his arm around the bend to turn the light on, and charged into the room. Everything in the world came to an abrupt halt. It was like he was having a bizarre out-of-body experience or a vivid dream. Surely he couldn't be seeing what he thought he was. It wasn't possible. There couldn't be any way that he was staring at an empty bed, could there? All the blood in his body rushed to his outer extremities as if he were physiologically preparing for a fight.

"Mack!" Coby screeched. "Mack, where are you? Ma—"

His screams ceased as soon as he saw it. Laying on the pillow, a small piece of white paper leered up at him malevolently. Coby ran over to the side of the bed and snatched the note up. The first thing he saw was the familiar insignia: An X with a curved line underneath it, drawn in red. The same one that had been on the postcard that had been dropped through the mail slot earlier that evening. Underneath the dead smiley face were five sentences:

NO NEED TO FRET, THE BOY'S ALIVE. MEET WITH ME AND HE SURVIVES. SAVE THIS NOTE, NO WATCHFUL EYES. COPS OR TRICKS, THE YOUNG ONE DIES.

1600 ELM STREET, TOLEDO.

Coby felt a blast of wooziness hit him as he read the note. He felt like he was going to vomit, and his hands shook. "Mack," he whispered weakly, as if simply summoning his kid brother would somehow rescue him from the darkness.

He didn't understand. Wasn't the wolf in a cell at the police department? Did he have a partner? Or had the police apprehended the wrong individual? A thousand thoughts jostled for the top position in his consciousness as he reread the note. The wolf clearly had Mack at the address he had provided. Coby's stomach clenched as he wondered whether Mack was alive or already dead. The wolf was obviously trying to lure Coby out and take him as his prey. Coby had no way of knowing whether Mack was alive or not, and with another pang in his chest, he realized that the wolf probably had no use for keeping Mack alive.

Most of the other parts of the note were clear. *Save this note, no watchful eyes.* The wolf was trying to cover himself so that no unwanted visitors would show up and save the day. He had no choice but to obey the command. If Mack was still alive and the cops showed up to the address thanks to the note, the wolf would probably kill him and Coby. Therefore, Coby had to take it with him. He crumpled up the note and shoved it in the pocket of his hoodie.

Panic continued to course through him as he began to pace around the room. The fear ballooning in his chest begged him to charge out to the two officers sitting in their patrol car outside and plead for help, but he knew he couldn't. A vision of the wolf plunging his knife into Sean's shoulder flashed across Coby's mind. If he was willing to kill Sean, why wouldn't he be willing to kill Mack? Coby couldn't ask for anyone's help. He had to do it on his own.

How was he supposed to go out to the address without the officers seeing him depart? The old Honda in the driveway his mom drove was his only means of transportation. But he couldn't just hop into the driver's seat and peel out with the police staking him out right across the street. Coby had to create some sort of diversion. Something that would beckon the cops away from their current vantage point. Hysteria continued to cloud Coby's vision, but he tried to streamline all his thoughts into concocting some sort of clandestine plan to distract the two men across the street.

Suddenly, he had an idea. Without a second thought, he tore out of Mack's room to the hallway, clambering down the stairs. Once he was back on the first floor, he turned and darted toward his parents' room. The shotgun that he had wielded earlier in the night was still propped up against the closet where he had left it. He quickly grabbed the gun and cradled it in his arms, making an about-face and charging back down the hallway toward the living room. He momentarily forayed into the kitchen to his left and snatched the Honda keys that were resting inside an empty porcelain ashtray. Coby tucked the keys in his pocket and charged back into the living room. With adrenaline beating through him like an 808 drum, he walked briskly to the sliding glass door, unlatched it, and slid it open.

Once he was outside, the cold shredded through him like a riptide. He took three deep breaths, watching the steam that his breathing produced while he clicked the safety button to enable the weapon in his hands to fire. As he pointed the shotgun at the sky, he looked over at his neighbor's house. The Geracys would probably be scared shitless at the sound of gunfire. Part of him doubted the plan. Perhaps there was another way to cause a ruckus that wouldn't be so dramatic and dangerous. But then Coby thought of Mack, tied up and bawling, waiting for his older brother to come and rescue him. That was all he needed to persuade him to pull the trigger. With a massive boom that cracked like a whip against the night sky, the shotgun pumped a shot into the air. The kickback rocked Coby, and he almost lost his balance. It took him a moment to regain his footing, but once he did, he pulled the trigger once more. Another boom erupted out of the muzzle of the gun, and Coby's eyes went blurry from looking directly at the flash of the shot exploding into motion. Instantly, he set the shotgun down in the grass and sprinted back into his house.

It only took Coby five seconds to make his way to the front door. He pressed his eyes to the peephole and looked across the street. His heart leapt as he saw the brawny officer already out of the car, jogging toward the source of the disturbance with his thinner colleague right in his wake. The two cops disappeared from view, and Coby could hear the sound of feet slapping against pavement as the men traveled through the alley on the side of the house, making their way to the backyard. Coby knew he only had a few seconds. He opened the front door, sprinted down the driveway, and fumbled with the keys to the car. It took him several long, panicked moments to get into the vehicle, but he finally found himself in the driver's seat, and quietly shut the door. With one more deep breath, Coby turned the key in the ignition and put the car in reverse.

11:51 p.m.

The black house across the street thudded with the rambunctious tones of hip-hop music. The blinds were drawn, and Amos could see a hive of people clustered about inside the house. They all were wearing masks and other flamboyant garb and looked to be having a marvelous time. Amos found a small shred of amusement at the fact he was probably going to put a serious damper on their night.

Stevie had an impish look on her face. "Looks like fun."

Amos shook his head and turned toward the passenger seat to look at her.

"You can probably go inside and have a drink with them. You could pass as a college kid."

"And you could pass as a geriatric, you old fuck," Stevie replied quickly. Amos couldn't help cracking a smile, but he tried to suppress his laughter. He wanted to keep Stevie's demeanor calm and purposeful instead of bubbly and vivacious. Ebullience wasn't conducive for an interview with someone who might have laid eyes on a murderer.

"Come on. Let's go."

They both opened their doors to the Ford Crown Victoria in unison and marched across the street. When they were on the front porch, Amos hammered loudly on the door. Inside, the dull roar of laughter and the general buzz of a party seemed to decrease in volume. Eventually, a disheveled, skinny young man wearing a grass skirt and a coconut bra answered the door. His large eyes seemed to swell in diameter as he saw the two people standing in front of him.

"Aloha," Stevie said snidely, eyeing the man's ensemble.

"Who the fuck are you?" His voice was throaty and deep as he looked as them with disdain.

Stevie bobbed her head forward like a snake lashing out. "The fucking police."

The man froze and his face became ashen. "The cops?"

"Yes. That's what police means," replied Stevie.

The man backed up. "Look, man, we ain't doing nothing wrong here. All us are over twenty-one."

"As much as I doubt that, I could really care

less how old you all are. We aren't here to bust your balls. We just want to talk. Do you live here?"

"Nah, I don't live here."

"Then why did you answer the door?"

The man shrugged. "I don't know. I'm drunk."

Amos gave a side-glance at Stevie, and he saw the corners of her mouth twitch.

"Do you know who *does* live here?"

"Uh, yeah. Like four people. Avery, for one."

"Avery? What is the last name?"

"Arnold."

"And where is she?"

The Hawaiian bro's face transformed into a smile. "Avery is a dude."

Stevie stomped her foot impatiently and knifed her upturned palm through the air. "Can you go and *get* this dude for us?"

"Uh, sure."

He turned around and stumbled into the house. Stevie frowned as the kid's foot caught on the rug beneath him, causing him to nearly cascade onto the floor. He caught his balance at the last second and kept walking.

"Let's hope Avery Arnold isn't quite as inebriated as our friend here," Amos muttered.

Within a minute, a tall young man with tan skin and a straight nose appeared in the doorframe. He wasn't wearing a Halloween costume, just a dark green flannel and jeans.

"Are you Avery?"

"Yes I am. What is the problem, sir?"

It took all Amos's being not to sigh in exasperation. Just from the one sentence he had uttered, Arnold gave off the impression of the quintessential kiss-ass Amos frequently ran into while he was trying to get information out of subjects, as he was inflecting an unnecessary amount of politeness and decorum into his voice.

"You live here, correct?"

"I do, sir."

"Do you have a job?"

"Y-yes, sir. I work at Staples."

Amos didn't miss the slight slur in his voice. Maybe he was drunk after all and just better at hiding it than his Hawaiian counterpart.

"What is your work week like?"

Arnold raised his eyebrows. "Have I done something wrong, officer?"

Amos shook his head. "No. Not at all. I'm speaking to you as a possible witness."

"A witness? A witness to what?"

"What is your work week like?" Amos repeated.

"It's never the same. I get different days off every week."

"Ah. Okay. This might be difficult then."

"Why?"

"This really has nothing to do with you. It has

to do with the house across the street."

Arnold furrowed his brow and glanced over Amos's shoulder at the Ledouxs' house.

"Does this have to do with when all those cops and other people were over there? When they marked it off as a crime scene?"

"No. Well, yes, but it doesn't specifically pertain to that. Unless you saw somebody over there in the days preceding it that you think might have been involved."

"I don't even know what that was," Arnold said quickly.

"Right. Okay. Yeah. We probably would've ended up talking to you because we would've canvassed the neighborhood for potential witnesses anyway."

"Witnesses to what? I'm confused."

"There is a killer in Newport," Stevie said, stepping in. Both Arnold and Amos looked over at her in surprise.

"Uh, Stev—"

"We still haven't caught him. He led us on a pretty wild goose chase tonight, and we thought we got him, but we didn't. Last week he left a scene behind at that house." Stevie pointed emphatically across the street. "There wasn't a body, but he did leave behind some DNA from a previous victim."

Arnold dropped his mouth open at a loss for words.

"We're talking to you because we want to know if you saw anybody enter or exit that house in the past few weeks. No one lives in it, see? So, no one should be inside of it. Except for the Mexican caretaker."

Stevie's disposition had taken a turn. Her body language was terse and the hand motions that accompanied her speech were short and direct. She seemed to be exhausted and growing impatient.

"Wait . . . *What?*"

"I'm not going to say it all again. Just have you seen anybody enter or exit that house? That is all we need to know."

"Well, I-I . . . You said there was a Mexican caretaker, right?"

"Yes."

"Well, I have seen a Mexican guy going in there."

"When? When did you see this?"

"Like, months ago," Arnold replied, stroking his dark brown hair as he thought.

"Okay, how about in the last few weeks?"

"Besides the police?"

Amos knew Stevie was going to come back with a snarky, sarcastic retort so he quickly jumped in. Amos touched her arm as he spoke before she had a chance. "Yes, Avery. Besides the police."

"Hmm. I'm not sure."

"You're not sure?"

"No. I mean, it isn't something I have really been paying attention to."

Stevie sarcastically chuckled in annoyance. Amos looked at her out of the corner of his eye.

"So, as far as you know, there wasn't anybody that went into the house?"

"Besides the police that day and night, no."

Amos felt his chest sink in disappointment. "Okay. Is there anyone else here that could help—"

"Night?"

Amos and Arnold's heads turned simultaneously toward Stevie.

"What?" Amos asked.

Something had suddenly lit up in Stevie's eyes. "He said the police that were there that night."

"And?"

"And there weren't any police there that night. The forensics team and the rest of the squad had cleared out by that afternoon."

Amos turned slowly back to Arnold. "You saw a cop go inside the house that night?"

"Y-yeah," Arnold replied, slurring slightly again. "I guess I shouldn't say night. It was like five o'clock, I think. I saw a guy go under the tape and go inside the house. I thought he was a cop because he showed up not long after everybody else was there. And he was dressed nice."

Amos could hear the percussion of his own heartbeat inside his ears. "What did this man look

314

like?"

Arnold shrugged. "I don't know. Tall. A little dumpy."

"Dumpy?"

"Yeah, like chubby. Oh! He had a mustache. A big, curly mustache. And glasses."

Amos felt his stomach clench. A few rapid images darted through his mind and the face materialized. The face was talking, exhibiting bizarre, erratic behavior. Amos recalled the impatience. The abrupt changes in mood. The hostility. He looked at Stevie, trying to share his surprise with her, but she just had a frown on her face. There was no trace of shock or wonder. After all, she hadn't met the man in question. She would have no way of knowing that Arnold had just given an accurate physical description of Gordon Dodd, the high school principal.

12:02 a.m.

"You and Ted talked to him, right?"

"Yeah. Yesterday morning."

"Did he seem suspicious?"

Amos froze, trying to recall the conversation he had with Dodd less than twenty-four hours ago. While he was thinking, he absentmindedly clicked his seat belt into place and turned the key in the ignition, firing up the car.

"He almost seemed bipolar. He would go from speaking in a normal tone to absolutely furious at the drop of a hat."

"What did he say about the whole thing? You told him about the case, right?"

"Yeah, we told him about Ledoux and Johnson. He didn't try and downplay that part, but he was really adamant that he wasn't going to warn his students about the threat."

Stevie's jaw twisted as she thought. "I wonder why that would be."

"I can't think of a logical reason. It was very very odd. There doesn't seem to be any logical reason for him trespassing onto a roped-off crime scene either. That's a smoking gun. If he's the guy, maybe he didn't warn his students because he didn't want Coby Conner's guard to be up."

"Ugh. I hope it isn't him."

"Why do you hope that?"

"Because of how screwed up it would be! The high school would be a game preserve of possible victims for him! He would be able to essentially shadow and prey on his intended victim for weeks."

"Hmm. Yeah, I see your point."

The car lurched forward and Stevie fell back into her seat a little as the Ford Crown Victoria zipped along.

"What next? Should we go try and speak with Dodd tomorrow?"

Amos gave Stevie an incredulous glance.

"Tomorrow? Why should we wait until tomorrow?"

"It's midnight."

"And if he's the guy, his entire plan revolved around abducting Coby Conner *tonight*."

"Coby has a protective detail at his house—"

"And if Dodd isn't at *his* house, then we need to alert that detail of the situation."

Stevie frowned. "So we're going to go over to Dodd's house and see if he's there?"

"That's the first step, yes."

"And what if he is?"

Before Amos could reply, his phone started vibrating in his pocket. He pulled it out and saw that Dozer was calling him.

"It's Dozer." Amos glanced over at Stevie ominously. With one hand still on the steering wheel, Amos unlocked his phone and answered the call.

"What's up, boss?"

"We got a problem."

Amos felt his stomach sink. "What is it?"

Dozer was breathing heavily and there was rustling in the background as if he were walking while speaking. "Coby Conner is no longer at his house."

"What?"

"Fifteen minutes ago, Officer Bosch and

Dunmire heard two gunshots come from the Conners' backyard. When they went to check it out, they found a Mossberg twelve-gauge double-barreled shotgun discarded in the grass. By the time they figured it out and went back around to the front of the house, the car that had been in the driveway was no longer there."

Amos's mind whirled and clicked at the new information. He subconsciously slowed the speed of the Ford Crown Victoria as if it would help him process the information better.

"So Coby fired the gun as a diversion so he could leave?"

"That's what we believe," Dozer replied, panting.

"Any idea where he might be headed?"

"No, but there is something else. Coby's younger brother, Mack, was supposed to be asleep in bed inside the house. But he isn't there either."

Amos felt his diaphragm clench in shock. "So Coby took Mack with him wherever they are going?"

"I don't know, Albert. I really don't know. Point is, we need everybody out looking for him. You included, since this is your case."

"What is the vehicle he's driving?"

"A white, late-model Honda CR-V. Plate GSF-617."

"Has anybody seen it?"

"Not yet." Dozer inhaled deeply.

"Jesus. Okay. We will start looking."

Amos waited for a response from Dozer, but none came. He pulled the phone away from his ear and looked down and saw that the call had already ended.

"What was that about?" Stevie looked distraught. Amos had a bit of difficulty tucking his phone in his pocket, and there were so many wild thoughts shooting through his brain that it was strenuous to string together coherent sentences while also focusing on the road. However, when he had finally relayed the information to her from Dozer, she became even more distressed.

"Where do you think he went?"

"I have no idea. But if he was desperate enough to fire a shotgun in the backyard to distract the officers out front, then something is seriously wrong."

Stevie's skin turned ashen as if she had come to a startling conclusion.

"What is it?" He said it softly because he was almost afraid to hear the answer.

"What if our guy kidnapped the little brother?"

Amos puckered his lips as he turned down Bates Way. His stomach rumbled uncomfortably and his fingers tingled.

"Even if that's true, that still wouldn't explain where Coby is going."

"Maybe the killer left a message with the brother's location to try and lure Coby out."

Amos pondered this for a moment, scratching his temple with his right hand while his left remained on the steering wheel.

"A message that our guys weren't able to decipher?"

Stevie shook her head vigorously. "I'm assuming if he was trying to bring Coby to a hidden location, he would probably tell him to take the message with him."

"Hmm, maybe."

"Wait, where are you going?"

Stevie looked at the road as if she had just found herself somewhere unexpected.

"To the station."

Stevie's eyebrows shot up to her hairline. "Why?"

"I'm dropping you off so you can get your own vehicle."

Stevie started stammering in response. "My own—what? Why? I don't—we're splitting up?"

"Yes. I'm sorry. I just need some space. It's not you, it's me."

"Oh, shut up. That isn't even funny!" Stevie spat. "Seriously, why are we splitting up? Where are you going?"

"*You're* going to try and find Coby Conner. Dozer's orders. I'm going to Dodd's house."

Stevie made a sarcastic, mocking face. "Oh yeah? Dozer specifically asked *me* to go find Coby? He called you, you schmuck. He wants us to go together."

Amos sighed as they came to a stop sign, and he glanced over again at his partner. She was looking at him defiantly.

"Listen, Stevie. I'm telling you, this is important. One of us needs to go to Dodd's house right now. I know it in my gut."

"Then send me! You're the lead on this case, and Coby is the primary vic. Or, he will be if someone doesn't find him. Don't you think it's more important for you to go after him?"

"I'm not sending you by yourself to Dodd's house."

"I can handle—"

"Damn it, Stevie, I know! I know! Stop arguing! We're wasting our time here!" Amos shouted as he pulled into the parking lot behind the police station.

"I just—"

"Just *go!*"

With an exasperated shake of her head, Stevie released her seatbelt, opened the passenger door, and got out of the car. Instead of walking away like Amos expected, she leaned back into the vehicle.

"Any clever ideas as to where I should look?"

"Start around his neighborhood and then make

your way toward the highway."

"Jesus," Stevie muttered. "Thank you for that insight."

She made a move to slam the door, but then leaned in quickly one more time. "I get that you're trying to protect me, but make sure to protect yourself. Just be careful, you idiot."

The door slammed shut, and Stevie stormed off toward her own company-issued vehicle. Amos exhaled after he realized that he had been holding his breath. Her brashness and irreverence were usually endearing, but in times of stress, they became difficult to manage. Amos put the car in reverse and searched for Dodd's address on the mobile data terminal that was in between the two front seats.

12:12 a.m.

Gordon Dodd's house was atop a steep, unpaved driveway that rested above the Agate Beach Wayside. The house itself was menacing; it was black with small windows and had three stories that stretched into the sky. From Amos's vantage point at the bottom of the driveway, it reminded him of a castle, towering above sea level, cold and unwelcoming.

Amos silently shut the door to the Ford Crown Victoria with a *click*. Even though he knew he would be knocking on Dodd's door, for some reason he didn't want to announce his presence sooner than he had to. His thighs burned as he climbed the sloping driveway, and as he scanned the black house, his stomach felt uneasy. Amos wasn't sure why, but it was almost as if some otherworldly force was warning him of impending danger. As his eyes passed over the small window on the topmost level of the house, he wondered if he was being watched at that very moment. There weren't any lights on inside the house, but Amos wasn't convinced that someone inside hadn't already noticed him approaching.

The top of the gravel driveway ended at a deck that looked like it was on the verge of collapse. It was covered in a layer of moisture and had weeds protruding from the cracks in the wood. The rest of the house was somewhat dilapidated as well, with loose shingles on the roof and rust on the front door. It was a little strange. Amos knew almost nothing about Gordon Dodd. Married. No kids. Apparently unfaithful. But he held an administrative job at a school, so it was surprising to see his house in such a sorry condition.

As Amos prowled up the steps, he heard a distinct creaking as the wood complained about his weight. Once he had scaled the miniature staircase and was on top of the deck, he noticed something unsettling: the front door wasn't all the way shut. A small sliver of darkness from the room beyond ogled at him. Unconsciously, Amos put his hand on his gun in the holster attached to his belt.

Biting his lip, Amos knocked on the door four times. As soon as he did, his heart fluttered in anticipation.

"Mr. Dodd? Are you there? Newport Police Department," Amos called loudly, even though the paranoia festering in his chest begged him to remain silent. There was no answer. Amos took a deep breath, trying to summon courage.

"Mr. Dodd? Open up, Newport Police Department," Amos called again, pounding on the door once more. His knocks unintentionally became more forceful, and the sliver of darkness between the door and the frame increased in size. After ten more seconds of penetrating silence, Amos threw caution to the wind, and gently pushed the door all the way ajar.

The first thing Amos saw was his own shadow against the opposing wall. He looked back out toward the night sky and saw the crescent moon casting light down on the neighborhood. Usually, moonlight was something Amos found pleasant and invigorating. However, tonight it felt much more eerie. With a deep breath, he crossed the threshold into the house.

Before he could get more than two steps onto the wooden floor, a tiny shape bolted across Amos's feet, skittering across the wood and darting out of the doorframe. Amos's chest constricted, but as he whirled about and laid eyes upon the small creature, his tension eased. A black cat trotted across the gravel.

"Jesus. You scared the shit out of me, friend."

The cat stopped in the grass and looked at Amos with its wide green eyes flashing in the darkness. With a nervous wag of its tail, the feline broke out into another run and slipped into the bushes that lined the driveway. Amos felt a stab of guilt as he watched the creature's tail slither through the leaves. Although it might be an outdoor cat, it likely had a curfew he had just unintentionally broken. *Oh well. He'll survive,* he thought. Amos turned his head back around.

"Mr. Dodd? Newport Police," Amos called again, but this time his voice was softer. It was almost as if he didn't want there to be a reply. Sure enough, his wish was granted. For a second, he stood in the silence staring at the shadow his body cast across the threshold. The dim moonlight from outside caused his outline to be rough and splotchy against the floor. From his current vantage point, he saw nothing else in the house, only the opposing wall.

As soon as he took one more step, a repugnant smell blasted into his nostrils. Amos tried to suppress the cough that gushed from his diaphragm, but he couldn't. The odor was too strong. He knew it instantly; it was the horrible scent of rotting human flesh. It was like wet garbage that was laced with the faintest hint of sweetness, as though someone had tried to mask rotting organic material with a puff of perfume. Amos held his breath and removed the gun from his holster. He wanted to use a flashlight as well, but he needed both hands on the gun for a steadier shot, so he simply stared into the opaque void in front of him, using the moonlight creeping in through the window as his guide.

There was a staircase ahead in the darkness, but Amos could tell that something downstairs was emitting the stench, because it seemed to be getting stronger as he moved further along away from the stairs. Along the wall next to the staircase, there was a series of framed photographs. Amos recognized Gordon Dodd in most of them, but there was also a woman Amos didn't know in the majority of them, probably Dodd's wife. Amos tiptoed across what he assumed was a living room, although it was hard to tell in the dark, and made his way down a narrow hallway. His hands shook as he held his gun at his ready, and Amos secretly hoped he wouldn't have to fire a shot. His accuracy would be completely null and void at the moment. With each step, the appalling smell grew greater in strength, and he knew he was almost there. To the left, there was an archway, and Amos thought he could see the faintest flicker of light gleaming through. He took one final beat to gather himself and ripped around the corner in a flash, brandishing his gun with as much steadiness as he could muster.

Amos's finger twitched, coming within a fraction of pulling the trigger as he saw the outline of a person sitting at the end of the dining room table that took up most of the room. But it was good he didn't, because it took him one second longer to realize that the person wasn't moving. And it wasn't Gordon Dodd. It was a woman. Or what had been a woman at one point in time. Five candles sitting on the table illuminated her lifeless face, and Amos focused on the image he knew would invade his dreams for years to come: instead of pupils, there were empty sockets, hollow and dark. The eyeballs had been scooped out clean. The woman's flesh was gray and drooped off her body so much that it looked like her skin was about to fall off, and the way her frizzy black hair curtained the flesh reminded Amos of the little girl from *The Exorcist*. Both her upper and bottom lips had gone the same way as her eyes, cut off and disposed somewhere where no one would find them. It was a blood-curdling effect; her mouth looked like it was ready for a dentist's X-ray. But the worst part was the mutilation that had been done to her jaw. Someone had taken a knife and slashed all the way up to her ears on both sides of her face. And now Amos realized what it was supposed to be: the killer's insignia come to life. That horizontal X with a curved line underneath.

Around the maimed mouth, there were still traces of blood. Oddly enough, Amos hadn't felt nauseous until he gazed upon the blood. Once he saw the crimson, the stomach acid began rising in his throat. He turned and charged down the hallway, frantically sprinting toward the exit, but vomit had already begun to leak out of his mouth. It dribbled along the wood floor, creating a trail as he ran. Thankfully, he managed to make it back out onto the front porch before the real eruption came, blowing out the contents of his stomach all over the Dodds' front lawn. His stomach seized over and over, to the point Amos wondered if he would ever not be vomiting again. As he continued to retch, Amos's eyes flickered up, and he saw the green pupils of the black cat that had been so eager to get out of the house gleaming at him from the bushes. It stared intensely, watching him lose his stomach contents over the lawn. And somehow, someway, it seemed to understand.

12:15 a.m.

Coby came within two feet of careening off the road as he rounded a gravelly corner. "Jesus Christ!" he screamed in panicked frustration. A mid-sized SUV wasn't suitable for going high speeds around sharp corners, but he couldn't slow down. He wouldn't slow down.

An automated female voice spoke to him from the GPS on the dashboard.

"In three hundred feet, keep left on Amber Alley." The voice, whom the GPS said was called Linda, put a weird inflection on the word *alley*. Coby wanted to smash his fist against it over and over until it no longer had a stupid automated voice that enunciated words incorrectly. In fact, he wanted to bash his fist into literally every inanimate object he could find. Every time he thought of Mack, helpless and in the arms of a predator, he would literally let out a shout of utter torture. This was his fault. He never should have left Mack alone. It had been his need to see Cassandra. His absolute infatuation had superseded everything else, including common sense. After all of the warning signs, he had *still* left for the party. He had still left to see her. And now he had paid the ultimate price. If something happened to Mack, it was one hundred percent on him. Coby didn't think he would be able to live with himself.

So far, the most ominous moment of the commute over to Toledo had been when Coby had sped past a mid-sized sedan poking its front end out of a side street. It was dark and there were no street lights illuminating the side of the road, but he was ninety percent positive the vehicle he had passed was a police officer on patrol. Yet, he never saw any flashing lights in his rearview. Or Coby had sped so fast he didn't notice them. Maybe he had unwittingly won a high-speed car chase.

Coby's heart was rattling like a small metallic orb trapped in a pinball machine. According to Linda, he was only one hundred feet away from his destination. Should he slow down? Surely the sound of a two-ton vehicle spitting gravel in every direction would give away the element of surprise. But could he use said element? The wolf had promised Mack would die if any "tricks" were attempted. He had to just hope the man was true to his word and would let Mack go.

Amber Alley was the narrowest road Coby had ever driven on. The trees on either side of the road were reaching out their greedy branches, hoping to envelope him in their wind-driven frenzy. Ahead, there was a fork in the road. Linda had said to stay on Amber Alley, but there wasn't a street sign that indicated which of the paths *was* Amber Alley. Oh well. Fifty-fifty shot. And as he chose the road on the right, something in the back of his mind told him this was indeed the correct track. Or at least the one he sought.

The road climbed upward, until it was steep. Coby slowed his pace a bit, easing off the gas pedal. He rounded a corner, and then two more. This road was like a geographically generated roller-coaster. Finally, after one more curve, the trees began to part. The CR-V shoved its way through the darkness, and Coby found himself in a massive clearing.

Thirty feet ahead, a gargantuan industrial building sat against the far edge of the trees. There was only one entrance to the building: a derelict, corroded door with a handle on the verge of falling off. Coby slowed his pace considerably, creeping the vehicle forward and eventually coming to a halt. There was still a considerable distance to the door to the building, but Coby didn't want to risk getting too close in case the killer's obliviousness to his presence remained. He quickly flipped off the headlights to the CR-V and stuffed the keys inside his pocket before opening the door and ducking out of the car.

Within five seconds, he was drenched. The rain was falling so hard that the droplets almost hurt. Coby burst into a full sprint, partly because adrenaline coursed through him, but he also wanted to get out of the rain. He ran so fast he nearly crashed into the door, but was able to stop his momentum just in time. Coby went to pull on the handle, but then noticed a flash of yellow drooping sadly on either side of the frame. He collected the material into his hands and read the bold black writing along the tape: POLICE LINE DO NOT CROSS.

Coby's heart jumped into his throat and his chest seized in fear. Were the cops already here? If so, would that mean Mack was already dead? But then, if they were here, why would the tape be broken? There definitely weren't any police vehicles in sight. Perhaps this was just a recent crime scene. Had the wolf killed someone else inside?

Coby let the tape go and took a deep breath. There was no time to dawdle and debate. He must go forward. It took a substantial amount of strength to pull the heavy door open, and he slipped through the opening before he could have any more second thoughts.

Inside, it was almost pitch-black. The only light that shone in the huge space in front of him was coming from at least fifty feet away. There was nothing else in the gigantic room, just whatever was emitting the illumination across the way. Coby tiptoed along, trying to make his eyes see what they couldn't. If there was ever a time to evolve into some transhuman, nocturnal species, now was it. It was so dark that it would be challenging to even notice movement. Yet, he looked around, trying to gobble up any indication of an outline of a human torso, or the glint of a knife in the darkness. There was nothing of the sort. Just the faint gleaming from the other side of the building.

Coby came closer and closer, and as his vision adjusted, he froze. They were faces. Faces shining in the black. But not actual faces. Petrified expressions leering in the darkness. Jack-o'-lanterns. *What on earth,* thought Coby.

His gait accelerated, and finally, he was directly in front of the pumpkins. There were four of them, and they appeared to offer a progression of emotions of sorts. The one on the far left was carved so it appeared to be frowning, with two spacious circles for eyes and a bent gap that looked like an upside-down rind of a watermelon. The second pumpkin was more stoic, with the same cavities for eyes, but instead of an expressive mouth, it had a straight-line chunk taken out of it to indicate ambivalence. The third one was smiling. And inside its mouth, it had jagged teeth. Teeth that looked demonic. Finally, there was the fourth one. Coby knew what it would be before he saw it. Sure enough, there were two large chunks cut out diagonally to form an X and a curved fissure underneath it forming a wild smile. The wolf's insignia. Coby stared at it for a long time. It was chilling but also completely absorbing. He couldn't take his eyes off it. If he had, he might have noticed the large figure gliding up behind him like a specter. But he didn't and thus, the knife was pressed firmly against his throat before he even knew what was happening.

"If you try and fight back I will hang you by your own intestines while your brother watches," the voice growled.

Coby's whole body felt heavier than lead. But, there was still a small leap in his stomach. *He's still alive!* That was the last thought he had before he felt the cold pinch on the side of his neck. In a matter of seconds, Coby Conner saw no more.

12:20 a.m.

Amos sat on the curb, breathing heavily. The world around him spun, and not metaphorically either; he was literally dizzy from the unsteadiness. In the distance, he heard the faint moaning of sirens. His cell phone sat next to his feet, still unlocked. As soon as he had finished talking to dispatch, his grip had melted away and the black iPhone had fallen to the ground. Since that moment, Amos had sat rocking back and forth on the curb, waiting for his colleagues to arrive. Occasionally, he would look up and see those same green eyes gleaming at him from under the bushes. But this time, when he looked back at the cat, it was gone. Perhaps the impending whine of sirens has scared it away.

The screech of tires against pavement cracked against Amos's eardrums. With an enormous amount of strain, Amos looked up and saw two cop cars speeding down the street toward him. Both came to a halt no more than ten feet away. Bosworth hopped out of the Chevy Tahoe, and

Lawrence Bonner crawled out of the passenger seat, his red hair rippling in the wind.

"Albert! Albert! Are you okay?"

Amos gave a brief bob of his head and swallowed to clear his throat. "Yeah. Yeah, I'll be alright."

"You called in a 12-49 A?"

Amos nodded again. "Yeah. She's inside. I think it's Gordon Dodd's wife."

Bonner placed both hands on his head. "Jesus Christ! Deidre?"

Amos looked up at Bonner. "You know her?"

"Yeah, she's a . . . family friend. Jesus. Are you sure it was her?"

"No. I mean, I don't know her. But there are pictures of Gordon Dodd and a woman hanging up in there, and that woman looks remarkably like the dead one in the kitchen. At least, I think she does. It's kind of hard to tell."

Bosworth looked down at Amos and snarled like he smelt something truly repellant. "Jesus . . . is it that bad?"

Amos felt his stomach grumble again, and for a moment, he thought he could still be sick. But it passed.

"Yeah. It's bad."

"Are you sure you're okay, Albert?"

Amos shook his head. "Well no, I'm not. I got sick over there on the lawn. But they don't pay me to be okay."

"Jesus, *Deidre!*" Bonner exclaimed again. "I hope you're wrong."

Amos just shrugged. "Hope so too. But somebody is still all carved up in there."

"You stay here, Albert," Bosworth said as though Amos was a small child. "Lawrence, let's go."

Bosworth walked briskly past him, and after hesitating, Bonner started to move in the same direction. Amos held out his hand to stop him.

"Wait. Hold on a sec. Maybe . . . If she was your friend. Perhaps you should stay out here."

Bonner looked down at him with panic in his eyes. He held still for a moment, and then took off in Bosworth's tracks.

Sirens continued to move through the night as more officers were on their way. A rattling on the ground drew Amos's attention away from Bonner, who had ducked into Dodd's house. His phone was vibrating against the pavement. From the screen, he could tell it was Stevie calling him. Amos reached down with quivering fingers and latched onto the shaking device. It was like doing a bicep curl to get the phone up to his ear.

"Stevie?"

"I told you we shouldn't have split up!"

Amos rubbed his fingers against his brow, trying to ease away some of the tension in his forehead. "I take it you heard then."

"I heard the dispatch a couple of minutes ago. Who was it?"

"Deidre Dodd. Gordon Dodd's wife. At least, I think."

"Jesus fuck. Was it bad?"

Amos swallowed thickly. "It wasn't good."

"Well, we definitely have a prime suspect now, don't we?"

"Yeah. Wait . . . How did you know that I was the one who called it in?"

"I just got off the phone with Dozer. He was trying to get ahold of you *because* you called it in. He thought we were still together."

"Why didn't he just call me?"

"He did! You didn't answer."

"Really? Well, I have to say, I'm not in the best state of mind at the moment. Are you on your way here now?"

There were a couple of beats of silence before Stevie replied. "No, I'm not. I'm on my way to Toledo."

Amos looked at the phone as though it had had some sort of technical error. Surely, he couldn't have heard her right. "Toledo?"

"Yes."

"Why are you going there?"

"Because that's where Coby Conner is going. And that's where our killer is."

Amos felt a thousand goose bumps rise on his arms.

"Why do you think that?"

Stevie started speaking faster and she sounded a bit like an auctioneer. "Because Dozer just told me Officer Hicks saw a white CR-V speeding past him on Highway 20 near mile marker forty-two. He said it matched the description of the one that just left Conner's house twenty minutes ago. He tried to follow in pursuit, but the kid evaded him."

"So why do you think he's in Toledo?"

Stevie made a clicking noise of impatience. "Think about it, Albert! If our guy has his brother and is trying to lure him out to a secluded spot, where do you think he might go? Where is a place where we know he has gone before where there is no danger of running into any resistance? A place that everybody left just a few hours ago thinking it was a diversion?"

Amos closed his eyes. *Of course.*

"Don't call it in."

"Huh?"

"Don't call it in."

Stevie made another strange noise. "What? Why? You think I'm wrong?"

"No, I think you're unequivocally right. But our guy either has some sort of police scanner or someone feeding him information, because he has been one step ahead of us this whole time. I don't want him to know we're coming."

"So you're going to leave the scene? Dozer won't like that."

Amos shrugged, even though he knew she couldn't see the gesture. "Oh well. This has to end, Stevie."

"Should we bring anybody else?"

Amos mulled it over for a few moments before coming to a decision.

"Yes. I'll call Ted."

"Okay. Yeah, that works. Three of us should be able to take him down, yeah?"

"I sure as heck hope so. Are you on the road right now?" Amos could tell from the sounds of wind gusting by that she was indeed behind the wheel.

"Yes. I'm still about ten minutes out."

"Okay. Okay . . . Alright, Stevie, listen to me. When you get there, stop before you get to the clearing and turn your headlights off. Wait for me and Teddy to get there, okay?"

Surprisingly, Stevie let out a bit of a chuckle, but didn't reply.

"I'm serious, Stevie. Don't go in that building until I get there."

Still no reply.

"Stevie?"

"Alright! Alright. I'll wait for you. Jesus."

"Don't be a hero. You hear me, Stevie

Hutchins? I ain't got no use for a dead hero."

Stevie laughed again. "Fine, Albert. I will wait."

It took Amos longer than it should've to connect his phone to the Bluetooth back in his car and dial Ted's number. His fingers still shook as the phone began to ring. He tried to steady them by taking a firm grip on the steering wheel. Five more police vehicles zoomed by; Amos wondered if any of them thought it was curious that an NPD-issued vehicle was *leaving* the scene. He didn't wave toward any of them. Calling attention to himself wasn't the best idea.

Ted answered the phone after four rings and sounded out of breath. "H-hello?"

"Teddy, where are you?"

There was some rustling from Ted's end of the line. "I'm six blocks away from the 12-49 that was just called in. Where are you?"

"Just leaving the 12-49 that was called in. And I was the one who called it in."

"Whoa! You found a body?"

"Yes."

"Who was it?"

"We believe it was Gordon Dodd's wife. It was

their house we found her at."

There was a long bout of silence as Ted seemed to be gathering his thoughts.

"Gordon Dodd . . . the guy we just talked to this morning? His *wife*? What were you doing at his house?"

"We got a tip he was seen breaking into Jamie Ledoux's house the day we found the deer. Our witness saw him later that evening."

"Oh my *God*."

"Yeah."

"Who was the witness?"

"Well, there are sort of two: Oscar Gutierrez and a kid named Avery Arnold. We ended up circling back to Gutierrez because . . . well, I'll explain the whole story in a bit."

"Jesus. Sounds like you've had a heck of a night."

"You could say that."

"So is Dodd . . . the *guy*?"

Amos again shrugged pointlessly. "The signs seem to be pointing that way, yes."

"Jesus. And we just talked to him this morning. Wait! Why are you leaving the scene?"

"That is why I'm calling you, Teddy. I think I know where our guy is."

Another long pause.

"You do?"

"Yes. And I want you to meet me there."

"Where do you think he is? And why don't you call it in?"

Amos sped up, and as he took a turn toward Highway 101, three more police cars with their lights flashing passed by. "The old industrial building in Toledo. Hicks saw Conner on milepost 42 going east on 20. Call it an educated guess, but I firmly believe that's where our perp is. As for why I didn't call it in, think it through. This guy has been ahead of us this whole time. He knows exactly what we're doing and when we do it. If I call it in, there's a good chance he'll know we're coming."

Again Ted took a while to reply. "Hmm. I don't know, Albert."

"Just trust me on this one, Teddy. It's the way our guy thinks. It's . . . homicidal poeticism in a way. He likes to be one step ahead of us at all times. It would be so fitting to do the final deed at the place he used to divert our attention away from Coby in the first place. He knows how much it would infuriate us to realize we had just been at the scene of the crime three hours before. That we were *that* close to catching him."

"I don't know, Albert," Teddy repeated. "That is assuming a lot. And what if you're wrong?"

"What if I am? Deidre Dodd isn't going anywhere. And nobody else seems to have any clue where Coby is. If we get there and there is nothing, then we will just turn around and come back."

Ted sighed a long exhale. Amos was certain he was going to say no.

"Fine. Fine. I will turn around."

"Thanks, Ted. Thanks. I think Stevie will feel more comfortable with you coming too."

"Stevie's coming?"

Amos thought he could hear a trace of annoyance in Ted's voice. "Yep. She's my partner, Teddy. Remember that."

"I know, I know. Is she with you now?"

"No. She's going to get there before me."

"Roger that. I might get there before you too. Is she going to wait for us?"

"Yeah." Amos didn't vocalize the other thought he had. *At least she said she was.*

"Okay. Okay. What was the address again?"

"1600 Elm Street."

"Got it. I'll be there in fifteen minutes."

"Okay. See you there."

Amos hit the END button on his cell phone, and as he did so, a drop of rain fell on his head. He looked up at the sky, seeing the black clouds signaling the impending storm. Right then, a whole river of nervous feelings washed through him. He was almost certain he, Ted, and Stevie were on the right track. But somehow, someway, it felt like the killer would still be one step ahead of them.

12:27 a.m.

As Amos twisted around the many curves of Highway 20 in the Ford Crown Victoria, the rain cascaded down at an alarming rate. It seemed like the farther east he went, the harder it fell. It was like that with most weather patterns along the coast; the farther away from the beach you got, the less temperate the conditions became. In the summer, it was always about ten degrees hotter when you got out to Toledo, and in the winter, it was frequently ten degrees cooler. Amos mused on the rain and how it obstructed his vision. His windshield wipers were turned to their highest frequency, and they still couldn't manage to brush all the water off the car. It made it so that he had to go quite a bit slower than his racing heart was urging him to go. Someone behind him in a Nissan Altima was getting uncomfortably close to his rear bumper; apparently, safety wasn't of the upmost importance to the cars' pilot. Amos had half a thought to pull over to the side of the road and let the man pass, but there wasn't any time to waste. Coby Conner could be on the verge of suffering the same fate as Deidre Dodd at this very moment.

It was almost unfathomable a person could be capable of performing such mutilation on someone else, especially someone that said person had loved at one point in time. But perhaps Gordon had been especially gruesome *because* of love. Didn't Ted say Dodd had been cheating on his wife? Was it possible he had become so dissatisfied with his wife that it wasn't enough to sleep with another woman, but he also had to take her life? She didn't fit the profile of the normal victim: a teenage boy or young man. Maybe Dodd lumped her in with the rest of his victims because he just wanted to get rid of her.

No, that didn't make sense at all. If he just wanted to be rid of Deidre, why would he take the time to concoct such an elaborate scene? And surely the killer hadn't murdered the woman *before* hacking away at her cheeks and eyes; he had to have done it while she was still breathing. The killer's particular brand of cruelty was not one to let any of his victims pass painlessly. Deidre had to have been tortured. And that sort of sadistic scheme didn't fit for someone he was trying to quickly dispose of. For that matter, why would Dodd dispose of his wife at all? Surely it would be a dead giveaway to the police that he was their man, and for a killer that thrived in living in the shadows and eluding all signs of suspicion, was it likely he would murder someone he was so closely tied to?

There was a piece of the puzzle that was missing. Someone had paid Tuck Parker to wear the wolf mask and strut around the neighborhood from which Coby Conner was supposed to be abducted. And that person had faked a Mexican accent while talking to Parker, to point Amos and his colleagues in the direction of Oscar Gutierrez, who had seen the real killer leaving in a truck. It seemed apparent now from the drunk college kid's testimony the killer had been hoping Gutierrez would watch someone leaving the house. And the person who was leaving the house was Gordon Dodd. So Dodd wanted Gutierrez to point the police toward . . . himself?

It had felt like someone had been orchestrating this whole act from behind the scenes. Like some demon in the shadows was pulling all the strings, and knew Amos's every move before he made it. Could it be possible this antagonist actually *did* know his every move, because he was literally beside him the whole time? Could the killer be . . . police?

Amos had only thought Tuck Parker was guilty for a short period. But maybe he would've kept him in custody if someone else hadn't jumped in and told him Parker wasn't the guy. After all, it was hard to discount a man wearing the same mask that Sean McVey had seen on the face of the person who had stabbed him, and in the very neighborhood where he had been stabbed, no less. In any other instance, it would've been a slam dunk. And yet, it hadn't been. Someone had gotten Amos to change his mind. Someone had pointed to the next landmark on the road map the killer was leading them on. Someone . . .

Dozer. It had been Dozer. Amos's boss had demonstrated how unlikely it was Parker had been the one who had attacked McVey. Amos thought about it for a single second before he almost cracked a smile. Scott Dozer? A police chief sneaking out every five years on Halloween and murdering somebody? The overweight, middle-aged hardhead who thought with his temper? No way. There was absolutely no way. If Amos hadn't been in such a dire situation, desperately trying to rescue a teenager and his kid brother from a homicidal maniac while he tried to navigate the rain and the asshole behind him riding his butt, he would've burst into laughter.

Yet, something poked at Amos's subconscious. It was like that feeling where a word or idea is on the tip of your tongue and you just can't quite vocalize it. Some clue lingering in the dark, waiting to jump out. What was it? What was bothering him about Dozer? He tried to visualize the man, reclining in his chair behind his desk, his tree-trunk arms folded down in front of him. The chief's beer gut slopping over his belt, contrasting with the massive biceps that bulged under the sleeves of his polo shirt.

The tattoo. There had been a tattoo on Dozer's right bicep. Amos had thought it had been the outline of a large dog. Now that he thought about it more, the visual recollection in his memory appeared more and more like a wolf.

Oh stop it, thought Amos as he banked right past Dairy Queen and passed the sign that said WELCOME TO TOLEDO. A tattoo proved nothing. And for all he knew, it really could've just been a dog. All the other evidence pointed toward someone much more cunning and clandestine, and for that matter, intelligent. It was probably ludicrous Amos was even considering a police officer at all, and there was sure as hell no way if it was an officer it would be Scott Dozer. Amos knew the man he worked for, and Dozer surely couldn't be capable of the horror he had witnessed over the past few hours. He just *couldn't* . . . could he?

12:33 a.m.

Amos curled the car around another corner on Amber Alley, inching up the steep hill like a mountain climber scaling the final summit of Mount Everest. He was almost to the clearing where Ted and Stevie were likely waiting for him, and nearly to the building where Coby, Mack, and the mysterious assassin could potentially be. Eerily enough, the rain had stopped. Even the wind had frozen in the trees and everything was still. It was like the terrain around him knew this was the last breath before the dive into the deep end of the pool.

As Amos reached the last slope of Amber

Alley, his heart sank. Neither Stevie nor Ted was parked there. They were either already in the clearing or inside the building itself. *Damn it, Stevie,* he thought. *Can't you follow directions just once? Just once.* Amos pumped the brakes of the car one last time and inhaled deeply. *Here we go.*

Amos pulled into the clearing, and he instantly knew something was wrong. There was another Crown Vic stationed only inches away from the building, with its lights blasting against the side of the structure. A hundred feet to the left, there was a red pickup parked against the line of trees. But what really made the hairs on Amos's arms stand on end was the huddled mass lying in the mud next to the truck. He didn't even know what it was at first, but some sixth sense had pulled the mental fire alarm in his head. It only took a few seconds of eyeing the outline of the crumpled shape to realize that it was a body.

"Oh Jesus!" Amos pushed the gearshift into park and ripped the keys out of the ignition. He stumbled when he got out of the car as his feet didn't gain any traction on the mud, but he was able to keep upright. He burst forward into a full sprint toward the body on the ground. Even from a distance, he could see that it wasn't Stevie. The shape of the torso was too muscular and large. It was a male.

Amos's lungs felt like they were about to split

open. He urged his legs to gallop along faster, but he just couldn't do it. He had never been an athlete. Nevertheless, in twenty seconds, he arrived next to the man on the ground. Amos bent over and pressed two fingers against the man's neck and felt a distinct series of thumps. He was alive. Amos's arms shot underneath the man's torso, and he felt something warm and wet. With an enormous effort, and the popping sound from his joints, Amos managed to complete the task. As soon as he did, his heart seemed to stop. It was Ted. And the warm substance that was on his fingers was blood.

Trying to ignore the nausea percolating in his gut, Amos leaned forward. "Teddy! Teddy! Are you okay? Can you hear me, buddy?"

Ted groaned loudly. A flowerlike pattern was darkening the black material of his sweatshirt, and there was more blood caked around his hairline. Amos's chest dropped like someone had poured lead down his throat. The man was dying.

"He g-got me. Al-burr. My ch-chest."

"I know, buddy. I know. I'm here, Teddy. You're going to be alright." Amos shot a quick glance over his shoulder, looking for the perp. His heart was thumping along wildly.

"D-didn't see him. Was trying to help . . ."

"Where did he go, Ted? Which way did he go?"

Ted could only manage a single word in

response. "Inside."

"Did you see Coby or Mack? Are they with him?"

Ted muttered back, and it sounded like a warped version of "I don't know."

"Okay. Okay. Alright, Ted, I'm going to be right back, okay? I'm going to take care of this. You're going to be okay." He had to get back to the car to call backup. Ted didn't have long. Amos wanted to put the man in a more comfortable position, but every second that elapsed was one moment closer to the man's death.

"I was trying to h-help," Ted said again. Amos wondered if he was concussed. It certainly looked like he had been on the wrong end of a blow to the head.

"I know, Teddy, I know."

"No! I was trying to help St-Stevie."

Time seemed to freeze as Amos processed what Ted has said, and at that moment, he was more afraid than he had ever been in his life. "Where is she, Ted? Where is she?"

Ted raised one quivering finger and pointed. Amos's head snapped back toward the industrial building, and he noticed the Crown Vic parked with its headlights on and windshield wipers going full blast even though the rain had stopped. It was too far away to tell for sure, but it did indeed look like someone was slumped over in the driver's seat.

"Oh Jesus. Oh Jesus."

Amos leapt to his feet and took off running again. His arms pistoned back and forth, gathering speed for his legs, which seemed to be on the verge of failing him. Each thigh burned like a slab of meat thrown haphazardly against the grills of a barbecue in the middle of summer. A stitch in his chest whined in protest; it felt like somebody had stuck a needle in between his shoulder and pectoral muscle. After many long strides toward Stevie's car, the mud got the best of him. With a great splatter like paint tossed against a canvas, Amos tumbled into the brown slop on the ground. Pain erupted in his knee joints, and he gave a scream of frustration, but not from the pain, just the time wasted. He scrambled back to his feet and tried to regain the same speed, but felt a stab in his knee. It seemed to buckle as he took another long stride, and Amos was sure that he had done some sort of structural damage. But it didn't matter now. All that mattered was his partner. Finally, he made it to the vehicle and saw her collapsed in the driver's seat.

Stevie's hands were bound by rope, and her forehead was pressed against the steering wheel. Her face was curtained by her dark hair, but Amos thought he could see a trickle of blood running down her chin. She was totally motionless, but Amos felt certain that she wasn't dead. At least not yet. Just unconscious.

"Stevie! Stevie!" Amos pulled on the door, even though he knew it would be locked. Sure enough, the door held stiff. He frantically knocked against the window, trying to make her stir, but she didn't budge. For a moment, he began to cock his arm back, ready to break the window. But then he stopped. He probably couldn't even bust it with his bare fist, and even if he did, he would shower Stevie in glass. The passenger window. He would have to try and destroy the passenger window. But there was still the problem of getting in. He hadn't brought a sap or a baton. What could he use? Amos looked back toward his own car. He was certain there was a crowbar in the trunk. He took one more glance down at Stevie's petrified person before discharging into yet another full tear.

Yep. There is definitely something wrong in there, thought Amos as he ran and his knee felt like it might snap. Perhaps a torn ligament or a sprain. The pain was overwhelming, but he ignored it as he darted over to his car. Amos's hand felt numb from the cold, so it was difficult to shove his hand in his pocket to try and finger his keys so that he could open the trunk. *Where are you, you little bastards?* He touched his phone, his wallet, and spare change. *Fuck, fuck, fuck.* Finally, he lassoed the keys around his fingers. He was so eager to rip them out that they caught on a thread in his pocket.

"God dammit!" They were stuck to his pants.

With a massive wrench, he ripped the keys away from the fabric. But the inertia of his pull outran his grip, and when his arm went rocketing upward, the keys flew out of his hand and into the night. He saw them glint for a second, but then they were gone. Amos cursed again, louder than he ever had in his life. Where had they landed? He bent over and combed the mud with his palms. No keys. It was as if they had evaporated.

Amos glanced over at his car. He had thought he would need the key to get into the back, but then he realized there was a button on the dashboard that would also pop the trunk. His mind was in such a frenzied state that things were taking twice as long to process. With a mad scramble, he opened the driver's side door and plopped onto the cushion. It only took a few seconds to find the button on the center console that seemed to mime an opening trunk. Amos pressed it, and heard a loud *thunk* as the back of the car cracked open. His knee wailed in agony again as he tore out of the car.

Amos flipped open the back of the car. The outline of the spare tire was visible underneath the thin carpet material of the trunk. But he didn't see a crowbar. Surely it had to be there. Where could it be?

A gargantuan blast split the night in two. Amos instinctively ducked and closed his eyes, and he heard a *whoosh* as something passed over him.

There was the feeling of heat scalding the bald spot on the top of his head as the object went flying, and then another loud crunch as it landed somewhere in the nearby vicinity. Amos opened his lids and turned his head. A tire, still billowing smoke, was burning near the tree line. He instantly felt numb, and though his heart was begging him to close his eyes again and stay that way forever, he turned toward where the initial boom had emitted from.

The remnants of an orange mushroom cloud spread out against the sky, and the Crown Vic across the clearing was wreathed in flame. The nearest wall of the building was caved in and threatening to collapse, while the vehicle fumed and raged with fire. Somewhere in that mess, Amos knew that the remains of Stevie's corpse were also ablaze.

Amos stood there for five minutes. Or it could've been only five seconds; he wasn't sure. All he knew was he was frozen in place, and his heart shattered into a thousand pieces as he watched the orange glow of the combusting Crown Vic. *Stevie,* he thought. *Oh God. Stevie.* Was he going into shock? It felt like he was already out of his body and drifting into the netherworld. He literally couldn't move. Or could he? It seemed impossible. Anguish pulsed through him, followed by something else. What was that? That heat permeating throughout his chest? It burned like he had just swallowed a shot of whiskey. Anger. Furious loathing. *You fucker. You fucking bastard.* The wolf had taken her from him. His partner. His Stevie. His fists clenched until they were white and his arms were shaking. *You goddamn bastard.*

The large shape rose behind him, but Amos took no notice of it. His eyes were fixed on the spot where he knew his partner lay, forever asleep. He barely felt the cold pinch against his neck, and he only caught a fleeting glimpse of the needle that had pierced him and the pointed gray nose that was resting above his shoulder. Amos thought of Stevie one last time before everything went black.

1:01 a.m.

Clink. Clink. Clink.

A faint sound of metal on metal.

Clink. Clink. Clink.

It reminded him of some sort of machinery on an assembly line.

Clink. Clink. Clink.

It was getting louder now.

Clink. Clink.

The noise stopped. With an enormous amount of exertion, Amos opened his eyes. For many moments, everything was fuzzy. The outlines of two people took shape in front of him; one sitting and one standing behind.

Clink.

The noise came from a knife smacking against the back of the chair Coby Conner was tied to. He was stripped of everything but his underwear, a pair of navy blue briefs that called attention to the paleness of his skin. His arms were bound behind the metal chair and a filthy rag was stuffed deep into his mouth. Coby's face was covered in sweat, and his eyes were wide as he looked at Amos. The large figure standing behind him continued to tap the knife against the back of the chair. *Clink. Clink. Clink.* The man in the wolf mask looked at Amos, and though he couldn't see beyond the gray veneer, Amos felt sure the man was smiling. *Clink. Clink.* Amos wanted to yell at the creature to stop it; quit making that grating noise, but he couldn't. He couldn't even move his lips. This time the paralysis wasn't metaphorical; he was literally petrified in place. What had the man injected him with?

"So nice of you to join us, Albert," the man said softly. The words sounded deep, warped and unnatural. It was like he was putting some strange inflection into his speech to hide his true voice. "I imagine the succinylcholine has taken full effect now. I gave you a concentrated dose. Your muscles have effectively lost their function for the time being. I did the same thing to Coby here. Unfortunately, I believe his is wearing off."

When the man in the mask finished this

sentence, he pressed the tip of the knife against Coby's shoulder, creating a small incision that instantly leaked red. Coby groaned loudly, and his foot tapped repeatedly against the ground.

"You see, at its peak, succinylcholine has paralytic effects. Coby seems to be moving, doesn't he? Which is perfect. It's more satisfying for me when they squirm."

Amos scanned the area around him, as his pupils were still functioning. He was in the middle of a massive empty room, with a ceiling forty feet high and the nearest end half a football field away. He could still see the markings of the sinister message the man had left for him earlier that evening on the far wall. *Nothing here except your eyes.* Also, not far from the message, he thought he saw faces gleaming in the darkness. Were those jack-o'-lanterns?

"Before we begin, let's play a game," said the man, standing up taller. He seemed huge, especially standing next to the diminutive teen. "Do you like games, Albert?"

Amos tried to move his lips, but drool ran down his chin. Everything was still fuzzy.

"I bet you do, Albert. I bet you do," said the man in the mask, pointing at Albert. "Okay, here's the game: Say my name. Say my name, and I will let both of you go. Guess wrong, and you will watch as I make our young friend here bleed out as slowly as I can. Quite literally death from a thousand cuts." The man gripped Coby by the shoulder for a brief second and gave him a small, menacing shake. "Understand? Give me your best guess, Albert. I know it's very difficult for you to speak, but I think you can manage one word."

Amos thought it over. He didn't have anything to lose. If he got it right, he felt sure that the man wouldn't honor his promise to let them go. But could he speak? Even one word seemed out of the realm of possibility.

"Come on, Albert."

Amos started twisting his lips and called upon his voice box with all his might. At first, a pathetic grunt was all that came out.

"What was that? I didn't quite catch that, Albert."

Amos's tongue felt like lead. But he finally managed to summon enough energy for one word.

"D . . . D . . . Dozer."

Silence. For several long seconds, the man just stared at Amos. Then, like a bevy of fireworks, he erupted into wild laughter. The howls of mirth went on for at least ten seconds and almost sounded inhuman. Finally, when the Wolfmask began to speak, the warped tone was gone, and Amos began to recognize the voice.

"Dozer? Scott Dozer? The police chief? Now *that*!"

His hand reached up and ripped off the mask in one fell swoop.

"*That* would be a helluva twist!" Ted Leery said with a malevolent smile.

1:03 a.m.

"You should see your face!"

For a minute, Amos waited for someone to wake him up from the dream. It had to happen any moment. But dreams were usually not this vivid, were they? He had to be already dead. Except he knew he wasn't. He could see the Calvin Klein logo on Coby's briefs turn red from the blood leaking down his torso, and Amos's stomach gurgled uncomfortably. He watched Ted laughing and looked as the creases on each cheek deepened with every passing guffaw. He was insane. Amos saw the knife dripping crimson and the discarded wolf mask on the ground. This was too detailed for his imagination.

"I can't even tell you how long I have been waiting for this moment, Albert."

"T-Teddy?"

The wild look of euphoria melted away, and Ted's face convulsed in fury. He took two strides forward and backhanded Amos across the jaw.

"Don't fucking call me that!"

Amos tasted iron in his mouth. Something hot

splashed onto his tongue as Ted grabbed him by the jaw and got two inches from his noise.

"Call me Teddy one more time and I will cut your tongue right out of your mouth, you fat fuck."

Ted released him, and then stepped back behind Coby while maintaining eye contact with Amos.

"Don't you ruin this for me, Albert! Don't you destroy this moment. I'm not your fucking Teddy bear!"

At this pun, Ted began to chuckle, and he patted his chest as if to ward off a cough. When he brought his hand up in the air, his appendages had a sticky-looking substance on them that had come from his shirt. Amos watched as Coby's eyes darted up to look at Ted's bloody fingers.

"This is nifty stuff. Don't get me wrong, not even I had the foresight to predict how this would unfold. That is the beauty of it though, isn't it? There is ecstasy in spontaneity. There is . . . euphoria in improvisation. And I kept any materials I thought I might need if I got in a tight spot. Pipe bombs. Guns. Rope." He held up the fingers that had touched his chest. "Pigs blood."

Ted twirled the knife around in his hand, marveling at the sharp end. "Euphoria in improvisation, indeed. As many times as I have gone through this night in my head, I can't say I ever saw myself faking an injury to set up an ambush. Nor did I ever see myself blowing up a fucking car. How *thrilling*! Oh! Oh . . ."

Coby recoiled as Ted walked past him towards Amos.

Ted put a pitying expression on his face in mockery. "Oh, Albert, I'm so sorry about Stevie. So, so sorry. It must have been hell to see that unfold. How did it feel to watch her body burn? To see the skin melt off her bones? Must have been awful. Just downright *awful*. I have to say though, that pales in comparison to what I'm going to do to our friend here."

On the word *friend*, Ted slashed downward with the hand holding the knife, striking Coby on the back. The boy screamed through his gag and slammed his eyes shut in utter agony.

"You see, Albert," Ted said over Coby's wails. "You deserve to watch this after all your incompetence. You messed this up, buddy. How did you not know that it was me? I'm almost insulted. How did it not give it away when I was the one who tipped you off about the man calling 911 to report a shooting out here in Toledo a few hours ago?"

Amos knew he couldn't move a muscle. But the feeling was still there. The pain. His mouth was on fire from when Ted had struck him, and he could taste the blood. But he couldn't swallow. How ironic it would be if he choked to death on his own congealed blood, after years of being hemophobic.

"How did you not know it was a police officer when Tuck Parker turned up wearing a mask matching this one, in the very neighborhood where the McVey boy had been stabbed?" Ted picked up his discarded mask on the ground and wiggled it around in the air for a second before dropping it again. "You're a detective, Albert. You really believed that big of a coincidence? A man whom you had just interviewed for a crime showing up days later, involved in *your* murder case? Dead giveaway, Al. Dead giveaway."

Ted brought the tip of the knife up to Coby's cheek. The boy was still whimpering, but his moans had grown a little quieter. He was shaking and streaks of tears stained his cheeks. When Ted started to cut diagonally across Coby's cheek, the cries amplified in volume once more. Ted retracted the blade and slung it in Amos's direction. Three speckles of Coby's blood landed directly on Amos's nose, and in that moment, Amos wished that he had been killed in the explosion too.

"Bull's-eye!" Ted shouted gleefully. "A direct hit! I'm surprised you're not puking, Albert. Damn . . . the first bit of spine you have showed in weeks, my friend."

Amos had been thinking the same thing. He was fragile. Impotent. And yet, somehow, he hadn't thrown up.

The malevolent smile on Ted's face had

returned. "Your stupidity was only matched by your cunt of a partner. For such a big mouth, she sure doesn't have the brain to match it, does she? I mean, she was just as instrumental in this as you were. I'm not sure I could've found a pair of detectives that I could've strung along better than you two. You watched as I arrested Parker, just minutes after I had stabbed McVey. You went and talked to Gutierrez, after Parker told you the man who had paid him to wear the mask had had a Mexican accent. You entered Dodd's home after finding out Oscar had seen Dodd at Jamie Ledoux's house on the same day I showed you the deer I hung from the ceiling. Every step I wanted you to take, you took."

Amos thought of the drunken college kid. He had been the one to relay the news about Dodd, not Gutierrez, which Ted remained ignorant of. It was a small shred of intel, but it put the slightest chink into the man's armor.

"I even gave you a massive hint this morning, Albert, and you still didn't catch on! Remember how I told you that Dodd had been cheating on his wife? Well, I have been texting Dodd on a burner for several weeks now, pretending to be Sonya Smith, his mistress. Sonya had stopped talking to him months ago, but Dodd believed it was her when he got the first text from the number he didn't recognize. And that was how I lured him to Ledoux's house. 'Sonya' was going to meet him there," Ted said, using air quotes with his fingers for the woman's name. "And I arranged the meeting right when Oscar was doing his checkup on Ledoux's house. If you're going to frame someone, Albert, you better get the details right."

The wheels began to turn faster in Amos's mind, but there was still a huge missing piece of the puzzle. The motive. Sure, the man was a homicidal maniac. But why young men? Why Halloween? Ted crept back around Coby's chair and crouched down so his face was right next to Amos's ear.

"You know what our colleagues are going to find when they see Dodd's car parked at the Agate Beach Wayside in the coming hours, don't you? They are going to find Dodd with a bullet in his head and a pistol in his hand. They will also find McKenzie Conner tied up unconscious in the trunk of the car. I wonder how they will see it, Albert. My guess is they will believe Dodd finally felt some sort of guilt for his murderous rampage, and committed suicide before he could give in to the impulse to kill Coby's ten-year-old brother."

Ted stood up and retreated over to Coby. Coby looked up at him, a miserable expression on his face.

"How else was I supposed to get him out here and have my way with him, Albert? I never wanted to get Mack involved, but after Coby escaped from the party, how else could I have lured him from the confines of his house?"

Amos began to put the timeline together in his head. Hadn't Ted been with them in the car when they apprehended Parker? But that was right after McVey had been stabbed. He could have easily discarded the knife somewhere in the neighborhood, and walked back to the scene of his own crime pretending to be an officer called to the disturbance. What about apprehending Mack? Ted had been at the station right after Parker had been apprehended. There was only a small window of time for him to travel back to the Conner household and abduct the child. But then Amos realized that Ted had left the station shortly after he had arrived. He had told them that he was going to interview possible witnesses around the house on Borneo Drive. Sure enough, when Amos began to think of all of the events that had taken place throughout the night, Ted always seemed to be missing at the crucial junctures.

"I don't hurt *kids,* Albert. The boy won't even have a bruise. I gave him a heavy dose of anesthetic. He was out the entire time I was transporting him to Dodd's car. Don't hold it against me, Al. It was the only way. I was just thankful that no one had found Dodd with his brains blown out before I put Mack in the trunk."

Suddenly, Ted pinched the right side of Coby's chest, holding the boy's nipple in between his fingers. With one hard slit, Ted completely uprooted the chunk of flesh and chucked it on the ground. For a fleeting moment, Coby's eyes widened but no noise came out of his mouth. Then a horrible scream cut the air in two. It went on for a solid ten seconds, fluctuating in volume and inflection every other beat. Amos stared deeply into the fresh hole next to Coby's sternum.

"Why do men even have nipples?" Ted spoke over Coby's frantic shrieks. Amos noticed in that moment that a large erection was pushing Ted's black jeans forward. He tried to look away, but his muscles were still unable to complete the simplest of motions. "We don't nurse or carry milk. In my opinion, I just did you a solid, kid."

Ted ruffled Coby's hair forcefully. "So, why do you think I picked Coby here, Albert? For that matter, why do you think my victim of choice is always a young male? It shouldn't be that hard to guess, but given your inability to deduce, well, *anything,* you still might not be able to come to the correct conclusion. Let me ask you this. Have you ever seen me with a woman, Albert?"

Although Amos couldn't feel much, he didn't miss the shivers spreading down his spine. He had wondered about Ted's love life before, but had not spent any substantial amount of time dwelling on it. Amos had just figured that the man kept that part of his life clandestine. Surely a handsome man such as

Ted Leery had no trouble seducing the ladies; perhaps he just didn't like to be as boisterous about his sexual exploits as most men. That had always seemed like the most likely conclusion. But it looked like Amos was wrong about that too.

"That's right, Al. I'm a fag. A fairy. A queen. How many gay serial killers do you think there have been, other than Dahmer? Probably not many. *Probably. Not. Many.*"

He punched out the last words by carving new incisions on Coby's arm. Two diagonal lines that formed a sideways X, and a curved line underneath it. Without warning, Coby's screams ceased. His eyes rolled upward, and his head slumped onto his left shoulder. A wad of drool spilled out onto his chin, and his skin was as pale as marble. Ted's face showed blank shock for several seconds, and he hurriedly pressed his fingers against Coby's neck. A relieved smile spread out over his face.

"Don't worry, Albert. No need to fret. He just passed out. Looks like his little mind has had enough for the moment."

Ted walked over to Amos and patted him on the shoulder, as if to console him. His pats morphed into rubs, and Amos found Ted looking deep into his eyes. When he spoke again, his voice was barely a whisper.

"There is something wrong with me, Albert." He forced his face to show mock-fear, with his lips quivering and his forehead wrinkled. "If I'm ever caught and I get the chair . . . do you think they will find malformations in my brain? Do you think the autopsy will show physical impairment? I don't know how else to explain it. Surely the psychology of a homosexual, narcissistic psychopath was created through some sort of . . . injury, right? The thing is, I've always been this way. So . . . have I been carrying around damaged goods for my entire life?"

Ted stood up straight, and then wiped the blood from his knife on Amos's cheek, giving him a small smile.

"It started with animals. The neighbors' cat. A little girl's rabbit that she brought to school. Dogs. I was always good at not getting caught. And killing all of the little forest friends was so easy. No strings attached. But then . . . it changed when I was sixteen. It evolved. You see, my father had found a gay porno mag under my mattress one day. And when I came home from school, he beat the shit out of me. Gave me two black eyes and a broken jaw. He was a little . . . old school, we will say. Religious. Cultivated the typical repressed Catholic family. The funniest thing about it was he had a miniature cross with Jesus on it hanging over our fireplace in the living room. I still remember it rattling against the wall as he pounded my head into the carpet."

Ted paced back and forth, looking down at the ground as he continued to speak. "Some diseased, dormant thing inside me had always been there. It had manifested itself into a passive curiosity with killing and death. But then, when he beat me, the monster woke up and realized its true potential. Ever since that day, I've had this burning sensation in my stomach. I would call it rage, but somehow that doesn't do it justice, you know? It's more like a wildfire of hate. Tearing through everyone and everything. And yet, it is also my sexuality. This festering plague that I have created gets me off, see? The clinical term is sadomasochism. But I like to say simply that I just get really *excited* by hate. And my father was the first one to suffer."

The man looked down at his knife, bit his bottom lip, and shook his head as he apparently reminisced on his abusive father.

"Two months after he had beaten me to a pulp, he went on his annual hunting trip. It was the second week in October when elk season had opened. We grew up in Michigan, right? And out there, there is rugged terrain. I don't mean the limp-dick country you find out here on the West Coast, but I mean *really rough terrain.* Deep in the woods, that's where he went. Looking for a ten-point buck. And you know where I was? Hiding in the bed of his truck. I waited until nightfall. Then he woke up with a gun to his temple. His own forty-five. I bound his hands with a zip tie. Then I cut off his balls and let him bleed out in his sleeping bag. I can still hear his screams rattling around in my ears out there on the Upper Peninsula."

Amos wished that he had the ability to fasten his ears shut, but he was listening with rapt attention. He hated every word that came out of Ted's mouth, and yet he was disturbingly fascinated with what the man was saying.

"That was my first experience setting up a scene for the police to find. I ripped up the tent and left only blood. The blood attracted animals who left tracks. After two weeks of searching, the authorities found the campsite. And they almost immediately concluded it had been an animal attack. But the food in the cooler was left there, so they figured it couldn't have been a bear. In the end, they surmised that a pack of wolves had killed my father."

At this, that same exhilarated, demonic smile illuminated Ted's face, and he reached down to pick up the wolf mask yet again. He held it above his head like a trophy, then chucked it into Amos's lap.

"And so the legend began! I assume that you have already figured out that they found what was left of Arthur Leery in the Hiawatha National Forest on Halloween day. October thirty-first, 1983. The day that the Wolfmask was truly born."

The Wolfmask? That was what he called

himself? Amos was perplexed by the overtly literal name. And yet, it also somehow fit the insane man standing in front of him, pouring out his soul.

Ted looked at the ceiling high above as if he was thinking. He let a long pause hang on the air before he continued, "Remember how you told me you looked in the surrounding counties for any other young men who had disappeared on Halloween, Albert? Again, you showed your absolute carelessness and negligence. For if you had tried a little bit harder. Looked a little bit longer. Even just gave a tiny bit more effort and checked the outlying counties, you would've found my trail."

Amos's stomach clenched. *God damn it. God damn you, you fucking bastard,* he thought. He had been waiting for this confession. And yet, it still made Amos feel like his heart was going to explode.

The man raised his right hand and ticked off fingers on his gloves. "Waylon Garrison, Curry County '08. Brian Booker, Clackamas County '09. Aaron Dixon, Harney County 2010. Brian Toomey, Clatsop County '11. Ian Amberson, Klamath County 2013. Justin French, Baker, '14. Doug Ryan, Jefferson County, 2015. Kyle Martin, Hood River, '16."

Ted stood up straight and waved the knife around with a flourish. "I have killed a young man on every single Halloween night since 2007. You thought I only struck every five years. But you were wrong. I only kill every five years in *Newport.*"

Ted walked back toward Coby and checked his pulse again, as if to make sure he hadn't made an error the first time. "So why do you think I have stepped out of the shadows this time, Albert? Why did I make such of a show of it this go-around? Do you think I just wanted to make fools out of my colleagues? There has to be more to it than that, right? I mean, why now? What makes young Coby here so special?"

Amos's mouth was almost totally slack now. It seemed hard to fathom that words had ever been formed by his lips before. He was inwardly cursing himself for not bringing backup with him, or at least alerting his colleagues to where they were going. It had seemed like such a brilliant plan at the time. A way to preserve the element of surprise. And yet, it looked like he had ended up signing his own death warrant with the decision. Escape seemed next to impossible.

"It all started in the late nineties. I had just moved out to the West Coast and joined the force. I passed my psychological exams with ease. Back then, they weren't as arduous as they are now. But I studied nonetheless. I read up on the types of questions they would ask me, and what they would be looking for. I have always been somewhat of an expert at disguising my true intentions anyway, but this was a good test of my gusto. And I passed with flying colors. Isn't that scary? A budding serial killer can pass a mandated psychological exam and become a police officer by reading a couple of books.

"Anyway, I moved out here for no reason in particular other than wanting to get as far away from Michigan as possible. Ninety-seven was my first year as a deputy, and I was just learning the ropes. In December of that year, I was on patrol north of town. I pulled over a woman who had been swerving all over the road. She was coming back to her apartment from her company Christmas party, and I guess she didn't want to spend the money on a cab. Anyway, when I stopped her, she was just a wreck. In tears, just wailing away. Kept begging me to let her go. Said she was going to lose her job if her boss found out she got a DUI. But she was *wasted,* man. Just completely gone. You know how drunk she was? She said she would fuck me if I let her go. Naturally, I warned her that bribing an officer was a felony and placed her under arrest. This was on a Friday night. Well, on Monday morning, I was sitting at my desk when IA shows up. Two suits. Kept using words like *ergo* and *discretion.* They told me the same woman had told her lawyers I had asked for sexual favors in exchange for not placing her under arrest, and when she had refused, I became volatile and had used excessive force while putting her in cuffs."

Coby was still slumped over, so he didn't move when Ted gripped the back of his chair and curled his knuckles so tight around the metal rungs that they turned white.

"I was placed on suspension while they investigated. Almost lost my job because of that lying cunt. I had to go to a hearing, Albert. Have you ever noticed people will automatically believe the accuser when said accuser is a female? Even though I was eventually cleared of wrongdoing, my reputation was tarnished, because everyone believed her. People looked at me like I was some sort of sex-craved freak. Took me twice as long as it should've to get promoted. All because some little bitch couldn't take accountability for her own fucking mistake."

Amos wasn't sure where Ted was going with this, or how it connected to the current situation. But since he was currently unable to form even the most rudimentary sentence, he was forced to listen as Ted rambled on.

"I think you realize now how vindictive I can be, don't you? Do you think I just let her get away with what she did, Albert? I wanted to make her suffer. I wanted to do the worst possible thing you can do to another human being. Death was too easy. I wanted her to look over her shoulder every time she left her house. I wanted her to have night sweats and panic attacks. I wanted to ruin her. How do you think I did it? What is the worst thing you can do to a woman, Al? I had to defile her. Violate her. Make it so she could no longer indulge in the best feeling on earth without crippling anxiety. But how does a homosexual man *rape* a heterosexual woman? Doesn't that sort of go against the laws of biology? To tell you the truth, Albert, it wasn't her pussy that kept me hard. It was her screams."

Amos's stomach rumbled. The nausea had returned, but his gut still wouldn't alleviate it by vomiting. *Just kill me,* he thought. *Just get it over with.*

"After they found her, they went through normal protocol. They did a swab, but since I wore a condom and gloves, there was no DNA left behind. She was interviewed for hours on multiple occasions, but they never caught the man who raped Dana Conner."

There they were again. The goose bumps. Amos felt prickles all along his arms and on the back of his neck. *No. No way. It can't be.*

Ted crept forward, smiling from ear to ear. "So now you know, don't you? Now you realize why this young man is the crown jewel. The grand finale. There is no way I can beat it, right? I mean . . . how will I top this? Where does Ted Leery turn after he murders his biological son, Coby Conner?"

1:10 a.m.

Amos felt a tingling sensation on the back of his neck. Mixed with the enormous shock of what Ted had just revealed was the revelation that some feeling was beginning to return to his body. His wrists were itching against the rope that held them to the stiff chair. The taste of blood lingered in his mouth. Like a miniature candle illuminating a world full of darkness, Amos began to feel the slightest feeling of hope. Ted hadn't bothered to remove the pistol attached to his belt; perhaps this was intentional. Knowing Amos couldn't move to reach the gun and free himself of Ted's wickedness was probably meant to create the greatest feeling of despair. But perhaps, just this once, one of Ted's plans would backfire, and Amos would be able to get off one shot at the menace in front of him.

"He doesn't really look like me, does he? He's more . . . plain. I guess he gets that from his mother. That woman was worse than ugly; she was just totally forgettable. Yeah, Coby doesn't have any sort of striking features like I do. He's missing the straight nose. The hard jawline. But he's mine. Months ago, when I was stalking him, I pulled DNA off of a soda can that he had thrown away and had one of the lab rats run a genetic comparison to my blood. It was a match. Hell, Dana and her husband didn't even meet until six months before she had him. That must have been an awkward conversation to have. I wonder if Coby has any sort of inkling of the secret Andrew and Dana Conner have been harboring from him."

It all made so much sense now. Ted had pulled off the proverbial mask and put on a horrible, theatrical performance for one reason only: he wanted to finally reveal his true nature to the world by making a show of killing his own offspring. Some final vicious circle where the man who was abused by his own father showed the world how terrible fathers can truly be. This moment was the culmination of ten years of planning; Amos could see it in the triumphant look on Ted's face. But it wasn't Ted Leery who was finally stepping out of the darkness. It was the Wolfmask. And Coby Conner, the child of this uncaged demon, would be the one to suffer. Perhaps Ted had no intention of living after this deed was done. He was cunning enough to know that virtually all serial killers have a short shelf life. Maybe this was his way of going out with all guns blazing. His final act of evil before he turned his own knife back on himself.

"Do you think he would've been at all like me, Albert? If I had let him live out his life, would he have shown any hints of the same behavior? I don't believe so. I'm a different breed, Albert. I have evolved. I have grown to see the innate futility of living. Humans are vain, stupid creatures. We all end up in the same place in the end, so why does everyone pretend that the so-called dark thoughts that we all have are indicative of evil? If we all have the capability to commit these heinous acts, is it really evil? How can we differentiate between light and dark if we all are inherently gray anyway? It's all arbitrary. Morality doesn't exist. We are in a game where the players decide the rules. I have realized that there is no act that is *good* or *evil,* Albert. Everything that happens is just a reaction to a previous action. Everything just *is*."

Amos began to move his fingers ever so slightly. It was a minute gesture, but it transformed the tiny candle of hope in his chest into a more substantive flame. *Reach, Albert. Reach.*

"Albert, are your fingers moving?"

Ted snatched Amos's right hand and squeezed the index and middle fingers on it. "What were you trying to touch? Your gun?"

Amos looked up at the man towering over him and was crushed by despair. The game was up.

"Here, give it a go. Try and reach it."

Amos blinked. Surely Ted was patronizing him.

Ted was wearing a playful expression, and his face was beset by a zany, demonic energy that transformed his features. For the first time, he looked ugly. "Seriously. Try and reach your gun."

Amos only had to look into the man's eyes one

more time to realize he was serious.

"*Wait!* One moment. I have an idea."

Ted released Amos and walked back toward Coby. He snapped a few times in front of the boy's nose, and then slapped him hard across the jaw. Coby's eyes opened slightly, and Amos could tell for a fleeting moment the kid didn't know where he was. Amos wished Coby could stay in that moment until Ted finally killed him.

"Hey, buddy, welcome back. I don't think you missed much. What do you think, Al?" That same exhilarated and twisted smile lit up Ted's face. Was he going to reiterate the truth about Coby's parentage?

Coby looked up at Ted, and then his eyes went to the ground. He could no longer face his tormenter.

Ted began leaning on Coby's shoulder. "I woke you up because we're going to play another game. We're going to see if Albert can reach his gun. If he can touch his fingers to it, he wins. If he can't, you lose *your* fingers. How does that sound?"

Coby screamed through his gag, "No, no, no!"

Ted ignored this and looked back over at Amos with that leering grin. "Okay, Albert. Go. Reach. I will give you ten seconds, and then I will start with his pinky. Okay . . . one, two . . ." Ted put a vicelike grip on Coby's fingers, ready to hack away.

Amos stretched his appendages with all his

might, but the distance between the tips of his fingers and the handle of the gun was gaping. He could feel a bead of sweat seeping down his cheek. He supposed that was good. The succinylcholine was ebbing away. The rope held firm, but his gun was just inches away. His fingers felt like they were going to snap off with as much strain as he was putting on them. *Almost there. Almost there.*

"Nine . . . ten."

Amos couldn't see the gory details of what was happening behind Coby's chair; all he knew was the boy withered in agony as Ted chopped away at one of the hands that was tied. Soon, the loudest primal cry Amos had ever heard from a human being ripped the air apart. Ted raised one gloved, fisted hand and then wound up his arm like a center fielder aiming for home plate. Amos felt a small thump against his chest, and then saw the tan-colored sausage that was dipped in red on the ground. Coby's pinky. He stared at the tiny body part for a long time. But curiously, he felt no nausea or sickness. All in his gut now was hate.

"Stop." Speaking was still difficult, but Amos managed to spit the one word out. Ted's laughter instantly dissipated, and his face became stony as Coby wailed away.

"What did you say?" Amos didn't think he could say it again. Fortunately, Ted continued, "Did you say *stop*?"

Ted rushed forward and cocked his fist back before slamming it into Amos's jaw. The force of the blow toppled the chair over, and Amos landed on his shoulder and the side of his face. The floor was hard and cold.

"I won't fucking stop, Albert! I won't!"

Ted sounded like a child. His face was contorted in rage, his white teeth grinding against each other. Amos felt a minor level of triumph mixed with the pain bristling on his face. Even though he was knotted in place, at least for a second he had gained the upper hand.

"This will stop when I say it stops! And I'm not going to kill you until you see this boy torn to shreds! You deserve it, you fat piece of shit! You're going to keep watching until it's over, Albert! You're going to see what this boy's insides look like! I'm going to hack and slice and cut at every part that I see fit! And then, when *I* decide I have had enough—I'm going to cut out his fucking heart and force it down your throat." Ted moved his blade towards Coby's face. It looked like he was going to slice off the boy's nose.

Without warning, a massive bang erupted, echoing around the expansive room. The first thing Amos saw was the flash of light. Then chunks of flesh and speckles of gray and white splattered onto the ground, washed over by a wave of crimson. A fold of scalp flapped through the air before the tall body crumpled. From his angle on the floor, Amos saw a gun moving forward in the darkness. A forty-five pistol to be exact. Then he caught a glimpse of two bloody, shaking hands gripping the SIG Sauer. The gun still pointed at Ted's motionless body on the ground.

"Might be hard to do that with a hole in your head, Teddy," Stevie Hutchins said with a snarl.

TWENTY-SEVEN DAYS
AFTER HALLOWEEN

Everything was wet. Water pooled up on the uneven parts of the sidewalk, and the leaves of every tree were sopping. The rain came down at a steady, predictable pace. A stream rushed unapologetically on either side of the street and eventually reached the storm drain where it tumbled down into the abyss of the sewer. The cloud cover had turned all Newport gray, and thus, everything much drearier. A small child in a bright yellow rain coated sprinted down the side of Tenth Court, heading toward the cul-de-sac ahead. He was carrying a small toy barely visible under the sleeves of the bulky jacket, but he clung to it with purpose.

Newport had finally let go of the last remnants of summer. The sun would likely only be seen sporadically until May. Rain would fall three or four times a week until late spring, and on the first day of warm sunshine at the end of the long winter, the residents of the city would all collectively act like small children on Christmas morning. But while the storms and blanketing gray covered the town for now, no one would complain. Each person would keep their heads down and go about their business, waiting for the clouds to pass, much like the child in the yellow jacket.

The kid stomped his orange boots through a puddle like it wasn't even there. His head was bowed as he sprinted, trying to parry the rain, and therefore, he took little to no notice of the Ford Crown Victoria giving a wide berth around him.

The windshield wipers were set to an intermittent beat; it wasn't quite enough to clear the glass of all visual obstruction, but the next-level up when the wipers smacked back and forth spastically was far more distracting in Amos' opinion. He drove the car at approximately ten miles per hour, partially to be safe but also to intentionally annoy the person sitting in the passenger seat.

"Speed up, gramps. You'll be dead by the time

we get there at this rate."

Amos tried to suppress his smile, but he wasn't totally successful; the grin tickled the corners of his lips before he was able to resume the stoic expression he had been holding.

With a quick glance at the rearview mirror, Amos saw the child in the yellow jacket pumping his arms furiously, trying to accumulate speed so he could expedite the process of getting out of the rain. But as Amos squinted, he saw a jubilant, cheesy grin from just under the hood. The boy looked like he was having the time of his life. Warmth spread through Amos's body. Over the past month, it had been the simplest of things that had made him the most content.

"Seriously though, Albert, go faster. My back is killing me."

"Sorry, Stevie. I didn't even think about that." Amos pumped the gas and brought the car to a more appropriate speed with a lurch.

Amos glanced over at his partner and saw her sitting on the edge of the seat, using her hands to press herself forward and avoid putting pressure on her back. There was a bit of a bulge poking through her black jacket. He knew that this was from the bandages; second-degree burns required a hefty amount of dressing while they healed. When the burns finally were remedied, there would be substantial scarring. But without the grafts the doctors had done, her skin would've ended up looking far worse.

Stevie would probably say losing the first layer of skin on her back was the most minor injury she had suffered. She had also lost two fingers on her left hand, had cracked several ribs, and a bark chip had pierced her right eyelid and scratched her retina. Amos could still see swelling around her eye and the flesh had turned a tinge of pale green; it had been purple for the first two weeks. Finally, along with the wounded eye, she had suffered a concussion when she had slammed against the gargantuan Douglas fir on the edge of the clearing. But all in all, she had been lucky.

After hitting her over the head with his clenched fist, Ted had inoculated her with a dose of succinylcholine. Amos would bet Ted had fully expected her to remain paralyzed in the car, but the drug had not been administered properly. The investigation had yielded that when he had pressed the needle against her neck, a bubble had likely formed in the tube, and only a small portion of it had gotten into her system. That was the theory at least, because they had only found the slightest hint of succinylcholine in her bloodstream afterward. It hadn't been nearly enough to totally petrify her in place, and when Amos had been desperately trying to wake her by pounding on the window, she had begun to stir. Seconds after, Amos had been busy frantically searching for his keys and then the crowbar, and thus, he had missed her crawling out of the driver's seat of the Crown Vic. His head was still down when she had limped to the edge of the blast radius, and Amos had instinctively ducked when he had heard the blast, so he didn't see Stevie's body get tossed through the air like a rag doll and land firmly against a tree twenty feet away. The collision had knocked her out once more, and she only regained consciousness a half hour later, just in time to use the knife on her belt to cut her bonds and make her way into the industrial building to lodge a bullet into Ted's skull.

"Have you taken a Vicodin today?"

"No."

"Well maybe you sh—"

"I've taken three," Stevie said happily. Amos gave her a reproachful grin, but this didn't seem to deter her pleasant mood.

"You know opiates are some of the most addictive drugs in the world," Amos said.

"I can see why. I feel fucking peachy."

"Stevie . . ."

"Oh relax, Al. I only mix them with liquor on Fridays."

Amos tried to hold in the laughter, but he couldn't suppress the tiny snort that ejected from his nose.

"I'll be fine, partner. I'm not worried about it."

"Yeah, you're not because you're high."

Stevie contemplated this for a second. "True."

Both erupted into laughter. Amos's instantly turned into a wheeze; he had caught some sort of viral infection in his lungs over the past week. It made it hurt to laugh, but he couldn't stop, and he didn't want to. If he could, he would stay chuckling with Stevie for the rest of his life. Those fifteen minutes he had spent in the chair thinking she was dead were the hollowest fifteen minutes of his life. And the relief he had felt when he saw her standing there holding the gun was one of the best things he had ever felt.

Laughter felt fresh now. For the past four weeks, Amos's life had been filled with sleepless nights. Insomnia was new to him, but every time he tried to doze, visions of all that had been lost prowled through his head. All the young men that Ted had killed. Gordon Dodd and his wife, Deidre. Ted's father, Arthur Leery, whose death was being investigated by the police in Escanaba, Michigan, as a homicide. And, perhaps the most affecting to Amos, the innocence of Coby Conner. Throughout his career as a cop, he had always felt worse while thinking about the living who had survived a harrowing event rather than the dead who were now at peace.

Amos had visited the boy several times in the hospital, and on two separate occasions, Coby had

had a panic attack midconversation. He also had admitted he only slept for one to two hours at a time, and he would frequently wake up covered in sweat and his own urine. The physical injuries he had suffered paled in comparison to the emotional trauma. The scars on his chest, back, and hands were visible, but the inner scars were much deeper.

Mack was somehow even worse than Coby. On the two occasions Amos had visited the Conners, the boy hadn't spoken a word to him. Dana had said he had barely spoken at all since Bosworth and two other officers had found him trembling in the trunk of Gordon Dodd's car. Bosworth had relayed to Amos that he had shielded the child's eyes from Dodd's lifeless body and mangled head in the front seat, but Amos wasn't so sure that this was the truth.

Other than when he was dwelling on others' pain while lying in bed at night, Amos tried to keep his mind occupied with other things, and he was mostly successful. Hell, Anita might have suffered emotionally on a greater scale than he had. On November 1, after hours at the police station, he had finally returned home. Anita had pulled open the door looking white as a ghost, and had instantly burst into tears and embraced him on the doorstep. She had held on for dear life for at least ten minutes, convulsing in his arms and wailing away. Amos hadn't even said anything; at the time, he didn't think he had the energy to speak.

The forensics teams had asked Amos to go back out to Toledo the day after he had come home to walk them through everything, but he refused. He would never set foot in that industrial building again. He didn't even want to travel out past Toledo. Besides, the lab guys didn't need his help. They had found every piece of physical evidence they needed to confirm that Ted was the culprit: two more identical wolf masks in the backseat of Ted's red Dodge Ram 1500, as well as empty beakers of blood in a cooler sitting in the bed of the truck. Part of the blood samples belonged to a pig, but the rest came from Luke Ledoux and Devin Johnson. The forensic techs had also found three pistols, two leftover pipe bombs, a rotten pumpkin Ted had apparently decided not to use in his smiley-face display, and several large knifes. One had Sean McVey's DNA on the tip of it.

The one thing that continued to baffle the Newport Police Department was the lack of bodies. Two weeks before, they had done a search of Ted's residence and found no traces of the boys he had killed. It was most peculiar, but a question that would go unanswered. The investigating detectives would just have to take Amos's word for who Ted had killed and list each missing persons case as a probable homicide.

Unsurprisingly, the confirmed list of young

men who had gone missing on Halloween night in the state of Oregon wasn't short. Amos cursed himself for this fact, but in all honesty, it was standard operating procedure to focus on one specific area while looking for trends in a homicide case, instead of an entire massive state. That was what Ted had banked on. Three days after Halloween, Amos, Lawrence Bonner, and Bosworth had begun calling the outlying counties Ted had listed in his confession. Sure enough, they had quickly found eight missing boys. All of them had had a non-Ted-Leery-involved explanation listed for their disappearances. Two were runaways, three were suspected suicides, and one was even being investigated as a homicide, with the chief suspect being the young man's adoptive father. The other three were all homeless and since no bodies had been recovered, the police had figured that the transients had simply moved on to another location. It was fairly incredible that none of the investigating departments had been able to see the rash of deaths as the work of a serial killer. But Ted had been that clever. Each disappearance had a built-in explanation, and since they were staggered in one-year intervals and all in different counties in a massive state, it would have taken more communication and some sort of all-encompassing oversight to make the connection. Each department was focused on their own jurisdiction, not on the state as a whole. And Ted knew how to cover his tracks. Without physical, noncircumstantial evidence, all that each department had was the date of the disappearances themselves. But people commit suicide and run away every day of the year. Was a detective supposed to think "serial killer" just because a death he or she was investigating had happened on a holiday?

The logistics of how Ted could commit each crime were not complicated. Every year except for 2007 and 2012, the man had taken a paid vacation during the last two weeks of October. He had claimed he was staying at a time-share in Arizona, and his given reason for always leaving midfall was because Fountain Hills was more temperate that time of year. No one had obviously probed into Ted's personal life; there had been no reason to. He was as normal as any other detective on the force. He went to work functions. He drank with the boys. He brought in doughnuts. There was sort of an unspoken rule that your personal life should be left at the door, and since Ted had appeared ordinary, why would anyone look into what he did with his own time?

The real question was: what had Ted been doing from 1997 when he arrived in Oregon to 2007 when Devin Johnson was killed? Surely a serial killer wouldn't take a ten-year hiatus. His claimed crimes only started a decade back. It was a mystery the NPD was already beginning to try and solve. It likely wouldn't have a resolution any time soon. Not with the way things were looking on the inside of the department.

For the second time in as many years, the NPD had been hit by an absolute shit-storm. The Nowhere Girls case in 2016 had left a black eye on the department, and the previous chief had been relieved of his duties, as many of his subordinates had committed gross negligence while handling the investigations of victims in the case. Reporters had flooded PR Director Tony Burke's inbox with emails and had blown up his phone day after day. Several times when Amos had walked into the station in the months after the Nowhere Girls was solved, a reporter had approached him and attempted to ask questions that Amos had politely declined to comment on. Such was the nature of the beast when you royally screw up a serial-homicide investigation, and everything was happening again. Reporters would question every move each officer had made, internal affairs would be at the station every day, and members of the community would call for heads to roll. Dozer was finding this out, and he faced even more heat, as the killer had ended up being one of his own. Unlike his predecessor, however, he wasn't going to be fired. The city council felt it would look bad to fire another police chief when they were the ones who had just chosen him, but Dozer's life had become such a living hell with everyone calling for his head that he had no choice but to step down. Select others beneath him would be terminated. If Amos hadn't been the one to track down Ted in the first place, he might be in danger of such a fate. Luckily for him, it was going to be a moot point in a few months.

The Ford Crown Victoria listed lazily to the right and came to a halt against the curve. Neither of the detectives inside moved at first. Amos thought it was because they were both apprehensive about the rain, but Stevie apparently had other things on her mind.

"Are you going to tell him?"

Amos scratched his right eyebrow distractedly. "What are you talking about?"

He had hoped his feigned ignorance would dupe Stevie, but her closed lips spread and her eyebrows raised in a skeptical expression.

"Don't play dumb. I know you're good at it, but save it for another time."

Amos sighed. "You know I can't, Stevie."

"Yes, you can."

"No, I really can't."

"Wouldn't you want to know?"

"It isn't my place."

"Then whose is it?"

"His parents."

Stevie shook her head irritably. "You know

they are never going to tell him. If they were going to, they would've already."

"Maybe that's for the best."

Stevie looked at him like he had just declared there was a bout of impending flatulence in his gut. "How do you figure?"

"Stevie, he's already on the brink of a mental breakdown, if you can even call what he's suffered already something other than that. How do you think it would affect him to hear a sadistic, sociopathic killer had confessed to being his father while he was knocked out?"

"Better now than later! Better to have him suffer the lowest point in his life here than to patch him up for a bit only to rip out his heart down the line!"

"I told you, it isn't my place. If you want to infringe on Dana and Andrew Conner's boundaries, so be it. But I'm not going to be the one to do so. Here, come on, we're wasting daylight."

Before Stevie could formulate a response, Amos opened the door, leapt out of the car, and quickly trekked up the driveway toward the Conner household. He didn't want to turn his head, because he knew if he did, he would see that famous Stevie snarl. Her footsteps clapped along from behind him, and he heard her mumbling something that was likely explicit. Within moments, he had ascended the three cinder steps to the Conners' front porch and pushed the doorbell twice.

The door opened and Andrew Conner stood there looking pleased to see them. He was a massive man; Amos would venture to guess he was around six foot six and his torso was made up of huge globs of muscle and fat. His skin had the slightest tinge of brown in it, and, according to Dana, this was due to some ancestral roots in the Pacific Islands. But Andrew had been whitewashed by his parents with the generic name and the general mannerisms of a Caucasian man. He didn't look even slightly like Coby, which led Amos to wonder if there was ever any sort of inkling in the boy's mind about his lineage.

"Hey, guys. Come on in, come on it," Andrew said with an eager beckoning gesture.

"Thanks, Mr. Conner." Amos gave him a curt nod.

"Man, call me Andrew! We're on a first name basis, aren't we, Albert?"

"Sorry. Force of habit." Amos smiled.

As the two detectives crossed over the threshold, Andrew gave one nod at Stevie. "How's it goin', Stevie? The eye is lookin' better."

Stevie smiled. "I don't know if that pun was intentional or not, but either way, two thumbs up!"

Andrew let out a booming laugh. It came in rhythmic staccato beats and had the traces of a wheeze intermingled within the mirth.

"Nah, as per usual, when I'm funny, it's completely by accident. Come on into the living room, guys, that's where everybody is."

Amos circled around the corner of the hallway and came into the living room with Stevie right in his wake. The blue couch was stuffed with bodies. Dana was on the far right, her shoulder-length blond hair looking a little frazzled. Coby was in the middle. His face no longer had the bandage he had been sporting, but his hand was still wrapped in a white club that protected the finger that the hospital had reattached after Ted had disposed of it. Finally, on the right, Mack was curled up in a ball, with his head drooping onto the arm of the couch. There was darkness around his eyes and his curly brown hair cloaked his face like a curtain. Andrew quickly moved across the room and sat on the rocking chair that was across from his other family members. Amos and Stevie took their seats next to Andrew.

"How's it going, buddy?" Stevie was the first one to speak, as per usual.

Coby shrugged in response. "Not bad, I guess."

Stevie shook her head. "You know, kid, I'm a detective. I can tell when someone is lying."

Coby squirmed on the couch and his face broke into an uncomfortable smile. "I'm just not sleeping very much."

"That will change," Stevie replied quickly. "There are actually statistics on that. The first couple of months after a traumatic event usually translate to insomnia. But then, like all things, it passes."

Amos gave a sideways glance at his partner. He wasn't sure if she was just making up the "statistics" part, or just saying it to console the boy. Either way, she made it sound good.

"And how are you, Mack?" Amos was the one to pose the question this time. The child looked up at Amos with a nervous glance and grunted. The word was deformed and almost indistinguishable, but Amos thought that he had said "okay." One thing was certain: Mack sure as hell didn't seem okay. He looked like there was barely any energy left in his body, and his skin was so pale it seemed to be on the verge of being translucent. It made Amos feel horrible and somewhat guilty to think about how traumatized Mack must've been.

"What about you two?" Amos directed the question first at Dana and then looked over at Andrew as well.

Dana sort of twitched like she was trying to shrug. "As good as we can be, I guess," she replied, apparently speaking for her husband too. "Although we may never go on vacation again. Hell, it's hard to even leave this house without these two by my side."

Amos nodded. "I understand. I get why you would feel like that. And I certainly don't want to tell you how to conduct your lives, but living in fear is no way to be. If we all went about our days preparing for something bad to happen, then nothing good would ever happen."

"Yeah, I know," Dana said softly, and she absentmindedly stroked Coby's hair.

"Again, it's totally understandable you would feel the way you feel. But living in a shell and always looking over your shoulder is the way . . . *he* . . . would want you to feel."

As soon as he said it, Amos knew he had crossed some sort of invisible line. Ted Leery was a taboo topic in the Conner household, and each person besides the two detectives suddenly had an expression on their faces akin to watching someone get thrown into a wood chipper. Silence blanketed the room.

Once again, Stevie came to the rescue. "It helps if you get back into a routine. Sitting around making yourselves miserable isn't going to help the healing process. When are you going back to school, Coby?"

Coby looked at her apprehensively. "I'm not sure."

"Are you scared about going back?"

Coby sat up a little straighter and his voice got an octave deeper when he responded. It was an involuntary action, but still rather hilarious to Amos. Stevie had that effect on most males; Amos could only imagine all the boys who had tried to subconsciously impress her in her life.

"Not scared, no. Just don't want everybody to ask me about what happened."

"Why the heck not? How many boys can say they survived an encounter with a serial killer? Girls love a badass, Coby."

Coby flushed red but also chuckled.

Andrew leaned forward and gave him a finger-point. "It's true, Cobes. That is why your mom married me."

Dana rolled her eyes while everyone laughed, and eventually, she began to chuckle as well. "Yeah, a real badass over there. Remember when you cried after watching *You've Got Mail*?"

"Lies," Andrew quipped with a shifty smile and a wink in Coby's direction.

After the collective laughter began to subside, Dana turned the conversation back toward Amos.

"How are things at the station? I remember last time you guys came over you said that things were pretty bad. Is the chief still going to resign?"

"I think so."

"That's ridiculous," Dana snapped. "How is he in any way to blame for what happened?"

Amos shrugged. "It did happen under his watch."

"Yeah, yeah, but we're the victims here, and none of us are pointing fingers at anyone other than

. . . him. He was the one who did it, and him alone."

"I understand. It just looks bad. Especially after what happened last year with the Nowhere Girls case and who was involved in that."

"Hmm," Dana said quietly. "Well, even if mistakes were made, we don't fault you, or Dozer or anyone else but him."

Amos considered her. Her shoulder-length blond hair was groomed so that nary a stray follicle could peek out. Her green eyes were soft and kind, and gave off the impression of someone who was good at being consoling. He knew little about her, except that she was a protective mother and a kind woman. Perhaps this polished version of Dana Conner had evolved from someone much different, and that was why she was so lenient about people making mistakes. What Ted had told him about her DUI arrest and subsequent false accusations had been true. She had broken the law, then lied to try and deflect the blame onto someone else. It had been a huge misstep, but Amos wasn't going to judge her. She had been a panicked woman in her twenties trying to dig out of a hole she had created. Amos was willing to bet that this series of events was the greatest regret she possessed. Regardless, what Ted had done to her was unconscionable, revolting, and downright inhuman.

Another query from Dana interrupted Amos's brief stupor. "So will there be any other casualties?"

"Oh, sure. I mean, there has to be. I don't want to say that we're going to have a completely new staff, but jobs will be lost. That's for sure."

"But obviously, you two aren't in any danger . . ."

"No, I don't think so. Even if I am, it won't matter anyway."

Out of the corner of his eye, Amos saw Stevie cringe. Two weeks before, she had been made aware of Amos's plans. Angry tears had been shed and she had even shouted at him, but then she had apologized for her outburst. Now she pretended like he had never told her at all, and whenever Amos brought it up, she acted like she was about to receive a surprise colonoscopy.

Another stretch of quiet hit the room before Dana replied. Each one of the Conners was staring at Amos and frowning. "What do you mean?"

Amos closed his eyes and sighed. "I'm retiring in the spring."

Dana's eyes narrowed even further. "Please tell me this was in the cards before this happened."

"If I told you that I would be lying."

Dana made a noise of irritation. "But why? You were the hero of this whole thing. Surely you would be like . . . revered around town for the role you played."

"That is not really how it works. And I wasn't the hero. She was." He indicated Stevie with a nod.

"You both were!"

Amos felt a little touched but also a little irritated. It was good to feel appreciated, but he didn't like being confronted about his life choices by someone he didn't even really know. Who was she to give pointers on his career?

When Amos didn't reply, Dana rubbed the arches of her eye sockets like she was trying to ward off a headache. "I just think you're making a mistake. You say that we shouldn't let . . . *him* . . . affect our lives. But then you're going to quit because of him? You are a hero, in my eyes. The only one who was clever enough to save our son. And now you are going to let him win?"

"I don't know how to explain it to you, Mrs. Conner," Amos replied, reverting back to the more formal way of addressing her as an expression of annoyance. "It doesn't really have anything to do with him. I mean, it does . . . but it has more to do with how we handled this whole thing. Two years in a row, Mrs. Conner. Two years in a row. That tells me plainly that we were doing something wrong. We let people get away with murder. And there are dozens of dead girls and boys who paid for it. I'm coming to the realization now the rules in place work more in the bad guys' favor than ours. Sometimes . . . procedure can be the death of justice. I'm not saying I'm completely getting out of this line of work. I'm just going to do it in a different avenue."

Now, even Stevie looked over at him like he had just grown two more heads. She hadn't yet been privy to this part of the plan.

Dana's mouth was now slightly agape like she was on the verge of a sneeze. "What do you mean? You're going to become a private investigator?"

Amos shrugged. "Something like that."

"A PI? Why do you think—"

"I don't want you to quit."

Everyone's heads turned toward Coby, as his voice had overtaken his mother's. The boy was sitting timidly on the edge of the couch, looking nervous for speaking out. Perhaps it was Amos's imagination, but Coby looked like he was shaking.

"I'm not quitting, bud. I'm retiring."

"But still. You saved me." Coby's forehead was screwed up like he was looking directly at the sun.

"I did. And you're safe now, whether I'm a detective or not."

Coby stared at him for a long time. The silence in the room was almost unbearable, but Amos didn't want to break it. He could tell that the boy was working up a reply.

"Am I?"

Coby's bottom lip trembled. All at once, the boy totally broke down. He threw his clubbed hand and his scarred cheek on his mother's shoulder and shook while releasing horrible, pained sobs. His whole body convulsed and the part of his face that was visible contorted in agony.

Dana stroked his hair and whispered, "It's okay. It's okay. I'm here."

She repeated the last three words several times. Amos felt an overwhelming bubble of pity in his stomach, and in that moment, he realized all that had been lost. Watching the broken child twist and turn in his mother's arms was what it had taken to get him to see how much had been torn beyond repair. The Conners and the two detectives had survived Ted Leery, but none of them would ever be quite whole again.

Amos leaned forward and Coby pulled away from Dana's shoulder. His eyes were swollen and red, and his face was stained with tears. And in that moment, he knew he had made the right decision about withholding the reality about Coby's parentage. This fractured child in front of him would spend years healing. If he knew the truth, he might not make it out alive. Amos made piercing eye contact with the boy and mustered as much strength as he could in his voice.

"Coby, no one is ever going to hurt you like that again. That is a promise."

When the two detectives departed the house, the weather had taken a turn for the better. The rain was no longer falling, and a piercing ray of sunshine had parted the clouds. On the top of the tree line in the distance, there were the traces of a rainbow. But it was faded, and the various colors could only be seen if you squinted. It reflected how Amos felt. The storm had passed, and there was hope for the future, albeit faint.

"So a private dick, huh?"

Amos looked over at Stevie, who was giving him a mischievous smile.

"Guess so. We will see."

"Do you have anything particular in mind?"

Amos shook his head. "No. Just kind of playing it by ear."

Stevie gave a slight roll of her eyes. She knew he was lying, but didn't grill him about it.

"I guess we will have to see what the future holds. Who knows? I might be a shit PI."

"You might be, yeah."

Amos laughed. "That isn't what you're supposed to say!"

Stevie chuckled and raised her palms toward the air. "Hey, sugarcoating isn't my thing. I'm just saying, you make a pretty good detective."

"Well, thank you, Stevie. That does genuinely make me feel good."

"It's not supposed to make you feel good, it's supposed to make you pull your head out of your ass."

Amos didn't reply to this, but he did give her a small smile as they got into the Ford Crown Victoria.

"What are you smirking at? I'm serious."

Amos sighed. "Stevie, my decision is made. Me and Anita talked for hours before we came to this decision."

"So what is the real reason you're doing this?"

Amos again faked a surprised expression, but it didn't fool her.

"Come on. You don't have to give me that 'structures becoming shackles' crap. I'm not going to badger you about this. You're obviously a big boy who makes his own decisions, and I know I'm not going to be able to change your mind. But since you're leaving me, I feel like I deserve an honest answer."

Amos exhaled deeply. She could always see right through him.

"Come on, Al. Just tell me."

He fastened his seatbelt into place and took a deep breath before giving her the explanation she was looking for.

"It was the day after Halloween. When I came home. I will never forget that look on Anita's face for the rest of my life. She was so scared. She clung to me like I might just disappear into thin air. I just . . . I can't do that to her again, Stevie. I just can't."

"Hmm. Fair enough."

Amos was slightly taken aback by this, so he just repeated the same exact thing, except in question form.

"Fair enough?"

"Yep. Fair enough. Although, if you're looking for a less, uh, hazardous occupation, I'm not sure a private investigator is the right way to go."

Amos gave a halfhearted shrug. "At least I won't be in the direct line of fire."

"If you say so."

Amos turned the key in the ignition and fired up the engine, simultaneously shifting into reverse. He looked back toward the tree line, trying to find the rainbow. But it had vanished.

"For the record, I don't think you actually will make a shit PI."

Amos grinned while looking into his rearview mirror. "I don't think you will make a shit informant either."

Stevie raised her eyebrows. "If you should be so lucky."

"Who knows? Maybe one day you could join me. We could start our own firm."

Stevie shook her head vigorously. "I could never be a PI. Subtlety is not my forte."

The two made eye contact, and Amos's smile

was now almost from ear to ear.

"Truer words have never been spoken, Stevie Hutchins."

FORTY-TWO DAYS
AFTER HALLOWEEN

The tourists had all cleared out. Summer was long gone, and the biting cold pushed the crowds away. Barely any traffic cluttered the streets, as Newport's residents were collectively at work, and Amos's path down Herbert Street was easy and unobstructed. He came to a halt next to the sidewalk and shifted the car into park. The heater on his dashboard turned off automatically, and for several seconds, he watched his breath steam up the windshield.

When he pulled open the door, a blast of cold stabbed through his black overcoat, causing an involuntary sound of discomfort to escape his lips. He hurried across the sidewalk and pulled the door to Sandcastle Toys open with more force than was necessary. A loud *ding* signaling his presence in the shop rang out and a voice called to him from close by.

"Hello, dear!"

Amos turned to look at the person who had greeted him. She was old and looked like an owl. The woman was perched on a stool behind a desk with an old-fashioned cash register on it and was giving him a kind, although somewhat disingenuous, smile. Amos could never remember this woman's name, but he knew she was the owner of the shop.

"Good morning. I'm here to see Maryanne."

The avian-looking woman's face fell, but this only lasted for a millisecond before she reverted back into the warm old-lady persona that she usually sported.

"Of course. She mentioned something about an appointment this morning. Up the stairs, dear, as always. Careful, those things are getting more and more rickety by the day."

Amos chuckled. "Thank you."

As promised, the stairs at the back of the shop did indeed appear precarious. They were steep wooden steps, and although Amos had made the climb a couple of times before, he didn't remember it being this much of a workout for his thighs. When he got to the top of the staircase, his breath was slightly ragged. *The treadmill is calling,* he thought.

There was a heavy wooden door at the top of the stairs, with a plaque plastered to it that read, *Maryanne Wiggins, PI.* Amos rapt on the door several times and tried to regain his breath as he waited. It wasn't long before the door swung open, and a middle-aged woman who looked like a hobbit stood in front of him.

"Maryanne, wow! You've lost weight since the last time I saw you."

Wiggins looked down at her body like it was something that didn't belong to her.

"Indeed, I have."

Amos gave her an encouraging grin, but she didn't say anything more at first. They both just stood there awkwardly for a couple of beats.

"Oh, am I supposed to comment on your physical appearance? Yes, okay, well . . . you've lost hair since the last time I saw you," she said, her voice wrought with phlegm.

Amos burst into laughter while Wiggins stayed straight-faced. "Happens to the best of us, Maryanne."

"Hasn't happened to me, yet. That would be a horrifying sight, wouldn't it? Well, come on in then.

I cleaned up just for you."

When Amos stepped into her office, he could tell she was being facetious. Boxes were stacked haphazardly across the floor, and the desk that took up most of the room was littered with random pieces of paper. The only thing somewhat organized was a large bookshelf next to the desk that contained dozens of black three-ring binders. Wiggins waddled through the room. Her right leg buckled every time she took a step. She had once explained the cause of this limp to Amos, but he couldn't remember the exact story. Something about a high-speed chase back when she had been a cop. She also held her right hand close to her body like it was dead weight. Amos knew this was due to nerve-damage stemming from her confrontation with the killer of the Nowhere Girls case.

Wiggins plopped into the chair closest to the far window, and Amos followed suit into the chair opposite of her.

"Heard you had a hell of an encounter with your buddy Leery."

"You could say that."

"How is the kid doing?"

Amos gave a noncommittal gesture, but it was more than enough to convey the message to the highly intuitive Wiggins.

"Not great, eh."

"Well, you can understand why."

"Absolutely," Wiggins replied, with a firm nod. "Frankly, it would be strange if he were okay. And the brother?"

"Worse," Amos said grimly.

"Yeah, well. He's only nine, isn't he?"

"Ten."

Wiggins stared at a point over Amos's shoulder, and her eyes misted over as she pondered Coby's younger brother.

"Aren't you going to ask how I'm doing?"

"No," Wiggins said simply. Amos laughed, and again, Wiggins remained stoic.

"You have never been one to beat around the bush, Maryanne."

Wiggins shook her head. "You're a cop, Albert. I already know how screwed up your psyche is. I don't need to ask."

"I won't be a cop for much longer."

Wiggins's face finally showed a bit of emotion. Surprise. "You're quitting?"

"Retiring. Officially."

"Aren't you a little young to retire?"

"Twenty-year man, Maryanne."

"And still younger than me."

"Do you know that for a fact?"

Wiggins shrugged. Amos expected to hear a question or two about what had motivated him to come to such a decision, but none came. Either Wiggins didn't care, or already partly sensed the

415

reason, or both.

"So how is business?"

Wiggins drummed the fingers of her left hand against the desk. "Busy. Annoyingly busy. Ever since the Nowhere Girls, my phone has been ringing off the hook. Half of my days are spent trying to decipher which cases are worth taking and which ones are nonsense. Unsurprisingly, the majority have been nonsense. A lot of weirdos around these parts, Albert. The other day I had a middle-aged man try and hire me to investigate his brother over a dispute that took place in a Port-a-Potty. And, in the most shocking development of the past decade, alcohol was involved."

"What did you tell him?"

"To stop drinking a twelve pack of Pabst Blue Ribbon before ten in the morning."

Amos chortled heartily and was surprised to even see Wiggins cracking a smile. It passed quickly though.

"How is the hand?"

Wiggins glanced down at her lame right hand. "Fine."

Amos pursed his lips and looked out the window behind her. The view of the town from her office was surprisingly beautiful; you could see the tops of every building and just beyond, the opaque blue of the ocean.

"Why have you come, Albert?"

Amos looked back at her and was met with piercing eye contact. It almost made him a little uncomfortable. He didn't answer at first.

"Surely you didn't arrange an appointment to exchange pleasantries with me. There are far more pleasant people to do that with. So why have you come, Albert?"

Amos sighed and rubbed his temple. Never one to beat around the bush, indeed.

"Well . . . I was wondering . . ."

Wiggins raised her eyebrows expectantly. But Amos continued to dawdle.

"Yes? You were wondering what?"

Amos exhaled one more uncomfortable sigh. Better to just come out and ask.

"Are you hiring?"

FIFTY-THREE DAYS
AFTER HALLOWEEN

Norma Osgood adjusted the IV bag in front of her, pulling it closer. Her glasses fell down her nose, and she brushed them back impatiently as she tried to move the IV. A bit of moisture was permeating through the plastic, and Norma shook her hand in disgust as the tips of her fingers touched the wetness. It was mostly just water, but Norma had always hated accidently touching something that she wasn't expecting to be damp. *Well, time to sterilize yet again,* she thought.

Norma pushed herself up from her kneeling position, using the bed to shift her weight. When you were obese, it was far more difficult to get your body to move with any sort of agility. Even simple movements put strain on your joints and pain in your feet. She hadn't always been this way. Hell, in high school, she hadn't even been 110 pounds. Then she had gotten married to a man who was head over heels for her, and eventually let herself go. Who was there to impress anymore? She had won. She had secured a wonderful life partner. Her weight wasn't going to drive Jean to leave. At least she hoped not. Now that she had had three kids, it was almost impossible to fathom being anything other than flabby and out of shape. Her metabolism was completely shot.

Norma glanced at the patient lying down beneath her. His skin was greenish-yellow and a string of drool ran down his chin. If not for the heart monitor propped next to him that told a different story, it would be safe to assume that he was dead, just based on his appearance.

A sharp pain in her back pinched as she straightened up. It was likely her sciatic nerve that was out of whack, or something along those lines. Whatever it was, it hurt like hell whenever she twisted her spine.

"Son of a bitch," she muttered under her breath.

"Same ol' Norma."

Norma whirled about toward the doorway. Martin Peabody strode over the threshold into room 312, looking at her skeptically. His balding head gleamed under the light emanating from a fluorescent fixture above, and his thick-rimmed glasses inflated his pupils.

"Dr. P! I thought you were still on vacation today!"

Peabody pursed his lips. "Clearly. Usually even you can control your crass tongue when I'm around."

Norma felt her cheeks flush and a spark of indignation in her chest.

"Just got back, actually," Peabody said quietly. "Was pretty anxious to do so. Two weeks in humid Aruba is enough to make a man lose his nerve."

Oh yeah, sounds awful, thought Norma with disdain. Although maybe for a bad-mannered narcissist, a tropical island really was hell.

"I made sure to make this my first stop. Naturally, I have been most curious about this one. Do you have his file?"

Norma reached over and gripped the manila envelope on the bedside table. She handed it to Peabody, who snatched it and started riffling through the pages as though he knew there to be a hundred-dollar bill tucked in somewhere.

"How closely have you been monitoring his neural activity?"

"Uh, what do you mean?"

Peabody looked at her like she was the most foolish person in the world. "Brain scans. How frequently have you been doing MRIs?"

"Just three times since the incident, I think."

"Jesus," Peabody muttered under his breath.

Norma felt another strike of burning anger. She was able to mostly contain it, but her voice was still traced with hints of ire as she responded.

"Does it really matter? Don't we know enough to hypothesize that he's never going to come out of a coma?"

Peabody smiled his usual condescending smile. "How could we possibly know that? This is not a science that's overtly predictable. One day he could be in a deep coma, and the next he could be awake and recall everything that has happened to him since he was three years old. Or he could be dead. The point is, we will have no answers without analysis. And we will have no analysis without tests."

"Personally, dead probably wouldn't be the worst option for this one."

Peabody frowned at her. "We don't get to decide that, Norma. We don't get to play God."

Norma shrugged in a gesture that said "suit yourself" as she looked down at the patient's heavily bandaged forehead. As her eyes passed over his pale face, a taboo and instantly shameful thought fluttered through her mind. Even in his current state, the patient was quite handsome. Trying to push this idea out of her mind, she moved the conversation forward.

"Won't he just be a vegetable anyway, even if he does wake up?"

Peabody was absorbed in a piece of paper that was inside the manila folder and didn't respond. After many seconds of silence, Norma concluded he was just going to ignore her. *Oh well,* she thought. *It's better than when he opens his mouth.*

"Gage."

Norma turned and looked at Peabody with a baffled expression. "Huh?"

"Phineas Gage. Have you ever heard the story of Phineas Gage?"

Norma looked down at the folder in his hands, as if it might contain the answer to Peabody's pop quiz. "Um, well . . ."

"Phineas Gage was a railroad worker in 1848 in Vermont," Peabody continued as though Norma had not spoken at all. "One day in September, he was using a three-and-a-half-foot tamping iron to pack explosive powder inside a hole, and the powder detonated. It propelled the iron through his cheek, severing his optic nerve and severely damaging his left frontal lobe before shooting out of the top of his skull."

"I imagine that didn't feel too good," Norma replied slyly. Peabody didn't even crack the slightest smile.

"Gage's untimely accident would've caused instantaneous death had the rod wobbled slightly more to the right or the back of his head. And yet, he survived."

"Wow." Norma said it like a stock response, although she was somewhat impressed by the tale.

"After the accident, Gage wasn't a vegetable at all. He still possessed average mental acuity, and was able to perform any remedial task asked of him. All that was altered was his behavior. He became so volatile afterward that those who knew him said he was basically a whole new and terrible person. Most of his coworkers couldn't stand to be around him, for he was incredibly profane and bellicose. And it was all due to a forty-six-inch tamping iron that scrambled his brain. The point is . . . you never know."

"But the scans yielded extensive damage."

"Yes, they did. To his left frontal lobe. Just like Gage."

Norma shrugged. "Well. He's never going to wake up. So this is all a moot point."

Peabody didn't say anything. He just continued to scan the documents in the manila folder unrelentingly. For a while, the two stood in silence. Norma found herself desperately wishing for Peabody to leave. Even in just a couple of minutes she had been subjected to enough of his horribleness.

Suddenly, a loud crash split the silence in two. Norma and Peabody both turned their heads in a synchronized motion toward the door. Through the window, they could see two people flitting around and bent over something on the ground. Peabody strode quickly across room 312 with Norma in his wake. He ripped the door open and found two nurses bent over collecting bloodied shards of glass off the floor. They were hurriedly picking up the pointed slivers and placing them on a small cart that was filled with tiny crimson beakers, three of which were now smashed on the ground.

"What the hell is going on out here?"

"Dr. P!" one of the nurses, who had a beautiful face and dark skin, looked up at him and panicked. "I thought you were on vaca—"

"What the hell is going on here, I said."

The other nurse, whose name was Cindy, barely made eye contact with Peabody as she replied. "Sorry, Doctor P. The cart tipped over. The floor was wet."

"And now it's even more wet, thanks to you two idiots!" Peabody's face had turned a startling shade of red. Like most narcissists, he was prone to bouts of unbridled, unremorseful rage.

The nurse with the dark skin, who was called Angie, began profusely apologizing, but was instantly refuted by Peabody.

"I don't want to hear it! You know, we really don't dole out that much responsibility to you people, and you *still* find a way to screw things up!"

Angie's voice shook, and her eyes welled with tears. "I-I'm sorry, Doctor. It was just an accident."

This only seemed to feed Peabody's fury. "You're a nurse, not a toddler. You aren't allowed to have accidents."

Norma was hoping Peabody's tirade was nearing an end, but next came the most vicious barb yet.

"How someone so *careless* ever got a nursing degree is beyond me."

Some fuse deep in the recesses of Norma's brain ignited. Months of pent-up frustration burst the dam, and when she spoke, she barely recognized the voice that came out of her mouth, for it was hoarse and quite loud.

"You have no right to speak to them like that, Martin! That is just ridiculous."

Peabody rounded about, and his face was absent of color. Part of him looked completely flabbergasted someone had finally stood up to him, but his face was also contorted in wrath. There were two beats of nothing while Peabody's mouth twisted and tried to form words, and then his response finally came out.

"Don't even get me started on you, Osgood!"

"You know, why don't you get started on me,

Martin? Why don't you?"

Peabody bellowed back at her with as much ferocity as he could muster, and the battle was on. Back and forth they went, screaming at the tops of their lungs and hurling vicious insults through the air like they were ninja stars. The two nurses in the hallway looked like they couldn't believe what was happening and both cowered away from the tornado of anger swirling about in front of them.

"You're just a goddamn narcissist! And you have absolutely no regard for other people's feelings!"

Peabody's eyes bulged and he looked like an irascible bug. "And you're a careless, mindless amateur!"

Norma volleyed out a barrage of sarcastic laughter. "Yeah, well, it's better to be a mindless amateur who is well-regarded by her colleagues than an asshole who is despised by everyone."

Peabody's face fell. For a fleeting moment, there was noticeable hurt in his expression, and Norma began to feel a prickle of guilt. But then he opened his mouth.

"Out. Get out."

"Wha—"

"Get out, you old hag!"

Norma stepped forward and was inches from Peabody's face. For several moments, she wasn't positive she wouldn't strike him. But then the two nurses got in between them, and their sparring match remained verbal. Norma's rage was so strong it overpowered the voice in her head telling her chances of keeping her job were lowering by the second.

"You truly are *disgusting,* Peabody. No wonder your wife left you."

Peabody's mouth flexed as he scrambled to find a barb that would truly wound the woman across from him. But all that he managed to admonish her with was another "Get out!"

Rooms along the corridor began to open and heads were peeking out. The scene called every eye in the hallway to it, and the two rivals continued to scream at each other. The shouts were deafening, the commotion frightening, and everyone remained oblivious to the heart monitor nearby that spiked dramatically every other second. The hollers boomed and echoed off the walls, and not a single person watched anything else. If they had looked inside room 312, they would've seen the patient's fingers twitch. But they didn't, and it was no surprise that no one noticed the moment that Ted Leery's eyes flickered open.

ALSO BY
ALEX URQUHART

The Nowhere Girls

On a sullen, overcast day on the Central Oregon Coast, a body is found pressed against the jagged rocks of Yaquina Bay. Thanks to several brooding texts received by her grandmother, twenty-one-year old Katie Deeds' death is ruled a suicide. Jonah Carr, a local feature reporter on his third year of the job, is assigned the story by his editor. Initially, nothing looks to be atypical or particularly noteworthy about the girl's demise. She was known as being wildly erratic and impulsive, and although her suicide came as a surprise to those who knew her, no one considers the possibility of foul play. However, through a series of interviews with those closest to Katie, Jonah uncovers an intricate plot shrouding the girl's passing, adding another layer to the mystery. Only two people recall seeing Katie on the night of her death and one is unwilling to talk. Simultaneously, Jonah makes a loose connection to a thirty-two-year-old cold case. Kylie Desmond was last seen walking alone in the early morning hours of August 12th, 1984. Then, in 1994, her skull was found in an abandoned car. She was one of five teenage girls who were murdered over an eleven-year period; each walking alone or in pairs on the same highway. The killer was never caught. Now, with the assistance of Private Investigator Maryanne Wiggins, Jonah must probe every link to the cases that the Newport Police Department has neglected, desperate to find any loose-ends to tie to the girls before another body is unearthed. Through his exploits, he starts to answer the question that has haunted the small coastal town for decades: Is there a serial killer living in their midst?